BORGES
A READER

A selection from the writings of Jorge Luis Borges

EDITED BY
EMIR RODRIGUEZ MONEGAL AND ALASTAIR REID

E. P. Dutton   New York

CONTENTS

INTRODUCTION

There is something tautological about a Borges reader, since everything that Borges writes is immediately transmuted into reading. The key to his work is his view of reading as a form of writing—or rewriting. In one of his most celebrated stories, "Pierre Menard, Author of the *Quixote*" (JLB 30),* he has thoroughly demonstrated that the reader of a classic becomes, in a sense, a collaborator in it—his reading will inevitably change the text. In a famous essay, "Kafka and His Precursors" (JLB 73), Borges has shown that the reading of Kafka's work has now pervaded the entire corpus of Western literature—we recognize Kafka's influence [signature] in every author.

Because reading is at the core of everything he writes, Borges has erased the old distinctions among fiction, poetry, and essay. He has written poems which are footnotes to scholarly works: "General Quiroga Rides to His Death in a Carriage" (JLB 2), and "The Golem (II)" (JLB 84), for example. He has published stories that pretend to be book reviews, like "The Approach to Al'Mutásim"; and some of his literary essays are closer to fiction than to conventional criticism: "The Enigma of Edward FitzGerald" (JLB 76) belongs to that ambiguous category. Everything Borges writes becomes reading, that is, literature. He belongs to that family of writers (Petronius, Rabelais, Cervantes, Sterne) who produce two texts at the same time. One text is transparent enough to make the reader forget he is actually reading—he literally "sees" two boys discovering the streets of decadent Rome in the *Satyricon,* imagines the oversized, infantile monsters of *Gargantua* and *Pantagruel,* follows a senile errant knight and his talkative squire on their journey through the plains of La Mancha, or laughs at the antics of two brothers incapable of coming to the point in *Tristram Shandy.* The second text is opaque, reflecting only itself, and forcing the reader to realize that what he is doing is reading; that is, he is performing a highly specialized task. He has to help Petronius to put together the fragments of his narrative as well as collaborate with Rabelais in giving shape to the drolleries of his monsters. He has to be ready to discuss the romances of chivalry with Cervantes and his characters, as well as the

---

*JLB followed by a number identifies the pertinent text by Borges. This reference number appears to the *right of the title,* and it is this number, not the page number, to look for in locating a particular poem, story, or essay by Borges.

theory of sentiment with Sterne. Instead of being a mere consumer, he becomes a collaborator—a writer in his own right.

The double discourse these writers practice—the discourse of parody, allegory, translation, and criticism—is what Borges also practices. But for the innocent reader Borges has still another appeal. His texts are about some of the basic dreams and nightmares man has produced in centuries of literary vigil: the madness of unreturned love (JLB 51); the fear of lacking a real identity (JLB 36); the horror of discovering one's own cowardice (JLB 79); the emptiness of fame and success (JLB 49); the illusions fostered by any "coherent" explanation of the world (JLB 34). In spite of despising the pathos of the existentialists, Borges shares with them a tragic view of the world. He communicates it, however, through irony and parody.

Playing with time, with personal identity, with some of our most cherished cultural values, he really makes diversions to hide the unbearable truth—that we do not know what we are, where we come from or where we are going. A lucid system of denials, contradictions, paradoxes, governed by an impeccable syntax —this is what Borges's texts seem to be about. At the same time, the elegance of his writings reasserts their permanence in a world in which everything is transient. The voice that insists in denying is, after all, a voice and not a silence.

To anthologize Borges is to admit defeat from the very beginning. Few writers' works are more intimately one. Thus, to select and discriminate implies breaking up the totality of his work. On the other hand, almost any text of his (like the bone an archeologist may find) can be used to reconstruct the whole body of his work. Keeping in mind these two contradictory propositions, we have attempted to compile an anthology which covers virtually his entire production, at the same time selecting not only some major texts but also some neglected and little-known ones. In spite of the generosity of many of his publishers in English, we could not secure permission to reproduce all the texts we wanted. The aficionado will notice some of the omissions, but, fortunately, they are so well known and so easily available that we count on the reader's memory to restore them to their proper places in this anthology. To compensate for these involuntary omissions, we have included many texts that have never before been translated into English and which, in many cases, have never been collected in book form anywhere. Those texts are marked in the Notes with a dagger.

To illustrate the texts and put them into perspective, Emir Rodriguez Monegal prepared the introductions to the parts and the Notes. The editing of the texts and supervision of the translations has been the charge of Alastair Reid.

E.R.M./A.R.

NOTE ON THE TRANSLATIONS

The translations in this collection come from a variety of hands, since the business of bringing Borges into English has gone on in piecemeal fashion since the 1950s (with the exception of E. P. Dutton's 12-title Borges program, begun in 1968). As a result, Borges has something of a patchwork existence in English, inevitably so unless we still believe in that fiction of fictions, the perfect translator, someone with the time, means, and selflessness to give Borges the unity and completeness in English that he has in Spanish. In the case of work already translated, we have used the best *available* version; in other cases, the work has been newly translated.*

Borges is not inexperienced as a translator. "Nothing," he wrote in *Las Versiones Homéricas* in 1932, "is as consubstantial with literature and its modest mystery as the questions raised by a translation." For him, reading is a form of translation. Borges's spoken English has an elusive accent which he not incorrectly refers to as Northumbrian. With time, however, one realizes that he really speaks English with the formal correctness, and mannerisms, of his chosen mentors, Chesterton and Stevenson. Speaking Spanish, he is infinitely more playful and ironic; but his written Spanish, with its flawless but paradoxical syntax, its sparse measure intruded on by the tentative and the vertiginous, and the pervasiveness of something like English understatement in his ironies, is so intrinsically his own that it can only be surmised in English, in this or that reflection or imitation. The very variety of the translators, however, may help the reader to intuit the inimitable spirit of the original, which must remain just out of reach of all of them.

---

*A List of Translators may be found on pages 365–366.

A YOUNG POET'S VOICE

While teaching himself German in Switzerland, 1917, Borges discovered some extraordinary poems by an American writer—Walt Whitman. Very soon, he obtained from London a copy of an English edition of the striking originals. For some time, the young man believed Whitman was poetry itself. He attempted to imitate him and dutifully wrote some cosmic verses (JLB 61, JLB 95). The simultaneous discovery of German expressionist poetry helped him to develop an avant-garde style and turn of mind. He believed in the brotherhood of poets and found in Schopenhauer (JLB 60) and Nietzsche (JLB 22, JLB 33), two mesmerizing masters. His contacts in Spain with disciples or readers of Apollinaire (JLB 55) and Tristan Tzara, of the Chilean Vicente Huidobro and Pierre Reverdy, confirmed his Modernist vocation. In Argentina, he rediscovered Buenos Aires, a town he had left when only fourteen, and attempted to catch its essences and appearances in poems of deliberate simplicity (JLB 4). Because he came from a long line of men who fought in the wars of Independence and the civil wars, he devoted some elegiac verses to family piety and to the history of Argentina (JLB 2, JLB 6). Conscientiously, the young Borges was attempting to be a truly national bard.

DAWN   [JLB 1]

In the deep universal night
scarcely dispelled by the flickering gaslamps
a gust of wind coming out of nowhere
stirs the silent streets
with a trembling presentiment
of the hideous dawn that haunts
like some lie
the tumbledown outskirts of cities all over the world.
Under the spell of the refreshing darkness

5

and intimidated by the threat of dawn,
I felt again that tremendous conjecture
of Schopenhauer and Berkeley
which declares the world
an activity of the mind,
a dream of souls,
without foundation or purpose or volume.
And since ideas
are not like marble, everlasting,
but ever-renewing like a forest or a river,
the previous speculation
took another form in the dawn,
and the superstition of the hour,
when the light like a vine
begins twining itself to walls still in shadow,
dominated my reason
and projected the following whim:
If all things are devoid of matter
and if this populous Buenos Aires
comparable to an army in complexity
is no more than a dream
arrived at in magic by souls working together,
there's a moment
in which the city's existence is at the brink of danger and disorder
and that is the trembling moment of dawn
when those who are dreaming the world are few
and only a handful of night owls preserve
ashen and sketchy
a vision of the streets
which they will afterward define for others.
The hour in which the persistent dream of life
is in danger of breaking down,
the hour in which God might easily
destroy all his work!

But once more the world comes to its own rescue.
The light streaks in inventing dirty colors
and with a tremor of remorse
for my complicity in the daily rebirth
I seek my house,
amazed and icelike in the white glare,
while a songbird holds the silence back
and the spent night
lives on in the eyes of the blind.

GENERAL QUIROGA RIDES TO HIS DEATH IN A CARRIAGE

[JLB 2]

The watercourse dry of puddles, not a drop of water left,
and a moon gone out in the cold shiver of the dawn,
and the countryside, poor as a church mouse, dying of hunger.

The coach swayed from side to side, creaking up the slope;
a great bulk of a coach, voluminous, funereal.
Four black horses with a tinge of death in their dark coats
were drawing six souls in terror and one wide awake and bold.

Alongside the postilions a black man was galloping.
To ride to your death in a carriage—what a splendid thing to do!
General Quiroga had in mind to approach the haunts of death
taking six or seven companions with slit throats as escort.

That gang from Córdoba, troublemakers, loudmouthed, shifty
(Quiroga was pondering), now what can they possibly do to me?
Here I am strong, secure, well set up in life
like the stake for tethering beasts to, driven deep in the pampa.

I, who have endured through thousands of afternoons
and whose name alone is enough to set the lances quivering,
will not lay down my life in this godforsaken wilderness.
Do the winds from the southwest die, by any chance? Do swords?

But when the brightness of day shone on Barranca Yaco
weapons without mercy swooped in a rage upon him;
death, which is for all, rounded up the man from La Rioja
and more than one thrust of the dagger invoked Juan Manuel de Rosas.

Now dead, now on his feet, now immortal, now a ghost,
he reported to the Hell marked out for him by God,
and under his command there marched, broken and bloodless,
the souls in purgatory of his soldiers and his horses.

MANUSCRIPT FOUND IN A BOOK OF JOSEPH CONRAD

[JLB 3]

In the shimmering countries that exude the summer,
the day is blanched in white light. The day
is a harsh slit across the window shutter,
dazzle along the coast, and on the plain, fever.

But the ancient night is bottomless, like a jar
of brimming water. The water reveals limitless wakes,
and in drifting canoes, face inclined to the stars,
man marks the limp time with a cigar.

The smoke blurs gray across the constellations
afar. The present sheds past, name, and plan.
The world is a few vague tepid observations.
The river is the original river. Man, the first man.

THE MYTHICAL FOUNDING OF BUENOS AIRES [JLB 4]

And was it along this torpid muddy river
that the prows came to found my native city?
The little painted boats must have suffered the steep surf
among the root-clumps of the horse-brown current.

Pondering well, let us suppose that the river
was blue then like an extension of the sky,
with a small red star inset to mark the spot
where Juan Díaz fasted and the Indians dined.

But for sure a thousand men and other thousands
arrived across a sea that was five moons wide,
still infested with mermaids and sea serpents
and magnetic boulders which sent the compass wild.

On the coast they put up a few ramshackle huts
and slept uneasily. This, they claim, in the Riachuelo,
but that is a story dreamed up in the Boca.
It was really a city block in my district—Palermo.

A whole square block, but set down in open country,
attended by dawns and rains and hard southeasters,
identical to that block which still stands in my neighborhood:
Guatemala—Serrano—Paraguay—Gurruchaga.

A general store pink as the back of a playing card
shone bright; in the back there was poker talk.
The corner bar flowered into life as a local bully,
already cock of his walk, resentful, tough.

The first barrel organ teetered over the horizon
with its clumsy progress, its habaneras, its wop.

8

The cart-shed wall was unanimous for YRIGOYEN.
Some piano was banging out tangos by Saborido.

A cigar store perfumed the desert like a rose.
The afternoon had established its yesterdays,
and men took on together an illusory past.
Only one thing was missing—the street had no other side.

Hard to believe Buenos Aires had any beginning.
I feel it to be as eternal as air and water.

HORSE-WAGON INSCRIPTIONS [JLB 5]

My reader needs to imagine a horse wagon. It is not hard to imagine a large one,
the rear wheels higher than the front ones, suggesting a reserve of power, the
criollo driver as forged as the object of wood and iron he rides in, his lips
distracted in a whistle or giving paradoxically gentle warnings to the workhorses,
to the following drivers and to the pointed frame (like a steady prow, for those
who need a comparison). It does not matter whether it is loaded or unloaded,
though when returning empty it seems less like a work vehicle and the driver's
seat appears more like a throne, as if retaining the military connotation that
belonged to the chariots of Attila's guerrilla empire. The street could be Montes
de Oca or Chile or Patricios or Rivera or Valentin Gomez, but Las Heras is best,
because of its heterogeneous traffic. The sluggish horse cart is perpetually off in
the distance, yet that very slowness is its triumph, as though any unusual turn
of speed might seem the frightened urgency of a slave, and its own sluggishness
a total possession of time, if not eternity. (That temporal possession is the *criollo's*
infinite capital, his only one. We can exalt delay as immobility, a possession of
space.) The horse wagon persists, an inscription on its side. The classicism of the
suburb has decreed it be so, and though that impartial, expressive slogan, superimposed on the visible expressions of resistance, form, fate, height, reality,
confirms the accusation of European lecturers that we are charlatans, I cannot
hide it, for it is the subject of this essay. For a long time I have been a collector
of these writings: barnyard epigraphy that suggests adventures and pastimes more
poetic than the actual collected works circulating in these Italianized times. I have
no intention of dumping this hodgepodge of homegrown wisdom out on the table,
only to exhibit a few. The project is one of rhetoric, as can be seen. It is well
known that those who established this discipline incorporated within it all the
uses of language, even the derisive or humble uses of the riddle, the pun, the
acrostic, the anagram, the labyrinth, the crossword, the emblem. Though the
latter, which is a symbolic figure and not language, has been included, I admit
that including a highway sign is going too far. It is an Indian variation of the

9

motto, a genre borne on their shields. Besides, the horse-wagon inscription should be assimilated with other writings so that the reader is not deceived into expecting wondrous conclusions from my observations. How could I dare propose such conclusions here, when they neither exist nor can be found in the carefully planned anthologies of Menendez y Pelayo or Palgrave?

One error is quite obvious: that of mistaking as a genuine horse-wagon motto the name of the establishment to which the cart belongs. *The Model of Villa Bollini,* a perfect example of inspirationless insolence, is one of those to which I refer; *Mother of the North,* a horse cart from Calle Saavedra, is another. This latter name is a fine one and we can suggest two explanations. One, the least believable, is to ignore the metaphor and imagine this cart giving birth to the North, pouring out houses and stores and paint shops, as it goes along on its inventive way. The other, as you have foreseen, praises origins. But names such as these correspond to a literary genre that is less homegrown and more commercially oriented: a genre that specializes in condensed masterpieces like the *Colossus of Rhodes* tailor shop on Villa Urquiza and the *Dormitologist* mattress factory on Belgrano, but not the subject I am pursuing.

Genuine horse-wagon literature is not very diverse. It is traditionally assertive—*The Flower of Vertiz Plaza, The Victor*—and usually pretty boring. For instance, *The Fishhook, The Suitcase, The Bludgeon.* I am starting to take a liking to this latter motto, but the feeling is erased when I remember another one, also from Saavedra, which describes its extensive journeys as voyages, a navigator of prairie roads and dust storms: *The Schooner.*

The inscriptions on delivery carts form a subspecies of this genre. Haggling over prices and gossiping among women has made them swallow their pride, and their glaring slogans tend toward compliant boasting or gallantry. *The Liberal, Long Live He Who Watches Over Me, The Basque from the South, The Hummingbird, The Milkman Yet-to-Come, The Kid, Till Tomorrow, The Record of Talcahuano, The Sun Shines on All* are some entertaining examples. *What Your Eyes Have Done to Me* and *Where Ashes Remain, There Was Fire,* reflect a more individual passion. *He Who Envies Me Dies Hopeless* must be a Spanish intromission. *I'm in No Hurry* is *criollo* through and through. The blandness or severity of the brief phrase often corrects itself as well, not just because it is catchy, but because such phrases abound. I have seen a little fruit cart which, besides its presumptuous name, *The Neighborhood Favorite,* declared in an arrogant couplet:

> I'll say it out loud and defend it too
> That nothing could make me jealous of you

and showed the figure of a couple dancing the tango in semidarkness, with the bold heading *Straightforward.* Such concise verbosity, such sententious frenzy, reminds me of the diction of the famous Danish statesman Polonius, from *Hamlet,* or that of the natural Polonius, Baltazar Gracián.

I will get back to the classical inscriptions. *The Half-Moon of Moron* is the motto of a very tall cart with railings of seaworthy iron, which I had the chance to contemplate one damp night in the very center of our Abasto Market, its twelve hooves and four wheels reigning over a profuse fermentation of fragrances. *Soli-*

tude is the name of a wagon I saw in the southern province of Buenos Aires, requiring one to keep a distance. Once again, *The Schooner* has the same effect, though not so obscure. *What Does the Ol' Woman Care If Her Daughter Loves Me* is impossible to omit, not so much for its missing wit as for its genuine barnyard tone. The same can be observed regarding *Your Kisses Were Mine,* an affirmation derived from a song, but which, written on a horse wagon, becomes embellished with insolence. *What're You Lookin' At, Jealous* has something effeminate and conceited about it. *I Feel Proud,* with its high driver's seat in the dignity of the sun, is far above the most effusive accusations of Boethius. *Here Comes Spider* is a beautiful announcement: *Fo' the Blonde Gal, Whenever* is even better, not just in its *criollo* apocope and in its implied preference for the brunette, but also for the ironic usage of the adverb *whenever,* which here means *never.* (I first encountered this contradictory *whenever* in an untranslatable *milonga,* which I regret not being able to reproduce in a low voice or mitigate modestly in Latin. I will illustrate in its place this similar song, of Mexican origin, as recorded in Rubén Campos's book, *Mexican Folklore and Music:* "They will take from me, they say/The paths where I often wander;/The paths they might take away,/But my love for it, whenever." *My life, whenever* was also a common exclamation of knife fighters who blocked their opponent's knife or stained club.) *The Branch Is Blossoming* is a reference to extreme serenity and magic. *Almost Nothing, You Should've Told Me,* and *Who Can Say* cannot be improved upon. They imply drama, they are in touch with reality, they correspond to frequent emotions—they are a part of destiny, forever. They are gestures captured in writing, an unceasing affirmation. Their allusiveness is that of a reserved conversationalist who cannot directly narrate or reason and who is satisfied with open-ended sentences, generalities, one-liners, as sinuous as they are short. But the top honor, the grand prize of this contest, goes to the opaque inscription *He Who Is Lost Doesn't Weep,* which kept Xul-Solar and me scandalously intrigued, though given to understanding the delicate mysteries of Browning, the weak ones of Mallarmé, and the heavy ones of Góngora. *He Who Is Lost Doesn't Weep;* I bestow this somber carnation upon the reader.

There is no fundamental literary atheism. I thought I did not believe in literature, and yet I have let myself be swayed by the temptation of gathering together these particles of the art. I am justified by two reasons. One is the democratic superstition that postulates reserved merit for any anonymous work, as though we all knew as a group what no single person knows, as though intelligence were nervous and performed better when no one was watching. The other is how easy it seems to judge something short. It offends us to think that our opinion about one line might not be the conclusive one. We place our faith in sentences rather than in chapters. It is inevitable in such a discussion to mention Erasmus, the incredulous questioner of proverbs.

This essay will begin to sound scholarly after a number of days. I cannot provide any bibliographic reference, except for this casual paragraph from one of my predecessors on the subject. It belongs to the dull drafts of classical poetry now known as free verse.

II

I remember it thus:

> Horse carts, inscriptions on their sides,
> Announced your day was beginning,
> And on the corners were shops so reverent,
> They seemed to be waiting an angel's appearance.

I much prefer horse-wagon inscriptions, flowers of the barnyard.

ISIDORO ACEVEDO [JLB 6]

The truth is that I know nothing about him
except for place-names and dates—
frauds and failings of the word—
and so with a certain mixture of hesitation and compassion I have rescued
   his last day,
not the one that others saw but his own,
and I want to sidestep my own life now to write about his.

Inveterate cardplayer and habitué of Buenos Aires backrooms,
born on the right side of the Arroyo del Medio and a follower of Alsina,
inspector of native produce in the old Westside markets,
police inspector of the third district,
when his homeland called him up he fought
in the battles at Cepeda and Pavón and the stockyard flats.

But my words should not take up his battles
when the vision he wrested from them was so much his own.

For in the same way that other men write verse
my grandfather elaborated a dream.

While a lung ailment ate away at him
and hallucinatory fevers distorted the face of the day,
he assembled the burning documents of his memory
for the forging of his dream.

This took place in a house on Calle Serrano
during that burnt-out summer of 1905.

His dream was of two armies
entering the shadow of battle;
he enumerated the commands, the colors, the units.
"Now the officers are reviewing their battle plans," he said in a voice you
   could hear,
and in order to see them he tried sitting up.

12

He seized a stretch of the prairie,
scouting it for broken terrain, where the infantry could hold their ground,
and for a flat place so that the cavalry charge could not be turned back.

He made a final levy,
rallying the thousands of faces that a man knows without really knowing at
the end of his years:
bearded faces now growing dim in daguerreotypes,
faces that lived and died next to his own at the battles of Puente Alsina and
Cepeda.

In the visionary defense of his country that his faith hungered for (and not
that his fever imposed),
he plundered his days
and rounded up an army of Buenos Aires ghosts
so as to get himself killed in the fighting.

That was how, in a bedroom that looked onto the garden,
he died out of devotion for his city.

It was in the metaphor of a journey that I was told of his death, and I did
not believe it.
I was a boy, who knew nothing then of dying; I was immortal,
and afterward for days I searched the sunless rooms for him.

THE RECOLETA   [JLB 7]

Death is scrupulous here; here, in this city of ports,
death is circumspect:
a blood-kinship of enduring and provident light
reaching out from the courts of the *Socorro,*
from the ash burned to bits in the braziers,
to the sugar-and-milk of a holiday treat
and a depth of patios like a dynasty.
Old sweetnesses, old rigors meet
and are one in the graveyards of *La Recoleta.*

At your summit, the portico's bravery,
a tree's blind solicitude,
birds prattling of death without ever suspecting it,
a ruffle of drums from the veterans' burial plot
to hearten the bypasser;
at your shoulder, hidden away, the tenements of the Northside,
the walls of the executioner, Rosas.

13

Here a nation of unrepresentable dead
thrives on decay under a suffrage of marble,
since the day that the earliest seed in your garden, destined for heaven,
Uruguay's child,
María de los Dolores Maciel, dropped off to sleep—
the least of your buried—in your waste desolation.

Here something holds me: I think
of the fatuous flowers that speak out so piously now in your name—
the leaf-yellow clay under the fringe of acacia,
memorial wreaths lifted up in your family crypts—
why do they stay here, in their sleepy and delicate way,
side by side with the terrible keepsakes of those whom we loved?

I put the hard question and venture an answer:
our flowers keep perpetual watch on the dead
because we all incomprehensibly know
that their sleepy and delicate presence
is all we can offer the dead to take with them in their dying,
without giving offense through the pride of our living
or seeming more alive than the dead.

be to display a continuum of vanishing images: a vineyard muletrain, the wild mules in it blinkered; a long, calm stretch of water, covered with fallen willow leaves; a dizzying specter, lofty on his high horse, wading over flooded flatlands; the wide countryside where absolutely nothing happens; the traces left by the stubborn trampling of cattle, up toward the northern stockyards; a peasant (dark against the early sky) who dismounts from his half-dead horse and, with his knife, completes the operation, slitting its broad neck; gray smoke scattered in the air. So it was, until the rise of Don Juan Manuel—the now mythical father of Palermo (not merely historical, as Groussac's Dominguez-Domenico was)—and that rise was unstintingly executed. A villa on the Barracas road, honeyed with time, was the norm then. But Rosas wanted to build: the house would be as a daughter to him—untasted, untainted by outlanders' destinies. Thousands of cartloads of black loam were brought from the "Rosas alfalfa holdings" (later known as Belgrano) to level and fertilize the clayey ground, until the untamed mud of Palermo, ingrate earth, conformed to his expectations.

In the 1840s, Palermo rose to the head of the republic; it became the dictator's court, and its name a black oath on the lips of the Unitarians. Not to tarnish the rest of its history, I leave this episode out. It is enough to mention "that great white house, which was called his Palace" (Hudson, *Far Away and Long Ago*, page 108), and the orange groves, and the little brick-walled reservoir with the iron railings, where El Restaurador's dinghy lightly made do with the curtailed navigation that Schiaffino remarked upon: "Rowing in such shallow water could not have been pleasant, and in so small an area it must have been somewhat like a pony ride. But Rosas accepted it calmly; if he lifted his eyes, he could see the forms, foreshortened against the sky, of the sentinels standing guard at the railing, keeping a watchful eagle eye on the horizon." That court was already on its way to open rupture: the crude and huddled adobe bivouac of the Hernandez division, and the fighting and frenzied settlements of dun-colored barracks, the Palermo Quarters. The sector, as is evident, was always a marked card, a two-headed coin.

This daring Palermo lasted twelve years—in the anxiety brought on by the rigorous presence of a fat blond man who roamed the trim streets in blue military uniform with red trouser stripes, a scarlet vest, and an extremely wide-brimmed hat, and who usually carried a long, thin cane, which he flourished as if it were an airy, graceful scepter. This obstinate man went out from Palermo one late afternoon, to command the simple stampede, or battle, lost before it began, that was joined in Caseros; and another Rosas came to Palermo—Justo José—with the mien of a wild bull and with an extravagant slouch hat banded in Mazorca-terrorist scarlet, and a splendid general's uniform. He came there, and, if Ascasubi's satirical leaflets have it right,

at the gates of Palermo
he called for a hanging:
two luckless fellows
swung from the ombus
(with the leaden donations

the firing squad gave them),
until they had rotted
and scattered the meadows.

Ascasubi then turns to the neglected troops of the Grand Army's Entre Ríos division:

Meanwhile, the mudflats
were heaped, near Palermo,
with Entre-rianos,
not a shirt to their backs.
A far cry from heaven
(for so tell the stories),
they ate of starved heifers
and sold off their weapons.

Countless unremembered days matured and withered on the blurred plains of time—solitary outposts rose up: the Penitenciaria in '77, Norte hospital in '82, Rivadavia hospital in '87—until finally we arrive at Palermo as it was just before the 1890s, when the Carriegos bought their house. It is of the Palermo of 1889 that I wish to write. I will tell all I know, and leave out nothing, because life is as diffident as transgression, and we have no idea what God himself would choose to underscore. Then, too, circumstantial evidence is always poignant.[1] At the risk of going over well-known events, I will write down everything, knowing full well that, in time, omission will itself be mislaid; this is mystery's poorest mannerism and its foremost characteristic.[2]

Beyond the Oeste branch rail line, which ran along Centroamerica Street, the neighborhood idled along amid auctioneer's flags, treading not only on undeveloped terrain but on the mangled bodies of villas, which had been brutally auctioned and were soon to be trampled by stores, coal yards, backyards, slums, barbershops, and vacant lots. There one can find the neighborhood's sunken garden—manic palm trees bordered by junk and railings—a mutilated, rundown relic of some fine villa.

---

[1] "Pathos is almost always found in the enumeration of minute circumstances," Gibbon observes in one of the final notes of Chapter 50 of the *Decline and Fall.*

[2] I maintain—with neither a prudish fear nor a fickle love of paradox—that it is only new countries that have a past; that is to say, an autobiographical memory of their past, a living history. If time is concatenation, we must recognize that where there is a greater density of events, more time has passed, and that this inconsequential hemisphere is thus richest in time. The conquest and colonization of this realm—four timid mud forts cling to the coastline, vigilant of the hanging horizon: the arced bows of renegades—were such an ephemeral operation that one of my grandfathers, in 1872, was able to command the last important battle against the Indians, thus completing, in the late nineteenth century, the sixteenth century's task of conquest. Nevertheless, why bring up long-dead outcomes? I have never experienced the mild weather of Granada, shadowed by towers a hundred times older than the fig trees, but still I have experienced it in Pampa and in Triunvirato, an insipid place whose roof tiles are English-style now, and whose brick kilns have been smoking for three years, and whose cattle farms have been chaotic for five. Time—a European emotion for old men, an emotion which is their crowning justification—passes more incautiously in these republics. Young people feel this in spite of themselves. Here we are of the same time as time, and we are time's brothers.

and the pampa wind attacked every south-facing door, leaving the entryways covered with thistles and bringing the all-destructive clouds of locusts, which the people attempted to exorcise by shouting,[3] and solitude, and the rain. This brink tasted of dust.

The nearer one came to the treacherous water, and to the forest, the rougher the neighborhood grew. The first things built on that land were the Norte slaughterhouses, which covered some eighteen blocks between boundary streets that would later be called Anchorena, Las Heras, Austria, and Beruti, and that are now left with no other name but La Tablada, the Meat Yard, a term I heard used by a driver who was ignorant of its earlier justification. I have asked the reader to imagine that vast precinct, its many blocks, for although the stockyards disappeared by 1870, they are typical of the place, parceled as it has been now into real estate: the cemetery, Rivadavia hospital, the prison, the marketplace, the municipal corral, the wool-cleaning plant, the brewery, the Hale place—all encircled by the wretchedness of broken fortunes. The Hale place was renowned for two reasons: for the pears that raggle-taggle neighborhood children raided clandestinely, and for the apparition that visited one side of Figuero Street, resting its unlikely head in the crook of a lamppost. To the actual dangers of the knife fighters' proud camaraderie one would have to add the less concrete dangers of a mythology of outlawry: "La Viuda" and the outlandish "Chancho de Lata," sordid as the depths—these were the most menacing beings in the neighborhood pantheon. That northern precinct had once been haunted; it is fitting that a rubbish of souls should be drawn to its air. There are still some recesses of Palermo that are kept from their downfall only by the scaffolding of dear, dead comrades.

As one went down Chavango Street (later renamed Las Heras), the last shop on the street was La Primera Luz—a name that, despite its allusion to the habits of early risers, gives the impression (rightly) of deserted, muddy blind alleys and then, finally, after an exhausted turning of corners, human light in a grocery store. Against the background of red Norte cemetery and the Penitenciaria prison, an unwhitewashed, blunt, shattered outpost rose from the dust, gradually—its notorious name: Tierra del Fuego. Shards of the origin, aggressive or solitary crossroads, furtive men who signal to each other in whistles, then suddenly scatter in the lateral light of the side streets—that was its nature. This neighborhood was the last crossroads. Evil men on horseback—their miter-style homburgs pulled low on their foreheads, wearing the baggy breeches of peasants—sustained, by inertia or impulse, a running battle of individual vendettas against the police. The frontier fighter's blade, without being long—brazen men could afford to wield a short knife—was better-tempered than the government-issue machetes, because of the state's predilection for higher cost and shoddy manufacture. And the arm that guided it was looking for trouble, and was better acquainted with the split-second moves of hand-to-hand combat. An example of such energy has survived the attrition of forty years:

---

[3]It was heretical to kill them, for they were marked with the sign of the cross—symbol of their provenance from and special distribution by the Lord.

21

> Get out of my way, I pray you,
> for I come from Tierra'el Juego.[4]

Fighting aside, this was, as well, the frontier of guitars.

As I write down these rescued events, I find myself thinking of a chance line from Browning's "Home Thoughts from the Sea"—"Here and here did England help me"—which he wrote while considering a sacrifice on the sea and the tall ship, maneuvering like a chessboard bishop, in which Nelson went down. I repeat the line, translating, too, the name of the homeland—for that of my native place is no less immediate to me than Browning's was to him—and it serves me as a symbol of solitary nights, of endless, ecstatic trampings through the city's infinite precincts. For Buenos Aires is unfathomably deep, and I have never given myself over to its streets without receiving, however great my disillusionment or anguish, unexpected consolation—now a sense of unreality, now a guitar in a hidden patio, now a brush with other lives. "Here and here did England help me"—here and here did Buenos Aires come to help me. And that is one of the reasons for this first chapter.

A VINDICATION OF THE CABALA [JLB 9]

This is not the first time it has been attempted, nor will it be the last time it fails, but it is distinguished by two facts. One is my almost complete ignorance of the Hebrew language; another is that I do not wish to vindicate the doctrine, but rather the hermeneutical or cryptographic procedures which lead to it. These procedures, as is well known, are the vertical reading of sacred texts, the reading referred to as *boustrophedon* (one line from left to right, the following line from right to left), the methodical substitution of certain letters of the alphabet for others, the sum of the numerical value of the letters, etc. It is easy to scoff at such operations. I prefer to attempt to understand them.

It is evident that their remote source is the concept of the mechanical inspiration of the Bible. This concept turns the evangelists and prophets into God's impersonal secretaries taking dictation, and is found with imprudent energy in the *Formula consensus helvetica* which claims authority for the consonants in the Scriptures and even for the diacritical marks which did not appear in the primitive versions. The necessary fulfillment in man of God's literary purposes is called either inspiration or enthusiasm, this last a word whose strictest meaning is to be possessed by a god. The Islamites can pride themselves on having exceeded that hyperbole, since they have resolved that the original Koran—the mother of books—is one of God's attributes like His pity or His wrath, and they judge it to be older than speech, older than creation. Likewise there are Lutheran

---

[4]Taullard, 233.

22

migrations, from a sailors' brothel in Tyre.[1] The thirty-three human years of Jesus Christ and his day's darkening into night on the cross were not sufficient expiation for the harsh Gnostics.

There remains to consider the other meaning of those obscure inventions. The vertiginous tower of heavens in the Basilidean heresy, the proliferation of its angels, the planetary shadow of the demiurges disrupting earth, the machinations of the inferior circles against the *pleroma,* the dense population, even though inconceivable or merely nominal, of that vast mythology, envisage the diminution of this world. Not our evil, but our central insignificance, is predicated in them. As in the swift west winds of the plain, the sky is impassioned and monumental and the earth is poor. That is the intention justifying the melodramatic cosmogony of Valentinus, which winds an infinite argument of two supernatural brothers who recognize each other, of a fallen woman, of a mighty mock intrigue among the bad angels, and of a final marriage. In this melodrama or popular serial-story, the creation of this world is a mere aside. Admirable idea: the world imaged as a process essentially futile, like a sideways, lost glimpse of old celestial episodes. Creation as a chance act.

The project was heroic; orthodox religious sentiment and theology loudly repudiate that possibility. The first creation, for them, is a free and necessary act of God. The universe, as Saint Augustine would have it understood, did not begin in time, but rather simultaneously with it, a judgment which denies all priority to the Creator. Strauss gives as illusory the hypothesis of an initial moment, for that would contaminate with temporality not only the following moments but also "precedent" eternity.

Throughout the first centuries of our era, the Gnostics disputed with the Christians. They were annihilated, but we can imagine their possible victory. Had Alexandria triumphed and not Rome, the extravagant and muddled stories that I have summarized here would be coherent, majestic, and perfectly ordinary. Pronouncements such as Novalis's "Life is a sickness of the spirit,"[2] or the despairing one of Rimbaud, "True life is absent; we are not in the world," would fulminate in the canonical books. Speculations, such as Richter's discarded one, about the stellar origin of life and its chance dissemination on this planet, would know the conditional assent of the pious laboratories. In any case, what better gift can we hope for, than to be insignificant? What greater glory for a God, than to be absolved of the world?

---

[1] Helen, dolorous daughter of God. That divine filiation does not exhaust the points of contact of her legend with Christ's. To him the followers of Basilides assigned an insubstantial body; of the tragic queen it was claimed that only her *eidolon* or simulacrum was snatched away to Troy. A beautiful specter redeemed us; another led to battles and Homer. See, for this Helenaic Docetism, Plato's *Phaedrus* and the work *Adventures Among Books* by Andrew Lang, pages 237–248.

[2] That dictum—*Leben ist eine Krankheit des Geistes, ein leidenschaftliches Tun*—owes its diffusion to Carlyle, who published it in his famous article in the *Foreign Review,* 1829. These and the *Prophetic Books* by William Blake are not momentary coincidences, but rather an essential rediscovery of the agonies and lights of Gnosticism.

Allow me to preface these notes on the Argentine citizen's most apparent defects. My limited subject is the mysterious, everyday Argentine city dweller, the man who worships the magnificent meat-packing and auctioneering professions, who travels by bus and considers this vehicle a lethal weapon, who despises the United States and is overjoyed that Buenos Aires competes with Chicago in the art of murder, who does not believe that Jews can be uncircumcised or hairless, who intuits a deep relationship between cigarettes and perverse or nonexistent virility, who exercises lovingly the shoulder-shrugging of his Catholic disbelief. This same urban specimen consumes, on festive evenings in brand-new traditional restaurants, whole barbecues consisting of indigestible portions of the inner organs of animals, and he prides himself also on being both an idealist and a wise guy, believing naïvely, of course, in the supremacy of the wise guy. I will not describe here the native *criollo,* a nonstop conversationalist and storyteller, known for his generous lack of prejudice. Today's *criollo,* the one from the province of Buenos Aires at least, is more a set of speech mannerisms than a man, whose behavior is sometimes meant to please, at other times purposely to annoy. The aging gaucho is a good example of this species. His pride and wit are subtle forms of servility because they confirm the popular image of the *criollo.* To know what he is really like, one must explore those regions where the inhabitants have not stylized or falsified him, Uruguay's northern provinces, for example. Let us return, then, to our everyday Argentine of the city streets. I will not define him in his entirety but will indicate, rather, his most obvious traits.

First, the poverty of his imagination. For the typical Argentine, anything unusual is monstrous, and therefore ridiculous. The dissident who lets his beard grow when everyone else is clean-shaven, or who prefers to don a top hat while in his neighborhood the folks are sporting broad brims, is a scandalous source of disbelief. In the local music halls, the Spaniard and the greenhorn are portrayed as colorful parodies of the *criollo* (our actors' inept performances help). These foreigners are not conceded the dignity of being wicked, but rather are fleeting objects of laughter, mere nobodies. Every effort they make is in vain. Even the seriousness of death is denied them. Their ghostly image corresponds, crudely, to our erroneous beliefs about all aliens. According to the majority, the foreigner is always in the wrong, an unforgivable, almost unreal creature. The worst foreigner of all, at the moment, is the Uruguayan, simply because Buenos Aires' eleven good lads were treated badly in a soccer game by Montevideo's eleven bad lads. If one makes the mistake of finding qualitative differences among these faceless outsiders, what will become of the real people? These so-called foreigners cannot be admitted as responsible members of mankind. The failure of that intense film *Hallelujah* before the audiences of this country, or rather, the failure of the extensive audiences of this country to appreciate *Hallelujah,* was inevitable. The incapacity to understand foreigners, exacerbated in this case because they were blacks, was added to another no less deplorable symptom, the intolerant mockery of true fervor. To neglect everything in the world that is not Argentine

28

is to demonstrate our superiority over other nations. A few months ago, after the expected outcome of a gubernatorial election, people began talking about Russian gold as if the internal politics of a province of this faded republic could excite Moscow's interest or even be perceived by the Russians. A willful megalomania nourishes these legends, and our ignorance is advertised in all our popular magazines, which are as neglectful of the five continents and seven seas as they are well disposed toward the expensive summer residents of Mar del Plata, who worship their own vile and cautious enthusiasm. Our view of home is even worse than our view of the world. The native's map of Buenos Aires is well known: it encompasses the downtown area, the North End (aseptically omitting its tenements), the South End and Belgrano. The rest is an inconvenient land of shadows, a vain conjectural bus stop for commuters to the outlying slums.

Another outstanding feature I shall discuss is the exuberant enjoyment of failure. In our movie theaters, crushed hopes are applauded as the material of high comedy. After a fight, our lively audiences find the loser's humiliation far more satisfying than the winner's good fortune. Toward the wretched end of a party in a heroic Sternberg film, tall gangster Bill Weed steps on dawn's dead streamers as he staggers toward his treacherous victim. The traitor, seeing Weed approach him awkwardly but steadfast, runs fearfully from apparent death. Abrupt peals of laughter celebrate his terror and remind us immediately that we are in the Southern Hemisphere. In the neighborhood movie houses, any hint of aggression is enough to excite the public. This ever-ready resentment, often articulated so joyously, does not have to leave our lips; it is always close to our hearts. Argentine women are quick to greet their friends' good fortunes with envious remarks, as if happiness were validated by the envy it provokes. (By the way, the most sincere Spanish compliment is *enviable.*)

Frequent poison-pen letters offer another illustration of the city slicker's capacity for hatred. In this category we must include the new, traceless, anonymous if not infamous phone call, usually an abusive message which cannot be returned, of course, to the self-effacing messenger. I do not know if this impersonal and modest literary genre is an Argentine invention, but it is practiced often and enthusiastically. Some gifted inhabitants of this city season the impudence of their emissions with the deliberate bad timing of their calls. Nor do our fellow citizens forget that great speed can be a form of good breeding and that insults hurled to pedestrians from a fast car are unimpeachable. True, the recipient is rarely identified and the short spectacle of his anger is quickly forgotten but isn't it always comforting to offend? I will add another curious subject of insult: sodomy. In all countries, an indivisible reprobation falls upon the two practitioners of this unimaginable contact. ". . . both of them have committed an abomination . . . their blood shall be upon them," says Leviticus (20:13, King James version). Not so with Buenos Aires' tough guys, who virtually venerate the active partner, because he took advantage of his companion. I hand over this fecal dialectic to the apologists for the wise guy, to those staunch supporters of backbiting and leg-pulling, all of which conceal so much hell.

Resentment and a poor imagination define our place in death. A relevant article by Unamuno on *The Imagination in Cochabamba* condones the latter. The former is supported by the unheard-of spectacle of a conservative government which is forcing the entire republic into socialism, merely to annoy and depress the liberals.

I have been an Argentine for many generations. Without any joy, I am resigned to these complaints.

THE POSTULATION OF REALITY [JLB 12]

Hume noted for all time that Berkeley's arguments do not admit the slightest reply and do not produce the slightest conviction. I would like, in order to eliminate Croce's arguments, a no less gracious and mortal sentence. Hume's does not serve my purpose because Croce's diaphanous doctrine has the power of persuasion, if nothing more. The result is unmanageability: it serves to cut short a discussion, not to resolve it.

Croce's formula, my reader will recall, is the identity of the esthetic and the expressive. I am not rejecting it, but I would like to observe that all writers of classical habit tend to shun the expressive. The fact has not been considered until now; I will explain myself.

The romantic, generally with little success, wishes to express incessantly; the classicist on rare occasions dispenses with begging the question. I diverge here from all historical connotations of the words "classicist" and "romantic"; by them I understand two archetypes of the writer (two approaches). The classicist does not distrust language; he believes in the adequate virtue of each one of its signs. He writes, for example:

> After the departure of the Goths, and the separation of the allied army, Attila was surprised at the vast silence that reigned over the plains of Chalons: the suspicion of some hostile stratagem detained him several days within the circle of his wagons, and his retreat beyond the Rhine confessed the last victory which was achieved in the name of the Western empire. Meroveus and his Franks, observing a prudent distance, and magnifying the opinion of their strength by the numerous fires which they kindled every night, continued to follow the rear of the Huns till they reached the confines of Thuringia. The Thuringians served in the army of Attila: they traversed, both in their march and in their return, the territories of the Franks; and it was perhaps in this war that they exercised the cruelties, which, about fourscore years afterwards, were revenged by the son of Clovis. They massacred their hostages, as well as their captives: two hundred young maidens were tortured with exquisite and unrelenting rage; their bodies were torn asunder by wild horses, or their bones were crushed under the weight of rolling wagons; and their unburied limbs were abandoned on the public roads, a prey to dogs and vultures. (Gibbon, *Decline and Fall of the Roman Empire,* XXXV)

30

The incisive "After the departure of the Goths" allows us to perceive the mediative character of this writing, generalized and abstract to the point of invisibility. The author proposes to us a play of symbols, rigorously organized without a doubt, but whose eventual animation remains our responsibility. He is not, in fact, expressive; he limits himself to recording a reality, not representing it. The prodigious events to whose posthumous allusion he invites us imply charged experiences, perceptions, reactions: these can be inferred from the narration, but they are not in it. To state it more precisely: he does not write of initial contacts with reality, but rather of their final conceptual elaboration. This is the classical method, the one always observed by Voltaire, by Swift, by Cervantes. I will transcribe a second, perhaps exaggerated, paragraph by this last:

> In short Lothario felt that while Anselmo's absence afforded time and opportunity he must press the siege of the fortress, and so he assailed her self-esteem with praises of her beauty, for there is nothing that more quickly reduces and levels the castle towers of fair women's vanity than vanity itself upon the tongue of flattery. In fact with the utmost assiduousness he undermined the rock of her purity with such engines that had Camilla been of brass she must have fallen. He wept, he entreated, he promised, he flattered, he importuned, he pretended with so much feeling and apparent sincerity, that he overthrew the virtuous resolves of Camilla and won the triumph he least expected and most longed for. (*Quixote,* I, Chapter 34)

Passages like the previous one make up the greater part of world literature, even of that which is least unworthy. To repudiate them in order to accommodate a formula would be misleading and ruinous. Within their notorious inefficacy, they are efficacious; that contradiction must be resolved.

I would suggest this hypothesis: imprecision is tolerable or plausible in literature because we are always inclined to it in reality. The conceptual simplification of complex states is often an instantaneous operation. The very act of perceiving, of heeding, is of a selective order; every attention, every fixation of our conscience, implies a deliberate omission of that which is uninteresting. We see and hear by means of remembrances, fears, foresight. In all corporal matters, unconsciousness is a necessity of physical acts. Our body knows how to articulate this difficult paragraph; it knows how to deal with stairs, with knots, with crossings, with cities, with rushing rivers, with dogs; it knows how to cross a street without being obliterated by the traffic; it knows how to procreate; it knows how to breathe; it knows how to sleep; it knows perhaps how to kill: our body, not our intellect. Our lives are a series of adaptations, that is to say, the educating of forgetfulness. It is notable that the first news of Utopia given to us by Thomas More should be his perplexed ignorance of the "true" length of one of its bridges . . .

I reread, for a better understanding of the classical, the paragraph by Gibbon, and I came across an almost imperceptible and certainly innocuous metaphor—that of the reign of silence. It is an attempt at expression—I do not know if well chosen or ill-fated—that does not seem suited to the strict legal discharge of the rest of his prose. Naturally, it is justified by its invisibility, its conventional nature. Its use permits us to define another of the marks of classicism: the belief that once an image has been forged, it constitutes public property. For the classical concept, the plurality of man and of time is incidental; literature is always one. The astonishing defenders of Góngora vindicated him of the charge of innovation by means of documentary proof of the perfectly erudite ancestry of his metaphors. The romantic discovery of personality was not even foreseen by them. Now, we are all so absorbed in it that the fact of denying or forgetting it is only one of the many facilities of *being personal.* With regard to the thesis that poetic language should be one, we can point out its evanescent resurrection at the hands of Arnold, who proposed to reduce the vocabulary of the Homeric translators to that of the authorized version of Scriptures, without any relief other than the eventual interjection of some of Shakespeare's liberties. Arnold's argument was the power and diffusion of the biblical words.

The reality that classical writers propose is a matter of confidence, like the paternity of a certain character of the *Lehrjahre.* The reality which the romantics attempt to exhaust is of a rather impositive nature: their constant method is that of emphasis, the partial lie. I do not ask for illustrations: all the pages of prose or verse that are professionally contemporary can be successfully examined.

The classical postulation of reality can assume three modes, very diversely accessible. The one most easily dealt with consists of a general imparting of the important facts. (Except for a few uncomfortable allegories, the above-quoted text by Cervantes is not a bad example of this first and spontaneous mode of classical method.) The second consists of imagining a more complex reality than the one stated to the reader and recounting its derivations and effects. I know of no better illustration than the opening of the heroic fragment by Tennyson, *Morte d'Arthur:*

> So all day long the noise of battle roll'd
> Among the mountains by the winter sea;
> Until King Arthur's table, man by man,
> Had fallen in Lyonnesse about their Lord,
> King Arthur: then, because his wound was deep,
> The bold Sir Bedivere uplifted him,
> Sir Bedivere the last of all his knights,
> And bore him to a chapel nigh the field,
> A broken chancel with a broken cross,
> That stood on a dark strait of barren land.
> On one side lay the Ocean, and on one
> Lay a great water, and the moon was full.

Three times this narration has postulated a more complex reality: the first time, by means of the grammatical artifice of the adverb "so"; the second—and finer —time, by means of the incidental manner of transmitting a fact: "because his wound was deep"; the third time, by means of the unexpected addition of "and the moon was full." Morris provides another effective illustration of this method. After relating the mythical abduction of one of Jason's oarsmen by the fleet-footed river divinities, he closes the story in this way:

. . . the gurgling river hid
The flushed nymphs and the heedless sleeping man.
But ere the water covered them, one ran
Across the mead and caught up from the ground
The brass-bound spear, and buckler bossed and round,
The ivory-hilted sword, and coat of mail,
Then took the stream; so what might tell the tale,
Unless the wind should tell it, or the bird
Who from the reed these things had seen and heard?

This final testimony from beings who have not even been mentioned previously is what concerns us at this point.

The third method, the most difficult and most effective, employs circumstantial invention. Let this very memorable passage from *La gloria de Don Ramiro* serve as an example: ". . . that spectacular bacon broth, served in a tureen with a padlock to defend it from the voracity of the pages"—so suggestive of genteel poverty, of the string of servants, of the big old house full of stairs and turns and different lights. I have stated a short, linear example, but I know of long, drawn-out works—the rigorous imaginative novels of Wells,[1] the exasperatingly truthful ones of Daniel Defoe, which use no other approach than the exposition or series of those laconic details with long-range consequences. I maintain the same of the cinematographic novels of Josef von Sternberg, which are also made up of significant moments. It is an admirable and difficult method, but its general applicability makes it less strictly literary than the two previous ones, particularly the second. The latter tends to function on the basis of pure syntax, pure verbal dexterity. The proof can be found in these lines by Moore:

> *Je suis ton amant, et la blonde*
> *Gorge tremble sous mon baiser.*

Their virtue lies in the transition from the possessive pronoun to the definite article, in the surprising use of "la." A reverse symmetry can be found in the following line from Kipling:

---

[1] Also *The Invisible Man*. That character—a solitary chemistry student during a desperate London winter—ends up by recognizing that the privileges of the invisible state do not outweigh the inconveniences. He must go barefoot and naked so that the city is not alarmed by an overcoat hurrying by and a pair of autonomous boots. A revolver in his transparent hand is impossible to hide, and so is the food he swallows until it has been digested. From dawn on, his nominal eyelids do not block the light and he must become accustomed to sleeping with his eyes open. Nor can he throw his ghostly arm over his eyes. In the street he is susceptible to traffic accidents and is in constant fear of being run over. He must flee London. He must take refuge in wigs, in dark glasses, in fake noses and in suspicious beards, in gloves . . . so that people do not see that he is invisible. Once discovered, he initiates in an inland village a miserable reign of terror. He wounds a man so that he will be respected. The commissioner of police has him tracked by dogs; they bring him to bay near the station and kill him.

Another very clever example of circumstantial phantasmagoria is Kipling's "The Finest Story in the World," included in *Many Inventions* (1893).

33

Little they trust to sparrow—dust that stop the seal in his sea!

Naturally, "his" is determined by "seal": "that stop the seal in *his* sea."

NARRATIVE ART AND MAGIC

[JLB 13]

Analyses of the technique of the novel have not, I think, been wholly exhausted. A historical reason for this continued neglect may be the greater antiquity of other genres; a more basic reason, however, is that the novel's many technical complexities are not easily disentangled from its plot. The analysis of a short story or elegy is served by a specialized vocabulary and aided by the facility of quoting brief, pertinent passages. The study of the novel, on the other hand, lacks such special terms, and the critic is hard put to it to find examples that immediately illustrate his arguments. I therefore ask indulgence for the cumbrousness of what follows.

I shall start out by considering from the viewpoint of the novel William Morris's *Life and Death of Jason* (1867). My aim is literary, not historical. I deliberately omit any references to the poem's classical origins. Let me only point out that the ancients—among them, Apollonius of Rhodes—had long since set the deeds of the Argonauts to verse, and mention an intermediate work dating from 1474, *Les faits et prouesses du noble et vaillant chevalier Jason,* not to be found in Buenos Aires, of course, but which English students may readily consult.

Morris's difficult task was to narrate realistically the fabled adventures of Jason, king of Iolchos. Line by line virtuosity, common enough in short lyrical pieces, was impossible in a narrative of over 10,000 lines. What was required, above all, was a strong appearance of factual truth, capable of producing that willing suspension of disbelief which, for Coleridge, is the essence of poetic conviction. Morris achieves this conviction; I want to find out how.

I take an example from Book I. Æson, the old king of Iolchos, gives his son over to the charge of the centaur Chiron. The problem lies in making the centaur believable. Morris solves it almost unwittingly by weaving in mention of this mythical race at the outset among the names of other strange wild beasts. "Where bears and wolves the centaurs' arrows find," he states quite matter of factly. This first incidental reference is followed some thirty lines later by another, which comes before any actual description. The old king orders a slave to take the child to the forest at the foot of the mountains, blow on an ivory horn to call forth the centaur—who will be, he tells him, "grave of face and large of limb"—and fall upon his knees before him. These commands go on, until we come to a third and somewhat negative mention of the centaur, of whom the king bids the slave to "have no whit of fear." Then, troubled by the fate of the son he is about to lose, Æson tries to imagine the boy's future life in the forests among the "quick-eyed centaurs"—an epithet which brings them to life and is justified by their wide-

extraordinary qualities. It was *not* colorless, nor was it of any one uniform color—presenting to the eye, as it flowed, every possible shade of purple, like the hues of a changeable silk. . . . Upon collecting a basinful, and allowing it to settle thoroughly, we perceived that the whole mass of liquid was made up of a number of distinct veins, each of a distinct hue; that these veins did not commingle; and that their cohesion was perfect in regard to their own particles among themselves, and imperfect in regard to neighboring veins. Upon passing the blade of a knife athwart the veins, the water closed over it immediately, as with us, and also, in withdrawing it, all traces of the passage of the knife were instantly obliterated. If, however, the blade was passed down accurately between the two veins, a perfect separation was effected, which the power of cohesion did not immediately rectify.

From the foregoing illustrations it may rightly be inferred that the main problem of the novel is that of causation. One kind of novel, the slow-moving psychological variety, attempts to frame an intricate chain of motives akin to those of real life. This, however, is not generally the case. In the adventure novel, cumbersome motivation of this kind is inappropriate; the same may be said for the short story and for the endless spectacular fictions made up in Hollywood, with the silvery images of Joan Crawford, that are read and reread the whole world over. A quite different sort of order rules them, one based not on reason but on association and suggestion—the ancient light of magic.

Magic—that craft, or ambition, of early man—has been reduced by Frazer to a convenient general law, the Law of Sympathy, which assumes that "things act on each other at a distance through a secret sympathy," either because their form is similar (imitative, or homeopathic, magic) or because of a previous physical contact (contagious, or contact, magic). An example of the second is Kenelm Digby's ointment, which was applied not to the bandaged wound but to the offending weapon that inflicted it—leaving the wound, free of the stringency of barbarous treatments, to heal itself. Of the first kind of magic, the examples are innumerable. The Indians of Nebraska donned creaking buffalo robes, with horns and manes, and day and night beat out a thunderous dance so as to call the buffalo. Medicine men in central Australia inflict a wound in their forearms that sheds blood so that the imitative sky will shed rain. The Malayans often torment or insult a wax image so that the enemy it resembles will die. Barren women in Sumatra adorn and hold in their laps a wooden image of a child so that their wombs will bear fruit. For the same reasons of similarity, among the ancient Hindus the yellow root of the curcuma plant was used for the cure of jaundice, and, locally in Argentina, a tea made of nettles was used to cure hives. A complete list of these savage, or ridiculous, examples is impossible; I think I have cited enough of them, however, to show that magic is not the contradiction of the law of cause and effect but its crown, or nightmare. The miraculous is no less strange in that world than it is in the world of astronomers. All of the laws of nature as well as those of imagination govern it. To the superstitious mind, there is a necessary link not only between a gunshot and a corpse but between a corpse and a tortured wax image, or the prophetic smashing of a mirror, or spilled salt, or thirteen people ominously seated at the same table.

This dangerous connection, this frenzied and clearly defined cause and effect, also holds good in the novel. Saracen historians, whose writings are the source of José Antonio Conde's *Historia de la dominación de los árabes en España,* do not write of a king or caliph that he died, but that "He was taken to the rewards and gifts," or that "He passed into the mercy of the All-Powerful," or that "He awaited his fate so many years, so many moons, and so many days." This fear that a terrible event may be brought on by its mere mention is out of place or pointless in the overwhelming disorder of the real world, though not in a novel, which should be a rigorous scheme of attentions, echoes and affinities. Every episode in a painstaking piece of fiction prefigures something still to come. Thus, in one of Chesterton's phantasmagorias, a man suddenly shoves a stranger out of the road to save him from an oncoming motorcar, and this necessary but alarming violence foreshadows the first man's later act of declaring the other man insane so that he may not be hanged for a murder. In another Chesterton story, a vast and dangerous conspiracy consisting of a single man (aided by false beards, masks, and aliases) is darkly heralded by the lines:

> As all stars shrivel in the single sun,
> The words are many, but The Word is one.

This comes to be unraveled at the end through a shift of capital letters:

> The words are many, but the word is One.

In a third story, the initial prototype—the passing mention of an Indian who throws his knife at another man and kills him—is the complete reverse of the plot: a man stabbed to death by his friend with an arrow beside the open window of a tower. A knife turned into an arrow, an arrow turned into a knife. Between the two, there is a long repercussion. Elsewhere, I have pointed out that the single preliminary mention of stage sets taints with a disquieting unreality the fine descriptions of dawn, the pampa, and nightfall that Estanislao del Campo has worked into his *Fausto.* This teleology of words and episodes is also omnipresent in good films. At the beginning of *The Show Down,* a pair of adventurers play cards for a prostitute, or a turn at her; at the end, one of them has gambled away the possession of the woman he really loves. The opening dialogue of *Underworld* concerns stool pigeons, the opening scene is a gunfight on an avenue; these bits foreshadow the whole plot. In *Dishonored,* there are recurring themes: the sword, the kiss, the cat, betrayal, grapes, the piano. But the most perfect example of an autonomous orb of confirmations, omens, and monuments is Joyce's preordained *Ulysses.* One need only look into Stuart Gilbert's study or, in its absence, into the dizzying novel itself.

Let me sum up the foregoing. I have pointed out two chains of cause and effect: the natural, which is the incessant result of endless, uncontrollable processes; and the magic, in which—clear and defined—every detail is an omen and a cause. In the novel, I think that the only possible integrity lies in the second. Let us leave the first to psychological fiction, where all things are plausible.

I propose for the reader's consideration this modest literary specimen:

> Once there were two balloons
> and I didn't know which to go up in.
> At once I went to the one
> that was making a hundred-year journey.
> It took me to a strange land
> where the mules did the plowing . . .

It is the beginning of a crude *milonga,* which degenerates into a cluster of fatuous incongruities, up to the image of the last line. It came to my ears in a country store near Arapey, at the beginning of 1931, and I reproduce it, confident that it is free of errors. To be innocently fond of it or to make fun of it both seem equally pointless. I prefer, at this point, to examine just how it works. As for what is behind it, vague and lost as it certainly is, I leave the final investigation of that to the Last Judgment—or to the brilliant and incisive Spitzer, "who works his way through the capillaries of the most characteristic idiomatic forms to the original esthetic impulses which brought them about." It is enough for me to explain the effects the lines produce in me.

Once there were two balloons. In this line, *once,* the conventional way of beginning fairy tales, and the native equivalent of the European *once upon a time,* sets up the mention of the balloons, which tend to suggest the marvels of the nineteenth century. That happy and sentimental anachronism is the first "effect" of the *milonga.* If Gracián had been the perpetrator of the verse, I would suspect something worse, a suggestion of spurious disharmony between the solitary nature of the occasion and the duality of the balloons.

And I didn't know which to go up in. Second shift. Suddenly, the untemporal circumstances of the previous line take us in a fanciful biographical direction.

At once I went to the one. Third shift. Blunt and unexpected decision.

That was making a hundred-year journey. Fourth shift, by means of which we come to know that the innocent *compadrito* of the *milonga* was already familiar with the balloons, and knew that one of them was undertaking a venerable expedition, conferring (or requiring) longevity on those who joined it. Nothing is said of the course of the other balloon, a no less admirable detail.

It took me to a strange land. Negative surprise, the surprise of there being no surprise, since a "strange land" is the least that can justify that journey.

Where the mules did the plowing. Here, for the first time, an actual marvel crops up, albeit not very felicitously. The image of mules plowing tries to introduce utter incongruity, but cheerfully misses doing so through the commonly unpleasant connotation of the two words.

So much for the analysis. I undertook it, not to pretend that the rather ordinary *milonga* had hidden felicities, but to show what any verbal form can set going in us. That intricate game of changes, of successful frustrations, of enthusiasms, exhausts for me the esthetic act. Those who discount it or gloss over it are ignoring literary particularity.

39

Another simple example, two lines from the lyric of a tango called "Villa Crespo," by, I think, Tagle Lara:

> Where are they now, those men and these minxes—
> red hat bands and wide hats that Requeña once knew?

Their concealed triumphs are fourfold. The first is the interrogative tone given to the regret, the question "Where are they?" to emphasize that they no longer exist. The second is the high tone of the word "men," here with the ring and authority of handsome men, standing out in opposition to the word "minxes" which follows. The third is the definition of that dark, *fin-de-siècle* crowd through its attributes: red hat bands and wide hats. The fourth is the substitution of the third person for the first, of the individual name for the vague "I knew."

I copy out a third example, this time one of respected origin, the 107th line of the first book of the twelve that make up *Paradise Lost.* It is as follows:

> and study of revenge, immortal hate

Here, the reciprocity of the elements is obvious: "study," a temperate and serious word, is opposed to "revenge," "immortal," with its majestic overtones, opposed to "hate."

A fourth example, a verse of a poem by Cummings.

> God's terrible face,
> brighter than a spoon,
> collects the image of one fatal word;
> so that my life (which like the sun and the moon)
> resembles something that has not occurred:
> i am a birdcage without any bird,
> a collar looking for a dog, a kiss
> without lips; a prayer lacking any knees
> but something beats within my shirt to prove
> he is undead who, living, no one is.
> I have never loved you dear as now i love.

Imperfect symmetry, a scheme frustrated and lightened by continual surprises, is the notorious rule in this verse. "Spoon" instead of "sword" or "star," "looking for" instead of "without," "shirt" in the place of "breast," the lower-case personal pronoun, "undead" for "alive," are the most obvious variations. . . . "The rose is without a why," we read in the first book of Silesius's *Cherubinischer Wandersmann.* I affirm the contrary, I insist that a close conspiring of whys is essential for the rose to be a rose. I think that there is always more than one reason for the sudden triumph of one line or the immediate failure of another. I believe in reasonable mysteries, not in crude miracles.

A fifth and last example, this time one of equivocation. I read on a street poster of Catholic persuasion:

> Youths of no experience believe in men.
> Grown-ups, who have lived, who have thought, believe in God.

I suspect that the necessity of being unequivocal ruined a good version, which I shall put back.

> The young, with no experience, believe in men.
> Men believe in God.

The counterbalancing of "the young" and "men" is more than enough to contain the words eliminated.

The obvious and dilatory analyses I have just traced out justify two conclusions: one, the value of rhetorical discipline, provided it is practiced with precision; the other, the final impossibility of an esthetic. If no word exists in vain, if a *milonga* heard in a country store is a world of attractions and repulsions, how can we elucidate that "tide of pomp, that beats upon the high shore of this world," the 1056 pages of the First Quarto attributed to one, Shakespeare? How to judge seriously what is judged in the mass by no other method than a wondrous emission of awestruck eulogies, without studying a single line?

The esthetic of the complete works should be put aside, that of its diverse instances should remain. In any case, the one should precede the other, as its justification.

Literature is fundamentally a syntactical matter. It is accidental, linear, sporadic and most everyday.

THE DREAD REDEEMER LAZARUS MORELL [JLB 15]

THE REMOTE CAUSE

In 1517, the Spanish missionary Bartolomé de las Casas, taking great pity on the Indians who were languishing in the hellish workpits of Antillean gold mines, suggested to Charles V, king of Spain, a scheme for importing blacks, so that they might languish in the hellish workpits of Antillean gold mines. To this odd philanthropic twist we owe, all up and down the Americas, endless things—W. C. Handy's blues; the Parisian success of the Uruguayan lawyer and painter of Negro genre, Don Pedro Figari; the solid native prose of another Uruguayan, Don Vicente Rossi, who traced the origin of the tango to Negroes; the mythological dimensions of Abraham Lincoln; the 500,000 dead of the Civil War and its $3,300,000 spent in military pensions; the entrance of the verb *to lynch* into the thirteenth edition of the dictionary of the Spanish Academy; King Vidor's impetuous film *Hallelujah;* the lusty bayonet charge led by the Argentine captain Miguel Soler, at the head of his famous regiment of "Mulattoes and Blacks," in the Uruguayan battle of Cerrito; the Negro killed by Martín Fierro; the deplorable Cuban rumba "The Peanut Vendor"; the arrested, dungeon-ridden Napoleonism of Toussaint L'Ouverture; the cross and the snake of Haitian voodoo rites and the blood of goats whose throats were slit by the *papaloi's* machete; the habanera, mother of the tango, another old Negro dance, of Buenos Aires and Montevideo, the *candombe.*

And, further, the great and blameworthy life of the nefarious redeemer Lazarus Morell.

THE PLACE

The Father of Waters, the Mississippi, the largest river in the world, was the worthy theater of this peerless scoundrel. (Álvarez de Pineda discovered the river, and its earliest explorer was Captain Hernando de Soto, the old conqueror of Peru, who helped while away the Inca chief Atahualpa's months of prison, teaching him the game of chess. When de Soto died, he was given the Mississippi's waters for a grave.)

The Mississippi is a broad-bosomed river, an immense, dim brother of the Paraná, the Uruguay, the Amazon, and the Orinoco. It is a river of muddy waters; each year, disgorged by it, over 400 million tons of silt profane the Gulf of Mexico. From time immemorial, so much muck has built up a delta, where gigantic swamp cypresses grow out of the debris of a continent in perpetual dissolution, and where labyrinths of mud and rushes and dead fish extend the bounds and the peace of this foul-smelling alluvial domain. Upstream, between the Arkansas and the Ohio, is another stretch of lowlands. Living there is a sallow race of squalid men, prone to fever, who avidly gape at stone and iron, for in their environs there is little but sand, timber, and muddy water.

THE MEN

At the beginning of the nineteenth century (the date that concerns us), the vast cotton plantations along the river were worked, from sunup to sundown, by blacks. These blacks slept on dirt floors in wooden cabins. Apart from mother-child relations, kinships were casual and unclear. They had first names, but they made do without family names. Nor could they read. Their soft, falsetto voices intoned an English of drawled vowels. They worked in rows, bent under the overseer's lash. When they ran away, full-bearded men, springing onto beautiful horses, tracked them down with snarling packs of hounds.

To successive layers of animal hopes and African fears there had been added the words of the Bible. Their faith, therefore, lay in Christ. They sang deeply and in chorus, "Go down, Moses." The Mississippi served them as a magnificent image of the paltry Jordan.

The owners of this hardworked land and of these black gangs were idle, greedy gentlemen with flowing locks, who lived in big mansions that overlooked the river—always with a white pine, Greek Revival portico. A good slave was worth a thousand dollars and did not last long. Some of them were thankless enough to fall ill and die. Out of such uncertainties, one had to wring the greatest return. This is why slaves were kept in the fields from first light to last; this is why plantations required yearly crops, such as cotton or tobacco or sugarcane. The soil, overworked and mismanaged by this greedy cultivation, was left exhausted within a short time, and tangled, miry wastes encroached upon the land.

42

On abandoned farms, on the outskirts of towns, among the thick canebrakes, and in the abject bayous, lived the poor whites. They were fishermen, occasional hunters, and horse thieves. They often begged bits of stolen food from the blacks, and even in their lowly condition these poor whites kept up a certain pride—that of their untainted, unmixed blood. Lazarus Morell was one of them.

THE MAN

The daguerreotypes of Morell usually published in American magazines are not authentic. This lack of genuine representations of so memorable and famous a man cannot be accidental. We may suppose that Morell resisted the camera, essentially, so as not to leave behind pointless clues, and, at the same time, to foster the mystery that surrounded him. We know, however, that as a young man he was not favored with looks, and that his eyes, which were too close together, and his straight lips were not prepossessing. Thereafter, the years conferred upon him that majesty peculiar to white-haired scoundrels and daring, unpunished criminals. He was an old Southern gentleman, despite a miserable childhood and an inglorious life. Versed in Scripture, he preached with unusual conviction. "I saw Lazarus Morell in the pulpit," noted the proprietor of a Baton Rouge gambling house, "and I listened to his edifying words and I saw the tears gather in his eyes. I knew that in God's sight he was an adulterer, a Negro-stealer, and a murderer, but my eyes wept, too."

Another fair record of these holy effusions is furnished by Morell himself. "I opened my Bible at random," he wrote, "and came upon a fitting verse from Saint Paul, and I preached an hour and twenty minutes. Nor was this time misspent by my assistant Crenshaw and his confederates, for they were outside rounding up all the hearers' horses. We sold them on the Arkansas side of the river, except for one spirited chestnut that I reserved for my own private use. He pleased Crenshaw as well, but I made him see that the animal was not for him."

THE METHOD

The stealing of horses in one state and selling them in another were barely more than a digression in Morell's criminal career, but they foreshadowed the method that now assures him his rightful place in a Universal History of Infamy. This method is unique not only for the peculiar circumstances that distinguished it but also for the sordidness it required, for its deadly manipulation of hope, and for its step-by-step development, so like the hideous unfolding of a nightmare. Al Capone and Bugs Moran were later to operate in a great city, with dazzling sums of money and lowly submachine guns, but their affairs were vulgar. They merely vied for a monopoly. As to numbers of men, Morell came to command some thousand—all sworn confederates. Two hundred of them made up the Heads, or Council, and they gave the orders that the remaining 800 carried out. All the risks fell upon these active agents, or strikers, as they were called. In the event of trouble, it was they who were handed over to justice or thrown into the Mississippi with a stone fixed securely about their feet. A good many of them were mulattoes. Their diabolical mission was the following:

Flashing rings on their fingers to inspire respect, they traveled up and down the vast plantations of the South. They would pick out a wretched black and offer him freedom. They would tell him that if he ran away from his master and allowed them to sell him, he would receive a portion of the money paid for him, and they would then help him escape again, this second time sending him to a free state. Money and freedom, the jingle of silver dollars together with his liberty —what greater temptation could they offer him? The slave became emboldened for his first escape.

The river provided the natural route. A canoe; the hold of a steamboat; a scow; a great raft as big as the sky, with a cabin at the point or three or four wigwams—the means mattered little, what counted was feeling the movement and the safety of the unceasing river. The black would be sold on some other plantation, then run away again to the canebrakes or the morasses. There his terrible benefactors (about whom he now began to have serious misgivings) cited obscure expenses and told him they had to sell him one final time. On his return, they said, they would give him part of both sales and his freedom. The man let himself be sold, worked for a while, and on his final escape defied the hounds and the whip. He then made his way back bloodied, sweaty, desperate, and sleepy.

FINAL RELEASE

The legal aspect of these doings must now be reviewed. The runaway slave was not put up for sale by Morell's gang until his first master had advertised and offered a reward to any man who would catch him. An advertisement of this kind warranted the person to take the property, if found. The black then became a property in trust, so that his subsequent sale was only a breach of trust, not stealing. Redress by a civil action for such a breach was useless, as the damages were never paid.

All this was very reassuring—but not entirely foolproof. The black, out of sheer gratitude or misery, might open his mouth. A jug of rye whiskey in some Cairo brothel, where the son of a bitch, born a slave, would squander those good dollars that they had no business letting him have, and their secret was spilled. Throughout these years, abolitionist agitators roamed the length and breadth of the North—a mob of dangerous madmen who opposed private property, preached the emancipation of slaves, and incited them to run away. Morell was not going to let himself be taken in by those anarchists. He was no Yankee, he was a Southern white, the son and grandson of whites, and he hoped one day to retire from business and become a gentleman and have his own miles of cotton fields and rows of bent-over slaves. He was not about to take pointless risks—not with his experience.

The runaway expected his freedom. Lazarus Morell's shadowy mulattoes would give out an order among themselves that was sometimes barely more than a nod of the head, and the slave would be freed from sight, hearing, touch, day, infamy, time, his benefactors, pity, the air, the hound packs, the world, hope, sweat, and himself. A bullet, a knife, or a blow, and the Mississippi turtles and catfish would receive the last evidence.

44

In the hands of reliable men, the business had to prosper. At the beginning of 1834, Morell had already "emancipated" some seventy blacks, and many others were ready to follow the lead of these lucky forerunners. The field of operations grew wider, and it became essential to take on new associates. Among those who swore to the oath was a young man from Arkansas, one Virgil Stewart, who very soon made himself conspicuous for his cruelty. Stewart was the nephew of a gentleman who had had many slaves decoyed away. In August 1834, this young man broke his oath and exposed Morell and his whole gang. Morell's house in New Orleans was surrounded by the authorities. Only due to their negligence, or perhaps through a bribe, was Morell able to make good an escape.

Three days passed. During this time, Morell remained hidden on Toulouse Street in an old house with courtyards that were filled with vines and statues. It seems that he took to eating little and would stalk up and down the dim, spacious rooms in his bare feet, thoughtfully smoking cigars. By a slave of the place, he sent two letters to Natchez and a third to Red River. On the fourth day, three men joined him, and they stayed until dawn, arguing over plans. On the fifth day, Morell got out of bed as it was growing dusk and, asking for a razor, carefully shaved off his beard. Then he dressed and left. At an easy pace, he made his way across the city's northern suburbs. Once in the country, skirting the Mississippi flats, he walked more briskly.

His scheme was foolhardy. He planned to enlist the services of the last men still to owe him honor—the South's obliging blacks. They had watched their companions run off and never seen them reappear. Their freedom, therefore, was real. Morell's object was to raise the blacks against the whites, to capture and sack New Orleans, and to take possession of the territory. Morell, brought down and nearly destroyed by Stewart's betrayal, contemplated a nationwide response—a response in which criminal elements would be exalted to the point of redemption and a place in history. With this aim, he started out for Natchez, where he enjoyed greater strength. I copy his account of that journey:

> I walked four days, and no opportunity offered for me to get a horse. The fifth day, about twelve, I stopped at a creek to get some water and rest a little. While I was sitting on a log, looking down the road the way that I had come, a man came in sight riding on a good-looking horse. The very moment I saw him, I was determined to have his horse. I arose and drew an elegant rifle pistol on him and ordered him to dismount. He did so. and I took his horse by the bridle and pointed down the creek, and ordered him to walk before me. He went a few hundred yards and stopped. I made him undress himself. He said, "If you are determined to kill me, let me have time to pray before I die." I told him I had no time to hear him pray. He dropped on his knees, and I shot him through the back of the head. I ripped open his belly and took out his entrails, and sunk him in the creek. I then searched his pockets, and found four hundred dollars and thirty-seven cents, and a number of papers that I did not take time to examine.

His boots were brand-new, and fitted me genteelly. I put them on and sunk my old shoes in the creek.

That was how I obtained the horse I needed, and directed my course for Natchez in much better style than I had been for the last five days.

THE DISRUPTION

Morell leading rebellions of blacks who dreamed of lynching him; Morell lynched by armies of blacks he dreamed of leading—it hurts me to confess that Mississippi history took advantage of neither of these splendid opportunities. Nor, contrary to all poetic justice (or poetic symmetry), did the river of his crimes become his grave. On January 2, 1835, Lazarus Morell died of a lung ailment in the Natchez hospital, where he had been interned under the name Silas Buckley. A fellow patient on the ward recognized him. On the second and on the fourth, the slaves of certain plantations attempted an uprising, but they were put down without a great deal of bloodshed.

THE ART OF VERBAL ABUSE [JLB 16]

A conscientious study of other literary genres has led me to believe in the greater value of insult and mockery. The aggressor, I tell myself, knows that the tables will be turned, and that "anything you say may be used against you," as the honest constables of Scotland Yard warn us. That fear is bound to produce special anxieties, which we disregard on more comfortable occasions. The critic would like to be invulnerable, and sometimes he is. After comparing the healthy indignations of Paul Groussac, the Franco-Argentine critic, with his ambiguous eulogies (not to mention the similar cases of Swift, Voltaire, and Johnson), I nourished or inspired in myself that hope of invulnerability. It vanished as soon as I left off reading those pleasant mockeries, in order to examine Groussac's method.

I noticed immediately one thing: the fundamental injustice and delicate error of my conjectures. The practical joker proceeds carefully, like a gambler admitting the fiction of a pack of cards, a corruptible paradise of two-headed people. The three kings of poker are meaningless in *truco,* the Argentine card game. The polemicist is also a creature of convention. For most people, the street formulas of insult offer a model of what polemics can become. The man in the street guesses that all people's mothers have the same profession, or he suggests that they move immediately to a general place that has several names, or he imitates a rude sound. A senseless convention has determined that the offended one is not himself but rather the silent and attentive listener. Language is not even needed. For example, Sampson's, "I will take the wall of any man or maid of Montague's," or Abram's, "Do you bite your thumb at us, sir?" were the legal tender of the troublemaker, around 1592, in Shakespeare's fraudulent Verona and in the beer halls, brothels, and bear-baiting pits of London. In Argentine schools, the middle finger and a show of tongue serve that purpose.

"Dog" is another very general term of insult. During the 146th Night of the *1001 Nights,* the discreet reader learns that the son of Adam, after locking the son of the lion in a sealed chest, scolded him thus: "O dog of the desert . . . Fate hath upset thee, nor shall caution set thee up."

A conventional alphabet of scorn also defines polemicists. The title *sir,* unwisely and irregularly omitted in spoken intercourse, is scathing in print. Commenting on the sonnets *perpetrated* by *Doctor Lugones* is equivalent to branding them as eternally unspeakable, and to refuting each and every one of his metaphors. At the first mention of *doctor* the demigod vanishes and is replaced by a vain Argentine gentleman who wears paper collars, gets a shave every other day, and is in danger of dying at any moment of a respiratory ailment. What remains is the central and incurable futility of man. But the sonnets also remain, their music awaiting a reader. An Italian, in order to rid himself of Goethe, concocted a brief article where he persisted in calling him *il signore Wolfgang.* This was almost flattery, since it meant that he didn't know there were solid arguments against Goethe.

Perpetrating a sonnet, concocting an article. Language is a repertory of these suitable snubs which are the ordinary currency of controversy. To say that a literary man has discharged a book, or has cooked it up or ground it out are easy temptations. The verbs of bureaucrats or storekeepers are much more effective: dispatch, circulate, sell. Combine these dry words with more effusive ones and the enemy is doomed to eternal shame. To a question about an auctioneer who also used to recite poetry, someone quickly responded that he was energetically auctioning off *The Divine Comedy.* The witticism is not overwhelmingly ingenious, but its mechanism is typical. As with all witticisms, it involves a mere confusion. The verb *auctioning* (supported by the adverb *energetically*) leaves one to understand that the incriminated gentleman is an irreparable and sordid auctioneer, and that his Dantesque diligence is an outrage. The listener readily accepts the argument because it is not presented as an argument. Were it correctly formulated, he would have to refute its validity. First of all, declaiming and auctioneering are related activities. Secondly, the old vocation of declaiming, an exercise in public speaking, could help the auctioneer at his task.

One of the satirical traditions (not despised by Macedonio Fernández, Quevedo, or George Bernard Shaw) is the unconditional inversion of terms. According to this famous prescription, doctors are accused inevitably of promoting contagion and death, court clerks of theft, executioners of encouraging longevity, tellers of adventure stories of numbing or putting the reader to sleep, wandering Jews of paralysis, tailors of nudism, tigers and cannibals of preferring a diet of rhubarb. A variety of that tradition is the innocent phrase which pretends at times to condone what it is destroying. For example: "The famous camp bed under which the general won the battle. The last film of the talented director René Clair was utterly charming. When we woke up . . ."

Another handy method is the abrupt change. For instance: a young priest of Beauty, a mind illuminated by Helenic light, an exquisite man with the taste

47

... of a mouse. Likewise, these Andalusian lyrics which quickly pass from inquiry to assault:

> A chair is made
> of many sticks.
> Shall I break it
> over your ribs?

Let me insist on the formal aspects of this game, its persistent and illicit use of confusing arguments. Seriously defending a cause and disseminating burlesque exaggerations, false generosity, tricky concessions, and patient contempt are not incompatible, but are so diverse that no one, until now, has managed to put them all together. Here are some illustrious examples: Set to demolish Ricardo Rojas's *History of Argentine Literature,* what does Paul Groussac do? The following, which all Argentine men of letters have relished: "After hearing resignedly two or three fragments in cumbersome prose of a certain tome publicly applauded by those who had barely opened it, I now consider myself authorized not to continue any further, consulting summaries or indexes of that bountiful history of what never organically existed. I am referring especially to the first and most indigestible part of the bulk (it occupies three of the four volumes). The mumblings of native half-breeds . . ." Groussac, with that good ill humor, fulfills the most eager ritual of satirical games. He pretends to be pained by the errors of the adversary (after hearing resignedly), allows one to glimpse the spectacle of abrupt scorn (first the word "tome," next "bulk"), uses terms of praise in order to assault (that *bountiful* history); and then, at last, he reveals his hand. He does not commit sins of syntax, which is effective, but does commit sins in his arguments. Criticizing a book for its size, insinuating that no one wants to deal with that ton of bricks, and finally professing indifference toward the idiocy of some gauchos or mulattoes, appears to be the reaction of a hoodlum, not of a man of letters.

Here is another of his famous diatribes: "It is regrettable that the publication of Dr. Piñero's legal brief may prove to be a serious obstacle to its circulation, and that this ripened fruit of a year and a half of diplomatic leisure may cause no other 'impression' than that of its printing. This shall not be the case, God willing, and insofar as it lies within our means, so melancholy a fate will be avoided . . ." Again the appearance of compassion, again the devilish syntax. Again, too, the marvelous banality of reproof: making fun of those few who could be interested in a particular document and its leisurely production.

An elegant defense of these shortcomings may conjure up the dark root of satire. Satire, according to recent beliefs, stems from the magic curse of wrath, not from reason. It is the relic of an unlikely state in that wounds inflicted upon the name fall upon the possessor.

The particle *ël* was trimmed off the angel Satanaël, God's rebellious firstborn who was adored by the Bogomiles. Without it, he lost his crown, splendor, and prophetic powers. His current dwelling is fire, and his host is the wrath of the Powerful. Inversely, the Cabalists tell that the seed of the remote Abraham was sterile until they interpolated in his name the letter *he,* which made him capable of begetting.

48

Swift, a man of radical bitterness, proposed in his chronicle of Captain Lemuel Gulliver's travels to defame humankind. The first voyages, to the tiny republic of Lilliput and to the elephantine land of Brobdingnag, are what Leslie Stephen suggests, an anthropometric dream which in no way grazes the complexities of our being, its passion and its rigor. The third and funniest voyage mocks experimental science through the well-known procedure of inversion: Swift's shabby laboratories want to propagate sheep without wool, use ice for the production of gunpowder, soften marble for pillows, beat fire into fine sheets, and make good use of the nutritious parts of fecal matter. (This book also includes a strong passage on the hardships of senility.) The fourth and last voyage shows clearly that beasts are more worthy than men. It presents a virtuous republic of talking, monogamous—that is, human—horses, with a proletariat of four-legged men who live in herds, dig for food, latch onto the udders of cows to steal milk, discharge their waste upon each other, devour rotten meat, and stink. The fable is self-defeating, as one can see. The rest is literature, syntax. In conclusion it says: "I am not in the least provoked at the sight of a lawyer, a pickpocket, a colonel, a fool, a lord, a gamester, a politician, a whore-master . . ." Certain words, in that good enumeration, are contaminated by their neighbors.

Two final examples. One is the celebrated parody of insult which we are told was improvised by Dr. Johnson: "Your wife, sir, under pretence of keeping a bawdy-house, is a receiver of stolen goods." The other is the most splendid verbal abuse I know, an insult so much more singular if we consider that it represents its author's only brush with literature: "The gods did not allow the poet Santos Chocano to defame the gallows by dying there. He is still alive, after having exhausted infamy." Defaming the gallows, exhausting infamy. Vargas Vila's discharge of these illustrious abstractions refuses any compromise with his subject, leaving him unharmed, unbelievable, quite unimportant, and possibly immortal. The most fleeting mention of Chocano is enough to remind anyone of the famous insult, obscuring with malign splendor all reference to him, down to the very last details and symptoms of his infamy.

I will attempt to summarize the former. Satire is no less conventional than poetic couplets or a distinguished sonnet by the Argentine José Maria Monner Sans, for which he was awarded a natural flower. Its method is the assertion of false arguments, its only law, the simultaneous invention of pranks. I almost forgot: satire also has the obligation of being memorable.

Let me add a certain virile reply recorded by De Quincey (*Writings,* eleventh volume, page 226). Someone flung a glass of wine in the face of a gentleman during a theological or literary debate. The victim did not show any emotion and said to the offender: "This, sir, is a digression: now, if you please, for the argument." (The author of that reply, a certain Dr. Henderson, passed away in Oxford around 1787, without leaving us any memory other than those just words, a sufficient and beautiful immortality.)

A popular tale, which I picked up in Geneva during the last years of World War I, tells of Miguel Servet's reply to the judges who had condemned him to the stake: "I will burn, but this is a mere event. We shall continue our discussion in eternity."

Fancy your coming out and asking me, of all people, about the late Francisco Real. Yes, I knew him, even if he wasn't from around here. His stamping ground was the Northside—that whole stretch from the Guadalupe pond to the old Artillery Barracks. I never laid eyes on him above three times, and they were all on the same night, but nights like that you don't forget. It was when La Lujanera decided to come around to my place and bed down with me, and when Rosendo Juárez disappeared from the Maldonado for good. Of course, you're not the sort of person that name would mean much to. But around Villa Santa Rita, Rosendo Juárez—or, as we called him, the Slasher—had quite a reputation. He was one of Don Nicolás Paredes's boys, just as Paredes was one of Morel's gang, and he was admired for the way he handled a knife. Sharp dresser, too. He always rode up to the whorehouse on a dark horse, his riding gear decked out in silver. There wasn't a man or dog around that didn't respect him—and that goes for the women as well. Everyone knew that he had at least a couple of killings to his credit. He usually wore a soft hat with a narrow brim and tall crown, and it would sit in a cocky way on his long hair, which he slicked straight back. Lady Luck smiled on him, as they say, and around Villa all of us who were younger used to ape him—even as to how he spit. But then one night we got a good look at what this Rosendo was made of.

All this may seem made up, but what took place on that particular night started when a flashy red-wheeled buggy, jamful of men, came barreling down one of those hard-packed dirt roads out between the brick kilns and the empty lots. Two men in black were making a lot of noise twanging on guitars, and the driver kept cracking his whip at the stray dogs that snapped at the horse's legs. Sitting quiet, directly in the middle, was a man wrapped in a poncho. This was the famous Butcher—he had picked up the name working in the stockyards— and it seemed he was out for a fight and maybe even a killing.

The night was cool and welcome. Two or three of the men sat on the folded hood as though they were parading along some downtown avenue in Carnival. Much more happened that night, but it was only later that we learned about these first doings. Our gang was there at Julia's fairly early. Her dance hall, between the Gauna road and the river, was really a big shed built of corrugated sheet iron. You could spot the place from several blocks off by the noise or by the red lamp hanging out front. Julia was a darky, but she was careful to see that things ran well. There were always plenty of musicians and good booze, not to mention dancing partners who were ready to go all night. But La Lujanera, who was Rosendo's woman, had the rest beat by a mile. She's dead now, and I can tell you that years go by when I don't give her a thought anymore, but you should have seen her in her day—what eyes! One look at her could cause a man to lose sleep.

The rum, the music, the women, Rosendo talking tough and slapping each of us on the back, which to me was a sign of real friendship—well, I was as happy as could be. I had a good partner, too, who was having an easy time following my steps. The tango took hold of us, driving us along, splitting us up, then

river flowing on blindly, a horse half asleep, the dirt roads, the kilns—and I began to realize that, in the middle of the ragweed and the dump heaps and that whole forsaken neighborhood, I had sprouted up no more than a weed myself. With our big mouths and no guts, what else would grow there but trash like us? Then I thought, no, that the worse the place the tougher it had to be.

At the dance hall, the music was still going strong, and on the breeze came a smell of honeysuckle. It was a nice night, all right, with so many stars—some on top of others—that looking at them made you dizzy. I tried to convince myself that what had happened meant nothing to me. Still, I couldn't get over Rosendo's cowardice and the newcomer's sheer bravery. Real had even managed to get hold of a woman for the night—for that night, for the next night, and maybe forever. God knows which way the two had headed; they couldn't have wandered far. By then they were probably going at it in some ditch.

When I got back, the dance was in full swing. I slipped quietly into the crowd, noticing that a few of our boys had left and that some of the Northsiders were dancing along with everyone else. But there was no pushing or shoving. The music sounded sleepy, and the girls tangoing with the outsiders appeared to have little to say.

I was on the lookout, but not for what happened. From outdoors, sounds came to us of a woman crying, followed by that voice that we all knew by then —but now it was low, somehow too low.

"Go on in," it told her.

There was more wailing.

"Open the door, you hear?" Now the voice sounded desperate. "Open it, you bitch—open it."

The battered door swung open and in came La Lujanera, alone and almost as though she were being herded.

"There must be a ghost out there," said the Redhead.

"A dead man, friend." It was the Butcher staggering in, his face looking like a drunk's. In the space we opened for him he took a couple of blind, reeling steps, then all at once he fell like a log. One of his friends rolled him over and propped up his head with his scarf, but that only got him smeared with blood. We could see a great gash in Real's chest. The blood was welling up and blackening the bright red neckerchief he wore under his scarf. One of the women brought rum and some scorched rags.

He was in no condition to explain. La Lujanera stared at him in a daze, her arms dangling by her sides. There was a single question on every face, and finally she got out the answer. She said that after leaving the hall they had gone to a little field and at that point a man appeared out of nowhere, challenged the Butcher to fight, and stabbed him. She swore she didn't know who the man was, but she said that he wasn't Rosendo. I wondered whether anyone would believe her.

The man at our feet was dying. It looked to me as though whoever had done the job had done it well. But the man hung on. When he knocked that second time, Julia had been brewing maté. The cup went clear around the circle and back to me before he breathed his last. As the end came, he said in a low voice, "Cover my face." All he had left was his pride; he didn't want us watching while his face went through its agony. Someone laid his hat over him, and that's how he died —not uttering a sound—under that high black crown. It was only when his chest stopped heaving that they dared uncover him. He had that exhausted look of the dead. In his day, from the Artillery Barracks all the way to the Southside, he'd been one of the bravest men around. As soon as I knew he was dead and couldn't talk, I stopped hating him.

"All dying takes is being alive," one of the girls in the crowd said. And another said, "A man's so full of pride, and now look—all he's good for is gathering flies."

The Northside gang began talking among themselves in low voices. Then two of them spoke out together, saying, "The woman killed him." After that, one of them loudly flung the accusation in her face, and the rest swarmed around her. Forgetting I had to be careful, I leaped in. What kept me from reaching for my knife I don't know. Almost everyone was gaping at me, and I said, putting them down, "Look at this woman's hands. Where would she get the strength or the nerve to knife a man?"

Then, coolly, I added, "Whoever would have dreamed that the deceased, who'd made a big name for himself in his own backyard, would end up like this? Especially out here where nothing ever happens?"

Nobody offered his hide for a whipping.

At that moment, in the dead silence, came the sound of approaching riders. It was the police. Everyone—some more, some less—had his own good reason for staying clear of the law. The best thing was to dump the body into the Maldonado. You remember the long window the knife had flown out of? Well, that's where the man in black went. Several of them lifted him up. Hands stripped him of every cent and trinket he had, and somebody even hacked off one of his fingers to steal his ring. They were very daring with a helpless corpse once a better man had laid him out. One good heave and the current did the rest. To keep him from floating, they may have cut out his intestines. I don't know—I didn't want to look. The old-timer with the gray mustache wouldn't take his eyes off me. Making the best of the commotion, La Lujanera slipped away.

When the police came in for a look around, the dance was going again. That blind fiddler could scrape some lively numbers on that violin of his—the kind of thing you never hear anymore. It was growing light outside. The fence posts on a nearby slope seemed to stand alone, the strands of wire still invisible in the early dawn.

Easy as can be, I walked the two or three blocks back to my own place. A candle was burning in the window, then all at once it went out. Let me tell you, I hurried when I saw that. Then, Borges, I put my hand inside my vest—here by the left armpit, where I always carry it—and took my knife out again. I turned the blade over, slowly. It was as good as new, innocent-looking, and there wasn't the slightest trace of blood on it.

All history knows that the cruelest of the rulers of the Sudan was Yaqub the Ailing, who delivered his country to the rapacity of Egyptian tax collectors and died in a palace chamber on the fourteenth day of the moon of Barmahat, in the year 1842. There are those who hold that the wizard Abd-er-Rahman al-Masmudi (whose name may be translated as the "Servant of the All-Merciful") slew him by means of a dagger or poison. That he died a natural death is more likely, however, since he was called the Ailing. Captain Richard F. Burton spoke to the wizard in 1853, and recounts the tale I quote here.[1]

It is true that as a consequence of the conspiracy woven by my brother Ibrahim, with the treacherous and useless support of the black chiefs of Kordofan, who betrayed him, I suffered captivity in the castle of Yaqub the Ailing. My brother perished by the sword, on the blood-red skin of Justice, but I flung myself at the hated feet of the Ailing, telling him that I was a wizard, and that if he spared my life I would show him shapes and appearances still more wonderful than those of the magic lantern. The tyrant demanded an immediate proof. I asked for a reed pen, a pair of scissors, a large leaf of Venetian paper, an inkhorn, a chafing dish with some live coals in it, some coriander seeds, and an ounce of benzoin. I cut up the paper into six strips, wrote charms and invocations on the first five, and on the remaining one wrote the following words, taken from the glorious Koran: "And we have removed from thee thy veil; and thy sight today is piercing." Then I drew a magic square in the palm of Yaqub's right hand, told him to make a hollow of it, and into the center I poured a pool of ink. I asked him if he saw himself clearly reflected in it, and he answered that he did. I told him not to raise his head. I dropped the benzoin and coriander seeds into the chafing dish, and I burned the invocations upon the glowing coals. I next asked him to name the image he desired to see. He thought a moment and said, "A wild horse, the finest of those that graze along the borders of the desert." Looking, he saw a quiet, green pasture, and a minute later a horse drawing near, lithe as a leopard, with a white spot on its face. He asked me for a drove of horses as handsome as the first one, and on the horizon he saw a cloud of dust, and then the drove. It was at this point that I knew my life was spared.

From that day on, with the first streak of light in the eastern sky, two soldiers would enter my cell and lead me to the Ailing's bedchamber, where the incense, the chafing dish, and the ink were already laid out. So it was that he demanded of me, and I showed him, all the visible things of this world. This man, whom I still hate, had in his palm everything seen by men now dead and everything seen by the living: the cities, the climates, the kingdoms into which the earth is divided; the treasures hidden in its bowels; the ships that ply its seas; the many instruments of war, of music, of surgery; fair women; the fixed stars and the planets; the colors used by the ungodly to paint their odious pictures; minerals and plants, with the secrets and properties they hold locked up in them; the silvery angels, whose only food is the praise and worship of the Lord; the awarding of prizes in schools; the

---

[1]From *The Lake Regions of Central Africa* (1860), Richard F. Burton.

idols of birds and kings buried in the heart of the pyramids; the shadow cast by the bull that holds up the world and by the fish that lies under the bull; the sandy wastes of Allah the All-Merciful. He saw things impossible to tell, like gaslit streets and the whale that dies on hearing the cry of a man. Once, he ordered me to show him the city called Europe. I let him see its main thoroughfare, and it was there, I believe, in that great stream of men—all wearing black and many using spectacles—that he first set eyes on the Man with the Mask.

This figure, at times in Sudanese garments and at times in uniform, but always with a veil over his face, from then on haunted the things we saw. He was never absent, and we dared not divine who he was. The images in the mirror of ink, at first fleeting or fixed, were more intricate now; they obeyed my commands without delay, and the tyrant saw them quite plainly. Of course, the growing cruelty of the scenes left us both in a state of exhaustion. We witnessed nothing but punishments, garrotings, mutilations—the pleasures of the executioner and of the merciless.

In this way, we came to the dawn of the fourteenth day of the moon of Barmahat. The circle of ink had been poured into the tyrant's hand, the benzoin and coriander cast into the chafing dish, the invocations burned. The two of us were alone. The Ailing ordered me to show him a punishment both lawful and unappealable, for that day his heart hungered to view an execution. I let him see the soldiers with their drums, the spread calfskin, the persons lucky enough to be onlookers, the executioner wielding the sword of Justice. Marveling at the sight of him, Yaqub told me, "That's Abu Kir, he who dealt justice to your brother Ibrahim, he who will seal your fate when it's given me to know the science of bringing together these images without your aid."

He asked me to have the doomed man brought forward. When this was done, seeing that the man to be executed was the mysterious man of the veil, the tyrant paled. I was ordered to have the veil removed before justice was carried out. At this, I threw myself at his feet, beseeching, "O king of time and sum and substance of the age, this figure is not like any of the others, for we do not know his name or the name of his fathers or the name of the city where he was born. I dare not tamper with the image, for fear of incurring a sin for which I shall be held to account."

The Ailing laughed, and when he finished he swore that he would take the guilt on his own head—if guilt there were. He swore this by his sword and by the Koran. I then commanded that the prisoner be stripped, and that he be bound on the calfskin, and that the mask be torn from his face. These things were done. At last, Yaqub's stricken eyes could see the face—it was his own. He was filled with fear and madness. I gripped his trembling hand in mine, which was steady, and I ordered him to go on witnessing the ceremony of his death. He was possessed by the mirror, so much so that he attempted neither to avert his eyes nor to spill the ink. When in the vision the sword fell on the guilty head, Yaqub moaned with a sound that left my pity untouched, and he tumbled to the floor, dead.

Glory be to Him, who endureth forever, and in whose hand are the keys of unlimited Pardon and unending Punishment.

56

Tom Castro is what I call him, for this was the name he was known by, around 1850, in the streets and houses of Talcahuano, Santiago, and Valparaiso, and it is only fitting now that he comes back to these shores—even if only as a ghost and as mere light reading—that he go by this name again. The registry of births in Wapping lists him as Arthur Orton, and enters the name under the date June 7, 1834. It is known that he was a butcher's son, that his childhood suffered the drabness and squalor of London slums, and that he felt the call of the sea. This last fact is not uncommon. Running away to sea is, for the English, the traditional break from parental authority—the road to adventure. Geography fosters it, and so does the Bible (Psalms, 107:23, 24): "They that go down to the sea in ships, that do business in great waters; These see the works of the Lord, and his wonders in the deep."

Orton ran away from his familiar, dirty, brick-red streets, went down to the sea in a ship, gazed at the Southern Cross with the usual disappointment, and deserted in the Chilean port of Valparaiso. As an individual, he was at once quiet and dull. Logically, he might (and should) have starved to death, but his dim-witted good humor, his fixed smile, and his unrelieved meekness brought him under the wing of a family called Castro, whose name he came to adopt. Of this South American episode no other traces are left, but his gratefulness does not seem to have flagged, since, in 1861, he reappears in Australia still using that name —Tom Castro. There, in Sydney, he made the acquaintance of a certain Ebenezer Bogle, a Negro servant. Bogle, without being especially handsome, had about him that air of authority and assurance, that architectural solidity typical of certain Negroes well along in years, in flesh, and in dignity. He had another quality, which most anthropology textbooks have denied his race—a capacity for sudden inspiration. In due time, we shall see proof of this. He was a well-mannered, upright person, whose primeval African lusts had been carefully channeled by the uses and misuses of Calvinism. Apart from receiving divine visitations (which will presently be described), Bogle was no different from other men, with nothing more distinctive about him than a long-standing, shamefaced fear that made him linger at street crossings—glancing east, west, south, and north—in utter dread of the vehicle that might one day take his life.

Orton first saw him early one evening on a deserted Sydney street corner, steeling himself against this quite unlikely death. After studying him for a long while, Orton offered the Negro his arm, and, sharing the same amazement, the two men crossed the harmless street. From that moment of a now dead and lost evening, a protectorate came into being—that of the solid, unsure Negro over the obese dimwit from Wapping. In September 1865, Bogle read a forlorn advertisement in the local paper.

THE IDOLIZED DEAD MAN

Toward the end of April 1854 (while Orton was enjoying the effusions of Chilean hospitality), the steamer *Mermaid,* sailing from Rio de Janeiro to Liverpool, went down in the waters of the Atlantic. Among those lost was Roger Charles Tichborne, an army officer brought up in France and heir of one of the leading Roman Catholic families of England. Incredible as it may seem, the death of this Frenchified young man—who spoke English with the most refined Parisian accent and awoke in others that incomparable resentment which only French intelligence, French wit, and French pedantry can touch off—was a fateful event in the life of Arthur Orton, who had never laid eyes on Tichborne. Lady Tichborne, Roger's anguished mother, refused to give credence to her son's death and had heartrending advertisements published in newspapers the world over. One of these notices fell into the soft, black hands of Ebenezer Bogle, and a masterly scheme was evolved.

THE VIRTUES OF DISPARITY

Tichborne was a gentleman, slight in build, with a trim, buttoned-up look, sharp features, darkish skin, straight black hair, lively eyes, and a finicky, precise way of speaking. Orton was an enormously fat, out-and-out boor, whose features could hardly be made out; he had somewhat freckled skin, wavy brown hair, heavy-lidded eyes, and his speech was dim or nonexistent. Bogle got it into his head that Orton's duty was to board the next Europe-bound steamer and to satisfy Lady Tichborne's hopes by claiming to be her son. The plan was outrageously ingenious. Let us draw a simple parallel. If an impostor, in 1914, had undertaken to pass himself off as the German emperor, what he would immediately have faked would have been the turned-up mustache, the withered arm, the authoritarian frown, the gray cape, the illustriously bemedaled chest, and the pointed helmet. Bogle was more subtle. He would have put forward a clean-shaven kaiser, lacking in military traits, stripped of glamorous decorations, and whose left arm was in an unquestionable state of health. We can lay aside the comparison. It is on record that Bogle put forward a flabby Tichborne, with an imbecile's amiable smile, brown hair, and an invincible ignorance of French. He knew that an exact likeness of the long-lost Roger Charles Tichborne was an outright impossibility. He also knew that any resemblances, however successfully contrived, would only point up certain unavoidable disparities. Bogle therefore steered clear of all likeness. Intuition told him that the vast ineptitude of the venture would serve as ample proof that no fraud was afoot, since an impostor would hardly have overlooked such flagrant discrepancies. Nor must the all-important collaboration of time be forgotten: fourteen years of Southern Hemisphere, coupled with the hazards of chance, can wreak change in a man.

A further assurance of success lay in Lady Tichborne's unrelenting, harebrained advertisements, which showed how unshakably she believed that Roger Charles was not dead and how willing she was to recognize him.

THE MEETING

Tom Castro, always ready to oblige, wrote Lady Tichborne. To confirm his identity, he cited the unimpeachable proof of two moles located close to the nipple of his left breast and that childhood episode—so painful, but at the same time so unforgettable—of his having been attacked by a nest of hornets. The letter was short and, in keeping with Tom Castro and Bogle, was wanting in the least scruples of orthography. In the imposing seclusion of her Paris hotel, the lady read and reread the letter through tears of joy, and in a few days' time she came up with the memories her son had asked for.

On January 16, 1867, Roger Charles Tichborne announced his presence in that same hotel. He was preceded by his respectful manservant, Ebenezer Bogle. The winter day was bright with sunshine; Lady Tichborne's weary eyes were veiled with tears. The Negro threw open wide the window blinds, the light created a mask, and the mother, recognizing her prodigal son, drew him into her eager embrace. Now that she really had him back, she could relinquish his diary and the letters he had sent her from Brazil—those cherished reflections that had nourished her through fourteen years of solitude. She handed them back with pride. Not a scrap was missing.

Bogle smiled to himself. Now he had a way to flesh out the compliant ghost of Roger Charles.

AD MAJOREM DEI GLORIAM

This glad reunion—which seems somehow to belong to a tradition of the classical stage—might well have crowned our story, rendering certain, or at least probable, the happiness of three parties: the real mother, the spurious son, the successful plotter. Fate (such is the name we give the infinite, ceaseless chain of thousands of intertwined causes) had another end in store. Lady Tichborne died in 1870, and her relatives brought suit against Arthur Orton for false impersonation. Unburdened by solitude or tears—though not by greed—they had never believed in the obese and nearly illiterate prodigal son who appeared, straight out of the blue, from the wilds of Australia. Orton counted on the support of his numerous creditors who, anxious to be paid what was owed them, were determined that he was Tichborne.

He also counted on the friendship of the family solicitor, Edward Hopkins, and of Francis J. Baigent, an antiquary intimately acquainted with the Tichborne family history. This, however, was not enough. Bogle reasoned that, to win the game, public opinion would have to be marshaled in their favor. Assuming a top hat and rolled umbrella, he went in search of inspiration along the better streets of London. It was early evening. Bogle perambulated about until a honey-colored moon repeated itself in the rectangular basins of the public fountains. The expected visitation was paid him. Hailing a cab, he asked to be driven to Baigent's flat. Baigent sent a long letter to the *Times,* certifying that the supposed Tichborne was a shameless impostor. He signed it with the name of Father Goudron of the Society of Jesus. Other equally papist accusations soon followed. Their effect was immediate: decent people everywhere were quick to discover that Sir Roger Charles was the target of an unscrupulous Jesuitical plot.

59

The trial lasted 190 days. Something like a hundred witnesses swore that the defendant was Tichborne—among them, four fellow officers in the 6th Dragoon Guards. The claimant's supporters kept on repeating that he was not an impostor for, had he been one, he would have made some effort to ape his model's youthful portraits. Furthermore, Lady Tichborne had identified him, and obviously a mother cannot be wrong. All went well, or more or less well, until a former sweetheart of Orton's took the stand to testify. Bogle was unshaken by this treacherous maneuver on the part of the "relatives"; assuming top hat and umbrella, he once again took to the London streets in search of a visitation. We will never know whether he found it. Shortly before reaching Primrose Hill, there loomed out of the dark the dreaded vehicle that had been in pursuit of him down through the years. Bogle saw it coming, he cried out, but salvation eluded him. Dashed violently against the stone pavement, his skull was split by the dizzying hooves.

THE SPECTER

Tom Castro was the ghost of Roger Charles Tichborne, but he was a sorry ghost animated by someone else's genius. On hearing the news of Bogle's death, he collapsed. He went on lying, but with failing conviction and obvious discrepancies. It was not hard to foresee the end.

On February 27, 1874, Arthur Orton, alias Tom Castro, was sentenced to fourteen years' penal servitude. In prison, he got himself liked; this was Orton's calling. Good behavior won him a four-year reduction of sentence. When this last touch of hospitality—prison—was behind him, he toured the hamlets and centers of the United Kingdom, giving little lectures in which he alternately pleaded his innocence or his guilt. Modesty and ingratiation were so deep-seated in him that many a night he would begin by exoneration and end by confession, always disposed to the leanings of his audience.

On April 2, 1898, he died.

THE MASKED DYER, HAKIM OF MERV [JLB 20]

If I am not mistaken, the chief sources of information concerning Mokanna, the Veiled (or, literally, Masked) Prophet of Khurasan, are only four in number: (a) those passages from the *History of the Caliphs* culled by Baladhuri; (b) the *Giant's Handbook,* or *Book of Precision and Revision,* by the official historian of the Abbasids, Ibn abi Tahir Taifur; (c) the Arabic codex entitled *The Annihilation of the Rose,* wherein we find a refutation of the abominable heresies of the *Dark Rose,* or *Hidden Rose,* which was the Prophet's holy book; and (d) some barely legible coins unearthed by the engineer Andrusov during excavations for the

Trans-Caspian Railway. These coins, now on deposit in the numismatic collection at Teheran, preserve certain Persian distichs which abridge or emend key passages of the *Annihilation.* The original *Rose* is lost, for the manuscript found in 1899 and published all too hastily by the *Morgenländisches Archiv* has been pronounced a forgery—first by Horn, and afterward by Sir Percy Sykes.

The Prophet's fame in the West is owed to a long-winded poem by Thomas Moore, laden with all the sentimentality of an Irish patriot.

THE SCARLET DYE

Along about the year 120 of the Hegira (A.D. 736), the man Hakim, whom the people of that time and that land were later to style the Prophet of the Veil, was born in Turkestan. His home was the ancient city of Merv, whose gardens and vineyards and pastures sadly overlook the desert. Midday there, when not dimmed by the clouds of dust that choke its inhabitants and leave a grayish film on the clusters of black grapes, is white and dazzling.

Hakim grew up in that weary city. We know that a brother of his father apprenticed him to the trade of dyer—that craft of the ungodly, the counterfeiter, and the shifty, who were to inspire him to the first imprecations of his unbridled career. In a famous page of the *Annihilation,* he is quoted as saying:

> My face is golden but I have steeped my dyes, dipping uncarded wool on second nights and soaking treated wool on third nights, and the emperors of the islands still compete for this scarlet cloth. Thus did I sin in the days of my youth, tampering with the true colors of God's creation. The Angel told me that the ram was not the color of the tiger, the Satan told me that the Almighty wanted them to be, and that He was availing Himself of my skill and my dyestuffs. Now I know that the Angel and the Satan both strayed from the truth, and that all colors are abominable.

In the year 146 of the Hegira, or Flight, Hakim was seen no more in Merv. His caldrons and dipping vats, along with a Shirazi scimitar and a bronze mirror, were found destroyed.

THE BULL

At the end of the moon of Sha'ban, in the year 158, the desert air was very clear, and from the gate of a caravan halting place on the way to Merv a group of men sat gazing at the evening sky in search of the moon of Ramadan, which marks the period of continence and fasting. They were slaves, beggars, horse dealers, camel thieves, and butchers of livestock. Huddled solemnly on the ground, they awaited the sign. They looked at the sunset, and the color of the sunset was the color of the sand.

From the other end of the shimmering desert (whose sun engenders fever, just as its moon engenders chills), they saw three approaching figures, which seemed to be of gigantic size. They were men, and the middle one had the head of a bull. When they drew near, it was plain that this man was wearing a mask and that his companions were blind.

Someone (as in the tales of *The 1001 Nights*) pressed him for the meaning of this wonder. "They are blind," the masked man said, "because they have looked upon my face."

THE LEOPARD

It is recorded by the Abbasids' official chronicler that the man from the desert (whose voice was singularly sweet, or so it seemed in contrast to his brutish mask) told the caravan traders that they were awaiting the sign of a month of penance, but that he was the preacher of a greater sign—that of a lifetime of penance and a death of martyrdom. He told them that he was Hakim, son of Osman, and that in the year 146 of the Flight a man had made his way into his house and, after purification and prayer, had cut off his head with a scimitar and taken it to heaven. Held in the right hand of the stranger (who was the angel Gabriel), his head had been before the Lord—in the highest heaven—who entrusted it with the mission of prophesying, taught it words so ancient that their mere utterance could burn men's mouths, and endowed it with a radiance that mortal eyes could not bear. Such was his justification of the mask. When all men on earth professed the new law, the Face would be revealed to them and they could worship it openly —as the angels already worshiped it. His mission proclaimed, Hakim exhorted them to a holy war—a *jihad*—and to their forthcoming martyrdom.

The slaves, beggars, horse dealers, camel thieves, and butchers of livestock shunned his call. One voice shouted out "Sorcerer!" and another "Impostor!"

Someone had a leopard with him—a specimen, perhaps, of that sleek, bloodthirsty breed that Persian hunters train—and it happened that the animal broke free of its bonds. Except for the masked prophet and his two acolytes, the rest of them trampled each other to escape. When they flocked back, the Prophet had blinded the beast. Before its luminous dead eyes, the men worshiped Hakim and acknowledged his supernatural powers.

THE VEILED PROPHET

It is with scant enthusiasm that the historian of the Abbasid caliphs records the rise of the Veiled Hakim in Khurasan. That province—much disturbed by the failure and crucifixion of its most famous chieftain—embraced the teachings of the Shining Face with fervor and desperation, and it lay down in tribute its blood and gold. (By then, Hakim had set aside his brutish effigy, replacing it with a fourfold veil of white silk embossed with precious stones. The symbolic color of the ruling dynasty, the Banu Abbas, was black; for his Protective Veil, for his banners and turbans, Hakim chose the very opposite color—white.) The campaign began well. In the *Book of Precision*, of course, the armies of the Caliph are everywhere victorious; but as the invariable result of these victories is the removal of generals or the withdrawal from impregnable fortresses, the chary reader can surmise actual truth. At the end of the moon of Rajab, in the year 161, the famed city of Nishapur opened its metal gates to the Masked One; at the beginning of 162, the city of Asterabad did the same. Hakim's military activity (like that of a more fortunate prophet) was limited to praying in a tenor voice, elevated toward the Divinity on the back of a reddish camel, in the very thick of battle. Arrows whistled all around without ever once striking him. He seemed to court danger. On the night a group of hated lepers gathered around his palace, he had them let in, kissed them, and given them silver and gold.

The petty tasks of government were delegated to six or seven devotees. Ever mindful of serenity and meditation, the Prophet kept a harem of 114 blind women, who did their best to satisfy the needs of his divine body.

THE ABOMINABLE MIRRORS

However indiscreet or threatening they may be, so long as their words are not in conflict with orthodox faith, Islam is tolerant of men who enjoy an intimacy with God. The Prophet himself, perhaps, might not have scorned this leniency, but his followers, his many victories, and the outspoken wrath of the Caliph—who was Mohammed al-Mahdi—drove him at last into heresy. This discord, though it led to his undoing, also made him set down the tenets of a personal creed, in which borrowings from old Gnostic beliefs are nonetheless detectable.

At the root of Hakim's cosmogony is a spectral god. This godhead is as majestically devoid of origin as of name or face. It is an unchanging god, but its image cast nine shadows which, condescending to creation, conceived and presided over a first heaven. Out of this first demiurgic crown there issued a second, with its own angels, powers, and thrones, and these founded a lower heaven, which was the symmetrical mirror of the first. This second conclave, in its turn, was mirrored in a third, and this in a lower one, and so on to the number 999. The lord of this lowermost heaven is he who rules us—shadow of shadows of still other shadows—and his fraction of divinity approaches zero.

The world we live in is a mistake, a clumsy parody. Mirrors and fatherhood, because they multiply and confirm the parody, are abominations. Revulsion is the cardinal virtue. Two ways (whose choice the Prophet left free) may lead us there: abstinence or the orgy, excesses of the flesh or its denial.

Hakim's personal heaven and hell were no less hopeless:

> Those who deny the Word, those who deny the Veil and the Face [runs a curse from the *Hidden Rose*], are promised a wondrous Hell: for each lost soul shall hold sway over 999 empires of fire; and in each empire, over 999 mountains of fire; and in each mountain, over 999 castles of fire; and in each castle, over 999 chambers of fire; and in each chamber, over 999 beds of fire; and in each bed he will find himself everlastingly tormented by 999 shapes of fire, which will have his face and his voice.

This is confirmed in another surviving versicle:

> In this life, ye suffer in a single body; in death and Retribution, in numberless numbers of bodies.

63

Heaven is less clearly drawn:

> Its darkness is never-ending, there are fountains and pools made of stone, and the happiness of this Heaven is the happiness of leave-taking, of self-denial, and of those who know they are asleep.

THE FACE

In the year 163 of the Flight (and fifth year of the Shining Face), Hakim was besieged at Sanam by the Caliph's army. There was no lack of provisions or martyrs, and the arrival of a host of golden angels was imminent. It was at this point that an alarming rumor made its way through the fortress. An adulteress in the harem, as she was strangled by the eunuchs, had cried out that the ring finger of the Prophet's right hand was missing and that all his other fingers lacked nails. This rumor spread among the faithful. From the top of a terrace, in the midst of his people, Hakim was praying to the Lord for a victory or for a special sign. Two captains, their heads bowed down, slavish—as if beating into a driving rain—tore away the Veil.

At first, there was a shudder. The Apostle's promised face, the face that had been to the heavens, was indeed white—but with that whiteness peculiar to spotted leprosy. It was so bloated and unbelievable that to the mass of onlookers it seemed a mask. There were no brows; the lower lid of the right eye hung over the shriveled cheek; a heavy cluster of tubercles ate away the lips; the flattened, inhuman nose was like a lion's.

Hakim's voice attempted one final stratagem. "Your unforgivable sins do not allow you to see my splendor—" it began to say.

Paying no heed, the captains ran him through with spears.

I, A JEW

Like the Druzes, like the moon, like death, like next week, the distant past forms part of those things that can be enriched by ignorance. It is infinitely supple and yielding; it offers itself to us much more than the future and poses fewer problems. One knows, moreover, that it is the chosen spot of mythology.

Who has not one day played at searching for his ancestors, imagining the prehistory of his race and blood? I have often played at that myself, and it has not displeased me to imagine myself often as a Jew. It is a matter of a simple hypothesis, a sedentary and modest adventure that can harm no one—not even the good repute of Israel—in view of the fact that my Judaism, like the songs of Mendelssohn, is without words. The journal *Crisol,* in its January 30 issue, chose to salute this retrospective hope and speaks of my "Jewish ancestry, maliciously hidden." (The participle and the adverb delight me.)

My name is Borges Acevedo. Ramos Mejía, in one of the notes to Chapter 15 of *Rosas y su tiempo* ("Rosas and His Times"), enumerates the names of the families of Buenos Aires at that time in order to demonstrate that all, or almost all, "came from Judeo-Portuguese roots." Acevedo figures in the list, the only document to support my Judaizing pretensions until the confirmation offered by *Crisol.* Captain Honorio Acevedo, however, devoted himself to detailed investigations that I cannot permit myself to ignore. They inform me that the first Acevedo to disembark on this continent was the Catalan Don Pedro de Acevedo, a farmer, settled in Pago de los Arroyos since 1728, the father and grandfather of cattle-raisers in the same province, a notable who figures in the annals of the parish of Santa Fe and in documents referring to the history of the vice-royalty—an ancestor, in short, irremediably Spanish.

Two hundred years without being able to discover the Israelite, 200 years without managing to set my hands on this ancestor.

I am grateful to *Crisol* for having impelled me to pursue these investigations, but I have less and less hope of ever ascending to the Altar of the Temple, to the Bronze Sea, to Heine, to Gleizer, the Argentine publisher, and the Ten Righteous Men, to Ecclesiastes, and Charlie Chaplin.

Statistically speaking, the Jews were very few. What would we think of someone in the year 4000 who discovers everywhere descendants of the inhabitants of the San Juan province [one of the least populated in Argentina]? Our inquisitors are seeking Hebrews, never Phoenicians, Numidians, Scythians, Babylonians, Huns, Vandals, Ostrogoths, Ethiopians, Illyrians, Paphlagonians, Sarmatians, Medes, Ottomans, Berbers, Britons, Libyans, Cyclops, or Lapiths. The nights of Alexandria, Babylon, Carthage, Memphis have never succeeded in engendering one single grandfather; it was only to the tribes of the bituminous Black Sea that such power was granted.

THE DOCTRINE OF CYCLES [JLB 22]

I

This doctrine (which its most recent inventor calls the eternal return) can be formulated thus:

"The number of all the atoms which make up the world is, although excessive, finite, and as such only capable of a finite (although also excessive) number of permutations. Given an infinite length of time, the number of possible permutations must be exhausted, and the universe must repeat itself. Once again you will be born of the womb, once again your skeleton will grow, once again this page will reach your same hands, once again you will live all the hours until the hour of your incredible death." Such is the customary order of the argument, from its insipid prelude to the enormous, threatening dénouement. It is usually attributed to Nietzsche.[1]

Before refuting the doctrine—an undertaking of which I am not sure I am capable—we must imagine, at least from afar, the superhuman numbers that it involves. I will begin with the atom. The diameter of an atom of hydrogen has been calculated, providing for error, at a hundred-millionth of a centimeter. This dizzying smallness does not mean that it is indivisible: on the contrary, Rutherford defines it with the image of a solar system made up of a central nucleus and a revolving electron 100,000 times smaller than the atom as a whole. Let us put aside the nucleus and the electron and consider a frugal universe made up of ten atoms. (We are dealing of course with a modest experimental universe: invisible, given that microscopes do not even suspect its existence; imponderable, since no scale will be able to measure it.) Let us also postulate—in accordance with Nietzsche's conjecture—that the number of changes in that universe equals the number of ways in which the ten atoms may be arranged by varying the order in which they are placed. How many different states can that world know before an eternal recurrence? The calculation is easy: simply multiply $1 \times 2 \times 3 \times 4 \times 5 \times 6 \times 7 \times 8 \times 9 \times 10$, a tedious operation which will give us the sum of 3,628,800. If an almost infinitesimal particle of the universe is capable of that variety, we can lend little or no credence to the monotony of the cosmos. I have considered ten atoms; in order to obtain two grams of hydrogen we would need considerably more than a billion billions. To compute the number of possible changes in that pair of grams—that is, to multiply a billion billions by each one of the whole numbers that precede it—is already an operation far beyond the human limits of my patience.

I do not know if my reader is convinced; I am not. The painless and chaste extravagance of enormous numbers creates without a doubt that peculiar pleasure common to all excess. Yet the regression remains more or less eternal, even though in very remote terms. Nietzsche could reply: "Rutherford's revolving electrons are a novelty for me, and so is the idea—so scandalous for a philologist —that an atom may be split. However, I never denied that the vicissitudes of matter were numerous; I only declared that they were not infinite." This likely answer from Friedrich Zarathustra obliges me to fall back on Georg Cantor and his heroic theory of aggregates.

Cantor destroys the foundation of Nietzsche's thesis. He affirms the perfect infinity of the number of points in the universe, and even of a meter of the universe, or a fraction of that meter. The operation of counting is nothing more

---

[1]Among the books consulted for this essay, I should mention the following: *Die Unschuld des Werdens,* Friedrich Nietzsche, Leipzig, 1931; *Also sprach Zarathustra,* Friedrich Nietzsche, Leipzig, 1892; *Introduction to Mathematical Philosophy,* Bertrand Russell, London, 1919; *The A B C of Atoms,* Bertrand Russell, London, 1927; *The Nature of the Physical World,* A. S. Eddington, London, 1928; *Die Philosophie der Griechen,* Dr. Paul Deussen, Leipzig, 1949; *Wörterbuch der Philosophie,* Fritz Mauthner, Leipzig, 1923; *La ciudad de Dios,* San Agustín, translation by Díaz de Beyral, Madrid, 1922.

for him than that of comparing two series. For example, if the oldest sons of all the houses of Egypt were killed by the Angel except those living in houses which had a red sign on the door, it is obvious that as many were saved as there were red marks, without it being necessary to enumerate how many marks there in fact were. Here the quantity is indefinite; there are other groupings in which it is infinite. The set of natural numbers is infinite, but it is possible to demonstrate that there are as many odd numbers as there are even.

1 corresponds to 2
3 corresponds to 4
5 corresponds to 6, etc.

The proof is as irreproachable as it is worthless, but it is no different from the following one which proves that there are as many multiples of 3018 as there are numbers—without excluding from these 3018 and its multiples.

1 corresponds to 3018
2   "   6036
3   "   9054
4   "   12,072, etc.

It is possible to affirm the same of its powers, even though the powers must be ratified as we progress in the series.

1 corresponds to 3018
2   " 3018^2 or 9,108,324
3   " etc.

A brilliant acceptance of these facts has inspired the formula that an infinite collection—for instance, the natural series of whole numbers—is a collection whose members can split off in turn into infinite series. (Better yet, to avoid any ambiguity: an infinite set is that set which can equal one of its partial sets.) In these elevated latitudes of enumeration, the part is no less copious than the whole; the exact quantity of points in the universe is the same as in a meter, or in a decimeter, or in the farthest stellar trajectory. The series of natural numbers is well ordered; in other words, the terms which form it are consecutive: 28 precedes 29 and follows 27. The series of the points in space (or of the instants in time) cannot be ordered in the same way; no number has an immediate successor or predecessor. It is like the series of fractions according to magnitude. What fraction shall we enumerate after ½? Not 51/100, because 101/200 is closer; not 101/200 because 201/400 is closer; not 201/400 because . . . The same thing happens with points, according to Georg Cantor. We can always insert others in infinite numbers. However, we should try not to imagine decreasing dimensions. Each point is already the end of an infinite subdivision.

This brush of Cantor's lovely game with Zarathustra's lovely game is fatal for Zarathustra. If the universe consists of an infinite number of terms then it is absolutely capable of an infinite number of combinations, and the need for a recurrence is invalidated. Only its mere possibility remains, calculated at zero.

67

In the autumn of 1883, Nietzsche wrote: "And this slow spider which creepeth in the moonlight, and this moonlight itself, and thou and I in this gateway whispering together, whispering of eternal things—must we not all have already existed? And must we not return and run in that other lane out before us, that long weird lane—must we not eternally return?—Thus did I speak, and always more softly, for I was afraid of mine own thoughts and arrear-thoughts." Three centuries before the cross, Eudemos wrote: "If we are to believe the Pythagoreans, the same things will return regularly and you will be with me once again and I will repeat this doctrine and my hand will play with this stick and all else will be the same." In the Stoic cosmogony, "Zeus feeds upon the world": the universe is consumed cyclically by the same fire which engendered it and rises up again from annihilation to repeat an identical history. Once again the various seminal particles are combined, once again they give form to rocks, trees, and men—and even to virtue and to days, since for the Greeks no noun was possible without some corporeality. Once again, each sword and each hero; once again, each night of meticulous insomnia.

Like all the other conjectures of the school of Porticus, this one about general repetition spread with time and its technical name, *apokatastasis,* was recorded in the Gospel, although for unknown reasons (Words of the Apostles, III, 21). Book Twelve of the *Civitas Dei* of Saint Augustine devotes several chapters to the rebuttal of such an abominable doctrine. The chapters (which I have before me now) are too involved to be summarized. However, the episcopal fury of their author seems directed at two targets: one, the showy uselessness of the circle; the other, the fact that reason should die like an acrobat on the cross, in interminable functions. Farewells and suicides lose their dignity if they are repeated; Saint Augustine must have thought the same of the crucifixion. This explains why he rejected the reasoning of the Stoics and the Pythagoreans so vehemently. They argued that God's knowledge is unable to comprehend infinite things and that the eternal rotation of the worldly process serves to familiarize God with it; Saint Augustine mocks their useless revolutions and affirms that Jesus is the straight path which permits us to flee from the circular labyrinths of such deceits.

In the chapter of his *Logica* which deals with the law of causality, John Stuart Mill declares that a periodic repetition of history is conceivable—but not true. He cites Virgil's "messianic eclogue":

Jam redit et Virgo, redeunt Saturnia regna . . .

Could Nietzsche, a Hellenist, possibly have been ignorant of his predecessors? Nietzsche, the author of fragments on the pre-Socratics—could he not have known of a doctrine learned by the disciples of Pythagoras? It is very difficult to believe that this is so—and besides, useless. It is true that Nietzsche, in a memorable note, has indicated the precise spot in which the idea of the eternal return came to him: a path in the woods of Silvaplana, near a vast pyramidal block, one noontime in August of 1881—"six thousand feet beyond men and time." It is true that the instant is one of Nietzsche's glories. He would write: "The moment in which I begot recurrence is immortal, for the sake of that moment alone I will endure recurrence." (*Unschuld des Werdens,* II, 1308) It is my opinion, however, that we must not postulate such surprising ignorance, nor any human confusion —human enough—between inspiration and memory, nor any crime of vanity. My key is of a grammatical, almost a syntactical nature. Nietzsche knew that the eternal return is one of those fables or fears or diversions that recur eternally, but he also knew that the most effective grammatical person is the first person. For a prophet, it is the only one. For reasons of voice and anachronism—or typography—it was impossible for Zarathustra to derive his inspiration from an epitome, or from the *Historia Philosophiae Graeco-Romanae* of Ritter and Preller, substitute professors. The prophetic style does not permit the use of quotation marks or erudite allegations to books and authors . . .

If my human flesh assimilates the brutal flesh of sheep, who will prohibit the human mind from assimilating mental states? From so much thinking about it and suffering it, the eternal return of all things belongs to Nietzsche, and not to a dead man who is little more than a Greek name. I will not insist: Miguel de Unamuno has already written his piece on the adoption of thoughts.

Nietzsche wanted men able to bear immortality. I say this with the words found in his personal notebooks, in the *Nachlass,* where he also wrote: "Ye fancy that ye will have a long rest ere your second birth takes place—but do not deceive yourselves! 'Twixt your last moment of consciousness and the first ray of the dawn of your new life no time will elapse—as a flash of lightning will the space go by, even though living creatures think it is billions of years, and are not even able to reckon it. Timelessness and immediate rebirth are compatible, once intellect is eliminated!"

Before Nietzsche, personal immortality was merely a hopeful equivocation, a confused project. Nietzsche proposes it as a duty and confers upon it the atrocious lucidity of an insomniac. "Not sleeping," I read in the classic treatise [*Anatomy of Melancholy*] by Robert Burton, "hardily crucifies the melancholy." We know for a fact that Nietzsche suffered from that crucifixion and had to seek salvation in the bitterness of chloral hydrate. Nietzsche wanted to be Walt Whitman; he wanted to fall in love with every detail of his destiny. He followed a heroic method; he unearthed the intolerable Greek hypothesis of eternal repetition and tried to extract from that mental nightmare an occasion for rejoicing. He looked for the most terrible idea in the universe and held it up for the delight of men. The facile optimist generally imagines that he is Nietzschean; Nietzsche confronts him with the circles of the eternal return and spits him from his mouth.

Nietzsche wrote: "We must not strive after distant and unknown states of bliss and blessings and acts of grace, but we must live so that we would fain live again and live forever so, to all eternity!" Mauthner objects that to attribute the slightest moral influence (that is, practice) to the thesis of the eternal return is to negate the thesis—since that is the same as imagining that something could happen differently. Nietzsche would respond that the formulation of the eternal return and its prolonged moral influence (that is, practice) and Mauthner's ruminations and his own refutation of Mauthner's ruminations are just so many necessary moments of world history, the work of atomic agitations. He could justly write what he had already written: "Even supposing the recurrence of the cycle is only a probability or a possibility, even a thought, even a possibility can shatter us and transform us. It is not only feelings and definite expectations that do this! See what effect the thought of eternal damnation has had!" And elsewhere, "From the moment when this thought begins to prevail all colors will change their hue and a new history will begin."

III

At times the sensation of having already lived a certain moment leaves us wondering. The partisans of the eternal return assure us that such is the case, and in these perplexing states they find a corroboration of their beliefs. They forget that memory implies a change that would negate the thesis, for time would continue to perfect it until that distant cycle in which the individual would be able to foresee his destiny and choose to act in another way. . . . Moreover, Nietzsche never spoke of a mnemonic confirmation of the return.

Nor did he speak—and this should be stressed also—of the finiteness of atoms. Nietzsche denies atoms; to him atomic structure seemed to be just a model of the world, made exclusively for the eyes and for arithmetic understanding. . . . In order to establish his thesis he spoke of a limited force developing itself in infinite time, yet incapable of an unlimited number of variations. He was not laboring without perfidy; first he warns us against the idea of an infinite force— "let us beware of such orgies of thought"—and then he generously concedes that time is infinite. Similarly, he enjoys availing himself of the concept of previous eternity. For example, an equilibrium of the cosmic force is impossible, since if it were not, it would already have operated in a previous eternity. Or: universal history has happened an infinite number of times . . . in a previous eternity. The invocation appears to be valid, but one must remember that previous eternity or *aeternitas a parte ante* (as the theologians called it) is nothing more than our natural inability to conceive of a beginning to time. We suffer from the same inability with regard to space, so that to invoke a previous eternity is as convincing as invoking a right hand infinity. I will state it in another manner: if time is infinite for the intuition, then space is also. The previous eternity has nothing to do with the real time which elapses. Let us go back to the first second and we will note that it requires a predecessor, and that predecessor another, and so on into infinity. In order to staunch this *regressus in infinitum,* Saint Augustine resolves that the first second in time coincides with the first second of creation: *non in tempore sed cum tempore incepit creatio.*

Nietzsche falls back on energy; the second law of thermodynamics declares that there are energy processes which are irreversible. Heat and light are merely forms of energy. In order to convert light into heat, simply project it onto a black surface. Heat, on the other hand, cannot return to its form as light. This proof, of an inoffensive and insipid aspect, annuls the circular labyrinth of the eternal return.

The first law of thermodynamics declares that the energy of the universe is constant; the second, that that energy tends to incommunication and disorder, although the total amount does not decrease. This gradual disintegration of the forces which compose the universe is called entropy. Once all different temperatures have been equalized, once the action of one body on another has been barred or compensated for, the world will be a fortuitous concurrence of atoms. In the deep center of the stars, that difficult and fatal balance has been accomplished. By dint of interchanges, the entire universe will achieve it, and it will be tepid and dead.

Light is losing its heat; the universe is becoming invisible, minute by minute. It is becoming lighter as well. At some point, it will be nothing but heat: balanced, immovable, equal heat. Then it will have died.

A final certainty, this time of a metaphysical order. If Zarathustra's thesis is accepted, I do not understand what prevents two identical processes from becoming agglomerated in one. Is mere succession enough, unverified by anyone? Without a special archangel to keep count, what does it mean that we are passing through the 13,514th cycle, and not the first of the series or number 322^{2000}? Nothing, as far as practice goes—which does no harm to the thinker. Nothing, as far as intelligence—which is serious.

CHESTERTON AND THE LABYRINTHS OF THE DETECTIVE STORY

[JLB 23]

The English know the agitation of two incompatible passions: the strange appetite for adventure and the strange appetite for legality. I write "strange," because for the *criollo* they are just that. Martín Fierro, sainted army deserter, and his cohort Cruz, sainted police deserter, would profess astonishment, not without cursing and laughter, over the British (and American) doctrine that the law is infallibly right; yet they would not dare to imagine that their miserable fate as cutthroats was interesting or desirable. Killing, to a *criollo*, is a *lamentable act,* one of man's misfortunes which in itself neither increases nor diminishes his virtue. Nothing could be more opposite to "Murder Considered as One of the Fine Arts" by the "morbidly virtuous" De Quincey, or to the "Theory of the Moderate Murder" by the sedentary Chesterton.

Both passions—for corporeal adventure, for rancorous legality—find satisfaction in the current detective narrative. Its prototypes are the past serials and present collections of the nominally famous Nick Carter, a smiling, hygienic athlete, engendered by the journalist John Coryell on a sleepless typewriter which dispatched 70,000 words a month. The genuine detective story—need I say it?—rejects with equal contempt physical risks and distributive justice. It serenely does without jails, secret stairways, remorse, gymnastics, fake beards, fencing, the bats of Charles Baudelaire, and even the element of chance. In the earliest example of the genre (*The Mystery of Marie Roget,* by Edgar Allan Poe, 1842) and in one of the most recent ones (*Unravelled Knots,* by the Baroness Orczy), the story is limited to the discussion and abstract resolution of a crime, perhaps quite distant from the event or after many years. The everyday methods of police investigation —fingerprints, interrogation, and confession—would seem like solecisms therein. One might object to the conventionality of this veto, but such a convention, in this instance, is irreproachable: it does not aim to avoid difficulties, but rather to impose them. It is not a convenience for the writer, like the illegible espionage works of Jean Racine or like scenic passages.

The detective novel to some degree borders on the character or psychological novel (*The Moonstone,* by Wilkie Collins, 1868, *Mr. Digwood and Mr. Lumb,* by Eden Phillpotts, 1934). The short story is of a strict, problematical nature; its code could be the following:

A. *A discretional maximum of six characters.* The imprudent infraction of this law is to blame for the confusion and tedium of all detective movies. In every one we are presented with fifteen strangers, and it is finally revealed that the heartless criminal is not Alpha who was looking through the keyhole, nor Beta who hid the money, nor the grieving Gamma who would sob in the corners of the hallway, but rather that insipid, young Upsilon, whom we had been confusing with Phi, who has such a striking resemblance to Tau, the substitute elevator operator. The stupor this fact produces is somewhat moderate.

B. *Resolution of all the loose ends to the mystery.* If my memory (or the lack of it) does not fail me, the varied infraction of this second law is the favorite defect of Conan Doyle. At times, it deals with a trifling amount of ashes, gathered behind the reader's back by the talented Holmes, and only derivable from a cigar made in Burma, which is sold in only one store, which is patronized by only one customer. At other times, the cheating is of greater consequence. It deals with a guilty party, terribly unmasked at the last moment, who turns out to be a stranger, an insipid, torpid interpolation. In pure detective stories, the criminal is one of the characters present from the beginning.

C. *Avaricious economy of means.* The final discovery that two characters in the plot are one and the same can be pleasing—as long as the instrument behind the change does not turn out to be a false beard or an Italian accent, but different names and circumstances. The adverse case—two individuals who are patched together in a third and who provide him ubiquity—runs the unavoidable risk of seeming clumsy.

D. *Priority of how over who.* The bunglers I have already execrated in section (A) revel in the story about a jewel placed within the reach of fifteen men—that is, of fifteen names, because we know nothing about their personalities—and then stolen by the sticky fingers of one of them. They have the impression that the deed of ascertaining to which name the sticky fingers belong is of considerable interest.

E. *Necessity and wonder of the solution.* The first establishes that the mystery should be a *determined* mystery, fit for only one solution. The second requires that the reader marvel over that solution, without resorting to the supernatural, of course, whose handiwork in this genre of fiction is a weakness and a felony. Also prohibited are hypnotism, telepathic hallucinations, portents, elixirs with unknown effects, ingenious pseudoscientific tricks, and lucky charms. Chesterton always performs the tour de force of proposing a supernatural explanation and then replacing it, losing nothing, with another one from this world.

The Scandal of Father Brown, Chesterton's most recent book (London, 1935), has suggested the foregoing guidelines to me. Out of the five series of chronicles of the humble clergyman, this one is probably the least successful. It contains, however, two stories that I would not like to see excluded from a Brownian anthology or canon: the third, "The Blast of the Book"; the eighth, "The Unsolvable Problem." The premise of the former is exciting: it deals with a damaged, supernatural book which causes the instantaneous disappearance of all those who open it. Somebody announces over the telephone that he has the book in front of him and that he is going to open it. The frightened listener "hears a kind of silent explosion." Another of the fulminated characters leaves a hole in a pane of glass; another, a rip in a canvas; another, his deserted wooden leg. The dénouement is good, but I can swear that his most devout reader foresaw it, while contemplating page 73. There is an abundance of traits very typical of G.K.: for instance, that gloomy masked man with the black gloves, who turns out to be an aristocrat totally opposed to nudism.

The settings for the crimes are admirable, as in all of Chesterton's books, and carefully and sensationally false. Has anyone ever brought into question the resemblance between the fantastic London of Stevenson and that of Chesterton, between the mourning gentleman and nocturnal gardens of the *Suicide Club* and those of the now five-part saga of Father Brown?

THE TRANSLATORS OF THE 1001 NIGHTS[1]   [JLB 24]

In Trieste in 1872, in a palace with damp statues and defective sanitation, a gentleman whose face had been dramatically enhanced by an African scar— Captain Richard Francis Burton, English consul—undertook a famous translation of the *Qitab alif laila wa laila,* the book which infidel Christians call *The 1001 Nights.* One of the secret aims of his labor was the annihilation of another gentleman (also with a dark Moorish beard, also weather-tanned) who was compiling a vast dictionary in England, and who died long before he could be

---

[1]Among the books consulted, I should enumerate the following: *Les Mille et une Nuits, contes arabes traduits,* by Jean Antoine Galland. Paris, n.d.; *The Thousand and One Nights,* commonly called *The Arabian Nights Entertainments.* A new translation from the Arabic by E. W. Lane. London, 1839; *The Book of the Thousand Nights and a Night.* A plain and literal translation by Richard F. Burton. London(?), n.d. Vols. VI, VII, VIII; *The Arabian Nights.* A complete [*sic*] and unabridged selection from the famous literal translation of R. F. Burton. New York, 1932; *Le Livre des Mille Nuits et une Nuit. Traduction litterale et complète du texte arabe,* by Dr. J. C. Mardrus. Paris, 1906; *Tausend und eine Nacht. Aus dem Arabischen übertragen,* by Max Henning. Leipzig, 1897; *Die Erzählungen aus den Tausendundein Nächten. Nach dem Arabischen Urtext der Calcutter Ausgabe vom Jahre 1839,* translated by Enno Littmann. Leipzig, 1928.

annihilated by Burton. This was Edward Lane, the Orientalist, author of a version of *The 1001 Nights* scrupulous enough to have supplanted the previous one, Galland's. Lane translated against Galland, Burton against Lane: in order to understand Burton one must understand that inimical dynasty.

GALLAND

Let me begin with its founder. It is well known that Jean Antoine Galland was a French Arabist who brought from Istanbul a patient collection of coins, a monograph on the spread of coffee, an Arabic copy of the *Nights,* and a Maronite supplement to it which came from a memory no less inspired than Scheherazad's own. To this obscure informant whose name, said to be Hanna, I should not wish to forget, we owe certain fundamental stories which the original does not know —of Aladdin, of the Forty Thieves, the one about Prince Ahmed and the sprite Peri Banu, that of Abu-al Hassan the Sleeper and Waker, that of the night-adventure of Harun al-Rashid, of the two sisters envious of the younger sister. The mere enumeration of those names is enough to prove that Galland establishes the canon, including stories that time was to make indispensable and that translators to come—his enemies—would not dare omit.

Another undeniable fact is that the happiest and most felicitous praise of *The 1001 Nights*—from Coleridge, De Quincey, Stendhal, Tennyson, Edgar Allan Poe, Newman—comes from readers of Galland's translation. Two hundred years and ten better translations have come and gone, but that man of Europe or the Americas who thinks of *The 1001 Nights* thinks invariably of that first translation. The epithet *Arabian Nights-like* (*Arabian-Nightly* suffers from vulgarity, *Arabian-Nocturnal* seems perverse) refers in no way to the erudite obscenities of Burton or Mardrus, and in every way to the jewels and magic spells of Galland.

Word for word, Galland's version is the worst written of all, the most fraudulent and weakest, but it was the most read. Those who became intimate with it came to know happiness and wonder. Its Orientalism, which now appears to us so slight, dazzled many of those who took snuff and plotted tragedies in five acts. Twelve elegant volumes appeared from 1707 to 1717, twelve innumerably read volumes, and they went into diverse languages, including Hindustani and Arabic. We, anachronistic readers of the twentieth century, perceive in them the cloying flavor of the eighteenth century and not the faint Oriental aroma which 200 years ago determined their newness and their glory. No one is to be blamed for the undetectedness of that aroma today, Galland least of all. Sometimes the changes of a language do it harm. In the preface of a German translation of *The 1001 Nights,* Dr. Weil fumed that the merchants of the unpardonable Galland supply themselves, each time the story requires them to cross the desert, with a "valise of dates." It could be argued that around 1710 the mere mention of dates was enough to blot out the image of the valise, but that is unnecessary. "Valise," then, was a subclass of "saddlebag."

There are other attacks. In a certain confused panegyric which survives in the *Morceaux choisis* of 1921, André Gide vituperates the licenses of Antoine Galland, the better to efface the literalness of Mardrus (whose candor is much

74

superior to his reputation), as *fin de siècle* as the former is eighteenth century, and much more unfaithful.

Galland's reserve is mundane; decorum inspires it, not morality. Let me copy down a few lines from the third page of the *Nights: "Il alla droit a appartement de cette princesse, qui, ne s'attendant pas a le revoir, avait reçu dans son lit un des derniers officiers de sa maison."* Burton makes the nebulous *officier* concrete: "a black cook, rank with kitchen grease and soot." Both, diversely, deform: the original is less ceremonious than Galland, and less greasy than Burton. (Effects of decorum: in the measured prose of Galland, the detail "had received in her bed" becomes brutal.)

LANE

Ninety years after the death of Galland, a very different translator of the *Nights* is born: Edward Lane. His biographers never cease repeating that he is a son of Dr. Theophilus Lane, prebendary of Hereford. That Genesene datum (and the awesome form that it calls up) will suffice us. For five studious years the Arabized Lane lived in Cairo, "almost exclusively among Muslims, speaking and hearing their idiom, shaping himself to their customs with the most perfect care, and received by all of them as an equal." However, neither the high Egyptian nights nor the opulent black coffee with cardamom seed, nor the frequent literary discussions with doctors of law nor the venerated muslin turban nor eating with his fingers made him forget his British modesty, the delicate solitude central to the lords of the world. Whence his most learned version is (or seems to be) an encyclopedia of evasion. The original is not professionally obscene; Galland corrects the occasional bawdry by supposing it in bad taste. Lane seeks it out and persecutes it like an inquisitor. His probity will make no pact with silence; he prefers an alarmed chorus of notes in a crabbed minor typeface, which mutter such things as these: "I pass over a most reprehensible episode. . . . I suppress a repugnant explanation. . . . Here a line too coarse for translation. . . . I necessarily suppress another anecdote. . . . From this point I give way to omissions. . . . Here the story of the slave Bukhayt, utterly unfit to be translated." Mutilation does not exclude death; there are stories rejected entire "because they cannot be purified without destruction." This responsible and total repudiation does not seem to me illogical; the subterfuge of the Puritan is what I condemn. Lane is a virtuoso of subterfuge, an undoubted precursor of Hollywood's stranger modesties. My notes furnish me with a couple of examples. On Night 391, a fisherman presents a fish to the king of kings, who desires to know whether the fish is male or female. He is told that it is a hermaphrodite. Lane finds a way to soften that improper conversation, translating that the king asked what species the animal belonged to, and that the clever fisherman responded that it was of a mixed species. On Night 217, a king with two wives is spoken of, who would lie one night with the first, the next night with the second, and thus were they all well pleased. Lane dilutes the felicity of that monarch, saying that he treated his wives "with impartiality. . . ." One reason is that he destined his work for "the little parlor-table," center of unalarming reading and circumspect conversation.

75

The oblique, passing carnal allusion is sufficient to make Lane forget his honor and abound in distortions and occultations; there is no other fault in him. Save for the particular taint of that temptation, Lane is a man of admirable faithfulness. He is without design, which is a positive advantage. He does not intend to flaunt the barbaric hues of the *Nights* like Captain Burton, nor to overlook or attenuate them either, like Galland. This latter domesticated his Arabs, so that they would not be utterly out of place in Paris; Lane is minutely Hagarene. Galland spurned all literal precision; Lane justifies his interpretation of every doubtful word. The first invokes an invisible manuscript and a dead Maronite woman; Lane gives edition and page. Galland does not concern himself with notes; Lane accumulates a chaos of clarifications which, organized, make up an independent volume. To differ: such is the necessity his precursor imposes on him. Lane will rise to it; for him, it will be enough not to abridge the original.

The elegant Newman-Arnold debate (1861–62), more memorable than its two interlocutors, has argued extensively the two general ways of translating. Newman in it defended the literal mode, the retention of all verbal singularities; Arnold, the strict elimination of distracting or hindering details. This proceeding may furnish the pleasures of uniformity and gravity; the other, continuous small wonders. Both are less important than the translator and his literary habits. To translate the spirit is an intention of such enormity, so phantasmal, that it can well turn out to be inoffensive; to translate the letter, a precision so extravagant that there is no risk in attempting it. Of more consequence than these infinite purposes is the conservation or suppression of certain particulars; of more consequence than those preferences and omissions is the syntactic movement. Lane's is pleasant, in keeping with the distinguished little parlor-table. In his vocabulary he commonly avoids the overuse of Latin words, though not because of any artifice of brevity. He is absentminded; on the threshold page of his translation he puts the adjective "romantic," a kind of futurism, in the mouth of a bearded Muslim of the twelfth century. At times the lack of sensitivity is happy for him, since it permits him the interpolation of very flat phrasing in a noble paragraph, with unwittingly good results. The richest example of that cooperation of heterogeneous words must be this one, which I submit: "And in this palace is the last information respecting lords collected in the dust." Another might be this invocation: "By the Living that dies not nor canst ever die, by the name of Him to whom belong glory and permanence." In Burton, the occasional precursor of the always-fabulous Mardrus, I would be suspicious of formulas so satisfactorily Oriental; in Lane, they are so scarce that I must suppose them to be involuntary, which is to say genuine.

The scandalous decorum of Galland's and Lane's versions has provoked a genre of mockeries which it is traditional to repeat. I myself have not failed that tradition. It is very well known that they were not faithful to the unfortunate man who saw the Night of Power, to the imprecations of a garbageman of the thirteenth century tricked by a dervish, and to the habits of Sodom. It is very well known that they disinfected the *Nights*.

Detractors argue that that process annihilates or injures the pretty ingenuousness of the original. They are in error: *The Book of a Thousand Nights and a Night* is not (morally) ingenuous; it is an adaptation of old stories of plebeian taste, coarse, from Cairo's middle classes. Save in the exemplary stories of *Sindbad,* the immodesties of *The 1001 Nights* have nothing to do with the freedom of the paradisal state. They are speculative ventures by the editor; his object is a guffaw, his heroes never rise above being porters, beggars, or eunuchs. The old amorous stories of the collection, those which recite cases of the desert or of the cities of Arabia, are not obscene, as no production of pre-Islamic literature is. They are impassioned and sad, and one of their preferred motifs is the death from love, that death which a judgment of the Ulemas has pronounced no less holy than that of a martyr who bears witness to the faith. . . . If we approve of that argument, the timidities of Galland and Lane will seem to us restitutions of a primitive text.

I know of another, better argument. To evade the erotic possibilities of the original is not one of the offenses the Lord will not forgive, when what is of primary importance is to project the magical atmosphere. To offer men a new *Decameron* is a commercial operation like so many others; to offer them an *Ancient Mariner* or *Bateau Ivre* merits another heaven. Enno Littmann observes that *The 1001 Nights* is, more than anything, a collection of marvels. The universal imposition of that sense of the marvelous on all Occidental minds is the work of Galland. Let there be no doubt of that. Less happy than we, the Arabs say they have little regard for the original; they know already the men, the customs, the talismans, the deserts, and the demons that those histories reveal to us.

BURTON

In some place in his work, Rafael Cansinos Asséns swears that he can salute the stars in fourteen classical and modern languages. Burton dreamed in seventeen idioms and tells that he had a command of thirty-five: Semitic, Dravidic, Indo-European, Amharic. . . . That wealth does not exceed its own definition; it is a trait which agrees with the rest, equally excessive. But there is no one less exposed to the repeated taunt of *Hudibras* against the doctors capable of saying absolutely nothing in several languages; Burton was a man who had much to say, and seventy-two volumes of his work go on saying it. Let me give some titles at random: *Goa and the Blue Mountains, System of Bayonet Exercises, A Personal Narrative of a Pilgrimage to Medina, The Lake Regions of Equatorial Africa, City of the Saints, Exploration of the Highlands of the Brazil, On a Hermaphrodite of the Cabo Verde Islands, Letters from the Battlefields of Paraguay, Ultima Thule, or a Summer in Iceland, To the Gold Coast for Gold, The Book of the Sword (First Volume), The Perfumed Garden of Nafzaní*—a posthumous work, committed to the fire by Lady Burton, as was *A Collection of Epigrams Inspired by Priapus.* The writer reveals himself through this catalog, that English captain, with a passion for geography and the innumerable ways of men that men know. I will not defame his memory by comparing him with Morand, a bilingual, sedentary, intellectual gentleman who goes up and down infinitely in the elevators of an always-same hotel, admiring the spectacle of a trunk. . . . Burton, disguised as an Afghan, had pilgrimaged to the holy cities of Arabia; his voice had prayed to the Lord to deny his bones and his skin, his painful flesh and his blood, to the Flame of Wrath and of Justice; his mouth, dried out by the *samún,* had left a kiss on the aerolite which is worshiped in the Ka'abah. That is a celebrated adventure; the possible rumor that an uncircumcised man, a *nazraní,* was profaning the shrine would have decided his death. Before, dressed as a dervish, he had practiced medicine in Cairo, not without varying it a bit with prestidigitation and magic, to gain the confidence of the sick. Around 1858 he had commanded an expedition to the secret sources of the Nile—a charge that he carried as far as the discovery of Lake Tanganyika. In that enterprise he caught a high fever; in 1855 the Somalis pierced his cheeks with a javelin. (Burton was coming from Harrar, which was a city closed to Europeans, in the interior of Abyssinia.) Nine years later, he tried the terrible hospitality of the ceremonious cannibals of Dahomey; on his return there was no lack of rumors (perhaps spread, certainly encouraged, by him) that he had "eaten strange flesh"—like Shakespeare's omnivorous proconsul.[2] Jews, democracy, the Ministry of Foreign Affairs, and Christianity were his favorite hatreds; Lord Byron and Islam, his worships. Of the solitary office of writing he had made something brave and plural: he attacked it beginning at daybreak, in a vast hall multiplied by eleven tables, each of them with the material for a book, some with a bright jasmine in a vase of water. He inspired illustrious friendships and loves; of the first I will mention only Swinburne, who dedicated to him the second series of *Poems and Ballads,* "in recognition of a friendship which I must always count among the highest honours of my life," and who lamented his decease with many stanzas. A man of words and heroic deeds, well might Burton take on the motto of the *Divan* of Almotanabí:

> The horse, the desert, the night know me,
> The guest, the sword, the paper, the pen.

It will be remarked that from the anthropophagous amateur to the sleeping polyglot, I have not rejected those characterizations of Richard Burton which with no lack of fervor we can call legendary. The reason is clear: the Burton of the legend is the translator of the *Nights.* I have sometimes suspected that the radical distinction between poetry and prose resides in the very different expectation of the one who reads it: the former presupposes an intensity which in the

---

[2]I allude to the Mark Antony invoked by Caesar's apostrophe:

> . . . on the Alps
> It is reported, thou didst eat strange flesh
> Which some did die to look on.

In those lines, I believe I can make out a somewhat inverted glimpse of the zoological myth of the basilisk, a serpent of mortal glance. Pliny (*Natural History,* eighth book, para. 33) tells us nothing of the posthumous powers of that ophidian, but the conjunction of seeing and ceasing to be *(vedi Napoli e poi mori)* must have influenced Shakespeare.

The glance of the basilisk was venomous; the Divinity, on the other hand, can kill by pure splendor—or pure irradiation of *mana.* The direct vision of God is intolerable. Moses covers his face on Mount Horeb, *for he feared to look on God;* Hakim, a prophet from Jorasan, wore a quadruple veil of white silk so as not to blind men. Cf. also Isaiah, 6:5, and I Kings, 19:13.

invariably invoked. Burton is lovingly prodigal with substitutions of that order. His vocabulary is no less disproportionate than his notes. Archaism coexists with argot, jail or navy slang with technical terms. He does not blush at his glorious hybridization of English; neither the Scandinavian repertory of Morris nor the Latin of Johnson have his nod, but rather the touch and repercussion of both. Neologisms and "foreignisms" abound: *castrato, inconséquence, hauteur, in gloria, bagnio, langue fourrée, pudonor, vendetta, Wazir.* Each of those words may be just, but their intercalation implies a falseness. Not a bad falseness, since those verbal antics—and others, syntactic—divert the sometimes wearisome course of the *Nights.* Burton can manage them; at the beginning he gravely translates *Sulayman* "Son of David (on the twain be peace!)"; later, when that majesty is familiar to us, he reduces it to *Solomon Davidson.* He makes of a king who for the other translators is "king of Samarcand in Persia," *a King of Samarcand in Barbarian-land,* of a buyer who for the rest is "choleric," *a man of wrath.* That is not all; Burton completely rewrites, with addition of circumstantial details and physiological features, the beginning of the history and the end. He thus inaugurates, around 1885, a proceeding whose perfection (or whose reductio ad absurdum) we will consider later in Mardrus. English is always more intemporal than French; the heterogeneous style of Burton has antiquated less than Mardrus's, which is of an obvious date.

DR. MARDRUS

A paradoxical destiny, Mardrus's. He is accorded the virtue "moral" by being the most faithful translator of *The 1001 Nights,* a book of admirable lasciviousness, which quality had been quietly withheld from its readers theretofore by the good breeding of Galland or the Puritanical niceties of Lane. One admires his genial literalness, shown very well in the subtitle "Literal and Complete Version of the Arabic Text," and by the inspiration of writing *Book of the Thousand Nights and a Night.* The history of that name is edifying; we might recall it before looking at Mardrus.

The *Meads of Gold and Mines of Gems* of Masudi describes a collection titled *Hézar Afsane,* Persian words whose direct import is *A Thousand Adventures,* but that people call *A Thousand Nights.* Another tenth-century document, the *Fihrist,* narrates the frame-story of the series: the king's desolate oath that each night he would wed a virgin whom at daybreak he would decapitate, and Scheherazad's resolution to distract him with marvelous stories, until over them both had rolled a thousand nights and she showed him their son. That invention—so superior to the foreshadowings and analogies of Chaucer's pious cavalcade or Giovanni Boccaccio's epidemic—is said to be posterior to the title, and to have been contrived with the aim of justifying it. . . . However that may be, the primitive figure 1000 soon rose to 1001. How did that additional night, which now we cannot do without, come to be, that *maquette* for Quevedo's ridicule—and later Voltaire's—of Pico della Mirandola's *Book of All Things and Many Other Things?* Littmann suggests a contamination of the Turkish phrase *bin bir,* whose literal sense is *one thousand one,* and whose employment is for *many.* Lane, at the

81

beginning of 1840, adduced a handsomer reason: the magic fear of even numbers. It is certain that the adventures of the title did not stop there. Antoine Galland from 1704 onward eliminated the repetitiousness of the original and translated *Thousand and One Nights.* It is this name which is now familiar in all the nations of Europe save England, which prefers the title *Arabian Nights.* In 1839 the editor of the Calcutta impression, W. H. M'Naghten, had the singular scruple to translate *Qitab alif laila wa laila, Book of the Thousand Nights and a Night.* That renewal through spelling did not go unnoticed. John Payne, in 1882, commenced publishing his *Book of the Thousand Nights and One Night;* Captain Burton, beginning in 1885, his *Book of the Thousand Nights and a Night;* J. C. Mardrus, from 1889, his *Livre des mille nuits et une nuit.*

I am seeking the passage that made me definitively doubt the faithfulness of that last-named. It belongs to the doctrinal history of the City of Brass, which takes up the end of Night 566 through part of 578 in all versions, but which Dr. Mardrus has remanded (his guardian angel will know the cause) to Nights 338–346. I do not insist; the inconceivable reform of an ideal calendar ought not exhaust our wonder. Scheherazad-Mardrus narrates: "The water followed four channels laid out with charming detours in the floor of the room, and the bed of each channel had a special hue: the first canal-bed was of pink porphyry; the second, topazes; the third, emeralds; and the fourth, turquoise, so that the water, according to the color of its bed, was dyed, and, irradiated by the soft light that filtered through the silken hangings above, cast over surrounding objects and the marble walls the deliciousness of a marine landscape."

As an attempt at visual prose in the manner of the *Portrait of Dorian Gray,* I accept (and even admire) that description; as a version "literal and complete" of a passage composed in the thirteenth century, I repeat that it alarms me infinitely. There are multiple reasons: a Scheherazad without Mardrus describes by enumerating the parts, not their interaction, and does not allege circumstantial details, such as that the color of the canal-bed shines through the water, does not define the quality of the light filtered by the silk, and does not allude to the Watercolorists' Salon in the final image. Another small flaw: "charming detours" is not Arabic; it is egregiously French. I do not know whether the foregoing reasons will altogether satisfy; for myself they are not enough, and so I had the indifferent courtesy to collate the three German versions—by Weil, Henning, and Littmann—and the two English ones—Lane's and Sir Richard Burton's—by which I confirmed that the original of the ten lines of Mardrus was this: "The four waterways emptied into a trough (or basin), which was of marble of diverse colors."

Mardrus's interpolations are not uniform. At times they are boldly anachronistic, as if suddenly Marchand were to discuss the retreat from the mission. For example: "They overlooked a dream-city . . . Thence sight, fixed on horizons drowned in the night, embraced palace cupolas, the terraces of houses, serene gardens climbing up in those bronze precincts; and canals illuminated by the stars passed in a 1000 bright circuits to the shadow of the foundations, while there in the background, a metal sea held in its cold breast the reflected fires of heaven." Or this, whose Gallicism is no less manifest: "A magnificent tapestry of glorious supplement the Oriental style. His interpolations, to me, merit every respect. He has some intruders into a meeting say, "We would not be like the morning, which disperses festive gatherings." Of a generous king he assures us that "the fire that burns for his guests brings to mind the Inferno and the dew of his beneficent hand is like the Deluge"; of another he tells us that "his hands were as liberal as the sea." Those nice apocrypha are not unworthy of Burton or Mardrus, and the translator destined them for the verse parts, where their lovely vivacity might be an ersatz or *succedaneum* for the original rhymes. With respect to the prose, I understand that he translated it tolerably well, with certain justified omissions, equidistant from hypocrisy and immodesty. Burton praised his work—"every way as faithful as a translation of popular temper can be." Not in vain was Dr. Weil a Jew "though librarian"; in his language I believe I can perceive something of the flavor of the Scriptures.

The second version (1895–97) dispenses with the charms of exactitude, but also with those of style. I speak of that one supplied by Henning, Leipzig Arabist, to the *Universalbibliothek* of Philipp Reclam. It is accused of being an expurgated version, though the publisher says the contrary. The style is insipid, stubborn. Its most unarguable virtue is probably its extensiveness. The Bulak and Breslau editions are represented, as are the manuscripts of Zotenberg and of the Supplementary Nights of Burton. Henning, translator of Sir Richard, is literarily superior to Henning, translator of Arabic, which is a mere confirmation of the primacy of Sir Richard over the Arabs. In the preface and at the end of the book the excellences of Burton are abundant—almost robbed of their authority by the report that Burton employed "the language of Chaucer, equivalent to medieval Arabic." The indication that Chaucer was *one* of the sources of the vocabulary of Burton would have been more reasonable. (Another is the *Rabelais* of Sir Thomas Urquhart.)

The third version, Greve's, derives from the English version of Burton and repeats it, with the exclusion of the encyclopedic notes. He published it before the Insel-Verlag War.

The fourth (1923–28) comes to supplant the former. It embraces six volumes, like the other, and it is signed by Enno Littmann, decipherer of the monuments of Axum, enumerator of the 283 Ethiopian manuscripts which are in Jerusalem, collaborator in the *Zeitschrift für Assyriologie*. Without the pleasing demurrals of Burton, his translation is of a total frankness. The most ineffable obscenities do not give him pause; he renders them all into his tranquil German, once in a rare while into Latin. He does not omit one word, not even those which register, 1000 times, the passage from each night to the following one. He disregards or refuses local color; his editors had to indicate to him that he should retain the name of Allah and not substitute God for it. Like Burton and John Payne, he translates Arabic verse into Occidental verse. He notes ingenuously that if after the ritual announcement, "Such a one pronounced these verses," there should follow a paragraph of German prose, his readers would be disconcerted. He supplies the notes necessary for the fine comprehension of the text—some twenty per volume, all brief. He is always lucid, readable, mediocre. He follows (so he tells us) the respiration local to Arabic. If there is no error in the *Encyclopaedia Britannica,* his translation is the best of the many circulating. I hear that Arabists agree; it comes to nothing that a mere literary man—and that, from a republic merely Argentine—prefers to dissent.

My reason is this: the versions of Mardrus and Burton, and even of Galland, may only be conceived of *after a literature.* Whatever their defects or their merits, those characteristic works presuppose a rich anterior process. In some way, the almost inexhaustible English process is shadowed forth in Burton—the hard obscenity of John Donne, the gigantic vocabulary of Shakespeare and Cyril Tourneur, Swinburne's tendency to archaism, the gross erudition of the treatise-writers of the seventeenth century, the energy and vagueness, the love of tempests and magic. In the merry paragraphs of Mardrus, *Salammbô* and LaFontaine, *The Wicker-work Woman* and the Russian ballet live together. In Littmann, like Washington incapable of lying, there is no other thing than German probity. It is little, it is so little. The intercourse between the *Nights* and Germany should have produced something more.

In the field of philosophy, as in novels, Germany possesses a fantastic literature—better said, *only* possesses a fantastic literature. There are marvels in the *Nights* that I would like to see rethought in German. In expressing that desire, I am thinking about the deliberate prodigies of the collection—the all-powerful slaves from a lamp or ring, Queen Lab who changes Muslims into birds, the copper boatman with talismans and formulas on his chest—and about those more general marvels which proceed from its collective nature, from the necessity of completing 1001 sections. Magic spells all exhausted, the copyists had to resort to historical or pious notices, whose inclusion seems to attest to the good faith of the rest. In one tone coexist the ruby which ascended to heaven and the first description of Sumatra, the features of the court of the Abbasideans and the silver angels whose feeding is the justification of the Lord. That mixture becomes poetic; the same may be said for certain repetitions. Is it not portentous that on Night 602 King Shahryar hears from the mouth of his queen his own story? In imitation of the general model, a story is wont to contain other stories, of no less extensiveness: stages within the stage as in the tragedy of *Hamlet,* elevations to the power of dream. A hard clear verse of Tennyson seems to define them:

Laborious orient ivory, sphere in sphere.

For the greatest wonder, the adventitious heads of the Hydra can be even more concrete than the body; Shahryar, fabulous king "of the Isles of China and Hindostan," receives tidings from Tarik bin Zyad, governor of Tangiers and victor in the battle of Guadelette. . . . The antechambers are a confusion of mirrors, the mask is beneath the face, so that no one knows which is the true man and which his idols. And nothing of that matters; that disorder is as trivial and acceptable as the inventions of a man when he first dozes off into dream.

Chance has played at symmetry, at contrast, at digression. What would a man, a Kafka, not do to organize, accentuate those games, remake them according to German deformation, according to the *Unheimlichkeit* of Germany?

86

never repeats a formula with the evident fear of being wrong; Chesterton is comfortable, hence, his almost ineffectual use of scholastic dialectic. He is, moreover, one of the few Christians who not only believe in Heaven, but who are interested in it and who thrive on restless conjectures and previsions regarding it. The event is unusual . . . I will never forget the visible discomfort of a certain group of Catholics, one afternoon when Xul-Solar spoke of angels and of their customs and appearances.

Chesterton—who can ignore it?—was an incomparable inventor of fantastic stories. Unfortunately, he sought to extract from them a moral, thus reducing them to mere parables. Fortunately, he never really succeeded in doing so.

CHESTERTON, DETECTIVE STORY WRITER

Edgar Allan Poe wrote stories of pure, fantastic horror or of pure *bizarrerie;* Poe was the inventor of the detective story. This is no less certain than the fact that he never combined the two genres. He never invoked the help of the sedentary French gentleman Auguste Dupin (from the Rue Dunot) to determine the precise crime of "The Man of the Crowd" or to elucidate the modus operandi of the specter that fulminated against the courtiers of Prospero, as well as this latter dignitary, during the famous epidemic of the Red Death. Chesterton, in the diverse narrations that constitute the five-part saga of Father Brown and those of the poet Gabriel Gale and those of the "Man Who Knew Too Much," executes, always, that tour de force. He presents a mystery, proposes a supernatural explanation and then replaces it, losing nothing, with one from this world. His dialogues, his narrative mode, his descriptions of characters and places, are excellent. This, naturally, seems sufficient for some to accuse him of "literature." A sad accusation for the learned! I hear from many mouths the legend that Chesterton, if you please, is a more illustrious writer than Edgar Wallace, but that the latter constructs his intolerable plots better. I promise my reader that those who say such things are lying and that the fiery depths of Hell will be their final dwelling place. In Chesterton's detective stories, everything is justified: the briefest and most fleeting episodes have subsequent projection. In one of his stories, one stranger assaults another so that the latter is not run over by a truck, and this alarming yet necessary violence prefigures its final act, of declaring him insane so that he cannot be executed for a crime. In another, a dangerous and vast conspiracy fomented by a single man (with the help of beards, masks, and pseudonyms) is foretold with horrid exactness in the couplet:

> As all stars shrivel in the single sun,
> The words are many, but The Word is one.

which is later deciphered, with a permutation of capitals:

> The words are many but the word is One.

In a third, the initial *marquette*—the unadorned mention of an Indian who throws his knife at another and kills him—is the strict reversal of the plot: a man stabbed by his friend with an arrow, on the top of a tower. A flying knife, an arrow used to stab . . . In another, there is a legend at the beginning: a blasphemous king raises with Satanic help a topless tower. God fulminates against the tower and makes it a bottomless pit, into which the king's soul is forever falling. This divine inversion somehow prefigures the silent rotation of a library, with two small cups, one with poisoned coffee, which kills the man who had intended it for his guest. (In the tenth issue of *Sur* magazine, I have attempted a study of the innovations and rigors Chesterton imposes upon the technique of detective stories.)

CHESTERTON, WRITER

I am certain that it is improper to suspect or concede merits of a literary nature in a man of letters. Truly informed critics never cease to point out that the most forgettable thing about a man of letters is his literature and that he can only be of interest as a human being—is art inhuman, therefore?—as an example of this country, of that date, or of such-and-such illnesses. Uncomfortably enough for me, I cannot share those concerns. I feel that Chesterton is one of the finest writers of our time, not just for his fortunate invention, visual imagination, and the childlike or divine happiness that pervades his works, but for his rhetorical virtues, for the pure merits of his skill. Those who have thumbed through Chesterton's work have no need of my demonstration; those who are ignorant of it can look over the following titles and perceive his fine verbal economy: "The Moderate Murderer," "The Oracle of the Dog," "The Salad of Colonel Clay," "The Blast of the Book," "The Vengeance of the Statue," "The God of the Gongs," "The Man with Two Beards," "The Man Who Was Thursday," "The Garden of Smoke." In that famous work *Degeneration,* which turned out to be such a fine anthology of the writers it tried to defame, Dr. Max Nordau ponders the titles of the French Symbolists: *Quand les violons sont partis, Les palais nomades, les illuminations.* Granted that few of them, if any, are provocative. Few people judge their acquaintance with *Les palais nomades* as necessary or interesting, yet many do with "The Oracle of the Dog." Of course, with the peculiar stimulus of Chesterton's titles, our conscience tells us that these names have not been invoked in vain. We know that in *Les palais nomades* there are no nomadic palaces; we know that "The Oracle of the Dog" will not lack a dog and an oracle, or a concrete, oracular dog. In like manner, "The Mirror of the Magistrate," which was popular in England around 1560, was nothing more than an allegorical mirror; Chesterton's "Mirror of the Magistrate" refers to a real mirror. . . . The foregoing does not insinuate that these somewhat parodistic titles indicate the level of Chesterton's style. It means that this style is omnipresent.

At one time (and in Spain) there existed the inattentive custom of comparing the names and works of Gomez de la Serna and Chesterton. Such an approximation is totally fruitless. They both intensely perceive (or register) the peculiar hue of a house, of a light, of an hour of the day, but Gomez de la Serna is chaotic. Inversely, limpidity and order are constant throughout Chesterton's writings. I dare to sense (according to M. Taine's geographical formula) the heaviness and disorder of British fog in Gomez de la Serna and Latin clarity in G. K.

There is something more terrible and marvelous than being devoured by a dragon; it is being a dragon. There is something stranger than being a dragon: being a man. Such elemental intuition, such a lasting fit of fear (and gratitude) shapes all of Chesterton's poems. Their fault (if they have one) is that each one has been formulated like some sort of justification or parable. They have been splendidly executed, but their plot is too apparent. Their distribution, their scaffolding, is too easily noticed. On occasion, on a rare occasion, there is an echo of Kipling:

> You have weighed the stars in the balance,
> and grasped the skies in a span:
> Take, if you must have answer,
> the word of a common man.

I feel, nevertheless, that *Lepanto* is one of the present-day works which future generations will not allow to die. A sense of vanity often detracts from heroic odes; this English acclamation of a victory of Spain's infantry and Italy's artillery does not run that risk. Its music, its gaiety, its mythology are admirable. It is a piece that is physically stirring, like the proximity of the sea.

VIRGINIA WOOLF: A CAPSULE BIOGRAPHY [JLB 27]

Virginia Woolf has been considered the leading English novelist. An exact ranking is not important, as literature is not a contest, but there is no question that she is one of the most delicate intellects and imaginations currently attempting promising experiments with the English novel.

Adelina Virginia Stephen was born in London in 1882. (The first name vanished without trace.) She is the daughter of Mr. Leslie Stephen, a compiler of biographies of Swift, Johnson, and Hobbes, books rarely attempting analysis and never invention, whose worth lies in the great clarity of their prose and the precision of their facts.

Adelina Virginia was the third of four children. The artist Rothenstein remembers her as "absorbed and silent, all dressed in black, with collar and cuffs of white lace." She was trained from infancy not to speak unless she had something to say. She was never sent to school, but one of her household tasks was the study of Greek. Sundays at her house were well attended, frequented by Meredith, Ruskin, Stevenson, John Morley, Gosse, and Hardy.

She spent her summers in Cornwall at the seashore, in a cottage lost in an enormous and rundown country estate with an orchard, terraces, and a greenhouse. This country estate reappears in a novel in 1927.

In 1912 Virginia Stephen married Mr. Leonard Woolf in London, and they acquired a printing press. They were attracted to typography, that sometimes traitorous accomplice of literature, and composed and edited their own books.

They were undoubtedly thinking of the glorious precedent of William Morris, printer and poet.

Three years later Virginia Woolf published her first novel, *The Voyage Out.* In 1919 *Night and Day* appeared; in 1922, *Jacob's Room.* This last book is already wholly characteristic. There is no plot in the narrative sense of that word; the theme is the character of one man studied not from within him, but indirectly through the objects and people surrounding him.

Mrs. Dalloway (1925) describes one woman's entire day; it is a reflection of Joyce's *Ulysses,* although much less overwhelming. *To the Lighthouse* (1927) uses the same technique: it shows several hours from several people's lives, so that in those hours we see their past and future. In *Orlando* (1928) there is also the preoccupation with time. The hero of this extremely original novel—undoubtedly Virginia Woolf's most intense work and one of the most singular and maddening of our age—lives for 300 years and is, at times, a symbol of England and particularly of its poetry. Magic, bitterness, and delight collaborate in this book. It is, moreover, a musical book, not only for the euphonic virtues of its prose, but for the very form of its composition, made up of a limited number of themes that return and combine with one another. What we hear in *A Room of One's Own* is also a musical piece in which dreams and reality alternate and find their equilibrium.

In 1931 Virginia Woolf published another novel, *The Waves.* The waves that lend their name to this book receive the interior soliloquy of the characters through the course of time and from the many vicissitudes of time. Each phase of their lives corresponds to a different hour from morning to night. There is no plot, no conversation, no action. The book nevertheless is moving. It is filled, like the rest of Virginia Woolf's work, with delicate physical touches.

WILLIAM FAULKNER: THREE REVIEWS [JLB 28]

THE UNVANQUISHED

It is a general rule that novelists do not present a reality, but rather its recollection. They write about real or believable events that have been revised and arranged by memory. (This process, of course, has nothing to do with the verb tenses which are used.) Faulkner, on the other hand, wants at times to re-create the pure present, not simplified by time nor even refined by attention. The "pure present" is no more than a psychological ideal; and therefore certain of Faulkner's disarrangements seem more confused—and richer—than the original events.

In previous works, Faulkner has played powerfully with time, deliberately shuffling chronological order, deliberately multiplying the labyrinths and ambiguities, so much so that there were those who insisted that he derived all his strength from those involutions. This novel—direct, irresistible, straightforward —finally destroys that suspicion. Faulkner does not attempt to explain his characters. He shows us what they feel, how they act. The events are extraordinary, but his narration of them is so vivid we cannot imagine them any other way. *"Le vrai peut quelquefois n'être pas vraisemblable"* ("The truth may not seem plausible."), Boileau has said. Faulkner lavishes implausibilities in order to appear truthful—and he succeeds. Or rather: the world he imagines is so real that it also encompasses the implausible.

William Faulkner has been compared to Dostoevsky. The comparison is not unjust, but Faulkner's world is so physical, so carnal, that, next to Colonel Bayard Sartoris or Temple Drake, the explanatory homicide Raskolnikov is as tenuous as one of Racine's princes. Rivers of brown water, rundown mansions, black slaves, equestrian wars—lazy and cruel: the peculiar world of *The Unvanquished* is consanguineous with this America and its history, and it is also *criollo*.

There are some books that touch us physically like the nearness of the sea or the morning. This—for me—is one of them.

ABSALOM, ABSALOM

I know of two kinds of writers: one whose obsession is verbal procedure, and one whose obsession is the work and passions of men. The former tends to receive the derogatory label "Byzantine" and to be exalted as a "pure artist." The other, more fortunate, has known such laudatory epithets as "profound," "human," "profoundly human," and the flattering abuse of "primal." The former is Swinburne or Mallarmé; the latter, Céline or Theodore Dreiser. Others, truly exceptional, exercise the joys and virtues of both categories. Victor Hugo remarked that Shakespeare embodied Góngora; we might also observe that he embodies Dostoevsky. . . . Among the great novelists, Joseph Conrad was the last, perhaps, who was as interested in the procedures of the novel as in the destiny and personality of his characters. The last, until Faulkner's sensational appearance on the scene.

Faulkner likes to present the novel through his characters. This method is not totally original: Robert Browning's *The Ring and the Book* (1868) details the same crime ten times, through ten mouths and ten souls, but Faulkner infuses an intensity in them which is almost intolerable. Infinite fragmentation, an infinite and black carnality, is encountered in this book. The theater is Mississippi; the heroes, men destroyed by envy, drink, solitude, and the erosions of hatred.

Absalom, Absalom is comparable to *The Sound and the Fury.* I know of no higher praise.

THE WILD PALMS

To my knowledge, no one has yet attempted a history of the forms of the novel, a morphology of the novel. Such a hypothetical and just history would emphasize the name of Wilkie Collins, who inaugurated the curious method of entrusting the narration of a work to the characters; of Robert Browning, whose vast narrative poem, *The Ring and the Book* (1868), details the same crime ten times, through ten mouths and ten souls; of Joseph Conrad, who at times showed two interlocutors guessing and reconstructing the story of a third. Also—with obvi-

93

ous justice—of William Faulkner. He, with Jules Romains, is one of the few novelists equally interested in the methods of the novel and the fate and character of its people.

In Faulkner's major works—*Light in August, The Sound and the Fury, Sanctuary*—the technical innovations seem necessary, inevitable. In *The Wild Palms,* they are less attractive than uncomfortable, less justifiable than exasperating. The book consists of two books, of two parallel (and opposed) stories that alternate with one another. The first, *Wild Palms,* is that of a man annihilated by carnality; the second, *Old Man,* that of a pale-eyed boy who tries to rob a train and to whom, after many blurred years of prison, the overflowing Mississippi grants a useless and atrocious freedom. This second story, admirable at times, interrupts again and again the difficult course of the first in long interpolations.

That William Faulkner is the leading novelist of our time is a conceivable affirmation. Of his works, *The Wild Palms* seems to me to be the least appropriate for becoming acquainted with him, but (like all of Faulkner's books) it contains pages of an intensity that clearly exceeds the possibilities of any other author.

THE TOTAL LIBRARY [JLB 29]

The caprice or fancy or utopia of the Total Library contains certain traits that could be confused with virtues. Actually, it is astonishing how long it took mankind to dream up the idea. Certain examples Aristotle attributes to Democritus and to Leucippus clearly prefigure it, but its late inventor is Gustav Theodor Fechner and its first expounder is Kurd Lasswitz. (Between Democritus of Abdera and Fechner flow—heavily laden—almost twenty-four centuries of European history.) Its connections are illustrious and multiple: it is related to atomism and combinatory analysis, to typography and to chance. In *The Race with the Tortoise* (Berlin, 1929), Dr. Theodor Wolff suggests that it is either a derivation from or a parody of Raymond Lull's mental machine; I would add that it is a typographical avatar of the doctrine of the eternal return which, adopted by the Stoics or by Blanqui,[1] by the Pythagoreans or by Nietzsche, eternally returns.

The most ancient of the texts that hint at it is alluded to in the first book of Aristotle's *Metaphysics.* I refer to the passage about Leucippus's cosmology: the formation of the world by the fortuitous conjunction of atoms. The writer observes that the atoms required by this conjecture are homogeneous and that their differences derive from position, order, or form. To illustrate those distinctions he adds: "A is different from N in form; AN from NA in order; Z from N in position." In the treatise *De Generatione et Corruptione,* he attempts to bring

---

[1] In *Sur* (No. 65, February 1940, pages 11–112), Borges reviews Neil Stewart's book about Louis Auguste Blanqui, whose *L'eternité par les astres* (1872) deals with the idea of the eternal return. Borges also refers to Blanqui in his preface to Adolfo Bioy Casares's novel *La invención de Morel* (1940).

the variety of visible things into accord with the simplicity of the atoms and he reasons that a tragedy is made up of the same elements as a comedy—that is, the twenty-six letters of the alphabet.

Three hundred years pass and Cicero composes an indecisive, skeptical dialogue and entitles it, ironically, *De Natura Deorum.* In the second book, one of the speakers argues:

> At this point must I not marvel that there should be anyone who can persuade himself that there are certain solid and indivisible particles of matter borne along by the force of gravity, and that the fortuitous collision of those particles produces this elaborate and beautiful world? I cannot understand why he who considers it possible for this to have occurred should not also think that, if a countless number of copies of the one-and-twenty letters of the alphabet, made of gold or what you will, were thrown together in some receptacle and then shaken out on to the ground, it would be possible that they should produce the *Annals* of Ennius, all ready for the reader. I doubt whether chance could possibly succeed in producing even a single verse! (Loeb Classical Library, pages 212–213)[2]

Cicero's typographical image was long-lived. Toward the middle of the seventeenth century, it appears in an academic discourse by Pascal; Swift, at the beginning of the eighteenth, stresses it in the preamble to his indignant "Trivial Essay on the Faculties of the Soul," which is a museum of commonplaces—as is the future *Dictionnaire des idées reçues* by Flaubert.

A century and a half later, three men vindicate Democritus and refute Cicero. Because such a huge period of time separates the litigants, the vocabulary and the metaphors of the polemic are different. Huxley (one of the men) does not say that the "golden letters" would finally compose a Latin verse if they were thrown a sufficient number of times; he says that a half-dozen monkeys, supplied with typewriters, would produce in a few eternities all the books in the British Museum.[3] Lewis Carroll (one of the other refuters) observes in the second part of his extraordinary dream novel *Sylvie and Bruno* (1893) that since the number of words in a language is limited, so is the number of their possible combinations, that is, of their books. "Soon [he says] literary men will not ask themselves, 'What book shall I write?' but 'Which book?' " Lasswitz, stimulated by Fechner, imagined the Total Library. He published his invention in the volume of fantastic tales *Traumkristalle.*

Lasswitz's basic idea is the same as Carroll's, but the elements of his game are the universal orthographic symbols, not the words of a language. The number of such elements—letters, spaces, punctuation marks—is reduced and can be reduced even further. The alphabet can do without the "q" (which is completely

---

[2]Since I do not have the original text at hand, I have copied this passage from Menéndez y Pelayo's Spanish translation (*Obras completas de Marco Tulio Cicerón,* Vol. III, page 88). Deussen and Mauthner mention a sack of letters but say nothing about their being made of gold; it is not impossible that the "illustrious bibliophage" has contributed the gold and removed the sack from the text.

[3]In absolute terms, one immortal monkey would be enough.

superfluous), the "x" (which is an abbreviation), and all the capital letters. The algorithms in the decimal system of enumeration can be eliminated or reduced to two, as they are in Leibniz's binary notation. Punctuation could be limited to the comma and the period. There would be no accents, as in Latin. By means of similar simplifications, Kurd Lasswitz arrives at twenty-five symbols (twenty-two letters, the space, the period, the comma), whose recombination and repetition would include everything it is possible to express: in all languages. The totality of such variations would take up a Total Library of astronomical size. Lasswitz urges mankind to construct that inhuman library, which chance would organize and which would itself eliminate intelligence. *(The Race with the Tortoise* by Wolff expounds the execution and the dimensions of that impossible enterprise.)

Everything would be in its blind volumes. Everything: the detailed history of the future, Aeschylus's *Egyptians,* the exact number of times the waters of the Ganges have reflected the flight of a falcon, the secret and true name of Rome, the encyclopedia Novalis would have composed, my dreams and musings at dawn on August 14, 1934, the proof of Pierre Fermat's theorem, the unwritten chapters of *Edwin Drood,* those same chapters translated into the language spoken by the Garamantes, the paradoxes Berkeley dreamed up about time and which he didn't publish, the iron books of Urizen, the premature epiphanies of Stephen Dedalus which before a cycle of 1000 years would be meaningless, the Gnostic preachings of Basilides, the song the sirens sang, the accurate catalog of the library, the proof that the catalog is fallacious. Everything: but because of a reasonable line or a reliable piece of news there would be millions of mad cacophonies, of verbal farragoes, and incoherences. Everything: but all of the generations of men will die out before the vertiginous shelves—the shelves which obliterate the daylight and in which chaos resides—ever grant them an acceptable page.

One of the mind's habits is the invention of horrible fancies. It has invented Hell, predestination, being predestined to Hell, the Platonic ideas, the chimera, the sphinx, the abnormal transfinite numbers (where the parts are no less abundant than the whole), masks, mirrors, operas, the monstrous Trinity: the Father, the Son, and the unresolvable Ghost, all articulated into one single organism.... I have tried to save from oblivion a minor horror: the vast, contradictory library, whose vertical deserts of books run the incessant risk of metamorphosis, which affirm everything, deny everything, and confuse everything—like a raving god.

PIERRE MENARD, AUTHOR OF THE QUIXOTE   [JLB 30]

The *visible* works left by this novelist are easily and briefly enumerated. It is therefore impossible to forgive the omissions and additions perpetrated by Madame Henri Bachelier in a fallacious catalog that a certain newspaper, whose Protestant tendencies are no secret, was inconsiderate enough to inflict on its wretched readers—even though they are few and Calvinist, if not Masonic and circumcised. Menard's true friends regarded this catalog with alarm, and even with a certain sadness. It is as if yesterday we were gathered together before the final marble and the fateful cypresses, and already error is trying to tarnish his memory. . . . Decidedly, a brief rectification is inevitable.

I am certain that it would be very easy to challenge my meager authority. I hope, nevertheless, that I will not be prevented from mentioning two important testimonials. The Baroness de Bacourt (at whose unforgettable *vendredis* I had the honor of becoming acquainted with the late lamented poet) has seen fit to approve these lines. The Countess de Bagnoregio, one of the most refined minds in the principality of Monaco (and now of Pittsburgh, Pennsylvania, since her recent marriage to the international philanthropist Simon Kautsch who, alas, has been so slandered by the victims of his disinterested handiwork), has sacrificed to "truth and death" (those are her words) that majestic reserve which distinguishes her, and in an open letter published in the magazine *Luxe* also grants me her consent. These authorizations, I believe, are not insufficient.

I have said that Menard's *visible* lifework is easily enumerated. Having carefully examined his private archives, I have been able to verify that it consists of the following:

a. A Symbolist sonnet which appeared twice (with variations) in the magazine *La conque* (the March and October issues of 1899).

b. A monograph on the possibility of constructing a poetic vocabulary of concepts that would not be synonyms or periphrases of those which make up ordinary language, "but ideal objects created by means of common agreement and destined essentially to fill poetic needs" (Nîmes, 1901).

c. A monograph on "certain connections or affinities" among the ideas of Descartes, Leibniz, and John Wilkins (Nîmes, 1903).

d. A monograph on the *Characteristica universalis* of Leibniz (Nîmes, 1904).

e. A technical article on the possibility of enriching the game of chess by means of eliminating one of the rooks' pawns. Menard proposes, recommends, disputes, and ends by rejecting this innovation.

f. A monograph on the *Ars magna generalis* of Ramón Lull (Nîmes, 1906).

g. A translation with prologue and notes of the *Libro de la invención y arte del juego del ajedrez* by Ruy López de Segura (Paris, 1907).

h. The rough draft of a monograph on the symbolic logic of George Boole.

i. An examination of the metric laws essential to French prose, illustrated with examples from

Saint-Simon (*Revue des langues romanes,* Montpellier, October 1909).

j. An answer to Luc Durtain (who had denied the existence of such laws) illustrated with examples from Luc Durtain (*Revue des langues romanes,* Montpellier, December 1909).

k. A manuscript translation of the *Aguja de navegar cultos* of Quevedo, entitled *La boussole des précieux.*

l. A preface to the catalog of the exposition of lithographs by Carolus Hourcade (Nîmes, 1914).

m. His work, *Les problèmes d'un problème* (Paris, 1917), which takes up in chronological order the various solutions of the famous problem of Achilles and the tortoise. Two editions of this book have appeared so far; the second has as an epigraph Leibniz's advice *"Ne craignez point, monsieur, la tortue,"* and contains revisions of the chapters dedicated to Russell and Descartes.

n. An obstinate analysis of the "syntactic habits" of Toulet (*N.R.F.,* March 1921). I remember that Menard used to declare that censuring and praising were sentimental operations which had nothing to do with criticism.

o. A transposition into Alexandrines of *Le cimetière marin* of Paul Valéry (*N.R.F.,* January 1928).

p. An invective against Paul Valéry in the *Journal for the Suppression of Reality* of Jacques Reboul. (This invective, it should be stated parenthetically, is the exact reverse of his true opinion of Valéry. The latter understood it as such, and the old friendship between the two was never endangered.)

q. A "definition" of the Countess of Bagnoregio in the "victorious volume"—the phrase is that of another collaborator, Gabriele d'Annunzio—which this lady publishes yearly to rectify the inevitable falsifications of journalism and to present "to the world and to Italy" an authentic effigy of her person, which is so exposed (by reason of her beauty and her activities) to erroneous or hasty interpretations.

r. A cycle of admirable sonnets for the Baroness de Bacourt (1934).

s. A manuscript list of verses which owe their
effectiveness to punctuation.[1]

Up to this point (with no other omission than that of some vague, circumstantial sonnets for the hospitable, or greedy, album of Madame Henri Bachelier)
we have the *visible* part of Menard's works in chronological order. Now I will
pass over to that other part, which is subterranean, interminably heroic, and
unequaled, and which is also—oh, the possibilities inherent in the man!—inconclusive. This work, possibly the most significant of our time, consists of the ninth
and thirty-eighth chapters of Part One of *Don Quixote* and a fragment of the
twenty-second chapter. I realize that such an affirmation seems absurd; but the
justification of this "absurdity" is the primary object of this note.[2]

Two texts of unequal value inspired the undertaking. One was that philologi-
cal fragment of Novalis—No. 2005 of the Dresden edition—which outlines the
theme of *total* identification with a specific author. The other was one of those
parasitic books which places Christ on a boulevard, Hamlet on the Cannebière,
and Don Quixote on Wall Street. Like any man of good taste, Menard detested
these useless carnivals, only suitable—he used to say—for evoking plebeian delight in anachronism, or (what is worse) charming us with the primary idea that
all epochs are the same, or that they are different. He considered more interesting,
even though it had been carried out in a contradictory and superficial way,
Daudet's famous plan: to unite in *one* figure, Tartarin, the Ingenious Gentleman
and his squire. . . . Any insinuation that Menard dedicated his life to the writing
of a contemporary *Don Quixote* is a calumny of his illustrious memory.

He did not want to compose another *Don Quixote*—which would be easy
—but *the Don Quixote*. It is unnecessary to add that his aim was never to produce
a mechanical transcription of the original; he did not propose to copy it. His
admirable ambition was to produce pages which would coincide—word for word
and line for line—with those of Miguel de Cervantes.

"My intent is merely astonishing," he wrote me from Bayonne on December
30, 1934. "The ultimate goal of a theological or metaphysical demonstration—the
external world, God, chance, universal forms—is no less anterior or common
than this novel which I am now developing. The only difference is that philosophers publish in pleasant volumes the intermediary stages of their work and that
I have decided to lose them." And, in fact, not one page of a rough draft remains
to bear witness to this work of years.

The initial method he conceived was relatively simple: to know Spanish well,
to reembrace the Catholic faith, to fight against Moors and Turks, to forget
European history between 1602 and 1918, and to *be* Miguel de Cervantes. Pierre

---

[1]Madame Henri Bachelier also lists a literal translation of a literal translation done by
Quevedo of the *Introduction à la vie dévote* of Saint Francis of Sales. In Pierre Menard's
library there are no traces of such a work. She must have misunderstood a remark of his
which he had intended as a joke.

[2]I also had another, secondary intent—that of sketching a portrait of Pierre Menard. But
how would I dare to compete with the golden pages the Baroness de Bacourt tells me she
is preparing, or with the delicate and precise pencil of Carolus Hourcade?

Menard studied this procedure (I know that he arrived at a rather faithful handling of seventeenth-century Spanish) but rejected it as too easy. Rather because it was impossible, the reader will say! I agree, but the undertaking was impossible from the start, and of all the possible means of carrying it out, this one was the least interesting. To be, in the twentieth century, a popular novelist of the seventeenth seemed to him a diminution. To be, in some way, Cervantes and to arrive at *Don Quixote* seemed to him less arduous—and consequently less interesting—than to continue being Pierre Menard and to arrive at *Don Quixote* through the experiences of Pierre Menard. (This conviction, let it be said in passing, forced him to exclude the autobiographical prologue of the second part of *Don Quixote*. To include this prologue would have meant creating another personage—Cervantes—but it would also have meant presenting *Don Quixote* as the work of this personage and not of Menard. He naturally denied himself such an easy problem), "My undertaking is not essentially different," he said in another part of the same letter. "I would only have to be immortal in order to carry it out." Shall I confess that I often imagine that he finished it and that I am reading *Don Quixote*—the entire work—as if Menard had conceived it? Several nights ago, while leafing through Chapter 26—which he had never attempted—I recognized our friend's style and, as it were, his voice in this exceptional phrase: the nymphs of the rivers, mournful and humid Echo. This effective combination of two adjectives, one moral and the other physical, reminded me of a line from Shakespeare which we discussed one afternoon:

> Where a malignant and turbaned Turk . . .

Why precisely *Don Quixote,* our reader will ask. Such a preference would not have been inexplicable in a Spaniard; but it undoubtedly was in a Symbolist from Nîmes, essentially devoted to Poe, who engendered Baudelaire, who engendered Mallarmé, who engendered Valéry, who engendered Edmond Teste. The letter quoted above clarifies this point. *"Don Quixote,"* Menard explains, "interests me profoundly, but it does not seem to me to have been—how shall I say it—inevitable. I cannot imagine the universe without the interjection of Edgar Allan Poe:

> Ah, bear in mind this garden was enchanted!

Or without the *Bateau Ivre* or the *Ancient Mariner,* but I know that I am capable of imagining it without *Don Quixote*. (I speak, naturally, of my personal capacity not of the historical repercussions of these works.) *Don Quixote* is an accidental book. *Don Quixote* is unnecessary. I can premeditate writing. I can write it without incurring a tautology. When I was twelve or thirteen years old I read it perhaps in its entirety. Since then I have reread several chapters attentively, but not the ones I am going to undertake. I have likewise studied the *entremeses,* the comedies, the *Galatea,* the exemplary novels, and the undoubtedly laborious efforts of *Pérsiles y Sigismunda* and the *Viaje al Parnaso.* . . . My general memory of *Don Quixote,* simplified by forgetfulness and indifference, is much the same as the imprecise, anterior image of a book not yet written. Once this image (which no one can deny me in good faith) has been postulated, my problems are undeniably considerably more difficult than those which Cervantes faced. My affable precursor did not refuse the collaboration of fate; he went along composing his immortal work a little *à la diable*, swept along by inertias of language and invention. I have contracted the mysterious duty of reconstructing literally his spontaneous work. My solitary game is governed by two polar laws. The first permits me to attempt variants of a formal and psychological nature; the second obliges me to sacrifice them to the 'original' text and irrefutably to rationalize this annihilation. . . . To these artificial obstacles one must add another congenital one. To compose *Don Quixote* at the beginning of the seventeenth century was a reasonable, necessary and perhaps inevitable undertaking; at the beginning of the twentieth century it is almost impossible. It is not in vain that three hundred years have passed, charged with the most complex happenings—among them, to mention only one, that same *Don Quixote.*"

In spite of these three obstacles, the fragmentary *Don Quixote* of Menard is more subtle than that of Cervantes. The latter indulges in a rather coarse opposition between tales of knighthood and the meager, provincial reality of his country; Menard chooses as "reality" the land of Carmen during the century of Lepanto and Lope. What Hispanophile would not have advised Maurice Bariès or Dr. Rodríguez Larreta to make such a choice! Menard, as if it were the most natural thing in the world, eludes them. In his work there are neither bands of gypsies, conquistadors, mystics, Philip the Seconds, nor autos-da-fé. He disregards or proscribes local color. This disdain indicates a new approach to the historical novel. This disdain condemns *Salammbô* without appeal.

It is no less astonishing to consider isolated chapters. Let us examine, for instance, Chapter 38 of Part One "which treats of the curious discourse that Don Quixote delivered on the subject of arms and letters." As is known, Don Quixote (like Quevedo in a later, analogous passage of *La hora de todos*) passes judgment against letters and in favor of arms. Cervantes was an old soldier, which explains such a judgment. But that the *Don Quixote* of Pierre Menard—a contemporary of *La trahison des clercs* and Bertrand Russell—should relapse into these nebulous sophistries! Madame Bachelier has seen in them an admirable and typical subordination of the author to the psychology of the hero; others (by no means perspicaciously) a *transcription* of *Don Quixote;* the Baroness de Bacourt, the influence of Nietzsche. To this third interpretation (which seems to me irrefutable) I do not know if I would dare to add a fourth; which coincides very well with the divine modesty of Pierre Menard: his resigned or ironic habit of propounding ideas which were the strict reverse of those he preferred. (One will remember his diatribe against Paul Valéry in the ephemeral journal of the superrealist Jacques Reboul.) The text of Cervantes and that of Menard are verbally identical, but the second is almost infinitely richer. (More ambiguous, his detractors will say; but ambiguity is a richness.) It is a revelation to compare the *Don Quixote* of Menard with that of Cervantes. The latter, for instance, wrote *(Don Quixote,* Part One, Chapter 9):

> . . . *la verdad, cuya madre es la historia, émula del tiempo, depósito de las acciones, testigo de lo pasado, ejemplo y aviso de lo presente, advertencia de lo por venir.*

[. . . truth, whose mother is history, who is the rival of time, deposi-
tory of deeds, witness of the past, example and lesson to the present, and
warning to the future.]

Written in the seventeenth century, written by the "ingenious layman"
Cervantes, this enumeration is a mere rhetorical eulogy of history. Menard, on
the other hand, writes:

> . . . la verdad, cuya madre es la historia, émula del tiempo, depósito
> de las acciones, testigo de lo pasado, ejemplo y aviso de lo presente, adver-
> tencia de lo por venir.

> [. . . truth, whose mother is history, who is the rival of time, deposi-
> tory of deeds, witness of the past, example and lesson to the present, and
> warning to the future.]

History, *mother* of truth; the idea is astounding. Menard, a contemporary
of William James, does not define history as an investigation of reality, but as its
origin. Historical truth, for him, is not what took place; it is what we think took
place. The final clauses—*example and lesson to the present, and warning to the
future*—are shamelessly pragmatic.

Equally vivid is the contrast in styles. The archaic style of Menard—in the
last analysis, a foreigner—suffers from a certain affectation. Not so that of his
precursor, who handles easily the ordinary Spanish of his time.

There is no intellectual exercise which is not ultimately useless. A philosophical doctrine is in the beginning a seemingly true description of the universe; as
the years pass it becomes a mere chapter—if not a paragraph or a noun—in the
history of philosophy. In literature, this ultimate decay is even more notorious.
"Don Quixote," Menard once told me, "was above all an agreeable book; now
it is an occasion for patriotic toasts, grammatical arrogance and obscene deluxe
editions. Glory is an incomprehension, and perhaps the worst."

These nihilist arguments contain nothing new; what is unusual is the decision
Pierre Menard derived from them. He resolved to outstrip that vanity which
awaits all the woes of mankind; he undertook a task that was complex in the
extreme and futile from the outset. He dedicated his conscience and nightly
studies to the repetition of a preexisting book in a foreign tongue. The number
of rough drafts kept on increasing; he tenaciously made corrections and tore up
thousands of manuscript pages.[3] He did not permit them to be examined, and he
took great care that they would not survive him. It is in vain that I have tried
to reconstruct them.

I have thought that it is legitimate to consider the "final" *Don Quixote* as
a kind of palimpsest, in which should appear traces—tenuous but not undecipherable—of the "previous" handwriting of our friend. Unfortunately, only a second

---

[3]I remember his square-ruled notebooks, the black streaks where he had crossed out words,
his peculiar typographical symbols, and his insectlike handwriting. In the late afternoon
he liked to go for walks on the outskirts of Nîmes; he would take a notebook with him
and make a gay bonfire.

Pierre Menard, inverting the work of the former, could exhume and resuscitate these Troys. . . .

"To think, analyze and invent," he also wrote me, "are not anomalous acts, but the normal respiration of the intelligence. To glorify the occasional fulfillment of this function, to treasure ancient thoughts of others, to remember with incredulous amazement that the *doctor universalis* thought, is to confess our languor or barbarism. Every man should be capable of all ideas, and I believe that in the future he will be."

Menard (perhaps without wishing to) has enriched, by means of a new technique, the hesitant and rudimentary art of reading: the technique is one of deliberate anachronism and erroneous attributions. This technique, with its infinite applications, urges us to run through the *Odyssey* as if it were written after the *Aeneid,* and to read *Le jardin du Centaure* by Madame Henri Bachelier as if it were by Madame Henri Bachelier. This technique would fill the dullest books with adventure. Would not the attributing of *The Imitation of Christ* to Louis Ferdinand Céline or James Joyce be a sufficient renovation of its tenuous spiritual counsels?

JOYCE AND NEOLOGISMS [JLB 31]

Laforgue, around 1883, procreated these beautiful and concise verbal monstrosities: *voluptés à vif, éternullité, chant-huant.* Groussac, that same year, alluded to the *japanesciences—japoniaiseries?—*that were overwhelming the Goncourt museum. Swinburne, in an exasperated work dated 1887, called Whitman's followers *Whitmaniacs.* Around 1900, someone from Buenos Aires (I believe Marcelino del Mazo) jokingly protested the numerous orchestras of *gríngaros.* Mariano Brull, only yesterday or the day before, constructed the word *jitanjáfora* which contains elements of Gitanjali, *gitanos* (gypsies), and amphoras. The ingenious English language (according to Jesperson) assembles *whirl* and *twist* and produces *twirl; blush* and *flash* and produces *flush.* Edward Lear—but why continue this catalog of precursors, destined to be incomplete? (I do not know if I should include Fischart, whose version of Rabelais's first book, dated 1575, is daringly called *Naupengeheurliche Geschichtklitterung* as well as *Affentheuerliche Geschichtschrift).*

It is well known that the most evident characteristic of "Work in Progress" (now entitled *Finnegans Wake)* is its methodical profusion of portmanteau words —to use the technical term of another precursor, Humpty Dumpty.[1] Within this profusion lies the novelty of James Joyce. So powerful and general are the judgmental inclinations (or so weak the esthetic ones) that practically none of Joyce's thousand and one commentators examine the neologisms he invented, and instead

[1]One reader of Carroll translated the ballad "Jabberwocky" into macaronic Latin. The first verse reads: *Coesper erat: Tunc lubriciles ultravia circum . . .*

In *coesper* are combined *vesper* and *coena; lubricus* and *graciles,* in *lubriciles.*

content themselves with proving, or disproving, that language requires new words. Here are some of those thought up by Joyce; I do not pretend they are his best. They are those that Stuart Gilbert has explained or those that I have deciphered while thumbing through the work's 628 pages.

Yahooth: yahoo + youth
Bompyre: bonfire + pyre
Merror: mirror + error
Pharoph: pharaoh + far off
Fairyociodes: variations + fairy + odes
Groud: grand + proud
Benighth me: beneath + night
Blue fonx: blue funk + blue fox
Clapplause: clap + applause
Voise: voice + noise
Silvamoonlake: silver + sylva
Ameising: amazing + ameise (ant)
Sybarate: sybarite + separate
Eithou: either + I + thou
Secular phoenish: finish + phoenix
Bannistars: banners + stars + banisters
Pursonal: purse + personal
Dontelleries: dentelleries + don't tell
Jinglish janglage: jingle jangle + English language

These monstrosities, thus isolated and disarmed, become somewhat melancholy. Some of them—the last three, for example—are mere *calembours* that fail to exceed the limited possibilities of Hollywood. Others—*clapplause, bompyre*—are tautologies. Another—*voise*—means a harsh voice, a voice that is almost a noise, yet the sound contradicts the author's intention. Another—*ameising*—requires some knowledge of German.[2] *Secular phoenish,* perhaps the most notable of all, alludes to one of the final lines in *Samson Agonistes,* in which the name *secular bird* is given to the phoenix of periodic deaths.

Another of Joyce's monstrosities, this time composed of phrases rather than separate words: "the animal that has two backs at midnight." Shakespeare and the sphinx of Thebes gathered the materials . . .

Laforgue, on occasion, transformed the pun into a lyrical or mournful instrument; in the vertiginous *Finnegans Wake* this procedure is constant. Here is one instance, where the play on words is terrible and majestic:

"Countlessness of livestories have netherfallen by this plage, flick as flowflakes, litters from aloft, like a waast wizzard all of whirlworlds. . . . Pride, O pride, thy prize!"

---

[2]The book's most celebrated sentence demands the same: "The walls are of rubimen and the glittergates of elfinbone." Ivory, in German, is *elfenbein,* which is probably a derivation of *Elefantenbein;* Joyce translates *elfinbone* literally: elf bone. In a similar manner the gospel manuscripts from the ninth century turned *margarita* (pearl) into *mere-grot:* sea stone.

It is like a sentence from *Urn Burial,* arduously attained after a century or a dream.

I am adding, while correcting the second proofs, a few ancient examples. Fischart, in his *Legend vom Ursprung des abgeführten, gevierten, vierhörnigen und viereckigten Hütleins,* dated 1580, nicknames the Jesuits *vierdächtig* (*vier* + *Dächer* + *verdächtig*). Shakespeare—carelessness, fatigue, typographical error? —writes in the tragedy *Troilus and Cressida* the monstrous name *Ariachne* (*Ariadne* + *Arachne*). That *vierdächtiger* Gracián gives the name *Falsirena* to an allegorical woman in his *Criticón* (Part One, Chapter 12).

AVATARS OF THE TORTOISE [JLB 32]

There is one concept that corrupts and perplexes all others. I am not speaking of evil, whose limited empire is that of ethics; I am speaking of the infinite. I once wished to compile its mobile history. The multifold Hydra (the swamp monster that has become the prefiguration or emblem of geometric progressions) would lend a becoming horror to its portal which would be crowned by the sordid nightmares of Kafka. The central chapters would not be unfamiliar to the conjectures of that remote German cardinal—Nicholas of Krebs, Nicholas of Cusa— who saw the circumference as a polygon composed of an infinite number of angles and wrote that an infinite line could be a straight line, a triangle, a circle, and a sphere (*De docta ignorantia,* I, 13). Five, seven years of metaphysical, theological, and mathematical apprenticeship would enable me to plan such a book properly. It is unnecessary to add that life denies me that hope, and even that adverb.

These pages belong in some way to that illusive *Biography of the Infinite.* Their aim is to record certain avatars of Zeno's second paradox.

Now let us recall that paradox.

Achilles runs ten times faster than the tortoise and gives it an advantage of ten meters. Achilles runs those ten meters, the turtle runs one; Achilles runs that meter, the turtle runs a decimeter; Achilles runs that decimeter, the turtle runs a centimeter; Achilles runs that centimeter, the turtle runs a millimeter; fleet-footed Achilles the millimeter, the turtle a tenth of a millimeter, and so on ad infinitum. Achilles never overtakes the tortoise. This is the customary version. Wilhelm Capelle (*Die Vorsokratiker,* 1935, page 178) translates the original text by Aristotle: "Zeno's second is referred to as Achilles. It reasons that the slower runner will not be overtaken by the faster one, since the pursuer must first pass through the point which the pursued has just left, so that the slower runner always has a certain advantage." As can be seen, the problem itself does not change, but I would like to know the name of the poet who endowed it with a hero and a tortoise. This argument owes its diffusion to those magical competitors and to the series:

$$10 + 1 + 1/10 + 1/100 + 1/1000 + 1 \ldots /10,000$$

Almost no one remembers the one which precedes it—the track—although the mechanism is identical. Movement is impossible (argues Zeno) since the moving object must cross a middle point in order to reach the final one, and before that, the middle of the middle, and before that, the middle of the middle of the middle, and before that . . .[1]

It is to Aristotle's pen that we owe the communication and first refutation of these arguments. He refutes with an almost disdainful brevity, but his recollection of them does inspire the famous "argument of the third man" against Platonic doctrine. That doctrine attempts to demonstrate that two individuals with common attributes (for example, two men) are merely temporal apparitions of an eternal archetype. Aristotle inquires if the many men and the Man—the temporal individuals and the archetype—possess common attributes. In that case, Aristotle affirms, it would be necessary to postulate another archetype which would embrace all of them, and later a fourth . . . Patricio of Azcárate, in a note on his translation of the *Metaphysics,* attributes the following presentation to one of Aristotle's disciples: "If what is affirmed of many things at once is a separate being different from the things which are affirmed (and this is what the Platonists maintain), there must be a third man. *Man* is the name applied to the individuals and the idea. There would be, therefore, a "third man," different from individual men and from the idea. At the same time there is a fourth man in a like relationship with the third and with the idea of the individual, then later a fifth, and so on ad infinitum. We postulate two individuals A and B who make up the genre C. We will then have $A + B = C$.

But, according to Aristotle, also:

$$A + B + C = D$$
$$A + B + C + D = E$$
$$A + B + C + D + E = F \ldots$$

Strictly speaking, two individuals are not needed: the individual and the genre are sufficient to determine the third man which Aristotle denounces. Zeno of Elea resorts to infinite regression as an argument against movement and numbers; his refuter, against universal forms.[2]

---

[1] A century later, the Chinese sophist Hui Tzu reasoned that a baton which was cut in half each day is interminable. (H. A. Giles, *Chuang Tzu,* 1889, page 453).

[2] In *Parmenides,* whose Zenonian character is unimpeachable, Plato contrives a similar argument to demonstrate that the one is really many. If the one exists, it partakes of being. Consequently, it consists of two parts which are being and the one. Yet each one of these parts is one and also is, so that each encloses two other parts, which encompass two others, ad infinitum. Russell (*Introduction to Mathematical Philosophy,* 1919, page 138) substitutes an arithmetic progression for Plato's geometrical progression. If the one exists, it partakes of being; but since being and the one are different, then two exists, and since being and two are different, then three exists, etc. Chuang Tzu (Arthur Waley, *Three Ways of Thought in Ancient China,* page 25) resorts to the same interminable *regressus* against the monists who declared that the 10,000 things (the universe) were a single thing. At any rate, he argues, the cosmic unity and the declaration of that unity are already two things; those two and the declaration of their duality are already three; those three and the declaration of their trinity are already four . . . Russell expresses the opinion that the vagueness of

The next of the avatars of Zeno registered in my disorderly notes is Agrippa, the skeptic. He denies that anything can be proven, since all proofs require a previous proof (*Hypotyposes,* I, 166). Empiricus Sextus argues similarly that all definitions are useless, since it would be necessary to define each one of the words being used and then define their definition (*Hypotyposes,* II, 207). Sixteen hundred years later Byron, in the dedicatory to *Don Juan,* would write of Coleridge, "I wish he would explain his Explanation."

Up until this point the *regressus in infinitum* has served to negate: Saint Thomas Aquinas appeals to it (*Summa theologica,* I, 2, 3) to affirm that God exists. He observes that there is nothing in the universe that does not have an efficient cause, and that cause is, of course, the effect of another previous cause. The world is an interminable linking of causes and each cause is an effect. Each state arises from a previous state and determines a following one. Yet the entire series could never have come into being, since the terms which make it up are conditional, that is to say, aleatory. Nevertheless, the world exists; and from this we can infer a noncontingent first cause that must be the divinity. This is the cosmological proof: Aristotle and Plato augur it; Leibniz rediscovers it.[3]

Hermann Lotze resorts to the *regressus* to question how an alteration in an object A can produce an alteration in an object B. He reasons that if A and B are independent, to postulate A's influence on B is to postulate a third element C, an element which in order to operate on B would require a fourth element D, which could not operate without E, which could not operate without F . . . In order to elude this multiplication of chimeras, he resolves that there can be only one object in the world: an infinite and absolute substance comparable to Spinoza's God. Transitive causes are reduced to immanent causes, to manifestations or modes of the cosmic substance.[4]

The case of F. H. Bradley is analogous, but perhaps even more alarming. This thinker (*Appearance and Reality,* 1897, pages 19–34) does not stop at combating causal relationships; he denies all relationships. Bradley asks if a relationship is related to its terms. The response is "yes," and he infers that this is to admit the existence of two other relationships, and then two more. In the axiom, "the part is less than the whole," he does not perceive two terms and the relationship "less than"; he perceives three ("part," "less than," "whole") whose association implies two other relationships and so on ad infinitum. In the statement, "John is mortal," he perceives three unconjugable concepts (the third is the copulative) which we shall never be able to unite. Bradley transforms all concepts into incommunicable, concrete objects. To refute him is to become contaminated by unreality.

Lotze inserts Zeno's periodic abysses between cause and effect; Bradley between subject and predicate, or between the subject and its attributes; Lewis

---

the term "being" is enough to invalidate the argument. He adds that numbers do not exist, that they are mere fictions of logic.

[3] An echo of this proof—now dead—reverberates in the first verse of the *Paradiso: La gloria di Colui che tutto move.*

[4] I am following James's exposition (*A Pluralistic Universe,* 1909, pages 55–60). Cf. Wentscher, *Fechner und Lotze,* 1924, pages 166–171.

Carroll (*Mind,* Vol. 4, page 278) between the second premise of the syllogism and its conclusion. He relates an interminable dialogue whose interlocutors are Achilles and the tortoise. Having reached the end of their endless race, the two athletes converse amiably about geometry. They consider this ratiocination:

a. Two things which equal a third are equal to one another.

b. The two sides of a triangle are equal to MN.

c. The two sides of the triangles are equal to one another.

The tortoise accepts premises (a) and (b) but denies that they justify the conclusion. He succeeds in having Achilles interpolate a hypothetical proposition:

a. Two things which equal a third are equal to one another.

b. The two sides of a triangle are equal to MN.

c. If (a) and (b) are valid, (z) is valid.

z. The two sides of a triangle are equal to one another.

Carroll observes that the Greek's paradox implies an infinite series of diminishing distances, while in his proposal the distances increase.

A final example, perhaps the most elegant of all, but also the one which differs least from Zeno. William James (*Some Problems of Philosophy,* 1911, page 182) denies that fourteen minutes can elapse, since beforehand seven must elapse, and before seven, three and a half, and before three and a half, one and three quarters minutes, and so on until the the end, until the invisible end, through the tenuous labyrinths of time.

Descartes, Hobbes, Leibniz, Mill, Renouvier, Georg Cantor, Gomperz, Russell, and Bergson have formulated explanations—not always inexplicable and useless—for the paradox of the tortoise. (I have recorded several.) As the reader has verified, its applications abound. The historical ones do not exhaust it; the dizzying *regressus in infinitum* is applicable perhaps to every subject. To esthetics —a given verse moves us for a given reason, a given reason for another given reason. . . . To the problem of knowledge—to know is to recognize, but it is necessary to have known in order to recognize. Yet to know is to recognize. How are we to judge this dialectic? Is it a legitimate instrument of inquiry or merely a bad habit?

It is hazardous to think that a coordination of words (for philosophy is nothing more than that) could resemble the universe. It is also hazardous to think that of those illustrious coordinations, one—albeit in an infinitesimal way—might resemble it a little more than the others. I have examined the combinations which enjoy a certain credibility. I venture to affirm that only in the one formulated by Schopenhauer have I glimpsed some trace of the universe. According to that doctrine, the world is a factory of the will. Art requires certain visible unrealities . . . always. Allow me to cite on: the metaphorical, or multiple, or carefully casual diction of the interlocutors of a play . . . Let us admit that which all idealists admit: the hallucinatory nature of the world. Let us do that which no idealist has done; let us search for the unrealities which confirm that nature. We will find them, I believe, in Kant's antinomies and in Zeno's dialectics.

"The greatest sorcerer," wrote Novalis in a memorable phrase, "would be he who bewitched himself to the point of taking his own phantasmagories for autonomous apparitions. Would that not be our case?" I surmise that this is so. We (the indivisible divinity who operates in us) have dreamed the world. We have dreamed it to be resistant, mysterious, visible, ubiquitous in space, and fixed in time; but we have permitted tenuous and eternal interstices of illogic a reason in its architecture in order to know that it is false.

SOME OF NIETZSCHE'S OPINIONS [JLB 33]

Glory is always a simplification and sometimes a perversion of reality; there is no famous man who has not been somewhat slandered by glory. In America and Spain, Arthur Schopenhauer is primarily the author of *Love, Woman and Death*: a rhapsody fabricated with sensational fragments by a Levantine editor. As for Friedrich Nietzsche, Schopenhauer's rebellious disciple, Bernard Shaw once observed (*Major Barbara,* London, 1905) that he was the universal victim of the phrase "blond beast" and that everybody attributed his fame and limited his work to a gospel for bullies. Despite the passage of time, Shaw's observation has not lost its validity, though one has to admit that Nietzsche has accepted and perhaps even nurtured that error. In his final years he aspired to the dignity of a prophet and knew that such a ministry is incompatible with a reasonable or explicit style. The most famous (not the best) of his works is a Jewish-German pastiche, a prophetic book more artificial and far less passionate than those by Blake. Parallel with the composition of his intentionally public works, Nietzsche made note in other books of the arguments capable of justifying such works. These arguments (plus all sorts of related meditations) have been organized and edited by Alfred Bacumler and comprise two volumes of 450 pages each. The work in general is entitled—somewhat basely—*The Innocence of Development,* and was published in 1913 by Alfred Kroner. "In his published books," writes the editor, "Nietzsche always speaks to an adversary, always reticently; in them his outer shell predominates, as the author himself has declared. On the other hand, his unpublished works (which span the period of 1870 to 1888) record the depth of his thought, and that is why they are not secondary works, but rather masterpieces."

This fragment—the 1072nd of the first volume—is a pathetic testimony to his loneliness: "What am I doing scribbling out these pages? Watching out for my old age: making a record, for that time when the soul can no longer undertake anything new, of the history of its adventures and ocean voyages. In the same way I save music for the age when I'm blind."

It is common to identify Nietzsche with the intolerances and aggressions of racism and exalt him (or defame him) as the precursor to that bloody pedantry. Let us see what Nietzsche—a solid European, after all—thought around 1880 of such problems. "In France," he notes, "nationalism has perverted character, in Germany spirit and good taste: in order to survive a great defeat—in all truth, a definitive defeat—one must be younger and healthier than the victor."

This final reservation should not lead us to believe that the victories of 1871 caused him to rejoice excessively. Fragment 1180 of the second volume declares: "To become enthusiastic over the principle, *Germany, Germany above all,* or over the German empire, we are not so stupid"; just before this he observes, *"Germany, Germany above all,* is perhaps the most meaningless motto that has ever been promulgated. Why Germany—I ask—if it doesn't seek, if it doesn't represent, if it doesn't mean anything greater than what other previous powers represented? All things considered, it is only another grand state, another folly of history."

He reacts to anti-Semitism with the following observations: "To find a Jew is a benefit, above all when he lives among Germans. Jews are an antidote to nationalism, the ultimate sickness of European reasoning. . . . In unstable Europe they are perhaps the strongest race: they surpass all of Western Europe in terms of the length of their evolutionary process. Their organization presupposes a richer development, a greater number of stages than that of other peoples. . . . Like any other organism, a race can only grow or perish: stagnation is impossible. A race that has not perished is a race that has grown incessantly. The length of their existence indicates the height of their evolution: the oldest race should also be the highest. In contemporary Europe the Jews have reached the supreme form of spirituality: ingenious comedy.

"With Offenbach, with Heinrich Heine, the potential of European culture has been surpassed: the other races don't have the possibility of being ingenious in this way. . . . In Europe the Jews are the oldest and purest race. That is why the beauty of the Jewish woman is unsurpassed."

When examined with a degree of impartiality, the foregoing paragraph is very vulnerable. His purpose is to refute (or disturb) German nationalism; his form is a hyperbolic affirmation of Jewish nationalism. This nationalism is the most exorbitant of all; the impossibility of invoking a country, an order, a flag, imposes upon him an intellectual Caesarism which usually exceeds the truth. The Nazi denies the participation of the Jew in German culture; the Jew, with equal injustice, pretends that German culture is Jewish culture. All things considered, Nietzsche's opinions were probably more impartial than his affirmations; I suspect that he was addressing, *in thought,* incredulous and easily provoked Germans.

On another occasion he wrote prophetically: "Germans believe that strength should be manifest through strictness and cruelty. It is hard for them to believe that there could be strength in serenity and quietness. They believe that Beethoven is stronger than Goethe; they are wrong about that."

This fragment—the 1168th—is perhaps pertinent to the present and even the future: "All truly Germanic people emigrated; present-day Germany is an advanced position of slaves and it is preparing the way for the Russianization of Europe." It is useless to add that such doctrine would attract few converts in the Germany of today. The country is ruled by Germanists who support the annexation of certain areas because of their Germanic race and certain other areas because of their inferior race. Such ethnological dangers affirm a Germanic predominance in Scandinavia, England, Holland, France, northern Italy, and America, a hypothesis that does not limit the representation of that ubiquitous race to Germany.

On another occasion Nietzsche said: "Bismarck is a slave. One only has to look at the faces of Germans: all those who had vigorous, productive blood emigrated, the lamentable population stayed behind. The weakhearted improved after an addition of foreign blood, principally that of slaves. The best blood in Germany is the blood from the villages, for example, Luther, Niebuhr, Bismarck."

To mobilize against Germany the paragraph I have just translated would be an oversimplified and unjust action. One of the superb capacities of German intellectuals—I do not know if the same applies to the French—is that of being unaffected by the superstitions of patriotism. In danger of seeming unjust, he prefers to be so with his own country. Nietzsche—we should not let ourselves be fooled by his Polish name—was very German. One of the admonitions we have read exhorts us not to confuse mere violence with strength. Zarathustra would not have thus spoken if he had had such a distinction in mind.

In the 1139th fragment, Nietzsche openly condemns Luther's work; nevertheless, in the 501st fragment he writes: "A man can perform an act that is worthy of merit, but it is impossible for an act to bestow merit upon a man." It is also impossible to formulate with fewer words the doctrine with which Martin Luther opposed the doctrine of salvation by works.

In that noisy and almost totally forgotten volume, *Degeneration,* which turned out to be such a fine anthology of the writers whom the author wished to defame, Max Nordau perceived the fragmentary character of Nietzsche's works as a demonstration of his incapacity to compose. Along with this reasoning (which is illicit to exclude, yet unimportant) we can propose another: Nietzsche's vertiginous mental richness, a richness which is even more surprising if we remember that practically his entire work deals with that subject upon which men have shown themselves to be the most ignorant and least inventive: ethics.

With the exception of Samuel Butler, no nineteenth-century author is as much our contemporary as Friedrich Nietzsche. Very little in his work has grown old, except, perhaps, that humanist veneration for classical antiquity which Bernard Shaw was the first to criticize. Also a kind of lucidity in the very heart of polemics, a sort of delicate censure, which our day and age seems to have forgotten.

TLÖN, UQBAR, ORBIS TERTIUS [JLB 34]

I owe the discovery of Uqbar to the conjunction of a mirror and an encyclopedia. The unnerving mirror hung at the end of a corridor in a villa on Goana Street, in Ramos Mejía; the misleading encyclopedia goes by the name of *The Anglo-American Cyclopaedia* (New York, 1917), and is a literal if inadequate reprint of the *Encyclopaedia Britannica* of 1902. The whole affair happened some five years ago. Bioy Casares had dined with me that night and talked to us at length about a great scheme for writing a novel in the first person, using a narrator who omitted or corrupted what happened and who ran into various contradictions, so that only a handful of readers, a very small handful, would be able to decipher the horrible or banal reality behind the novel. From the far end of the corridor, the mirror was watching us; and we discovered, with the inevitability of discoveries made late at night, that mirrors have something grotesque about them. Then Bioy Casares recalled that one of the heresiarchs of Uqbar had stated that mirrors and copulation are abominable, since they both multiply the numbers of men. I asked him the source of that memorable sentence, and he replied that it was recorded in *The Anglo-American Cyclopaedia,* in its article on Uqbar. It so happened that the villa (which we had rented furnished) possessed a copy of that work. In the final pages of Volume XLVI, we ran across an article on Upsala; in the beginning of Volume XLVII, we found one on Ural-Altaic languages; but not one word on Uqbar. A little put out, Bioy consulted the index volumes. In vain he tried every possible spelling—Ukbar, Ucbar, Ooqbar, Ookbar, Oukbahr. . . . Before leaving, he informed me it was a region in either Iraq or Asia Minor. I must say that I acknowledged this a little uneasily. I supposed that this undocumented country and its anonymous heresiarch had been deliberately invented by Bioy out of modesty, to substantiate a phrase. A futile examination of one of the atlases of Justus Perthes strengthened my doubt.

On the following day, Bioy telephoned me from Buenos Aires. He told me that he had in front of him the article on Uqbar, in Volume XLVI of the encyclopedia. It did not specify the name of the heresiarch, but it did note his doctrine, in words almost identical to the ones he had repeated to me, though, I would say, inferior from a literary point of view. He had remembered: "Copulation and mirrors are abominable." The text of the encyclopedia read: "For one of those gnostics, the visible universe was an illusion or, more precisely, a sophism. Mirrors and fatherhood are abominable because they multiply it and extend it." I said, in all sincerity, that I would like to see that article. A few days later, he brought it. This surprised me, because the scrupulous cartographic index of Ritter's *Erdkunde* completely failed to mention the name of Uqbar.

The volume which Bioy brought was indeed Volume XLVI of *The Anglo-American Cyclopaedia.* On the title page and spine, the alphabetical key was the same as in our copy, but instead of 917 pages, it had 921. These four additional pages consisted of the article on Uqbar—not accounted for by the alphabetical cipher, as the reader will have noticed. We ascertained afterward that there was no other difference between the two volumes. Both, as I think I pointed out, are reprints of the tenth *Encyclopaedia Britannica.* Bioy had acquired his copy in one of a number of book sales.

We read the article with some care. The passage remembered by Bioy was perhaps the only startling one. The rest seemed probable enough, very much in keeping with the general tone of the work and, naturally, a little dull. Reading it over, we discovered, beneath the superficial authority of the prose, a fundamental vagueness. Of the fourteen names mentioned in the geographical section, we recognized only three—Khurasan, Armenia, and Erzurum—and they were dragged into the text in a strangely ambiguous way. Among the historical names, we recognized only one, that of the impostor, Smerdis the Magician, and it was invoked in a rather metaphorical sense. The notes appeared to fix precisely the frontiers of Uqbar, but the points of reference were all, vaguely enough, rivers and craters and mountain chains in that same region. We read, for instance, that the southern frontier is defined by the lowlands of Tsai Haldun and the Axa delta, and that wild horses flourish in the islands of that delta. This, at the top of page 918. In the historical section (page 920), we gathered that, just after the religious persecutions of the thirteenth century, the orthodox sought refuge in the islands, where their obelisks have survived, and where it is a common enough occurrence to dig up one of their stone mirrors. The language and literature section was brief. There was one notable characteristic: it remarked that the literature of Uqbar was fantastic in character, and that its epics and legends never referred to reality, but to the two imaginary regions of Mlejnas and Tlön. . . . The bibliography listed four volumes, which we have not yet come across, although the third—Silas Haslam: *History of the Land Called Uqbar,* 1874—appears in the library catalogs of Bernard Quaritch.[1] The first, *Lesbare und lesenswerthe Bemerkungen über das Land Ukkbar in Klein-Asien,* is dated 1641, and is a work of Johann Valentin Andreä. The fact is significant; a couple of years later I ran across that name accidentally in the thirteenth volume of De Quincey's *Writings,* and I knew that it was the name of a German theologian who, at the beginning of the seventeenth century, described the imaginary community of Rosae Crucis—the community which was later founded by others in imitation of the one he had preconceived.

That night, we visited the National Library. Fruitlessly we exhausted atlases, catalogs, yearbooks of geographical societies, memoirs of travelers and historians —nobody had ever been in Uqbar. Neither did the general index of Bioy's encyclopedia show the name. The following day, Carlos Mastronardi, to whom I had referred the whole business, caught sight, in a bookshop on Corrientes and Talcahuano, of the black and gold bindings of *The Anglo-American Cyclopaedia.* . . . He went in and looked up Volume XLVI. Naturally, there was not the slightest mention of Uqbar.

Some small fading memory of one Herbert Ashe, an engineer for the southern railroads, hangs on in the hotel in Adrogué, between the luscious honeysuckle and the illusory depths of the mirrors. In life, he suffered from a sense of unreality, as do so many Englishmen; dead, he is not even the ghostly creature he was then. He was tall and languid; his limp squared beard had once been red. He was, I understand, a widower, and childless. Every few years he went to England to visit

---

[1]Haslam has also published *A General History of Labyrinths.*

—judging by the photographs he showed us—a sundial and some oak trees. My father and he had cemented (the verb is excessive) one of those English friendships which begin by avoiding intimacies and eventually eliminate speech altogether. They used to exchange books and periodicals; they would beat one another at chess, without saying a word. . . . I remember him in the corridor of the hotel, a mathematics textbook in his hand, gazing now and again at the passing colors of the sky. One afternoon, we discussed the duodecimal numerical system (in which 12 is written 10). Ashe said that as a matter of fact, he was transcribing some duodecimal tables, I forget which, into sexagesimals (in which 60 is written 10), adding that this work had been commissioned by a Norwegian in Rio Grande do Sul. We had known him for eight years and he had never mentioned having stayed in that part of the country. . . . We spoke of rural life, of *capangas,* of the Brazilian etymology of the word *"gaucho"* (which some old people in the east still pronounce *gaúcho*), and nothing more was said—God forgive me—of duodecimal functions.

In September 1937 (we ourselves were not at the hotel at the time), Herbert Ashe died of an aneurysmal rupture. Some days before, he had received from Brazil a stamped, registered package. It was a book, an octavo volume. Ashe left it in the bar where, months later, I found it. I began to leaf through it and felt a sudden curious lightheadedness, which I will not go into, since this is the story, not of my particular emotions, but of Uqbar and Tlön and Orbis Tertius. In the Islamic world, there is one night, called the Night of Nights, on which the secret gates of the sky open wide and the water in the water jugs tastes sweeter; if those gates were to open, I would not feel what I felt that afternoon. The book was written in English, and had 1001 pages. On the yellow leather spine, and again on the title page, I read these words: *A First Encyclopaedia of Tlön. Volume XI. Hlaer to Jangr.* There was nothing to indicate either date or place of origin. On the first page and on a sheet of silk paper covering one of the colored engravings there was a blue oval stamp with the inscription: *Orbis Tertius.* It was two years since I had discovered, in a volume of a pirated encyclopedia, a brief description of a false country; now, chance was showing me something much more valuable, something to be reckoned with. Now, I had in my hands a substantial fragment of the complete history of an unknown planet, with its architecture and its playing cards, its mythological terrors and the sound of its dialects, its emperors and its oceans, its minerals, its birds, and its fishes, its algebra and its fire, its theological and metaphysical arguments, all clearly stated, coherent, without any apparent dogmatic intention or parodic undertone.

The eleventh volume of which I speak refers to both subsequent and preceding volumes. Néstor Ibarra, in an article (in the *N.R.F.*), now a classic, has denied the existence of those corollary volumes; Ezequiel Martínez Estrada and Drieu La Rochelle have, I think, succeeded in refuting this doubt. The fact is that, up until now, the most patient investigations have proved fruitless. We have turned the libraries of Europe, North, and South America upside down—in vain. Alfonso Reyes, bored with the tedium of this minor detective work, proposes that we all take on the task of reconstructing the missing volumes, many and vast as they were: *ex ungue leonem.* He calculates, half seriously, that one generation of

lives and the most tenuous details of them, is the handwriting produced by a minor god in order to communicate with a demon. Another maintains that the universe is comparable to those code systems in which not all the symbols have meaning, and in which only that which happens every 300th night is true. Another believes that, while we are asleep here, we are awake somewhere else, and that thus every man is two men.

Among the doctrines of Tlön, none has occasioned greater scandal than the doctrine of materialism. Some thinkers have formulated it with less clarity than zeal, as one might put forward a paradox. To clarify the general understanding of this unlikely thesis, one eleventh-century[3] heresiarch offered the parable of nine copper coins, which enjoyed in Tlön the same noisy reputation as did the Eleatic paradoxes of Zeno in their day. There are many versions of this "feat of specious reasoning" which vary the number of coins and the number of discoveries. Here is the commonest:

> On Tuesday, X ventures along a deserted road and loses nine copper coins. On Thursday, Y finds on the road four coins, somewhat rusted by Wednesday's rain. On Friday, Z comes across three coins on the road. On Friday morning, X finds two coins in the corridor of his house. [The heresiarch is trying to deduce from this story the reality, that is, the continuity, of the nine recovered coins.] It is absurd, he states, to suppose that four of the coins have not existed between Tuesday and Thursday, three between Tuesday and Friday afternoon, and two between Tuesday and Friday morning. It is logical to assume that they *have* existed, albeit in some secret way, in a manner whose understanding is concealed from men, in every moment, in all three places.

The language of Tlön is by its nature resistant to the formulation of this paradox; most people do not understand it. At first, the defenders of common sense confined themselves to denying the truth of the anecdote. They declared that it was a verbal fallacy, based on the reckless use of two neological expressions, not substantiated by common usage, and contrary to the laws of strict thought—the verbs *to find* and *to lose* entail a *petitio principii,* since they presuppose that the first nine coins and the second are identical. They recalled that any noun—*man, money, Thursday, Wednesday, rain*—has only metaphorical value. They denied the misleading detail "somewhat rusted by Wednesday's rain," since it assumes what must be demonstrated—the continuing existence of the four coins between Thursday and Tuesday. They explained that equality is one thing and identity another, and formulated a kind of reductio ad absurdum, the hypothetical case of nine men who, on nine successive nights, suffer a violent pain. Would it not be ridiculous, they asked, to claim that this pain is the same one each time?[4] They said that the heresiarch was motivated mainly by the blasphemous intention

---

[3] A century, in accordance with the duodecimal system, signifies a period of 144 years.

[4] Nowadays, one of the churches of Tlön maintains platonically that such and such a pain, such and such a greenish-yellow color, such and such a temperature, such and such a sound, etc., make up the only reality there is. All men, in the climactic instant of coitus, are the same man. All men who repeat one line of Shakespeare *are* William Shakespeare.

of attributing the divine category of *being* to some ordinary coins; and that sometimes he was denying plurality, at other times not. They argued thus: if equality entails identity, it would have to be admitted at the same time that the nine coins are only one coin.

Amazingly enough, these refutations were not conclusive. After the problem had been stated and restated for a hundred years, one thinker no less brilliant than the heresiarch himself, but in the orthodox tradition, advanced a most daring hypothesis. This felicitous supposition declared that there is only one Individual, and that this indivisible Individual is every one of the separate beings in the universe, and that those beings are the instruments and masks of divinity itself. X is Y and is Z. Z finds three coins because he remembers that X lost them. X finds only two in the corridor because he remembers that the others have been recovered. . . . The eleventh volume gives us to understand that there were three principal reasons which led to the complete victory of this pantheistic idealism. First, it repudiated solipsism. Second, it made possible the retention of a psychological basis for the sciences. Third, it permitted the cult of the gods to be retained. Schopenhauer, the passionate and clear-headed Schopenhauer, advanced a very similar theory in the first volume of his *Parerga und Paralipomena.*

The geometry of Tlön has two somewhat distinct systems, a visual one and a tactile one. The latter system corresponds to our geometry; they consider it inferior to the former. The foundation of visual geometry is the surface, not the point. This system rejects the principle of parallelism, and states that, as man moves about, he alters the forms which surround him. The arithmetical system is based on the idea of indefinite numbers. It emphasizes the importance of the concepts *greater* and *lesser,* which our mathematicians symbolize as $>$ and $<$. It states that the operation of counting modifies quantities and changes them from indefinites into definites. The fact that several individuals counting the same quantity arrive at the same result is, say their psychologists, an example of the association of ideas or the good use of memory. We already know that in Tlön the source of all-knowing is single and eternal.

In literary matters too, the dominant notion is that everything is the work of one single author. Books are rarely signed. The concept of plagiarism does not exist; it has been established that all books are the work of one single writer, who is timeless and anonymous. Criticism is prone to invent authors. A critic will choose two dissimilar works—the *Tao Tê Ching* and *The 1001 Nights,* let us say —and attribute them to the same writer, and then with all probity explore the psychology of this interesting *homme de lettres.* . . .

The books themselves are also odd. Works of fiction are based on a single plot, which runs through every imaginable permutation. Works of natural philosophy invariably include thesis and antithesis, the strict pro and con of a theory. A book which does not include its opposite, or "counterbook," is considered incomplete.

Centuries and centuries of idealism have not failed to influence reality. In the very oldest regions of Tlön, it is not an uncommon occurrence for lost objects to be duplicated. Two people are looking for a pencil; the first one finds it and says nothing; the second finds a second pencil, no less real, but more in keeping with his expectation. These secondary objects are called *hrönir* and, even though awkward in form, are a little larger than the originals. Until recently, the *hrönir* were the accidental children of absentmindedness and forgetfulness. It seems improbable that the methodical production of them has been going on for almost a hundred years, but so it is stated in the eleventh volume. The first attempts were fruitless. Nevertheless, the modus operandi is worthy of note. The director of one of the state prisons announced to the convicts that in an ancient riverbed certain tombs were to be found, and promised freedom to any prisoner who made an important discovery. In the months preceding the excavation, printed photographs of what was to be found were shown the prisoners. The first attempt proved that hope and zeal could be inhibiting; a week of work with shovel and pick succeeded in unearthing no *hrön* other than a rusty wheel, postdating the experiment. This was kept a secret, and the experiment was later repeated in four colleges. In three of them the failure was almost complete; in the fourth (the director of which died by chance during the initial excavation), the students dug up—or produced—a gold mask, an archaic sword, two or three earthenware urns, and the moldered mutilated torso of a king with an inscription on his breast which has so far not been deciphered. Thus was discovered the unfitness of witnesses who were aware of the experimental nature of the search. . . . Mass investigations produced objects which contradicted one another; now, individual projects, as far as possible spontaneous, are preferred. The methodical development of *hrönir,* states the eleventh volume, has been of enormous service to archeologists. It has allowed them to question and even to modify the past, which nowadays is no less malleable or obedient than the future. One curious fact: the *hrönir* of the second and third degrees—that is, the *hrönir* derived from another *hrön,* and the *hrönir* derived from the *hrön of a hrön*—exaggerate the flaws of the original; those of the fifth degree are almost uniform; those of the ninth can be confused with those of the second; and those of the eleventh degree have a purity of form which the originals do not possess. The process is a recurrent one; a *hrön* of the twelfth degree begins to deteriorate in quality. Stranger and more perfect than any *hrön* is sometimes the *ur,* which is a thing produced by suggestion, an object brought into being by hope. The great gold mask I mentioned previously is a distinguished example.

Things duplicate themselves in Tlön. They tend at the same time to efface themselves, to lose their detail when people forget them. The classic example is that of a stone threshold which lasted as long as it was visited by a beggar, and which faded from sight on his death. Occasionally, a few birds, a horse perhaps, have saved the ruins of an amphitheater. (1940. *Salto Oriental.*)

POSTSCRIPT. 1947.
I reprint the foregoing article just as it appeared in the *Anthology of Fantastic Literature, 1940,* omitting no more than some figures of speech, and a kind of burlesque summing up, which now strikes me as frivolous. So many things have happened since that date. . . . I will confine myself to putting them down.

In March 1941, a manuscript letter by Gunnar Erfjord came to light in a volume of Hinton, which had belonged to Herbert Ashe. The envelope bore the postmark of Ouro Preto. The letter cleared up entirely the mystery of Tlön. The text of it confirmed Martínez Estrada's thesis. The elaborate story began one night in Lucerne or London, in the early seventeenth century. A benevolent secret society (which counted Dalgarno and, later, George Berkeley among its members) came together to invent a country. The first tentative plan gave prominence to "hermetic studies," philanthropy, and the Cabala. Andreä's curious book dates from that first period. At the end of some years of conventicles and premature syntheses, they realized that a single generation was not long enough in which to define a country. They made a resolution that each one of the master-scholars involved should elect a disciple to carry on the work. That hereditary arrangement prevailed; and after a hiatus of two centuries, the persecuted brotherhood reappeared in America. About 1824, in Memphis, Tennessee, one of the members had a conversation with the millionaire ascetic Ezra Buckley. Buckley listened with some disdain as the other man talked, and then burst out laughing at the modesty of the project. He declared that in America it was absurd to invent a country, and proposed the invention of a whole planet. To this gigantic idea, he added another, born of his own nihilism[5]—that of keeping the enormous project a secret. The twenty volumes of the *Encyclopaedia Britannica* were then in circulation; Buckley suggested a systematic encyclopedia of the imaginary planet. He would leave the society his mountain ranges with their gold fields, his navigable rivers, his prairies where bull and bison roamed, his Negroes, his brothels, and his dollars, on one condition: "The work will have no truck with the impostor Jesus Christ." Buckley did not believe in God, but nevertheless wished to demonstrate to the nonexistent God that mortal men were capable of conceiving a world. Buckley was poisoned in Baton Rouge in 1828; in 1914, the society forwarded to its collaborators, 300 in number, the final volume of the *First Encyclopaedia of Tlön.* The edition was secret; the forty volumes which comprised it (the work was vaster than any previously undertaken by men) were to be the basis for another work, more detailed, and this time written, not in English, but in some one of the languages of Tlön. This review of an illusory world was called, provisionally, *Orbis Tertius,* and one of its minor demiurges was Herbert Ashe, whether as an agent of Gunnar Erfjord, or as a full associate, I do not know. The fact that he received a copy of the eleventh volume would favor the second view. But what about the others? About 1942, events began to speed up. I recall with distinct clarity one of the first, and I seem to have felt something of its premonitory character. It occurred in an apartment on Laprida Street, facing a high open balcony which looked to the West. From Poitiers, the Princess of Faucigny Lucinge had received her silver table service. Out of the recesses of a crate, stamped all over with international markings, fine immobile pieces were emerging —silver plate from Utrecht and Paris, with hard heraldic fauna, a samovar. Among them, trembling faintly, just perceptibly, like a sleeping bird, was a magnetic compass. It shivered mysteriously. The princess did not recognize it. The blue needle longed for magnetic north. The metal case was concave. The letters on the dial corresponded to those of one of the alphabets of Tlön. Such was the first intrusion of the fantastic world into the real one.

---

[5]Buckley was a freethinker, a fatalist, and an apologist for slavery.

A disturbing accident brought it about that I was also witness to the second. It happened some months afterward, in a grocery store belonging to a Brazilian, in Cuchilla Negra. Amorim and I were on our way back from Sant' Anna. A sudden rising of the Tacuarembó River compelled us to test (and to suffer patiently) the rudimentary hospitality of the general store. The grocer set up some creaking cots for us in a large room, cluttered with barrels and wineskins. We went to bed, but were kept from sleeping until dawn by the drunkenness of an invisible neighbor, who alternated between shouting indecipherable abuse and singing snatches of *milongas,* or rather, snatches of the same *milonga.* As might be supposed, we attributed this insistent uproar to the fiery rum of the proprietor. . . . At dawn, the man lay dead in the corridor. The coarseness of his voice had deceived us; he was a young boy. In his delirium, he had spilled a few coins and a shining metal cone, of the diameter of a die, from his heavy gaucho belt. A serving lad tried to pick up this cone—in vain. It was scarcely possible for a man to lift it. I held it in my hand for some minutes. I remember that it was intolerably heavy, and that after putting it down, its oppression remained. I also remember the precise circle it marked in my flesh. This manifestation of an object which was so tiny and at the same time so heavy left me with an unpleasant sense of abhorrence and fear. A countryman proposed that it be thrown into the rushing river. Amorim acquired it for a few pesos. No one knew anything of the dead man, only that "he came from the frontier." Those small and extremely heavy cones, made of a metal which does not exist in this world, are images of divinity in certain religions in Tlön.

Here I conclude the personal part of my narrative. The rest, when it is not in their hopes or their fears, is at least in the memories of all my readers. It is enough to recall or to mention subsequent events, in as few words as possible; that concave basin which is the collective memory will furnish the wherewithal to enrich or amplify them. About 1944, a reporter from the Nashville, Tennessee, *American* uncovered, in a Memphis library, the forty volumes of the *First Encyclopaedia of Tlön.* Even now it is uncertain whether this discovery was accidental, or whether the directors of the still nebulous *Orbis Tertius* condoned it. The second alternative is more likely. Some of the more improbable features of the eleventh volume (for example, the multiplying of the *hrönir*) had been either removed or modified in the Memphis copy. It is reasonable to suppose that these erasures were in keeping with the plan of projecting a world which would not be too incompatible with the real world. The dissemination of objects from Tlön throughout various countries would complement that plan. . . .[6] The fact is that the international press overwhelmingly hailed the "find." Manuals, anthologies, summaries, literal versions, authorized reprints, and pirated editions of the Master Work of Man poured and continue to pour out into the world. Almost immediately, reality gave ground on more than one point. The truth is that it hankered to give ground. Ten years ago, any symmetrical system whatsoever which gave the appearance of order—dialectical materialism, anti-Semitism, Nazism—was enough to fascinate men. Why not fall under the spell of Tlön and

---

[6]There remains, naturally, the problem of the *matter* of which some of these objects consisted.

submit to the minute and vast evidence of an ordered planet? Useless to reply that reality, too, is ordered. It may be so, but in accordance with divine laws—I translate: inhuman laws—which we will never completely perceive. Tlön may be a labyrinth, but it is a labyrinth plotted by men, a labyrinth destined to be deciphered by men.

Contact with Tlön and the ways of Tlön have disintegrated this world. Captivated by its discipline, humanity forgets and goes on forgetting that it is the discipline of chess players, not of angels. Now, the conjectural "primitive language" of Tlön has found its way into the schools. Now, the teaching of its harmonious history, full of stirring episodes, has obliterated the history which dominated my childhood. Now, in all memories, a fictitious past occupies the place of any other. We know nothing about it with any certainty, not even that it is false. Numismatics, pharmacology, and archeology have been revised. I gather that biology and mathematics are awaiting their avatar. . . . A scattered dynasty of solitaries has changed the face of the world. Its task continues. If our foresight is not mistaken, a hundred years from now someone will discover the hundred volumes of the *Second Encyclopaedia of Tlön.*

Then, English, French, and mere Spanish will disappear from this planet. The world will be Tlön. I take no notice. I go on revising, in the quiet of the days in the hotel at Adrogué, a tentative translation into Spanish, in the style of Quevedo, which I do not intend to see published, of Sir Thomas Browne's *Urn Burial.*

PROLOGUE TO THE INVENTION OF MOREL [JLB 35]

Around 1880 Stevenson observed that the adventure story was regarded as an object of scorn by the British reading public, who believed that the ability to write a novel without a plot, or with an infinitesimal, atrophied plot, was a mark of skill. In *La deshumanización del arte* (1925), José Ortega y Gasset, seeking the reason for that scorn, said, "I doubt very much whether an adventure that will interest our superior sensibility can be invented today" (page 96), and added that such an invention was "practically impossible" (page 97). On other pages, on almost all the other pages, he upheld the cause of the "psychological" novel and asserted that the pleasure to be derived from adventure stories was nonexistent or puerile. That was undoubtedly the prevailing opinion of 1880, 1925, and even 1940. Some writers (among whom I am happy to include Adolfo Bioy Casares) believe they have a right to disagree. The following, briefly, are the reasons why.

The first of these (I shall neither emphasize nor attenuate the fact that it is a paradox) has to do with the intrinsic form of the adventure story. The typical psychological novel is formless. The Russians and their disciples have demonstrated, tediously, that no one is impossible. A person may kill himself because he is so happy, for example, or commit murder as an act of benevolence. Lovers may separate forever as a consequence of their love. And one man can inform on another out of fervor or humility. In the end such complete freedom is tantamount to chaos. But the psychological novel would also be a "realistic" novel, and have us forget that it is a verbal artifice, for it uses each vain precision (or each languid obscurity) as a new proof of verisimilitude. There are pages, there are chapters in Marcel Proust that are unacceptable as inventions, and we unwittingly resign ourselves to them as we resign ourselves to the insipidity and the emptiness of each day. The adventure story, on the other hand, does not propose to be a transcription of reality: it is an artificial object, no part of which lacks justification. It must have a rigid plot if it is not to succumb to the mere sequential variety of *The Golden Ass,* the *Seven Voyages of Sindbad,* or the *Quixote.*

I have given one reason of an intellectual sort; there are others of an empirical nature. We hear sad murmurs that our century lacks the ability to devise interesting plots. But no one attempts to prove that if this century has any ascendancy over the preceding ones it lies in the quality of its plots. Stevenson is more passionate, more diverse, more lucid, perhaps more deserving of our unqualified friendship than is Chesterton; but his plots are inferior. De Quincey plunged deep into labyrinths on his nights of meticulously detailed horror, but he did not coin his impression of "unutterable and self-repeating infinities" in fables comparable to Kafka's. Ortega y Gasset was right when he said that Balzac's "psychology" did not satisfy us; the same thing could be said of his plots. Shakespeare and Cervantes were both delighted by the antinomian idea of a girl who, without losing her beauty, could be taken for a man; but we find that idea unconvincing now. I believe I am free from every superstition of modernity, of any illusion that yesterday differs intimately from today or will differ from tomorrow; but I maintain that during no other era have there been novels with such admirable plots as *The Turn of the Screw, Der Prozess, Le Voyageur sur la terre,* and the one you are about to read, which was written in Buenos Aires by Adolfo Bioy Casares.

Another popular genre in this so-called plotless century is the detective story, which tells of mysterious events that are later explained and justified by a reasonable occurrence. In this book Adolfo Bioy Casares easily solves a problem that is perhaps more difficult. The odyssey of marvels he unfolds seems to have no possible explanation other than hallucination or symbolism, and he uses a single fantastic but not supernatural postulate to decipher it. My fear of making premature or partial revelations restrains me from examining the plot and the wealth of delicate wisdom in its execution. Let me say only that Bioy renews in literature a concept that was refuted by Saint Augustine and Origen, studied by Louis Auguste Blanqui, and expressed in memorable cadences by Dante Gabriel Rossetti:

> I have been here before,
> But when or how I cannot tell:
> I know the grass beyond the door,
> The sweet keen smell,
> The sighing sound, the lights around the shore.

In Spanish, works of reasoned imagination are infrequent and even very rare. The classicists employed allegory, the exaggerations of satire, and, sometimes, simple verbal incoherence. The only recent works of this type I remember are a story of *Las fuerzas extrañas* and one by Santiago Dabove: now unjustly forgotten. *The Invention of Morel* (the title alludes filially to another island inventor, Moreau) brings a new genre to our land and our language.

I have discussed with the author the details of his plot. I have reread it. To classify it as perfect is neither an imprecision nor a hyperbole.

THE CIRCULAR RUINS   [JLB 36]

And if he left off dreaming about you . . .
—*Through the Looking Glass,* VI

No one saw him disembark in the unanimous night, no one saw the bamboo canoe sink into the sacred mud, but in a few days there was no one who did not know that the taciturn man came from the south and that his home had been one of those numberless villages upstream in the deeply cleft side of the mountain, where the Zend language has not been contaminated by Greek and where leprosy is infrequent. What is certain is that the gray man kissed the mud, climbed up the bank without pushing aside (probably, without feeling) the blades which were lacerating his flesh, and crawled, nauseated and bloodstained, up to the circular enclosure crowned with a stone tiger or horse, which sometimes was the color of flame and now was that of ashes. This circle was a temple which had been devoured by ancient fires, profaned by the miasmal jungle, and whose god no longer received the homage of men. The stranger stretched himself out beneath the pedestal. He was awakened by the sun high overhead. He was not astonished to find that his wounds had healed; he closed his pallid eyes and slept, not through weakness of flesh but through determination of will. He knew that this temple was the place required for his invincible intent; he knew that the incessant trees had not succeeded in strangling the ruins of another propitious temple downstream which had once belonged to gods now burned and dead; he knew that his immediate obligation was to dream. Toward midnight he was awakened by the inconsolable shriek of a bird. Tracks of bare feet, some figs, and a jug warned him that the men of the region had been spying respectfully on his sleep, soliciting his protection, or afraid of his magic. He felt a chill of fear and sought out a sepulchral niche in the dilapidated wall where he concealed himself among unfamiliar leaves.

The purpose that guided him was not impossible, though supernatural. He wanted to dream a man; he wanted to dream him in minute entirety and impose him on reality. This magic project had exhausted the entire expanse of his mind; if someone had asked him his name or to relate some event of his former life, he would not have been able to give an answer. This uninhabited, ruined temple suited him, for it contained a minimum of visible world; the proximity of the workmen also suited him, for they took it upon themselves to provide for his frugal needs. The rice and fruit they brought him were nourishment enough for his body, which was consecrated to the sole task of sleeping and dreaming.

At first, his dreams were chaotic; then in a short while they became dialectic in nature. The stranger dreamed that he was in the center of a circular amphitheater which was more or less the burned temple; clouds of taciturn students filled the tiers of seats; the faces of the farthest ones hung at a distance of many centuries and as high as the stars, but their features were completely precise. The man lectured his pupils on anatomy, cosmography, and magic: the faces listened anxiously and tried to answer understandingly, as if they guessed the importance of that examination which would redeem one of them from his condition of empty illusion and interpolate him into the real world. Asleep or awake, the man thought over the answers of his phantoms, did not allow himself to be deceived by impostors, and in certain perplexities he sensed a growing intelligence. He was seeking a soul worthy of participating in the universe.

After nine or ten nights he understood with a certain bitterness that he could expect nothing from those pupils who accepted his doctrine passively, but that he could expect something from those who occasionally dared to oppose him. The former group, although worthy of love and affection, could not ascend to the level of individuals; the latter preexisted to a slightly greater degree. One afternoon (now afternoons were also given over to sleep, now he was only awake for a couple of hours at daybreak) he dismissed the vast illusory student body for good and kept only one pupil. He was a taciturn, sallow boy, at times intractable, whose sharp features resembled those of his dreamer. The brusque elimination of his fellow students did not disconcert him for long; after a few private lessons, his progress was enough to astound the teacher. Nevertheless, a catastrophe took place. One day, the man emerged from his sleep as if from a viscous desert, looked at the useless afternoon light which he immediately confused with the dawn, and understood that he had not dreamed. All that night and all day long, the intolerable lucidity of insomnia fell upon him. He tried exploring the forest, to exhaust his strength; among the hemlock he barely succeeded in experiencing several short snatches of sleep, veined with fleeting, rudimentary visions that were useless. He tried to assemble the student body but scarcely had he articulated a few brief words of exhortation when it became deformed and was then erased. In his almost perpetual vigil, tears of anger burned his old eyes.

He understood that modeling the incoherent and vertiginous matter of which dreams are composed was the most difficult task that a man could undertake, even though he should penetrate all the enigmas of a superior and inferior order; much more difficult than weaving a rope out of sand or coining the faceless wind. He swore he would forget the enormous hallucination which had thrown him off at first, and he sought another method of work. Before putting it into execution, he spent a month recovering his strength, which had been squandered by his delirium. He abandoned all premeditation of dreaming and almost immediately succeeded in sleeping a reasonable part of each day. The few times that he had dreams during this period, he paid no attention to them. Before resuming his task, he waited until the moon's disk was perfect. Then, in the afternoon, he purified himself in the waters of the river, worshiped the planetary gods, pronounced the prescribed syllables of a mighty name, and went to sleep. He dreamed almost immediately, with his heart throbbing.

He dreamed that it was warm, secret, about the size of a clenched fist, and of a garnet color within the penumbra of a human body as yet without face or sex; during fourteen lucid nights he dreamed of it with meticulous love. Every night he perceived it more clearly. He did not touch it; he only permitted himself to witness it, to observe it, and occasionally to rectify it with a glance. He perceived it and lived it from all angles and distances. On the fourteenth night he lightly touched the pulmonary artery with his index finger, then the whole heart, outside and inside. He was satisfied with the examination. He deliberately did not dream for a night; he then took up the heart again, invoked the name of a planet, and undertook the vision of another of the principal organs. Within a year he had come to the skeleton and the eyelids. The innumerable hair was perhaps the most difficult task. He dreamed an entire man—a young man, but one who did not sit up or talk, who was unable to open his eyes. Night after night, the man dreamed him asleep.

In the Gnostic cosmogonies, demiurges fashion a red Adam who cannot stand; as clumsy, crude, and elemental as this Adam of dust was the Adam of dreams forged by the wizard's nights. One afternoon, the man almost destroyed his entire work, but then changed his mind. (It would have been better had he destroyed it.) When he had exhausted all supplications to the deities of the earth, he threw himself at the feet of the effigy which was perhaps a tiger or perhaps a colt and implored its unknown help. That evening, at twilight, he dreamed of the statue. He dreamed it was alive, tremulous: it was not an atrocious bastard of a tiger and a colt, but at the same time these two fiery creatures and also a bull, a rose, and a storm. This multiple god revealed to him that his earthly name was Fire, and that in this circular temple (and in others like it) people had once made sacrifices to him and worshiped him, and that he would magically animate the dreamed phantom, in such a way that all creatures, except Fire itself and the dreamer, would believe it to be a man of flesh and blood. He commanded that once this man had been instructed in all the rites, he should be sent to the other ruined temple whose pyramids were still standing downstream, so that some voice would glorify him in that deserted edifice. In the dream of the man that dreamed, the dreamed one awoke.

The wizard carried out the orders he had been given. He devoted a certain length of time (which finally proved to be two years) to instructing him in the mysteries of the universe and the cult of fire. Secretly, he was pained at the idea of being separated from him. On the pretext of pedagogical necessity, each day he increased the number of hours dedicated to dreaming. He also remade the right shoulder, which was somewhat defective. At times, he was disturbed by the impression that all this had already happened. . . . In general, his days were happy; when he closed his eyes, he thought: *Now I will be with my son.* Or, more rarely: *The son I have engendered is waiting for me and will not exist if I do not go to him.*

Gradually, he began accustoming him to reality. Once he ordered him to place a flag on a faraway peak. The next day the flag was fluttering on the peak. He tried other analogous experiments, each time more audacious. With a certain bitterness, he understood that his son was ready to be born—and perhaps impatient. That night he kissed him for the first time and sent him off to the other temple whose remains were turning white downstream, across many miles of inextricable jungle and marshes. Before doing this (and so that his son should never know that he was a phantom, so that he should think himself a man like any other) he destroyed in him all memory of his years of apprenticeship.

His victory and peace became blurred with boredom. In the twilight times of dusk and dawn, he would prostrate himself before the stone figure, perhaps imagining his unreal son carrying out identical rites in other circular ruins downstream; at night he no longer dreamed, or dreamed as any man does. His perceptions of the sounds and forms of the universe became somewhat pallid: his absent son was being nourished by these diminutions of his soul. The purpose of his life had been fulfilled; the man remained in a kind of ecstasy. After a certain time, which some chroniclers prefer to compute in years and others in decades, two oarsmen awoke him at midnight; he could not see their faces, but they spoke to him of a charmed man in a temple of the north, capable of walking on fire without burning himself. The wizard suddenly remembered the words of the god. He remembered that of all the creatures that people the earth, Fire was the only one who knew his son to be a phantom. This memory, which at first calmed him, ended by tormenting him. He feared lest his son should meditate on this abnormal privilege and by some means find out he was a mere simulacrum. Not to be a man, to be a projection of another man's dreams—what an incomparable humiliation, what madness! Any father is interested in the sons he has procreated (or permitted) out of the mere confusion of happiness; it was natural that the wizard should fear for the future of that son whom he had thought out entrail by entrail, feature by feature, in a thousand and one secret nights.

His misgivings ended abruptly, but not without certain forewarnings. First (after a long drought) a remote cloud, as light as a bird, appeared on a hill; then, toward the south, the sky took on the rose color of leopard's gums; then came clouds of smoke which rusted the metal of the nights; afterward came the panic-stricken flight of wild animals. For what had happened many centuries before was repeating itself. The ruins of the sanctuary of the god of Fire was destroyed by fire. In a dawn without birds, the wizard saw the concentric fire licking the walls. For a moment, he thought of taking refuge in the water, but then he understood that death was coming to crown his old age and absolve him from his labors. He walked toward the sheets of flame. They did not bite his flesh, they caressed him and flooded him without heat or combustion. With relief, with humiliation, with terror, he understood that he also was an illusion, that someone else was dreaming him.

PORTRAIT OF THE GERMANOPHILE [JLB 37]

Etymology's implacable detractors reason that the origins of words do not show what they mean now; its defenders can reply that origins always show what words do not mean now. They show, for example, that pontiffs are not builders of pontoons; that miniatures are not painted with minium; that crystal is not made of ice; that a leopard is not a cross between a panther and a lion; that a candidate need not be clothed in white; that sarcophagi are not the opposite of vegetarians; that alligators are not lizards; that rubrics are not red like rubor; that the discoverer of America was not Amerigo Vespucci, and that Germanophiles are not devotees of Germany.

The aforesaid is not a falsehood, nor even an exaggeration. I have been naïve enough to converse with many Argentine Germanophiles; I have tried to talk about Germany and German indestructibility; I have mentioned Hölderlin, Luther, Schopenhauer, and Leibniz; I have ascertained that the Germanophile interlocutor barely identified those names and preferred to talk about a more or less antarctic archipelago that the English discovered in 1592 and whose relation to Germany I have yet to understand.

Complete ignorance of the Germanic, however, does not exhaust the definition of our Germanophiles. There are other distinctive characteristics perhaps as necessary as the first. One of them: the Germanophile is quite unhappy that the railroad companies of a certain South American republic have English stockholders. He is also distressed by the rigors of the South African war of 1902. He is anti-Semitic as well: he wishes to expel from our country a Slavo-Germanic community in which names of German origin predominate (Rosenblatt, Gruenberg, Nierenstein, Lilienthal) and which speaks a German dialect—Yiddish or Jüdisch.

Perhaps one could infer from the preceding that the Germanophile is really an Anglophobe. He is perfectly ignorant about Germany but resigns himself to enthusiasm for a country at war with England. We shall see that such is the truth, but not the whole truth, nor even its most significant part. To demonstrate this I will reconstruct, reducing it to its essentials, a conversation I have had with many Germanophiles in which I swear never to involve myself again, because the time granted to mortals is not infinite and the fruit of these discussions is vain.

Invariably my interlocutor begins by condemning the Treaty of Versailles, imposed by mere force on Germany in 1919. Invariably I illustrate this condemnatory verdict with a text by Wells or Bernard Shaw, who denounced that implacable document in the hour of victory. The Germanophile never rejects this text. He proclaims that a victorious country must dispense with oppression and vengeance. He proclaims that it was natural that Germany should want to nullify that outrage. I share his opinion. Afterward, immediately afterward, the inexplicable occurs. My prodigious interlocutor reasons that the old injustice suffered by Germany authorizes it in 1940 to destroy not only England and France (why not Italy?), but also Denmark, Holland, Norway—all completely free of blame for that injustice. In 1919, Germany was badly treated by its enemies: that all-powerful reason permits it to burn, destroy, and conquer all the nations of Europe and perhaps the globe. . . . The reasoning is monstrous, as can be seen.

I timidly point out this monstrosity to my interlocutor. The latter ridicules my outdated scruples and alleges Jesuit or Nietzschean reasons: the end justifies the means; necessity knows no law; there is no law other than the will of the strongest. The Reich is strong: the Reich's air forces have destroyed Coventry, etc. I murmur that I am resigned to passing from the morality of Jesus to that of Zarathustra or Hormiga Negra, but that our rapid conversion prohibits us from pitying Germany for the injustice which it suffered in 1919. On that date, which he does not want to forget, England and France were strong. There is no law other than the will of the strongest; consequently, those calumnied nations proceeded very well in wanting to destroy Germany, and one cannot censure them for anything other than having been indecisive (and even culpably merciful) in the execution of that plan. Disdaining these arid abstractions, my interlocutor initiates or outlines the panegyric of Hitler—that providential man whose indefatigable discourses preach the extinction of all charlatans and demagogues and whose incendiary bombs, unmitigated by wordy declarations of war, announce from the firmament the ruin of rapacious imperialism. Afterward, immediately afterward, the second marvel occurs. It is of a moral nature and almost unbelievable.

I always discover that my interlocutor idolizes Hitler, not in spite of the zenithal bombs and the fulminous invasions, the machine guns, accusations, and perjuries, but because of those customs and those instruments. He is cheered by wickedness and atrocity. Germanic victory does not matter to him; he wants the humiliation of England, the satisfactory burning of London. He admires Hitler as yesterday he admired his precursors in Chicago's criminal underworld. The discussion becomes impossible because the villainies I impute to Hitler are delights and merits for him. The apologists of Amigas, Ramírez, Quiroga, Rosas, or Urquiza pardon or mitigate their crimes; Hitler's defender derives a special pleasure from them. The Hitlerist is always a spiteful man, and a secret and sometimes public admirer of vicious cleverness and cruelty. Because of his imaginative penury, he is a man who postulates that the future cannot differ from the present, and that Germany, victorious until now, cannot begin to lose. He is the cunning man who longs to be on the winners' side.

It is not impossible that Adolf Hitler has some justification; I know that Germanophiles do not.

THE CYCLICAL NIGHT [JLB 38]

They knew it, the fervent pupils of Pythagoras:
that stars and men revolve in a cycle,
that fateful atoms will bring back the vital
gold Aphrodite, Thebans, and agoras.

In future epochs the centaur will oppress
with solid uncleft hoof the breast of the Lapith;
when Rome is dust the Minotaur will moan
once more in the endless dark of its rank palace.

129

Every sleepless night will come back in minute
detail. This writing hand will be born from the same
womb, and bitter armies contrive their doom.
(Edinburgh's David Hume made this very point.)

I do not know if we will recur in a second
cycle, like numbers in a periodic fraction;
but I know that a vague Pythagorean rotation
night after night sets me down in the world

on the outskirts of this city. A remote street
which might be either north or west or south,
but always with a blue-washed wall, the shade
of a fig tree, and a sidewalk of broken concrete.

This, here, is Buenos Aires. Time, which brings
either love or money to men, hands on to me
only this withered rose, this empty tracery
of streets with names recurring from the past

in my blood: Laprida, Cabrera, Soler, Suárez . . .
names in which secret bugle calls are sounding,
invoking republics, cavalry, and mornings,
joyful victories, men dying in action.

Squares weighed down by a night in no one's care
are the vast patios of an empty palace,
and the single-minded streets creating space
are corridors for sleep and nameless fear.

It returns, the hollow dark of Anaxagoras;
in my human flesh, eternity keeps recurring
and the memory, or plan, of an endless poem beginning:
"They knew it, the fervent pupils of Pythagoras . . ."

THE LOTTERY IN BABYLON [JLB 39]

Like all men in Babylon I have been a proconsul; like all, a slave; I have also
known omnipotence, opprobrium, jail. Look: the index finger of my right hand
is missing. Look again: through this rent in my cape you can see a ruddy tattoo
on my belly. It is the second symbol, Beth. This letter, on nights of full moon,
gives me power over men whose mark is Ghimel; but it also subordinates me to
those marked Aleph, who on moonless nights owe obedience to those marked
Ghimel. In a cellar at dawn, I have severed the jugular vein of sacred bulls against
a black rock. During one lunar year, I have been declared invisible: I shrieked

and was not heard, I stole my bread and was not decapitated. I have known what the Greeks did not: uncertainty. In a bronze chamber, faced with the silent handkerchief of a strangler, hope has been faithful to me; in the river of delights, panic has not failed me. Heraclitus of Pontica admiringly relates that Pythagoras recalled having been Pyrrho, and before that Euphorbus, and before that some other mortal. In order to recall analogous vicissitudes I do not need to have recourse to death, nor even to imposture.

I owe this almost atrocious variety to an institution which other republics know nothing about, or which operates among them imperfectly and in secret: the lottery. I have not delved into its history; I do know that the wizards have been unable to come to any agreement; of its powerful designs I know what a man not versed in astrology might know of the moon. I come from a vertiginous country where the lottery forms a principal part of reality: until this very day I have thought about all this as little as I have about the behavior of the indecipherable gods or about the beating of my own heart. Now, far from Babylon and its beloved customs, I think of the lottery with some astonishment and ponder the blasphemous conjectures murmured by men in the shadows at twilight.

My father related that anciently—a matter of centuries; of years?—the lottery in Babylon was a game of plebeian character. He said (I do not know with what degree of truth) that barbers gave rectangular bits of bone or decorated parchment in exchange for copper coins. A drawing of the lottery was held in the middle of the day: the winners received, without further corroboration from chance, silver-minted coins. The procedure, as you see, was elemental.

Naturally, these "lotteries" failed. Their moral virtue was nil. They did not appeal to all the faculties of men: only to their hope. In the face of public indifference, the merchants who established these venal lotteries began to lose money. Someone attempted to introduce a slight reform: the interpolation of a certain small number of adverse outcomes among the favored numbers. By means of this reform, the purchasers of numbered rectangles stood the double chance of winning a sum or of paying a fine often considerable in size. This slight danger —for each thirty favored numbers there would be one adverse number—awoke, as was only natural, the public's interest. The Babylonians gave themselves up to the game. Anyone who did not acquire lots was looked upon as pusillanimous, mean-spirited. In time, this disdain multiplied. The person who did not play was despised, but the losers who paid the fine were also scorned. The company (thus it began to be known at that time) was forced to take measures to protect the winners, who could not collect their prizes unless nearly the entire amount of the fines was already collected. The company brought suit against the losers: the judge condemned them to pay the original fine plus costs or to spend a number of days in jail. Every loser chose jail, so as to defraud the company. It was from this initial bravado of a few men that the all-powerful position of the company —its ecclesiastical, metaphysical strength—was derived.

A short while later, the reports on the drawings omitted any enumeration of fines and limited themselves to publishing the jail sentences corresponding to each adverse number. This laconism, almost unnoticed at the time, became of capital importance. *It constituted the first appearance in the lottery of nonpecuni-*

ary elements. Its success was great. Pushed to such a measure by the players, the company found itself forced to increase its adverse numbers.

No one can deny that the people of Babylonia are highly devoted to logic, even to symmetry. It struck them as incoherent that the fortunate numbers should be computed in round figures of money while the unfortunate should be figured in terms of days and nights in jail. Some moralists argued that the possession of money does not determine happiness and that other forms of fortune are perhaps more immediate.

There was another source of restlessness in the lower depths. The members of the sacerdotal college multiplied the stakes and plumbed the vicissitudes of terror and hope; the poor, with reasonable or inevitable envy, saw themselves excluded from this notoriously delicious exhilaration. The just anxiety of all, poor and rich alike, to participate equally in the lottery, inspired an indignant agitation, the memory of which the years have not erased. Certain obstinate souls did not comprehend, or pretended not to comprehend, that a new order had come, a necessary historical stage. . . . A slave stole a crimson ticket, a ticket which earned him the right to have his tongue burned in the next drawing. The criminal code fixed the same penalty for the theft of a ticket. A number of Babylonians argued that he deserved a red-hot poker by virtue of the theft; others, more magnanimous, held that the public executioner should apply the penalty of the lottery, since chance had so determined. . . .

Disturbances broke out, there was a lamentable shedding of blood; but the people of Babylon imposed their will at last, over the opposition of the rich. That is: the people fully achieved their magnanimous ends. In the first place, it made the company accept complete public power. (This unification was necessary, given the vastness and complexity of the new operations.) In the second place, it forced the lottery to be secret, free, and general. The sale of tickets for money was abolished. Once initiated into the mysteries of Bel, every free man automatically participated in the sacred drawings of lots, which were carried out in the labyrinths of the gods every seventy nights and which determined every man's fate until the next exercise. The consequences were incalculable. A happy drawing might motivate his elevation to the council of wizards or his condemnation to the custody of an enemy (notorious or intimate), or to find, in the peaceful shadows of a room, the woman who had begun to disquiet him or whom he had never expected to see again. An adverse drawing might mean mutilation, a varied infamy, death. Sometimes a single event—the tavern killing of C, the mysterious glorification of B—might be the brilliant result of thirty or forty drawings. But it must be recalled that the individuals of the company were (and are) all-powerful and astute as well. In many cases, the knowledge that certain joys were the simple doing of chance might have detracted from their exellence; to avoid this inconvenience the company's agents made use of suggestion and magic. Their moves, their management, were secret. In the investigation of people's intimate hopes and intimate terrors, they made use of astrologers and spies. There were certain stone lions, there was a sacred privy called Qaphqa, there were fissures in a dusty aqueduct which, according to general opinion, *led to the company;* malign or benevolent people deposited accusations in these cracks. These denunciations were incorporated into an alphabetical archive of variable veracity.

Incredibly enough, there were still complaints. The company, with its habitual discretion, did not reply directly. It preferred to scribble a brief argument—which now figures among sacred scriptures—in the debris of a mask factory. That doctrinal piece of literature observed that the lottery is an interpolation of chance into the order of the world and that to accept errors is not to contradict fate but merely to corroborate it. It also observed that those lions and that sacred recipient, though not unauthorized by the company (which did not renounce the right to consult them), functioned without official guarantee.

This declaration pacified the public unease. It also produced other effects, not foreseen by the author. It deeply modified the spirit and operations of the company. (I have little time left to tell what I know; we have been warned that the ship is ready to sail; but I will attempt to explain it.)

Improbable as it may be, no one had until then attempted to set up a general theory of games. A Babylonian is not highly speculative. He reveres the judgments of fate, he hands his life over to them, he places his hopes, his panic terror in them, but it never occurs to him to investigate their labyrinthian laws nor the gyratory spheres which disclose them. Nevertheless, the unofficial declaration which I have mentioned inspired many discussions of a juridico-mathematical nature. From one of these discussions was born the following conjecture: If the lottery is an intensification of chance, a periodic infusion of chaos into the cosmos, would it not be desirable for chance to intervene at all stages of the lottery and not merely in the drawing? Is it not ridiculous for chance to dictate the death of someone, while the circumstances of his death—its silent reserve or publicity, the time limit of one hour or one century—should remain immune to hazard? These eminently just scruples finally provoked a considerable reform, whose complexities (intensified by the practice of centuries) are not understood except by a handful of specialists, but which I will attempt to summarize, even if only in a symbolic manner.

Let us imagine a first drawing, which eventuates in a sentence of death against some individual. To carry out the sentence, another drawing is set up, and this drawing proposes (let us say) nine possible executioners. Of these executioners, four can initiate a third drawing which will reveal the name of the actual executioner, two others can replace the adverse order with a fortunate order (the finding of a treasure, let us say), another may exacerbate the death sentence (that is: make it infamous or enrich it with torture), still others may refuse to carry it out. . . .

Such is the symbolic scheme. In reality, *the number of drawings is infinite.* No decision is final, all diverge into others. The ignorant suppose that an infinite number of drawings requires an infinite amount of time; in reality, it is quite enough that time be infinitely subdivisible, as is the case in the famous parable of the Tortoise and the Hare. This infinitude harmonizes in an admirable manner with the sinuous numbers of chance and of the celestial archetype of the lottery adored by the Platonists. . . .

A certain distorted echo of our ritual seems to have resounded along the Tiber: Aelius Lampridius, in his *Life of Antoninus Heliogabalus,* tells of how this emperor wrote down the lot of his guests on seashells, so that one would receive ten pounds of gold and another ten flies, ten dormice, ten bears. It is only right to remark that Heliogabalus was educated in Asia Minor, among the priests of the eponymous god.

There are also impersonal drawings, of undefined purpose: one drawing will decree that a sapphire from Taprobane be thrown into the waters of the Euphrates; another, that a bird be released from a tower roof; another, that a grain of sand be withdrawn (or added) to the innumerable grains on a beach. The consequences, sometimes, are terrifying.

Under the beneficent influence of the company, our customs have become thoroughly impregnated with chance. The buyer of a dozen amphoras of Damascus wine will not be surprised if one of them contains a talisman or a viper. The scribe who draws up a contract scarcely ever fails to introduce some erroneous datum; I myself, in making this hasty declaration, have falsified or invented some grandeur, some atrocity; perhaps, too, a certain mysterious monotony. . . .

Our historians, the most discerning in the world, have invented a method for correcting chance. It is well known that the operations of this method are (in general) trustworthy; although, naturally, they are not divulged without a measure of deceit. In any case, there is nothing so contaminated with fiction as the history of the company. . . .

A paleographic document, unearthed in a temple, may well be the work of yesterday's drawing or that of one lasting a century. No book is ever published without some variant in each copy. Scribes take a secret oath to omit, interpolate, vary.

The company, with divine modesty, eludes all publicity. Its agents, as is only natural, are secret. The orders which it is continually sending out do not differ from those lavishly issued by impostors. Besides, who can ever boast of being a mere impostor? The inebriate who improvises an absurd mandate, the dreamer who suddenly awakes to choke the woman who lies at his side to death, do they not both, perhaps, carry out a secret decision by the company? This silent functioning, comparable to that of God, gives rise to all manner of conjectures. One of them, for instance, abominably insinuates that the company is eternal and that it will last until the last night of the world, when the last god annihilates the cosmos. Still another conjecture declares that the company is omnipotent, but that it exerts its influence only in the most minute matters: in a bird's cry, in the shades of rust and the hues of dust, in the catnaps of dawn. There is one conjecture, spoken from the mouths of masked heresiarchs, to the effect that *the company has never existed and never will.* A conjecture no less vile argues that it is indifferently inconsequential to affirm or deny the reality of the shadowy corporation, because Babylon is nothing but an infinite game of chance.

FRAGMENT ON JOYCE

[JLB 40]

Among the works that I have never written or will write (but that somehow justify me, even mysteriously or rudimentarily) is a story about eight or ten pages long, the profuse rough draft of which is entitled "Funes the Memorious," and which in even rougher drafts is called "Ireneo Funes." The protagonist of this doubly unreal fiction is, around 1884, a normally unfortunate country boy from Fray Bentos or Junín. His mother irons for a living; as for his problematical father, it is implied that he was a drifter. The truth of the matter is that the boy has the blood and silence of an Indian. In his childhood he was expelled from school for slavishly copying a couple of chapters, with illustrations, maps, vignettes, capital letters, and even a printing error. . . . He dies before reaching the age of twenty. He is incredibly idle: he has spent practically his whole life on a cot, his eyes fixed on the distant fig tree or on a spiderweb. At his wake, the neighbors recall the insignificant events of his story: a visit to the corrals, another to the brothel, another to somebody's ranch. . . . Somebody provides an explanation. The deceased was perhaps the only lucid man on earth. His perception and memory were infallible. We, at a glance, perceive three wineglasses on a table; Funes, all the leaves and clusters of grapes that constitute the wine. He knew the forms of the southern clouds at daybreak on April 30, 1882, and in his memory he could compare them to the seams of a book bound in Spain that he had once handled as a child. He could reconstruct all his dreams, all his daydreams. He died of a pulmonary congestion and his incommunicable life had been the richest in the world.

As for the magical country boy in my story, it is fitting to state that he is a precursor of supermen, a suburban and partial Zarathustra; what is undeniable is that he is a monstrosity. I have mentioned him because the consecutive, undeviating reading of the 400,000 words in *Ulysses* would require analogous monstrosities. (I will not suggest anything about those required by *Finnegans Wake:* to me no less inconceivable than C. H. Hilton's fourth dimension or the Nicene Creed.) Everyone knows that for the unprepared reader, Joyce's vast novel is undecipherably chaotic. Everyone also knows that its official interpreter, Stuart Gilbert, has shown that every one of its eighteen chapters corresponds to an hour of the day, an organ of the body, an art, a symbol, a color, a literary technique, and one of the adventures of Ulysses, son of Laertes, from the seed of Zeus. The mere announcement of such imperceptible, laborious congruities has sufficed for the entire world to venerate the work's severe construction and classical discipline. Among these voluntary ties, the most acclaimed has been the most insignificant: James Joyce's contacts with Homer, or (simply) with the senator for the Department of Justice, M. Victor Bérard.

Obviously more admirable, undoubtedly, is his multitudinous diversity of styles. Like Shakespeare, like Quevedo, like Goethe, like no other writer, Joyce is less a man of letters than a literature. He achieves this, incredibly, in the confines of only one volume. His writing is intense: Goethe's never was; it is delicate: Quevedo was never aware of that virtue. Like the rest of the world I have never read all of *Ulysses,* but I happily read and reread some scenes: the dialogue on Shakespeare, the *Walpurgisnacht* in the brothel, the questions and answers from the catechism: . . . "They drank in jocoserious silence Epp's massproduct, the creature cocoa." And from another passage: "A dark horse riderless, bolts like a phantom past the winningpost, his mane moonfoaming, his

eyeballs stars." And still another: "Bridebed, childbed, bed of death, ghostcan-
dled."[1]

Plenitude and indigence live side by side in Joyce. Lacking the talent to
construct (which his gods failed to bestow upon him and which he was obliged
to supplant with arduous symmetries and labyrinths), he was blessed with a
verbal knack, a gifted omnipresence in words, which can be compared without
exaggeration or inaccuracy to that in *Hamlet* or *Urn Burial....Ulysses* (everyone
knows it) is the story of one single day, on the edge of one lone city. In that
voluntary limitation it is licit to perceive something more than an Aristotelian
elegance; it is licit to infer that for Joyce, every day was in some secret way the
irreparable Day of Judgment; every place Hell or Purgatory.

ABOUT THE PURPLE LAND [JLB 41]

This novel, W. H. Hudson's first, is reducible to a formula so ancient that it can
almost comprise the *Odyssey;* so fundamental that the name formula subtly
defames and degrades it. The hero begins his wandering, and his adventures
encounter him along the way. *The Golden Ass* and the fragments of the *Satyricon*
belong to this nomadic, random genre, as do *Pickwick* and *Don Quixote, Kim* of
Lahore and *Segundo Sombra* of Areco. I do not believe there is any justification
for calling those books picaresque novels: first, because of the unfavorable connotation of the term; second, because of its local and temporal limitations (Spain,
sixteenth and seventeenth centuries). Further, the genre is complex. Disorder,
incoherence, and variety are not inaccessible, but they must be governed by a
secret order, which is revealed by degrees. I have recalled several famous examples; perhaps all show obvious defects.

Cervantes utilizes two types of characters: an emaciated, tall, ascetic, mad,
and grandiloquent nobleman; a corpulent, short, gluttonous, sane, and colloquial
peasant. That very symmetrical and persistent disharmony finally deprives them
of reality, lowers them to the stature of circus figures. (In the seventh chapter of
El Payador our own Lugones already insinuated that reproach.) Kipling invents
Kim, the little friend of the whole world, who is completely free: a few chapters
later, impelled by some sort of patriotic perversion, he gives him the horrible
occupation of a spy. (In his literary autobiography, written about thirty-five years
later, Kipling shows that he is impenitent and even unaware of the implications.)
I note those defects without animadversion; I do it to judge *The Purple Land* with
equal sincerity.

The most elementary of the sort of novels I am considering aim at a mere
succession of adventures, mere variety: the seven voyages of Sindbad the Sailor

---

[1]The French version is not so successful: *Lit nuptial, lit de parturition, lit de mort aux
spectrales bougies.* The blame lies with the language, naturally incapable of compound
voices.

are perhaps the best example, for the hero is just an underling, as impersonal and passive as the reader. In other novels (which are scarcely more complex) the function of the events is to reveal the hero's character, and even his absurdities and manias; that is the case in the first part of *Don Quixote*. In others (which correspond to a later stage) the movement is dual, reciprocal; the hero changes the circumstances, the circumstances change the hero's character. That is the case with the second part of the *Quixote,* with Mark Twain's *Huckleberry Finn,* with *The Purple Land.* The latter actually has two plots. The first, the visible one: the adventures of the young Englishman Richard Lamb in the Banda Oriental. The second, the intimate, invisible one: the assimilation of Lamb, his gradual conversion to a barbarous morality that reminds one of Rousseau a little and anticipates Nietzsche a little. His *Wanderjahre* are also *Lehrjahre.* Hudson was personally acquainted with the rigors of a semibarbarous, pastoral life; Rousseau and Nietzsche knew such a life only through the sedentary volumes of the *Histoire générale des voyages* and the Homeric epics. The foregoing statement does not mean that *The Purple Land* is flawless. It suffers from an obvious defect, which may logically be attributed to the hazards of improvisation: the vain and tedious complexity of certain adventures. I am thinking of the ones near the end of the book: they are so complicated that they weary the attention but do not hold it. In those onerous chapters Hudson appears not to understand that the book is successive (almost as purely successive as the *Satyricon* or the *Buscón*) and benumbs it with useless artifices. This is a common mistake; for example, Dickens tends toward similar prolixities in all his novels.

The Purple Land is perhaps unexcelled by any work of gaucho literature. It would be deplorable if we let a certain topographical confusion and three or four errors or errata (*Camelones* for *Canelones, Aria* for *Arias, Gumesinda* for *Gumersinda*) conceal that truth from us. *The Purple Land* is essentially *criollo,* native to South America. The fact that the narrator is an Englishman justifies certain explanations and certain emphases required by his readers, which would be anomalous in a gaucho accustomed to such things. In No. 31 of *Sur,* Ezequiel Martínez Estrada wrote:

> Never before has there been a poet, a painter, or an interpreter of things Argentine like Hudson, nor will there ever be again. Hernández is one part of the cosmorama of our life that Hudson sang, described, and explained. . . . The final pages of *The Purple Land* express the maximum philosophy and the supreme justification of America in the face of Western civilization and the refinements of culture.

As we see, Martínez Estrada did not hesitate to prefer Hudson's total output to the most notable of the canonical books of our gaucho literature. Incomparably more vast is the scope of *The Purple Land.* The *Martín Fierro* (notwithstanding the canonization proposed by Lugones) is less the epic of our origins—in 1872! —than the autobiography of a cutthroat, adulterated by bravado and lamentation that seem to prophesy the tango. Ascasubi's work is more vivid, it has more joy, more passion, but those traits are fragmentary and secret in three incidental volumes of 400 pages each. In spite of the variety of its dialogues, *Don Segundo*

Sombra is marred by the propensity to exaggerate the most innocent tasks. No one is unaware that the narrator is a gaucho; and therefore to indulge in the kind of dramatic hyperbole that converts the herding of bulls into an exploit of war is doubly unjustified. Güiraldes assumes an air of solemnity when he relates the everyday work of the country. Hudson (like Ascasubi, like Hernández, like Eduardo Gutiérrez) describes with complete naturalness events that may even be atrocious.

Someone will observe that in *The Purple Land* the gaucho has only a lateral, secondary role. So much the better for the accuracy of the portrayal, we reply. The gaucho is a taciturn man, the gaucho does not know, or he scorns, the complex delights of memory and introspection. To depict him as autobiographical and effusive is to deform him.

Another of Hudson's adroit strokes is his treatment of geography. Born in the province of Buenos Aires in the magic circle of the pampa, he nonetheless chooses to write about the purple land where the revolutionary horsemen used their first and last lances: the Banda Oriental. Gauchos from the province of Buenos Aires are the rule in Argentine literature: the paradoxical reason for that is the existence of a large city, Buenos Aires, the point of origin of famous writers of gaucho literature. If we look to history instead of to literature, we shall see that the glorification of the gaucho has had but little influence on the destinies of their province, and none on the destinies of their country. The typical organism of gaucho warfare, the revolutionary horseman, appears in Buenos Aires only sporadically. The authority falls to the city, to the leaders of the city. Only rarely does some individual—Hormiga Negra in legal documents, Martín Fierro in literature—attain, with the rebellion of a fugitive, a certain notoriety with the police.

As I have said, Hudson selects the Banda Oriental as the setting for his hero's escapades. That propitious choice permits him to enlist chance and the diversification of war to enrich Richard Lamb's destiny—and chance favors the opportunities for vagabond love. Macaulay, in the article about Bunyan, marveled that one man's imaginings would become, years later, the personal memories of many other men. Hudson's imaginings remain in the memory: British bullets that resound in the Paysandú night; the oblivious gaucho who enjoys his smoke of strong tobacco before the battle; the girl who surrenders to a stranger on the secret shore of a river.

Improving the perfection of a phrase divulged by Boswell, Hudson says that many times in his life he undertook the study of metaphysics, but happiness always interrupted him. That sentence (one of the most memorable I have encountered in literature) is typical of the man and the book. In spite of the bloodshed and the separations, *The Purple Land* is one of the very few happy books in the world. (Another, which also is about America, also nearly paradisaic in tone, is Mark Twain's *Huckleberry Finn*.) I am not thinking of the chaotic debate between pessimists and optimists; I am not thinking of the doctrinal happiness the pathetic Whitman inexorably imposed on himself; I am thinking of the happy disposition of Richard Lamb, of the hospitality with which he welcomed every vicissitude of life, whether bitter or sweet.

One last observation. To perceive or not to perceive the *criollo* nuances may be quite unimportant, but the fact is that of all the foreigners (not, of course, excluding the Spaniards) no one perceives them like the Englishman—Miller, Robertson, Burton, Cunningham, Grahame, Hudson.

CITIZEN KANE   [JLB 42]

Citizen Kane (called, in Argentina, *The Citizen*) has at least two story levels. The first, simple to the point of banality, sets out to attract the applause of the groundlings. This is its essence: a vain millionaire collects statues, gardens, palaces, swimming pools, diamonds, cars, libraries, men, and women; like an earlier collector (whose observations are usually ascribed to the Holy Ghost) he discovers that these miscellaneous and abundant objects are vanity of vanities, all is vanity. At the point of death, he yearns for one single thing in the whole universe: an appropriately humble sled, a plaything of his childhood!

The second level is far superior. It unites a memory of Koheleth with that of another nihilist, Franz Kafka. The theme, at the same time metaphysical and investigatory, psychological and allegorical, is the investigation of the secret being of a man, through the things he has brought into being, the words he has pronounced, the many lives he has run through. The manner is that of Joseph Conrad in *Chance* (1914) and of that fine film, *The Power and the Glory:* the rhapsody of heterogeneous scenes, in no chronological order. Endlessly, oppressively, Orson Welles shows fragments of the life of Charles Foster Kane and invites us to make connections and to reconstruct the life. The forms of multiplicity and disconnection abound in the film. The first scenes record the treasures accumulated by Charles Foster Kane; in one of the last scenes, a poor woman, well off and suffering, works away at a vast jigsaw puzzle on the floor of a palace that is also a museum. Finally we understand that the pieces are not governed by a secret unity: the languid Charles Foster Kane is a sham, a chaos of mere appearances. (A possible corollary, already envisaged by David Hume, Ernst Munch, and our own Macedonio Fernández: no man knows who he is, no man is anyone.) In one of Chesterton's stories (I think it is "The Head of Caesar"), the hero remarks that nothing is as terrifying as a labyrinth without a center. This film is precisely that labyrinth.

We all know that a party, a great enterprise, a lunch with writers or journalists, a cordial atmosphere of spontaneous friendliness, are fundamentally terrifying. *Citizen Kane* is the first film to depict them with some sense of that truth.

In general, the film sustains its vast argument. There are shots of admirable depth, shots whose deep planes are as precise and to the point as their immediate ones, as in the draperies of the Pre-Raphaelites.

I venture to suggest, however, that *Citizen Kane* will last as certain films of Griffith or Pudovkin "last"; nobody denies their worth, but nobody goes back to see them. They suffer from gigantism, from pedantry, from tedium. *Citizen Kane* is less intelligent than agreeable, genial, in the darkest and most Germanic sense of that dubious word.

DR. JEKYLL AND EDWARD HYDE, TRANSFORMED [JLB 43]

Hollywood has, for the third time, defamed Robert Louis Stevenson. This defamation is entitled *Dr. Jekyll and Mr. Hyde* and it was perpetrated by Victor Fleming who repeats the esthetic and moral errors of Mamoulian's version (or perversion) with unfortunate fidelity. In the 1886 novel, Dr. Jekyll is morally dual, as are all men, while his hypostasis—Edward Hyde—is wicked through and through. In the 1941 film, Dr. Jekyll is a young pathologist who practices chastity, while his hypostasis—Hyde—is a rake with sadistic and acrobatic tendencies. The Good, for Hollywood thinkers, is betrothal to the well-bred, well-heeled Miss Lana Turner; Evil (which so preoccupied David Hume and the heresiarchs of Alexandria) is illicit cohabitation with Fröken Ingrid Bergman or Miriam Hopkins. It is useless to observe that Stevenson is wholly innocent of this limitation or deformation of the problem. In the final chapter of the work he states Jekyll's defects: sensuality and hypocrisy. In 1888, in one of the *Ethical Studies,* he attempts to enumerate "all the manifestations of the truly diabolic" and proposes this list: "envy, malice, lies, mean silence, libellous truths, the slanderer, the petty tyrant, the querulous poisoner of domestic life." (I would contend that ethics do not encompass sexual matters unless they are contaminated by treason, covetousness, or vanity.)

The structure of the film is even more rudimentary than its theology. In the book, the identity of Jekyll and Hyde is a surprise; the author saves it for the end of the ninth chapter. The allegorical narration feigns to be a detective story. No reader guesses that Hyde and Jekyll are the same person; even the title makes us postulate that they are two. Nothing would be easier than transferring this approach to the cinema. Let us imagine a case for the police: two actors, recognizable to the public, will figure in the plot (let us say, George Raft and Spencer Tracy). They can use analogous words; they can mention facts that presuppose a common past; when the problem becomes undecipherable, one of them imbibes the magic drug and changes into the other. (Of course, the satisfactory execution of this plan would involve two or three phonetic readjustments: the modification of the names of the protagonists.) More civilized than I, Victor Fleming manages to avoid all surprise and all mystery. In the opening scenes of the film, Spencer Tracy fearlessly downs the versatile potion and is transformed into Spencer Tracy with a different wig and negroid features.

Going beyond Stevenson's dualistic parable and approaching *The Colloquy of the Birds,* which was composed (in the twelfth century of our age) by Farid ud-din Attar, we can conceive of a pantheistic film whose numerous characters are resolved finally in the One, which is everlasting.

I see that the fourteenth edition of the *Encyclopaedia Britannica* has omitted the article about John Wilkins. The omission is justified if we remember how trivial it was (twenty lines of biographical data: Wilkins was born in 1614, Wilkins died in 1672, Wilkins was the chaplain of the Prince Palatine, Charles Louis; Wilkins was appointed rector of one of the colleges of Oxford; Wilkins was the first secretary of the Royal Society of London, etc.); but not if we consider the speculative work of Wilkins. He abounded in happy curiosities: he was interested in theology, cryptography, music, the manufacture of transparent beehives, the course of an invisible planet, the possibility of a trip to the moon, the possibility and the principles of a world language. It was to this last problem that he dedicated the book *An Essay Towards a Real Character and a Philosophical Language* (600 pages in quarto, 1668). Our National Library does not have a copy of that book. To write this article I have consulted *The Life and Times of John Wilkins* by P. A. Wright Henderson (1910), the *Wörterbuch der Philosophie* by Fritz Mauthner (1924), *Delphos* by E. Sylvia Pankhurst (1935), and *Dangerous Thoughts* by Lancelot Hogben (1939).

At one time or another, we have all suffered through those unappealable debates in which a lady, with copious interjections and anacoluthia, swears that the word "luna" is more (or less) expressive than the word "moon." Apart from the self-evident observation that the monosyllable "moon" may be more appropriate to represent a very simple object than the disyllabic word "luna," nothing can be contributed to such discussions. After the compound words and derivatives have been taken away, all the languages in the world (not excluding Johann Martin Schleyer's *volapük* and Peano's romancelike *interlingua*) are equally inexpressive. There is no edition of the Royal Spanish Academy *Grammar* that does not ponder "the envied treasure of picturesque, happy and expressive words in the very rich Spanish language," but that is merely an uncorroborated boast. Every few years the Royal Academy issues a dictionary to define Spanish expressions. In the universal language conceived by Wilkins around the middle of the seventeenth century each word defines itself. Descartes had already noted in a letter dated November 1629 that by using the decimal system of numeration we could learn in a single day to name all quantities to infinity, and to write them in a new language, the language of numbers.[1] He also proposed the formation of a similar, general language that would organize and contain all human thought. Around 1664 John Wilkins began to undertake that task.

Wilkins divided the universe into forty categories or classes, which were then subdivisible into differences, subdivisible in turn into species. To each class he assigned a monosyllable of two letters; to each difference, a consonant; to each species, a vowel. For example, *de* means element; *deb,* the first of the elements,

---

[1]Theoretically, the number of systems of numeration is unlimited. The most complex (for the use of divinities and angels) would record an infinite number of symbols, one for each whole number; the simplest requires only two. Zero is written o, one 1, two 10, three 11, four 100, five 101, six 110, seven 111, eight 1000. . . . It is the invention of Leibniz, who was apparently stimulated by the enigmatic hexagrams of the Yi tsing.

fire; *deba,* a portion of the element of fire, a flame. In a similar language invented by Letellier (1850) *a* means animal; *ab,* mammalian; *abi,* herbivorous; *abiv,* equine; *abo,* carnivorous; *aboj,* feline; *aboje,* cat; etc. In the language of Bonifacio Sotos Ochando (1845) *imaba* means building; *imaca,* brothel; *imafe,* hospital; *imafo,* pesthouse; *imari,* house; *imaru,* country estate; *imede,* pillar; *imedo,* post; *imego,* floor; *imela,* ceiling; *imogo,* window; *bire,* bookbinder, *birer,* to bind books. (I found this in a book published in Buenos Aires in 1886: the *Curso de lengua universal* by Dr. Pedro Mata.)

The words of John Wilkins's analytical language are not stupid arbitrary symbols; every letter is meaningful, as the letters of the Holy Scriptures were meaningful for the Cabalists. Mauthner observes that children could learn Wilkins's language without knowing that it was artificial; later, in school, they would discover that it was also a universal key and a secret encyclopedia.

After defining Wilkins's procedure, one must examine a problem that is impossible or difficult to postpone: the meaning of the fortieth table, on which the language is based. Consider the eighth category, which deals with stones. Wilkins divides them into the following classifications: ordinary (flint, gravel, slate); intermediate (marble, amber, coral); precious (pearl, opal); transparent (amethyst, sapphire); and insoluble (coal, clay, and arsenic). The ninth category is almost as alarming as the eighth. It reveals that metals can be imperfect (vermilion, quicksilver); artificial (bronze, brass); recremental (filings, rust); and natural (gold, tin, copper). The whale appears in the sixteenth category: it is a viviparous, oblong fish. These ambiguities, redundancies, and deficiencies recall those attributed by Dr. Franz Kuhn to a certain Chinese encyclopedia entitled *Celestial Emporium of Benevolent Knowledge.* On those remote pages it is written that animals are divided into (a) those that belong to the emperor, (b) embalmed ones, (c) those that are trained, (d) suckling pigs, (e) mermaids, (f) fabulous ones, (g) stray dogs, (h) those that are included in this classification, (i) those that tremble as if they were mad, (j) innumerable ones, (k) those drawn with a very fine camel's-hair brush, (l) others, (m) those that have just broken a flower vase, (n) those that resemble flies from a distance. The Bibliographical Institute of Brussels also resorts to chaos: it has parceled the universe into 1000 subdivisions: number 262 corresponds to the pope; number 282, to the Roman Catholic Church; number 263, to the Lord's Day; number 268, to Sunday schools; number 298, to Mormonism; and number 294, to Brahmanism, Buddhism, Shintoism, and Taoism. It also tolerates heterogeneous subdivisions, for example, number 179: "Cruelty to animals. Protection of animals. Moral implications of duelling and suicide. Various vices and defects. Various virtues and qualities."

I have noted the arbitrariness of Wilkins, of the unknown (or apocryphal) Chinese encyclopedist, and of the Bibliographical Institute of Brussels; obviously there is no classification of the universe that is not arbitrary and conjectural. The reason is very simple: we do not know what the universe is. "This world," wrote David Hume, ". . . was only the first rude essay of some infant deity who afterwards abandoned it, ashamed of his lame performance; it is the work only of some dependent, inferior deity, and is the object of derision to his superiors; it is the production of old age and dotage in some superannuated deity, and ever since his death has run on . . ." (*Dialogues Concerning Natural Religion,* V, 1779). We must go even further; we must suspect that there is no universe in the organic, unifying sense inherent in that ambitious word. If there is, we must conjecture its purpose; we must conjecture the words, the definitions, the etymologies, the synonymies of God's secret dictionary.

But the impossibility of penetrating the divine scheme of the universe cannot dissuade us from outlining human schemes, even though we are aware that they are provisional. Wilkins's analytical language is not the least admirable of those schemes. It is composed of classes and species that are contradictory and vague; its device of using the letters of the words to indicate divisions and subdivisions is, without a doubt, ingenious. The word "salmon" does not tell us anything about the object it represents; "zana," the corresponding word, defines (for the person versed in the forty categories and the classes of those categories) a scaly river fish with reddish flesh. (Theoretically, a language in which the name of each being would indicate all the details of its destiny, past and future, is not inconceivable.)

Hopes and utopias aside, these words by Chesterton are perhaps the most lucid ever written about language:

> Man knows that there are in the soul tints more bewildering, more num-
> berless, and more nameless than the colours of an autumn forest; . . . Yet
> he seriously believes that these things can every one of them, in all their
> tones and semi-tones, in all their blends and unions, be accurately repre-
> sented by an arbitrary system of grunts and squeals. He believes that an
> ordinary civilized stockbroker can really produce out of his own inside
> noises which denote all the mysteries of memory and all the agonies of
> desire. *(G. F. Watts,* 1904, page 88)

ALMAFUERTE

[JLB 45]

Slightly more than half a century ago, a young man from Entre Ríos, who used to come to our house every Sunday, recited to us in the study, underneath the bluish globes of gas, an almost endless and certainly incomprehensible string of verse. That friend of my parents was a poet and the theme he customarily favored was that of poor slum dwellers, but the poem which he recited to us that evening was not his own work and it somehow seemed to envelop the entire universe. It would not surprise me if the circumstances I have enumerated are mistaken; perhaps instead of Sunday it was Saturday and electric lights had already replaced gas. What I am certain about is the brusque revelation afforded me by that verse. Until that evening, language had been nothing more to me than a means of communication, a tedious mechanism of signs; the poetry of Almafuerte which Evaristo Carriego recited to us revealed that it could also be music, passion, and illusion. Housman has written that poetry is something we feel physically, with our flesh and blood; I owe my first experience of that curious, magic fever to

Almafuerte. With time, other poets and other languages darkened and distorted him; Hugo was erased by Whitman and Liliencron by Yeats, yet I have remembered Almafuerte on the banks of the Guadalquivir and the Rodano.

Almafuerte's defects are evident and they border on parody in any given moment; what cannot be doubted is his inexplicable poetic force. This paradox, this intimate problem which is manifest through an occasionally vulgar form, has always interested me; among the works that I have never written or will write, but that somehow justify me, even in an illusory or ideal way, is one which would be befittingly entitled "Theory on Almafuerte." Rough drafts in a past style prove that such a hypothetical book has visited me since 1932. It contains one hundred pages at the most; imagining it any longer would make it seem unnecessarily unreal. No one should regret that it does not exist or that it only exists in the immobile, strange world formed by possible objects; the summary I will now outline can be compared to the memory of an extensive book after a number of years. Moreover, its condition as an unwritten book is singularly to its advantage; the subject examined deals less with an author's style than with his spirit, less with a work's denotation than with its connotation. The general theory on Almafuerte is preceded by a particular conjecture about Pedro Bonifacio Palacios. The theory (I hasten to affirm) can do without the conjecture.

It is well known that Palacios, all during his long life, was a chaste man. The love and happiness common to other men seem to have aroused within him a sort of sacred horror, which assumed the form of contempt or severe reprobation. The reader can verify this point by consulting Bonastre's polemic work (*Almafuerte*, 1920) and the refutation (*Almafuerte y Zoilo*, 1920) which Antonio Herrero penned. Moreover, Almafuerte's own personal testimony is more valid than any discussion; let us read the final lines from the first poem he wrote, entitled "In the Abyss":

> I am such a one
> of whom you must speak ill,
> because you will have to dwell
> in endless humiliation.
> I am the soul, the vision,
> brother of Lucifer;
> like him, I rant and swear.
> I share his impotence,
> and on my countenance
> the laurel's curse I wear!
>
> I am a thistle planted
> in rubble and quicklime,
> the flowering of pride,
> pride at its most sublime.
> I am a spore cast down
> behind the starred parade,
> wretched bird of the yard
> that flies where the eagle flies . . .

Shadow's shadow that cries
to be an immortal shade!

And every time that I laugh,
I think it is someone else,
and as if I were taming a horse,
I don't treat myself as myself.
I am the very void,
infertile and rigid,
like that dust-desert
where all the grass dies . . .
I'm a dead man who tries
not to be taken for dead!

Obviously more important than the misfortune declared in the foregoing verses is the valiant acceptance of that misfortune. Others—Boileau, Kropotkin, Swift—were familiar with the loneliness which surrounded Palacios; no one has conceived, as he has, a general doctrine of frustration, a vindication, and a mysticism. I have pointed out Almafuerte's central loneliness; he managed to convince himself wholly that failure was not one of his stigmas, but rather the substantial and final destiny of all mankind. Thus he has left in writing: "Man's happiness has never entered into God's plan" and "Do not ask for more than justice, though it is better not to ask for anything" and "Despise everything, for everything is aware of its despicable condition."[1] Almafuerte's pure pessimism exceeds the limits of Ecclesiastes and Marcus Aurelius; the latter two revile the world, but they praise and admire a righteous man, he who identifies himself with God. Not so Almafuerte, for whom virtue is a chance consequence of universal forces:

I shunned the lucky man, the potentate,
the honest, the harmonious, the robust,
because I thought they had been touched by fate,
as any lucky poker-player must!

the Missionary tells us.

Spinoza condemned repentance, judging it to be a form of sadness; Almafuerte, forgiveness. He condemned it because there is something pedantic about it, something of holier-than-thou condescension, of fear of the final judgment given to one man by another:

When the Son of God, Ineffable,
pardoned, out of Golgotha, the perverse,
He spread the most unimaginable wrong
across the whole face of the Universe!

---

[1]Blake had similarly written: "As air for the bird and sea for the fish, thus contempt for the contemptible." *Marriage of Heaven and Hell,* 1793.

Even more explicit are these two lines:

> I am not the Christ-God who forgives you.
> Better than that: I am the Christ who loves you!

Almafuerte, in order to demonstrate complete compassion, would have liked to be as dark as a blind man, as useless as a cripple, and—why not?—as infamous as a villain. We have already said that he felt frustration was the final goal of all destiny; the more beaten down the man, the taller he stands; the more insignificant, the more he resembles this world, which is certainly not moral. Thus he could sincerely write:

> I worshiped, since I like servility,
> that One who in the end fell from grace,
> the unredeemable cross of clay he bore,
> the lightless night that covered his abyss.

In another section from the same poem, he says of a murderer:

> Where does he hide his wolf's excitement?
> Where does he ply his tragic energy?
> He gives me the position of a lookout
> while he plots out his crime and robbery!

From the poem "God Bless," which outlines or prefigures this same idea, it suffices me to copy the final lines:

> To him who suffers night and day,
> and in the night until sleep comes
> the sense of his own misery,
> the great cross of his sufferings—
> I bow to him, I bend my knee,
> I kiss his feet, I say "God bless!"
> Black Christ, rank saint, and Job within,
> the infamous cup of Bitterness!

Almafuerte should have been born in an adverse period of time. During the early Christian era, in Asia Minor or Alexandria, he would have been the leader of a heresy, a dreamer of secret redemptions, and a weaver of magic formulas; during a totally barbaric age, a prophet of shepherds and warriors, an Antonio Conselheiro,[2] a Mohammed; during a totally civilized age, a Butler or a Nietzsche. Fate placed him in the suburbs of the province of Buenos Aires; it reduced him to the years 1854–1917; it surrounded him with dirt, dust, alleyways, wooden shacks, committees, peers who were ignorant at best. He read very little and also read too much; he often perused verses of Cipriano de Valera's version of the

---

[2] Euclydes da Cunha (*Os sertoes*, 1902) narrates that for Conselheiro, prophet of the northern *sertanejos*, virtue "was a superior reflection of vanity, almost an unrighteousness." Almafuerte would have shared that opinion. On the eve of a desperate battle, T. E. Lawrence (*Seven Pillars of Wisdom*, LXXIV) preached to the tribe of the area of the serahin a vindication of defeat and failure, identical to that already given by Almafuerte.

Scriptures, but also Parliamentary debates and exhaustive articles. In South America during those years, there were only two possibilities—that of catechism, with its three-in-one divinity and its ecclesiastical hierarchy, and the black labyrinth of blind atoms joined together throughout all eternity, as was taught by Büchner and Spencer. Almafuerte chose the latter; he was a mystic without a God and without faith. He despised what Bernard Shaw called "heaven's corruptness"; he honestly believed that happiness was undesirable. His opinions lie waiting in the dark corners of his work, for example, in this doctrine: "The perfect state of man is a state of anxiety, of longing, of infinite sadness."

Federico de Onís *(Anthology of Spanish and Hispanic-American Poetry,* 1934) has stated that Almafuerte's ideology is vulgar. This prologue attempts to prove just the opposite. A number of Argentine writers produce a rhetoric no less splendid than his and obviously more lucid and constant, yet no one is more intellectually complex; no one has rejuvenated, as he has, the themes of ethics.

The Argentine poet is a craftsman or, better yet, an artisan; his labor corresponds to a decision, not to a necessity. Almafuerte, on the other hand, is organic, as Sarmiento was, as Lugones very seldom was. His deformities are in plain sight, yet his zeal and conviction redeem him.

ON THE ORIGINS OF THE DETECTIVE STORY [JLB 46]

ROGER CAILLOIS: *Le roman policier.* (Editions des Lettres Françaises, Buenos Aires: 1941). I do not believe in history; I know nothing of sociology; I do believe I understand something of literature, since I discover in myself no other passion than that of letters, and almost no other exercise. In Caillois's monograph, the literary aspect (judgments, summaries, censures, approbations) seems to me to be very sound; the historical-sociological aspect, very unconvincing. (I have already stated my limitations.)

On page 14 of his treatise, Caillois attempts to derive the *roman policier* from concrete circumstances: Fouché's anonymous spies, the horror of the idea of disguised and ubiquitous policemen. He mentions Balzac's novel, *Une tenebreuse affaire,* and Gaboriau's serialized stories. He adds, "The exact chronology is not important." If exact chronology were important, it would not be unwarranted to recall that *Une tenebreuse affaire* (a work that vaguely prefigures the detective novels of our time) dates from 1841, that is to say the year in which *The Murders in the Rue Morgue*—a perfect specimen of its genre—appeared. As for the "precursor" Gaboriau—his first novel, *L'affaire Lerouge,* dates from 1863—it is more likely that the prehistory of the detective genre is found in the mental habits and irretrievable *Erlebnisse* of Edgar Allan Poe, its inventor, not in the aversion produced toward 1799 by Fouché's *agents provocateurs.*

Another minor objection: Caillois is too willing to believe in the probity of the individuals of the Crime Club. He judges them by the code drawn up by Miss Dorothy L. Sayers . . . which amounts to judging the premiere of a film by the hyperboles of the program, toothpaste by the statements on the tube, or the Argentine government by the Argentine constitution. Nicholas Blake and Milard Kennedy belong to the Crime Club; other more alarming individuals are J. J. Connington, Carter Dickson, and the aforementioned Miss Sayers. The first, in order to enrich literature, resorts to ballistics, toxicology, dactyloscopy, tattooing, agoraphobia, and diseases of the skin; the second, in order to elucidate a crime perpetrated in an elevator, perpetrates a suicidal pistol that, having fired its fatal shot, falls modestly into pieces; the third has contributed to an anthology of works by Stevenson and Chesterton, Hawthorne and Wilkie Collins, a personal story whose plot I will not keep from the reader. A man meets up with himself in two or three tragic circumstances. Alarmed by this duplication, he turns to the opportune detective, Lord Peter Wimsey. The aristocrat arrives at the ingenious truth: a twin brother.

Oscar Wilde has observed that rondeaus and triolets prevent literature from being at the mercy of genius. At this point one could observe the same of detective fiction. Whether mediocre or awful, the detective story is never without a beginning, a plot, and a dénouement. The literature of our time is exhausted by interjections and opinions, incoherences and confidences; the detective story represents order and the obligation to invent. Roger Caillois skillfully analyzes its role as rational game, lucid game.

I have read (and written) many pages on the detective genre. None seems as precise as these by Caillois. I do not exclude the excellent treatise by Francois Fosca, *Histoire et technique du roman policier* (Paris, 1937).

MELVILLE   [JLB 47]

In the winter of 1851 Melville published *Moby-Dick,* the infinite novel that brought about his fame. The story grows page by page until it assumes the dimensions of the cosmos: at the beginning the reader might consider the subject to be the miserable life of whale harpooners; then, that the subject is the madness of Captain Ahab, bent on pursuing and destroying the white whale; finally, that the whale and Ahab and the pursuit which exhausts the oceans of the planet are symbols and mirrors of the universe. To insinuate that the book is symbolic, Melville declares emphatically that it is not and that no one should "scout at Moby-Dick as a monstrous fable or, still worse and more detestable, a hideous and intolerable allegory" (*Moby-Dick,* chapter 45). The usual connotation of the word "allegory" seems to have confused the critics; they all prefer to limit themselves to a moral interpretation of the work. Thus, E. M. Forster (*Aspects of the Novel,* chapter 7) summarizes the spiritual theme as, more or less, the following: "a battle against evil conducted too long or in the wrong way." I agree, but the symbol of the whale is less apt to suggest that the cosmos is evil than to suggest its vast inhumanity, its beastly or enigmatic stupidity. In some of his stories, Chesterton compares the atheists' universe to a centerless labyrinth. Such is the universe of *Moby-Dick:* a cosmos (a chaos) not only perceptibly malignant as the Gnostics had intuited, but also irrational, like the cosmos of the Lucretian hexameters.

Moby-Dick is written in a romantic dialect of English, a vehement dialect which alternates or conjugates the procedures of Shakespeare, Thomas De Quincey, Browne, and Carlyle; "Bartleby," in a calm and evenly jocular language deliberately applied to an atrocious subject, seems to foreshadow Kafka. There is, however, a secret and central affinity between both fictions. Ahab's monomania troubles and finally destroys all the men on board; Bartleby's candid nihilism contaminates his companions and even the stolid gentleman who tells his tale and endorses his imaginary tasks. Melville seems to be saying, "It's enough for one man to be irrational for others and the universe itself to be so as well." Universal history prolifically confirms that terror.

"Bartleby" belongs to the volume titled *The Piazza Tales* (New York and London, 1896). One of its readers, John Freeman, observed that "Bartleby" would not be fully understood until Joseph Conrad published certain analogous pieces almost a half-century later; I would remark that Kafka's work casts a curious ulterior light on "Bartleby." Melville's story already defines a genre which, around 1919, Franz Kafka would reinvent and further explore: the fantasies of behavior and feelings or, as they are now wrongly called, psychological tales. Furthermore, the first pages of "Bartleby" are not anticipations of Kafka but rather allude to or repeat Dickens. . . . In 1849 Melville published *Mardi,* an inextricable and almost illegible novel, with an essential plot, however, that prefigures the obsessions and mechanism of *The Castle, The Trial*, and *Amerika:* the subject is an infinite chase on an infinite sea.

I have stated Melville's affinities with other writers. But this is not to demean his achievements. I am following one of the laws of description or definition, that of relating the unknown to the known. Melville's greatness is unquestionable, but his glory is recent. Melville died in 1891; twenty years after his death the eleventh edition of the *Encyclopaedia Britannica* considers him a mere chronicler of sea life; Lang and George Saintsbury, in 1922 and 1914, fully ignore him in their histories of English literature. Afterward he was rediscovered by Lawrence of Arabia and D. H. Lawrence, Waldo Frank and Lewis Mumford. In 1921 Raymond Weaver published the first American monograph: *Herman Melville, Mariner and Mystic;* John Freeman, in 1926, the critical biography *Herman Melville.*

Vast populations, towering cities, erroneous and clamorous publicity have conspired to make unknown great men one of America's traditions. Edgar Allan Poe was one of these men; so was Melville.

CONJECTURAL POEM [JLB 48]

Dr. Francisco Laprida,
assassinated September 22, 1829,
by the irregulars of Aldao,
reflects before he dies:

The bullets whine on the last afternoon.
The wind is up, and full of ashes,
dispersing the day and the formless
war, and victory belongs to them,
to the barbarians: the gauchos have won.
And Francisco Narciso de Laprida, I,
who studied canon law and civil,
whose voice declared the independence
of these harsh provinces, am overthrown,
covered with blood and sweat,
without fear or hope, lost,
fleeing south through the farthest outskirts.
I'm like that captain in *Purgatorio*
fleeing afoot and leaving a trail of blood,
blinded and felled by death
where a dark river loses its name:
that's the way I'll fall. Today's the end.
The lateral night of the plains
lies in ambush to waylay me. I hear the hoofs
of my own hot death, searching me out,
I longed to be something else, a man of
sentiments, books, judgment,
and now will lie in a swamp under the open sky.
And yet, a secret joy inexplicably
exalts me. I've met my destiny,
my final South American destiny.
The manifold labyrinth my steps
wove through all these years since childhood
has brought me to this ruinous afternoon.
Now at this last point I find
the recondite code and cipher to my days,
the fate of Francisco de Laprida,
the missing letter, the perfect
form known to God from the start.
In the mirror of this night I find
the unexpected mien of my eternity.
The circle's closing. Thus may it be.
My feet are treading the shadows of pikes
pointed at me. The taunts of death,
the riders, the horses and their manes
are circling around me, hovering, the first
blow of the hard iron to rip at my chest,
the intimate knife at my throat . . .

So the Platonic Year
Whirls out new right and wrong,
Whirls in the old instead;
All men are dancers and their tread
Goes to the barbarous clangour of a gong.
—W. B. Yeats, *The Tower*

Under the influence of the flagrant Chesterton (contriver and embellisher of
elegant mysteries) and of the court counsellor Leibniz (who invented preestab-
lished harmony), I have imagined the following argument, which I shall doubtless
develop (and which already justifies me in some way), on profitless afternoons.
Details, revisions, adjustments are lacking; there are areas of this history which
are not yet revealed to me; today, January 3, 1944, I dimly perceive it thus:

The action transpires in some oppressed and stubborn country: Poland,
Ireland, the republic of Venice, some state in South America or the Balkans.
. . . *Has transpired,* we should say, for although the narrator is contemporary,
the narrative related by him occurred toward the middle or beginning of the
nineteenth century. Let us say, for purposes of narration, that it was in Ireland,
in 1824. The narrator is named Ryan; he is a great-grandson of the young, heroic,
handsome, assassinated Fergus Kilpatrick, whose sepulcher was mysteriously
violated, whose name embellishes the verse of Browning and Hugo, whose statue
presides over a gray hill amid red moors.

Kilpatrick was a conspirator, a secret and glorious captain of conspirators; he
was like Moses in that, from the land of Moab, he descried the Promised Land but
would not ever set foot there, for he perished on the eve of the victorious rebellion
which he had premeditated and conjured. The date of the first centenary of his
death draws near; the circumstances of the crime are enigmatic; Ryan, engaged in
compiling a biography of the hero, discovers that the enigma goes beyond the
purely criminal. Kilpatrick was assassinated in a theater; the English police could
find no trace of the killer; historians declare that the failure of the police does not in
any way impugn their good intentions, for he was no doubt killed by order of those
same police. Other phases of the enigma disquiet Ryan. These facets are of cyclic
character: they seem to repeat or combine phenomena from remote regions, from
remote ages. Thus, there is no one who does not know that the bailiffs who
examined the hero's cadaver discovered a sealed letter which warned him of the
risk of going to the theater on that particular night: Julius Caesar, too, as he walked
toward the place where the knives of his friends awaited him, was handed a
message, which he never got to the point of reading, in which the treason was
declared, and the names of the traitors given. In her dreams, Caesar's wife,
Calpurnia, saw a tower, which the senate had dedicated to her husband, fallen to
the ground; false and anonymous rumors throughout the land were occasioned, on
the eve of Kilpatrick's death, by the burning of the round tower of Kilgarvan—an
event which might have seemed an omen, since Kilpatrick had been born at
Kilgarvan. These parallels (and others) in the history of Caesar and the history of

an Irish conspirator induce Ryan to assume a secret pattern in time, a drawing in which the lines repeat themselves. He ponders the decimal history imagined by Condorcet; the morphologies proposed by Hegel, Spengler, and Vico; the characters of Hesiod, who degenerate from gold to iron. He considers the transmigration of souls, a doctrine which horrifies Celtic belles lettres and which the very same Caesar attributed to the Britannic Druids; he thinks that before the hero was Fergus Kilpatrick, Fergus Kilpatrick was Julius Caesar. From these circular labyrinths he is saved by a curious species of proof which immediately plunges him into other labyrinths even more inextricable and heterogeneous: certain words spoken by a mendicant who conversed with Fergus Kilpatrick on the day of his death were prefigured in the tragedy of *Macbeth*. That history should have imitated history was already sufficiently marvelous; that history should imitate literature is inconceivable. . . .

Ryan discovers that in 1814, James Alexander Nolan, the oldest of the hero's comrades, had translated into Gaelic the principal dramas of Shakespeare, among them *Julius Caesar*. In the archives he also finds a manuscript article by Nolan on *Festspiele* of Switzerland: vast and roving theatrical representations these, which require thousands of actors and which reiterate historic episodes in the same cities and mountains where they occurred. Still another unpublished document reveals that a few days before the end, Kilpatrick, presiding over his last conclave, had signed the death sentence of a traitor, whose name has been blotted out. This sentence scarcely harmonizes with Kilpatrick's pious attitude. Ryan goes deeper into the matter (the investigation covers one of the hiatuses in the argument) and he succeeds in solving the enigma.

Kilpatrick was brought to his end in a theater, but he made of the entire city a theater, too, and the actors were legion. And the drama which was climaxed by his death embraced many days and many nights. Here is what happened:

On August 2, 1824, the conspirators gathered. The country was ripe for rebellion. But somehow every attempt always failed: there was a traitor in the group. Fergus Kilpatrick ordered James Nolan to uncover this traitor. Nolan carried out his orders: before the gathering as a whole, he announced that the traitor was Kilpatrick himself. He demonstrated the truth of his accusation with irrefutable proofs; the conspirators condemned their president to death. The latter signed his own death sentence; but he implored that his condemnation not be allowed to hurt the fatherland.

Nolan thereupon conceived his strange project. Ireland idolized Kilpatrick; the most tenuous suspicion of his disgrace would have compromised the rebellion; Nolan proposed a plan which would make Kilpatrick's execution an instrument for the liberation of the fatherland. He suggested the condemned man die at the hands of an unknown assassin, in circumstances deliberately dramatic, which would engrave themselves upon the popular imagination and which would speed the revolt. Kilpatrick swore to collaborate in a project which allowed him the opportunity to redeem himself and which would add a flourish to his death.

Pressed for time, Nolan was unable to integrate the circumstances he invented for the complex execution; he was forced to plagiarize another dramatist, the enemy-Englishman William Shakespeare. He repeated scenes from *Macbeth,* and from *Julius Caesar.* The public—and the secret—presentation took several days. The condemned man entered Dublin, discussed, worked, prayed, reproved, spoke words which seemed (later) to be pathetic—and each one of these acts, which would eventually be glorious, had been foreordained by Nolan. Hundreds of actors collaborated with the protagonist; the role of some was stellar, that of others ephemeral. What they said and did remains in the books of history, in the impassioned memory of Ireland. Kilpatrick, carried away by the minutely scrupulous destiny which redeemed and condemned him, more than once enriched the text (Nolan's text) with words and deeds of his own improvisation. And thus did the popular drama unfold in time, until, on August 6, 1824, in a theater box hung with funereal curtains, which foreshadowed Abraham Lincoln's, the anticipated pistol shot entered the breast of the traitor and hero, who could scarcely articulate, between two effusions of violent blood, some prearranged words.

In Nolan's work, the passages imitated from Shakespeare are the *least* dramatic; Ryan suspects that the author interpolated them so that one person, in the future, might realize the truth. He understands that he, too, forms part of Nolan's plan. . . . At the end of some tenacious caviling, he resolves to keep silent his discovery. He publishes a book dedicated to the glory of the hero; this, too, no doubt was foreseen.

A COMMENT ON AUGUST 23, 1944   [JLB 50]

That crowded day gave me three heterogeneous surprises: the *physical* happiness I experienced when they told me that Paris had been liberated; the discovery that a collective emotion can be noble; the enigmatic and obvious enthusiasm of many who were supporters of Hitler. I know that if I question that enthusiasm I may easily resemble those futile hydrographers who asked why a single ruby was enough to arrest the course of a river; many will accuse me of trying to explain a chimerical occurrence. Still, that was what happened and thousands of persons in Buenos Aires can bear witness to it.

From the beginning, I knew that it was useless to ask the people themselves. They are changeable; through their practice of incoherence they have lost every notion that incoherence should be justified: they venerate the German race, but they abhor "Saxon" America; they condemn the articles of Versailles, but they applaud the marvels of the Blitzkrieg; they are anti-Semitic, but they profess a religion of Hebrew origin; they laud submarine warfare, but they vigorously condemn acts of piracy by the British; they denounce imperialism, but they vindicate and promulgate the theory of *Lebensraum;* they idolize San Martín, but they regard the independence of America as a mistake; they apply the canon of Jesus to the acts of England, but the canon of Zarathustra to those of Germany.

I also reflected that every other uncertainty was preferable to the uncertainty of a dialogue with those siblings of chaos, who are exonerated from honor and piety by the infinite repetition of the interesting formula *I am Argentine.* And further, did Freud not reason and Walt Whitman not foresee that men have very little knowledge about the real motives for their conduct? Perhaps, I said to myself, the magic of the symbols *Paris* and *liberation* is so powerful that Hitler's partisans have forgotten that these symbols mean a defeat of his forces. Wearily, I chose to imagine that fickleness and fear and simple adherence to reality were the probable explanations of the problem.

Several nights later a book and a memory enlightened me. The book was Shaw's *Man and Superman;* the passage in question is the one about John Tanner's metaphysical dream, where it is stated that the horror of Hell is its unreality. That doctrine can be compared with the doctrine of another Irishman, Johannes Scotus Erigena, who denied the substantive existence of sin and evil and declared that all creatures, including the Devil, will return to God. The memory was of the day that is the exact and detested opposite of August 23, 1944: June 14, 1940. A certain Germanophile, whose name I do not wish to remember, came to my house that day. Standing in the doorway, he announced the dreadful news: the Nazi armies had occupied Paris. I felt a mixture of sadness, disgust, malaise. And then it occurred to me that his insolent joy did not explain the stentorian voice or the abrupt proclamation. He added that the German troops would soon be in London. Any opposition was useless, nothing could prevent their victory. That was when I knew that he too was terrified.

I do not know whether the facts I have related require elucidation. I believe I can interpret them like this: for Europeans and Americans, one order—and only one—is possible: it used to be called Rome and now it is called Western culture. To be a Nazi (to play the game of energetic barbarism, to play at being a Viking, a Tartar, a sixteenth-century conquistador, a gaucho, a redskin) is, after all, a mental and moral impossibility. Nazism suffers from unreality, like Erigena's hells. It is uninhabitable; men can only die for it, lie for it, kill and wound for it. No one, in the intimate depths of his being, can wish it to triumph. I shall hazard this conjecture: *Hitler wants to be defeated.* Hitler is collaborating blindly with the inevitable armies that will annihilate him, as the metal vultures and the dragon (which must not have been unaware that they were monsters) collaborated, mysteriously, with Hercules.

THE ALEPH [JLB 51]

O God! I could be bounded in a nutshell,
and count myself a King of infinite space. . . .
—*Hamlet,* II, 2

But they will teach us that Eternity is the Standing still of the Present Time, a *Nunc-stans* (as the Schools call it); which neither they, nor any else understand, no more than they would a *Hic-stans* for an Infinite greatness of Place.
—*Leviathan,* IV, 46

On the burning February morning Beatriz Viterbo died, after braving an agony that never for a single moment gave way to self-pity or fear, I noticed that the sidewalk billboards around Constitution Plaza were advertising some new brand or other of American cigarettes. The fact pained me, for I realized that the wide and ceaseless universe was already slipping away from her and that this slight change was the first of an endless series. The universe may change but not me, I thought with a certain sad vanity. I knew that at times my fruitless devotion had annoyed her; now that she was dead, I could devote myself to her memory, without hope but also without humiliation. I recalled that April 30th was her birthday; on that day to visit her house on Garay Street and pay my respects to her father and to Carlos Argentino Daneri, her first cousin, would be an irreproachable and perhaps unavoidable act of politeness. Once again I would wait in the twilight of the small, cluttered drawing room, once again I would study the details of her many photographs: Beatriz Viterbo in profile and in full color; Beatriz wearing a mask, during the Carnival of 1921; Beatriz at her first communion; Beatriz on the day of her wedding to Roberto Alessandri; Beatriz soon after her divorce, at a luncheon at the Turf Club; Beatriz at a seaside resort in Quilmes with Delia San Marco Porcel and Carlos Argentino; Beatriz with the Pekingese lapdog given her by Villegas Haedo; Beatriz, front and three-quarter views, smiling, hand on her chin. . . . I would not be forced, as in the past, to justify my presence with modest offerings of books—books whose pages I finally learned to cut beforehand, so as not to find out, months later, that they lay around unopened.

Beatriz Viterbo died in 1929. From that time on, I never let an April 30 go by without a visit to her house. I used to make my appearance at seven-fifteen sharp and stay on for some twenty-five minutes. Each year, I arrived a little later and stayed a little longer. In 1933, a torrential downpour coming to my aid, they were obliged to ask me to dinner. Naturally, I took advantage of that lucky precedent. In 1934, I arrived, just after eight, with one of those large Santa Fe sugared cakes, and quite matter-of-factly I stayed to dinner. It was in this way, on these melancholy and vainly erotic anniversaries, that I came into the gradual confidences of Carlos Argentino Daneri.

Beatriz had been tall, frail, slightly stooped; in her walk there was (if the oxymoron may be allowed) a kind of uncertain grace, a hint of expectancy. Carlos Argentino was pink-faced, overweight, gray-haired, fine-featured. He held a minor position in an unreadable library out on the edge of the Southside of Buenos Aires. He was authoritarian but also unimpressive. Until only recently, he took advantage of his nights and holidays to stay at home. At a remove of two generations, the Italian "s" and demonstrative Italian gestures still survived in him. His mental activity was continuous, deeply felt, far-ranging, and—all in all —meaningless. He dealt in pointless analogies and in trivial scruples. He had (as did Beatriz) large, beautiful, finely shaped hands. For several months he seemed to be obsessed with Paul Fort—less with his ballads than with the idea of a towering reputation. "He is the Prince of poets," Daneri would repeat fatuously. "You will belittle him in vain—but no, not even the most venomous of your shafts will graze him."

On April 30, 1941, along with the sugared cake I allowed myself to add a bottle of Argentine cognac. Carlos Argentino tasted it, pronounced it "interesting," and, after a few drinks, launched into a glorification of modern man.

"I view him," he said with a certain unaccountable excitement, "in his inner sanctum, as though in his castle tower, supplied with telephones, telegraphs, phonographs, wireless sets, motion-picture screens, slide projectors, glossaries, timetables, handbooks, bulletins. . . ."

He remarked that for a man so equipped, actual travel was superfluous. Our twentieth century had inverted the story of Mohammed and the mountain; nowadays, the mountain came to the modern Mohammed.

So foolish did his ideas seem to me, so pompous and so drawn out his exposition, that I linked them at once to literature and asked him why he didn't write them down. As might be foreseen, he answered that he had already done so—that these ideas, and others no less striking, had found their place in the Proem, or Augural Canto, or, more simply, the Prologue Canto of the poem on which he had been working for many years now, alone, without publicity, without fanfare, supported only by those twin staffs universally known as work and solitude. First, he said, he opened the floodgates of his fancy; then, taking up hand tools, he resorted to the file. The poem was entitled "The Earth"; it consisted of a description of the planet, and, of course, lacked no amount of picturesque digressions and bold apostrophes.

I asked him to read me a passage, if only a short one. He opened a drawer of his writing table, drew out a thick stack of papers—sheets of a large pad imprinted with the letterhead of the Juan Crisóstomo Lafinur Library—and, with ringing satisfaction, declaimed:

> Mine eyes, as did the Greek's, have known men's towns and fame,
> The works, the days in light that fades to amber;
> I do not change a fact or falsify a name—
> The *voyage* I set down is . . . *autour de ma chambre.*

"From any angle, a greatly interesting stanza," he said, giving his verdict. "The opening line wins the applause of the professor, the academician, and the Hellenist, to say nothing of the would-be scholar, a considerable sector of the public. The second flows from Homer to Hesiod (generous homage, at the very outset, to the father of didactic poetry), not without rejuvenating a process whose roots go back to Scripture—enumeration, congeries, conglomeration. The third —Baroque? decadent? example of the cult of pure form?—consists of two equal hemistichs. The fourth, frankly bilingual, assures me the unstinted backing of all minds sensitive to the pleasures of sheer fun. I should, in all fairness, speak of the novel rhyme in lines two and four, and of the erudition that allows me— without a hint of pedantry!—to cram into four lines three learned allusions covering thirty centuries packed with literature—first to the *Odyssey,* second to *Works and Days,* and third to the immortal bagatelle bequeathed us by the frolicking pen of the Savoyard, Xavier de Maistre. Once more I've come to realize that modern art demands the balm of laughter, the scherzo. Decidedly, Goldoni holds the stage!"

He read me many other stanzas, each of which also won his own approval and elicited his lengthy explications. There was nothing remarkable about them. I did not even find them any worse than the first one. Application, resignation, and chance had gone into the writing; I saw, however, that Daneri's real work lay not in the poetry but in his invention of reasons why the poetry should be admired. Of course, this second phase of his effort modified the writing in his eyes, though not in the eyes of others. Daneri's style of delivery was extravagant, but the deadly drone of his metric regularity tended to tone down and to dull that extravagance.[1]

Only once in my life have I had occasion to look into the 15,000 alexandrines of the *Poly-Olbion,* that topographical epic in which Michael Drayton recorded the flora, fauna, hydrography, orography, military and monastic history of England. I am sure, however, that this limited but bulky production is less boring than Carlos Argentino's similar vast undertaking. Daneri had in mind to set to verse the entire face of the planet, and, by 1941, had already dispatched a number of acres of the state of Queensland, nearly a mile of the course run by the River Ob, a gasworks to the north of Veracruz, the leading shops in the Buenos Aires parish of Concepción, the villa of Mariana Cambaceres de Alvear in the Belgrano section of the Argentine capital, and a Turkish baths establishment not far from the well-known Brighton aquarium. He read me certain long-winded passages from his Australian section, and at one point praised a word of his own coining, the color "celestewhite," which he felt "actually *suggests* the sky, an element of utmost importance in the landscape of the continent down under." But these sprawling, lifeless hexameters lacked even the relative excitement of the so-called Augural Canto. Along about midnight, I left.

Two Sundays later, Daneri rang me up—perhaps for the first time in his life. He suggested we get together at four o'clock "for cocktails in the saloon-bar next door, which the forward-looking Zunino and Zungri—my landlords, as you doubtless recall—are throwing open to the public. It's a place you'll really want to get to know."

More in resignation than in pleasure, I accepted. Once there, it was hard to find a table. The "saloon-bar," ruthlessly modern, was only barely less ugly than what I had expected; at the nearby tables, the excited customers spoke breathlessly of the sums Zunino and Zungri had invested in furnishings without a second thought to cost. Carlos Argentino pretended to be astonished by some feature or other of the lighting arrangement (with which, I felt, he was already familiar), and he said to me with a certain severity, "Grudgingly, you'll have to admit to the fact that these premises hold their own with many others far more in the public eye."

He then reread me four or five different fragments of the poem. He had revised them following his pet principle of verbal ostentation: where at first "blue" had been good enough, he now wallowed in "azures," "ceruleans," and "ultramarines." The word "milky" was too easy for him; in the course of an impassioned

---

[1] Among my memories are also some lines of a satire in which he lashed out unsparingly at bad poets. After accusing them of dressing their poems in the warlike armor of erudition, and of flapping in vain their unavailing wings, he concluded with this verse: "But they forget, alas, one foremost fact—BEAUTY!"
Only the fear of creating an army of implacable and powerful enemies dissuaded him (he told me) from fearlessly publishing this poem.

description of a shed where wool was washed, he chose such words as "lacteal," "lactescent," and even made one up—"lactinacious." After that, straight out, he condemned our modern mania for having books prefaced, "a practice already held up to scorn by the Prince of Wits in his own graceful preface to the *Quixote.*" He admitted, however, that for the opening of his new work an attention-getting foreword might prove valuable—"an accolade signed by a literary hand of renown." He next went on to say that he considered publishing the initial cantos of his poem. I then began to understand the unexpected telephone call; Daneri was going to ask me to contribute a foreword to his pedantic hodgepodge. My fear turned out unfounded; Carlos Argentino remarked, with admiration and envy, that surely he could not be far wrong in qualifying with the epithet "solid" the prestige enjoyed in every circle by Álvaro Melián Lafinur, a man of letters, who would, if I insisted on it, be only too glad to dash off some charming opening words to the poem. In order to avoid ignominy and failure, he suggested I make myself spokesman for two of the book's undeniable virtues—formal perfection and scientific rigor—"inasmuch as this wide garden of metaphors, of figures of speech, of elegances, is inhospitable to the least detail not strictly upholding of truth." He added that Beatriz had always been taken with Álvaro.

I agreed—agreed profusely—and explained for the sake of credibility that I would not speak to Álvaro the next day, Monday, but would wait until Thursday, when we got together for the informal dinner that follows every meeting of the Writers' Club. (No such dinners are ever held, but it is an established fact that the meetings do take place on Thursdays, a point which Carlos Argentino Daneri could verify in the daily papers, and which lent a certain reality to my promise.) Half in prophecy, half in cunning, I said that before taking up the question of a preface I would outline the unusual plan of the work. We then said goodbye.

Turning the corner of Bernardo de Irigoyen, I reviewed as impartially as possible the alternatives before me. They were: (a) to speak to Álvaro, telling him this first cousin of Beatriz's (the explanatory euphemism would allow me to mention her name) had concocted a poem that seemed to draw out into infinity the possibilities of cacophony and chaos; (b) not to say a word to Álvaro. I clearly foresaw that my indolence would opt for (b).

But first thing Friday morning, I began worrying about the telephone. It offended me that that device, which had once produced the irrecoverable voice of Beatriz, could now sink so low as to become a mere receptacle for the futile and perhaps angry remonstrances of that deluded Carlos Argentino Daneri. Luckily, nothing happened, except the inevitable spite touched off in me by this man, who had asked me to fulfill a delicate mission for him and then had let me drop.

Gradually, the phone came to lose its terrors, but one day toward the end of October it rang, and Carlos Argentino was on the line. He was deeply disturbed, so much so that at the outset I did not recognize his voice. Sadly but angrily he stammered that the now unrestrainable Zunino and Zungri, under the pretext of enlarging their already outsized "saloon-bar," were about to take over and tear down his house.

"My home, my ancestral home, my old and inveterate Garay Street home!" he kept repeating, seeming to forget his woe in the music of his words.

It was not hard for me to share his distress. After the age of fifty, all change becomes a hateful symbol of the passing of time. Besides, the scheme concerned a house that for me would always stand for Beatriz. I tried explaining this delicate scruple of regret, but Daneri seemed not to hear me. He said that if Zunino and Zungri persisted in this outrage, Doctor Zunni, his lawyer, would sue ipso facto and make them pay some $50,000 in damages.

Zunni's name impressed me; his firm, although at the unlikely address of Caseros and Tacuarí, was nonetheless known as an old and reliable one. I asked him whether Zunni had already been hired for the case. Daneri said he would phone him that very afternoon. He hesitated, then with that level, impersonal voice we reserve for confiding something intimate, he said that to finish the poem he could not get along without the house because down in the cellar there was an Aleph. He explained that an Aleph is one of the points in space that contains all other points.

"It's in the cellar under the dining room," he went on, so overcome by his worries now that he forgot to be pompous. "It's mine—mine. I discovered it when I was a child, all by myself. The cellar stairway is so steep that my aunt and uncle forbade my using it, but I'd heard someone say there was a world down there. I found out later they meant an old-fashioned globe of the world, but at the time I thought they were referring to the world itself. One day when no one was home I started down in secret, but I stumbled and fell. When I opened my eyes, I saw the Aleph."

"The Aleph?" I repeated.

"Yes, the only place on earth where all places are seen from every angle, each standing clear, without any confusion or blending. I kept the discovery to myself and went back every chance I got. As a child, I did not foresee that this privilege was granted me so that later I could write the poem. Zunino and Zungri will not strip me of what's mine—no, and a thousand times no! Legal code in hand, Dr. Zunni will prove that my Aleph is inalienable."

I tried to reason with him. "But isn't the cellar very dark?" I said.

"Truth cannot penetrate a closed mind. If all places in the universe are in the Aleph, then all stars, all lamps, all sources of light are in it, too."

"You wait there. I'll be right over to see it."

I hung up before he could say no. The full knowledge of a fact sometimes enables you to see all at once many supporting but previously unsuspected things. It amazed me not to have suspected until that moment that Carlos Argentino was a madman. As were all the Viterbos, when you came down to it. Beatriz (I myself often say it) was a woman, a child, with almost uncanny powers of clairvoyance, but forgetfulness, distractions, contempt, and a streak of cruelty were also in her, and perhaps these called for a pathological explanation. Carlos Argentino's madness filled me with spiteful elation. Deep down, we had always detested each other.

On Garay Street, the maid asked me kindly to wait. The master was, as usual, in the cellar developing pictures. On the unplayed piano, beside a large vase that held no flowers, smiled (more timeless than belonging to the past) the large photograph of Beatriz, in gaudy colors. Nobody could see us; in a seizure of tenderness, I drew close to the portrait and said to it, "Beatriz, Beatriz Elena, Beatriz Elena Viterbo, darling Beatriz, Beatriz now gone forever, it's me, it's Borges."

Moments later, Carlos came in. He spoke dryly. I could see he was thinking of nothing else but the loss of the Aleph.

"First a glass of pseudo-cognac," he ordered, "and then down you dive into the cellar. Let me warn you, you'll have to lie flat on your back. Total darkness, total immobility, and a certain ocular adjustment will also be necessary. From the floor, you must focus your eyes on the nineteenth step. Once I leave you, I'll lower the trapdoor and you'll be quite alone. You needn't fear the rodents very much—though I know you will. In a minute or two, you'll see the Aleph—the microcosm of the alchemists and Cabalists, our true proverbial friend, the *multum in parvo!*"

Once we were in the dining room, he added, "Of course, if you don't see it, your incapacity will not invalidate what I have experienced. Now, down you go. In a short while you can babble with *all* of Beatriz's images."

Tired of his inane words, I quickly made my way. The cellar, barely wider than the stairway itself, was something of a pit. My eyes searched the dark, looking in vain for the globe Carlos Argentino had spoken of. Some cases of empty bottles and some canvas sacks cluttered one corner. Carlos picked up a sack, folded it in two, and at a fixed spot spread it out.

"As a pillow," he said, "this is quite threadbare, but if it's padded even a half-inch higher, you won't see a thing, and there you'll lie, feeling ashamed and ridiculous. All right now, sprawl that hulk of yours there on the floor and count off nineteen steps."

I went through with his absurd requirements, and at last he went away. The trapdoor was carefully shut. The blackness, in spite of a chink that I later made out, seemed to me absolute. For the first time, I realized the danger I was in: I'd let myself be locked in a cellar by a lunatic, after gulping down a glassful of poison! I knew that back of Carlos's transparent boasting lay a deep fear that I might not see the promised wonder. To keep his madness undetected, to keep from admitting that he was mad, *Carlos had to kill me.* I felt a shock of panic, which I tried to pin to my uncomfortable position and not to the effect of a drug. I shut my eyes—I opened them. Then I saw the Aleph.

I arrive now at the ineffable core of my story. And here begins my despair as a writer. All language is a set of symbols whose use among its speakers assumes a shared past. How, then, can I translate into words the limitless Aleph, which my floundering mind can scarcely encompass? Mystics, faced with the same problem, fall back on symbols: to signify the godhead, one Persian speaks of a bird that somehow is all birds; Alanus de Insulis, of a sphere whose center is everywhere and circumference is nowhere; Ezekiel, of a four-faced angel who at one and the same time moves east and west, north and south. (Not in vain do I recall these inconceivable analogies; they bear some relation to the Aleph.) Perhaps the gods might grant me a similar metaphor, but then this account would

160

become contaminated by literature, by fiction. Really, what I want to do is impossible, for any listing of an endless series is doomed to be infinitesimal. In that single gigantic instant I saw millions of acts both delightful and awful; not one of them amazed me more than the fact that all of them occupied the same point in space, without overlapping or transparency. What my eyes beheld was simultaneous, but what I shall now write down will be successive, because language is successive. Nonetheless, I'll try to recollect what I can.

On the back part of the step, toward the right, I saw a small iridescent sphere of almost unbearable brilliance. At first I thought it was revolving; then I realized that this movement was an illusion created by the dizzying world it bounded. The Aleph's diameter was probably little more than an inch, but all space was there, actual and undiminished. Each thing (a mirror's face, let us say) was infinite things, since I distinctly saw it from every angle of the universe. I saw the teeming sea; I saw daybreak and nightfall; I saw the multitudes of America; I saw a silvery cobweb in the center of a black pyramid; I saw a splintered labyrinth (it was London); I saw, close up, unending eyes watching themselves in me as in a mirror; I saw all the mirrors on earth and none of them reflected me; I saw in a backyard of Soler Street the same tiles that thirty years before I'd seen in the entrance of a house in Fray Bentos; I saw bunches of grapes, snow, tobacco, lodes of metal, steam; I saw convex equatorial deserts and each one of their grains of sand; I saw a woman in Inverness whom I shall never forget; I saw her tangled hair, her tall figure, I saw the cancer in her breast; I saw a ring of baked mud in a sidewalk, where before there had been a tree; I saw a summer house in Adrogué and a copy of the first English translation of Pliny—Philemon Holland's—and all at the same time saw each letter on each page (as a boy, I used to marvel that the letters in a closed book did not get scrambled and lost overnight); I saw a sunset in Querétaro that seemed to reflect the color of a rose in Bengal; I saw my empty bedroom; I saw in a closet in Alkmaar a terrestrial globe between two mirrors that multiplied it endlessly; I saw horses with flowing manes on a shore of the Caspian Sea at dawn; I saw the delicate bone structure of a hand; I saw the survivors of a battle sending out picture postcards; I saw in a showcase in Mirzapur a pack of Spanish playing cards; I saw the slanting shadows of ferns on a greenhouse floor; I saw tigers, pistons, bison, tides, and armies; I saw all the ants on the planet; I saw a Persian astrolabe; I saw in the drawer of a writing table (and the handwriting made me tremble) unbelievable, obscene, detailed letters, which Beatriz had written to Carlos Argentino; I saw a monument I worshiped in the Chacarita cemetery; I saw the rotted dust and bones that had once deliciously been Beatriz Viterbo; I saw the circulation of my own dark blood; I saw the coupling of love and the modification of death; I saw the Aleph from every point and angle, and in the Aleph I saw the earth and in the earth the Aleph and in the Aleph the earth; I saw my own face and my own bowels; I saw your face; and I felt dizzy and wept, for my eyes had seen that secret and conjectured object whose name is common to all men but which no man has looked upon—the unimaginable universe.

I felt infinite wonder, infinite pity.

"Feeling pretty cockeyed, are you, after so much spying into places where you have no business?" said a hated and jovial voice. "Even if you were to rack your brains, you couldn't pay me back in a hundred years for this revelation. One hell of an observatory, eh, Borges?"

Carlos Argentino's feet were planted on the topmost step. In the sudden dim light, I managed to pick myself up and utter, "One hell of a—yes, one hell of a—"

The matter-of-factness of my voice surprised me. Anxiously, Carlos Argentino went on.

"Did you see everything—really clear, in colors?"

At that very moment I found my revenge. Kindly, openly pitying him, distraught, evasive, I thanked Carlos Argentino Daneri for the hospitality of his cellar and urged him to make the most of the demolition to get away from the pernicious metropolis, which spares no one—believe me, I told him, no one! Quietly and forcefully, I refused to discuss the Aleph. On saying goodbye, I embraced him and repeated that the country, fresh air, and quiet were the great physicians.

Out on the street, going down the stairways inside Constitution station, riding the subway, every one of the faces seemed familiar to me. I was afraid that not a single thing on earth would ever again surprise me; I was afraid I would never again be free of all I had seen. Happily, after a few sleepless nights, I was visited once more by oblivion.

POSTSCRIPT. MARCH 1, 1943.

Some six months after the pulling down of a certain building on Garay Street, Procrustes & Co., the publishers, not put off by the considerable length of Daneri's poem, brought out a selection of its "Argentine sections." It is redundant now to repeat what happened. Carlos Argentino Daneri won the Second National Prize for Literature.[2] First Prize went to Dr. Aita; Third Prize, to Dr. Mario Bonfanti. Unbelievably, my own book *The Sharper's Cards* did not get a single vote. Once again dullness and envy had their triumph! It's been some time now that I've been trying to see Daneri; the gossip is that a second selection of the poem is about to be published. His felicitous pen (no longer cluttered by the Aleph) has now set itself the task of writing an epic on our national hero, General San Martín.

I want to add two final observations: one, on the nature of the Aleph; the other, on its name. As is well known, the Aleph is the first letter of the Hebrew alphabet. Its use for the strange sphere in my story may not be accidental. For the Cabala, that letter stands for the *En Soph,* the pure and boundless godhead; it is also said that it takes the shape of a man pointing to both heaven and earth, in order to show that the lower world is the map and mirror of the higher; for Cantor's *Mengenlehre,* it is the symbol of transfinite numbers, of which any part is as great as the whole. I would like to know whether Carlos Argentino chose

---

[2] "I received your pained congratulations," he wrote me. "You rage, my poor friend, with envy, but you must confess—even if it chokes you!—that this time I have crowned my cap with the reddest of feathers; my turban with the most *caliph* of rubies."

162

that name or whether he read it—applied to another point where all points converge—in one of the numberless texts that the Aleph in his cellar revealed to him. Incredible as it may seem, I believe that the Aleph of Garay Street was a false Aleph.

Here are my reasons. Around 1867, Captain Burton held the post of British consul in Brazil. In July 1942 Pedro Henríquez Ureña came across a manuscript of Burton's, in a library at Santos, dealing with the mirror which the Oriental world attributes to Iskander Zu al-Karnayn, or Alexander Bicornis of Macedonia. In its crystal the whole world was reflected. Burton mentions other similar devices—the sevenfold cup of Kai Kosru; the mirror that Tariq ibn-Ziyad found in a tower (*1001 Nights*, 272); the mirror that Lucian of Samosata examined on the moon (*True History*, I, 26); the mirrorlike spear that the first book of Capella's *Satyricon* attributes to Jupiter; Merlin's universal mirror, which was "round and hollow . . . and seem'd a world of glas" (*The Faerie Queene*, III, 2, 19)—and adds this curious statement: "But the aforesaid objects (besides the disadvantage of not existing) are mere optical instruments. The Faithful who gather at the mosque of Amr, in Cairo, are acquainted with the fact that the entire universe lies inside one of the stone pillars that ring its central court. . . . No one, of course, can actually see it, but those who lay an ear against the surface tell that after some short while they perceive its busy hum. . . . The mosque dates from the seventh century; the pillars come from other temples of pre-Islamic religions, since, as ibn-Khaldun has written: 'In nations founded by nomads, the aid of foreigners is essential in all concerning masonry.' "

Does this Aleph exist in the heart of a stone? Did I see it there in the cellar when I saw all things, and have I now forgotten it? Our minds are porous and forgetfulness seeps in: I myself am distorting and losing, under the wearing away of the years, the face of Beatriz.

THE FLOWER OF COLERIDGE [JLB 52]

Around 1938 Paul Valéry wrote that the history of literature should not be the history of the authors and the accidents of their careers or of the career of their works, but rather the history of the Spirit as the producer or consumer of literature. He added that such a history could be written without the mention of a single writer. It was not the first time that the Spirit had made such an observation. In 1844 one of its amanuenses in Concord had noted: "I am very much struck in literature by the appearance that one person wrote all the books; . . . there is such equality and identity both of judgment and point of view in the narrative that it is plainly the work of one all-seeing, all-hearing gentleman" (Emerson, *Essays: Second Series*, "Nominalist and Realist," 1844). Twenty years earlier Shelley expressed the opinion that all the poems of the past, present, and future were episodes or fragments of a single infinite poem, written by all the poets on earth.

163

Those considerations (which are, of course, implicit in pantheism) could give rise to an endless debate. I am invoking them now to assist me in a modest plan: to trace the history of the evolution of an idea through the heterogeneous texts of three authors. The first one is by Coleridge; I am not sure whether he wrote it at the end of the eighteenth century or at the beginning of the nineteenth: "If a man could pass through Paradise in a dream, and have a flower presented to him as a pledge that his soul had really been there, and if he found that flower in his hand when he awoke—Ay!—and what then?"

I wonder what my reader thinks of that imagining. To me it is perfect. It seems quite impossible to use it as the basis of other inventions, for it has the integrity and the unity of a *terminus ad quem,* a final goal. And of course it is just that; in the sphere of literature as in others, every act is the culmination of an infinite series of causes and the cause of an infinite series of effects. Behind Coleridge's idea is the general and ancient idea of the generations of lovers who begged for a flower as a token.

The second text I shall quote is a novel that Wells drafted in 1887 and rewrote seven years later, in the summer of 1894. The first version was entitled *The Chronic Argonauts* (here "chronic" was the etymological equivalent of "temporal"); the definitive version of the work was called *The Time Machine.* In that novel Wells continued and renewed a very ancient literary tradition: the foreseeing of events. Isaiah *sees* the destruction of Babylon and the restoration of Israel; Aeneas, the military destiny of his descendants, the Romans; the prophet of the *Edda Saemundi,* the return of the gods who, after the cyclical battle in which our world will be destroyed, will discover that the same chess pieces they were playing with before are lying on the grass of a new meadow. Unlike those prophetic spectators, Wells's protagonist travels physically to the future. He returns tired, dusty, and shaken from a remote humanity that has divided into species who hate each other (the idle *eloi,* who live in dilapidated palaces and ruinous gardens; the subterranean and nyctalopic *morlocks* who feed on the *eloi*). He returns with his hair grown gray and brings with him a wilted flower from the future. This is the second version of Coleridge's image. More incredible than a celestial flower or the flower of a dream is the flower of the future, the unlikely flower whose atoms now occupy other spaces and have not yet been assembled.

The third version I shall mention, the most improbable of all, is the invention of a much more complex writer than Wells, although he was less gifted with those pleasant virtues that are usually called classical. I am referring to the author of *The Abasement of the Northmores,* the sad and labyrinthine Henry James. When he died, he left the unfinished novel *The Sense of the Past,* an imaginative work which was a variation or elaboration of *The Time Machine.* [1] Wells's protagonist travels to the future in an outlandish vehicle that advances or recedes in time as other vehicles do in space; James's protagonist returns to the past, to the eigh-

---

[1] I have not read *The Sense of the Past,* but I am acquainted with the competent analysis of it by Stephen Spender in his book *The Destructive Element* (pages 105–110). James was a friend of Wells; to learn more about their relationship, consult the latter's vast *Experiment in Autobiography.*

teenth century, by identifying himself with that period. (Both procedures are impossible, but James's is less arbitrary.) In *The Sense of the Past* the nexus between the real and the imaginative (between present and past) is not a flower, as in the previous stories, but a picture from the eighteenth century that mysteriously represents the protagonist. Fascinated by this canvas, he succeeds in going back to the day when it was painted. He meets a number of persons, including the artist, who paints him with fear and aversion, because he senses that there is something unusual and anomalous in those future features. James thus creates an incomparable *regressus in infinitum,* when his hero Ralph Pendrel returns to the eighteenth century because he is fascinated by an old painting, but Pendrel's return to this century is a condition for the existence of the painting. The cause follows the effect, the reason for the journey is one of the consequences of the journey.

Quite probably Wells was not acquainted with Coleridge's text; Henry James knew and admired the text of Wells. If the doctrine that all authors are one is valid, such facts are insignificant.[2] Strictly speaking, it is not necessary to go that far; the pantheist who declares that the plurality of authors is illusory finds unexpected support in the classicist, to whom that plurality matters but little. For classical minds the literature is the essential thing, not the individuals. George Moore and James Joyce have incorporated in their works the pages and sentences of others; Oscar Wilde used to give plots away for others to develop; both procedures, although they appear to be contradictory, may reveal an identical artistic perception—an ecumenical, impersonal perception. Another witness of the profound unity of the Word, another who denied the limitations of the individual, was the renowned Ben Jonson, who, when writing his literary testament and the favorable or adverse opinions he held of his contemporaries, was obliged to combine fragments from Seneca, Quintilian, Justus Lipsius, Vives, Erasmus, Machiavelli, Bacon, and the two Scaligers.

One last observation. Those who carefully copy a writer do it impersonally, do it because they confuse that writer with literature, do it because they suspect that to leave him at any one point is to deviate from reason and orthodoxy. For many years I thought that the almost infinite world of literature was in one man. That man was Carlyle, he was Johannes Becher, he was Whitman, he was Rafael Cansinos-Asséns, he was De Quincey.

HENRY JAMES [JLB 53]

Son of the Swedenborgian convert of the same name and brother of the famous psychiatrist who founded pragmatism, Henry James was born in New York,

---

[2]About the middle of the seventeenth century the epigrammatist of pantheism, Angelus Silesius, said that all the blessed are one (*Cherubinischer Wandersmann,* V, 7) and that every Christian must be Christ (ibid., V, 9).

April 15, 1843. The father wanted his sons to be cosmopolitan—citizens of the world in a stoic sense of the word—and he provided for their education in England, France, Geneva, and Rome. In 1860 Henry returned to America, where he undertook and abandoned the vague study of law. From 1864 onward he dedicated himself to literature, with growing self-denial, lucidity, and happiness. He lived in London and in Sussex as of 1869. His later trips to America were occasional and were never beyond New England. In July 1915 he adopted British citizenship because he understood that the moral duty of his country was to declare war on Germany. He died February 28, 1916. "Now, at last, that distinguished thing, death," he said in his dying hour.

The definitive edition of his works covers thirty-five volumes edited meticulously by himself. The main part of that scrupulous accumulation consists of stories and novels. It also includes a biography of Hawthorne, whom he always admired, and critical studies of Turgenev and Flaubert, close friends of his. He had little regard for Zola and, for complex reasons, for Ibsen. He protected Wells, who corresponded gratefully. He was Kipling's best man. The complete works comprise studies of a most diverse nature: the art of narrative, the discovery of as yet unexplored themes, literary life as a subject, indirect narrative procedures, the evil and the dead, the risks and virtues of improvisation, the supernatural, the course of time, the need to be interesting, the limits that the illustrator must impose upon himself so as not to compete with the text, the unacceptability of dialect, point of view, the first-person narration, reading aloud, the representation of unspecified evil, the American exiled in Europe, man exiled in the universe . . . These analyses, duly organized in a volume, would form an enlightening rhetoric.

He presented several comedies on the London stage, which were greeted with hisses and Bernard Shaw's respectful disapproval. He was never popular; the English critics offered him a distracted and frigid glory that usually excluded the effort of reading him.

"The biographies of James," Ludwig Lewisohn wrote, "are more significant for what they omit than for what they contain."

I have visited some literatures of the East and West; I have compiled an encyclopedic anthology of fantastic literature; I have translated Kafka, Melville, and Bloy; I know of no stranger work than that of Henry James. The writers I have enumerated are, from the start, amazing; the universe postulated by their pages is almost professionally unreal. James, before revealing what he is, a resigned and ironic inhabitant of Hell, runs the risk of appearing to be no more than a mundane novelist, less colorful than others. As we read his first pages, we are annoyed by some ambiguities, some superficial features; after a while we realize that those deliberate faults enrich the book. Of course we are not dealing here with that utter vagueness of the Symbolists, whose imprecisions, by eluding meaning, can mean anything. We are dealing with the voluntary omission of a part of the novel, which allows us to interpret it in one way or another; both premeditated by the author, both defined. Thus we shall never know, in "The Lesson of the Master," if the advice given to the disciple is or is not treacherous; if in "The Turn of the Screw" the children are victims or agents of the ghosts which in turn could be demons; in *The Sacred Fount*, which of the ladies who

166

pretend to investigate the mystery of Gilbert Long is the protagonist in that mystery; in "The Abasement of the Northmores," the final destiny of Mrs. Hope's project. I want to point out another problem of this delicate story of revenge: the intrinsic merits or demerits of Warren Hope, whom we have met only through his wife's eyes.

James has been accused of resorting to melodrama; this is because the facts, to him, merely exaggerate or emphasize the plot. Thus in *The American,* Madame Belleregarde's crime is incredible in itself, but acceptable as a sign of the corruption of an ancient family. Thus, in that story titled "The Death of the Lion," the demise of the hero and the senseless loss of the manuscript are merely metaphors which declare the indifference of those who pretend to admire him. Paradoxically, James is not a psychological novelist. The situations in his books do not emerge from his characters: the characters have been fabricated to justify the situations. With Meredith, the opposite occurs.

There are many critical studies of James. One can consult Rebecca West's monograph (*Henry James,* 1916), *The Craft of Fiction* (1921) by Percy Lubbock, the special issue of *Hound and Horn* corresponding to the months April–May 1934, *The Destructive Element* (1935) by Stephen Spender, and the passionate article by Graham Greene in the collective work, *The English Novelists* (1936). That article ends with these words: ". . . Henry James, as solitary in the history of the novel as Shakespeare in the history of poetry."

OUR POOR INDIVIDUALISM   [JLB 54]

The illusions of patriotism are limitless. In the first century of our era Plutarch ridiculed those who declared that the moon of Athens was better than the moon of Corinth; in the seventeenth century Milton observed that God usually revealed Himself first to His Englishmen; at the beginning of the nineteenth, Fichte declared that to have character and to be German were, obviously, the same thing. Here in Argentina, nationalists are much in evidence; they tell us they are motivated by the worthy or innocent desire to foment the best Argentine traits. But they do not really know the Argentine people; in speeches they prefer to define them in terms of some external fact—the Spanish conquistadors, say, or an imaginary Catholic tradition or "Saxon imperialism."

Unlike North Americans and almost all Europeans, the Argentine does not identify himself with the state. That can be explained by the fact that, in this country, the governments are usually exceedingly bad, or the state is an inconceivable abstraction;[1] the truth is that the Argentine is an individual, not a citizen. Aphorisms like Hegel's—"The State is the reality of the moral idea"—seem like a vicious joke. Films made in Hollywood repeatedly portray as admirable the man

---

[1]The state is impersonal; the Argentine can think only in terms of a personal relationship. Therefore, he does not consider stealing public funds a crime. I am simply stating a fact; I do not justify or condone it.

(generally a reporter) who tries to make friends with a criminal so he can turn him over to the police later; the Argentine, for whom friendship is a passion and the police something like a mafia, feels that this "hero" is an incomprehensible cad. He agrees with Don Quixote that "no one is without sin" and that "good men should not be the executioners of the others" (*Don Quixote,* I, 22). More than once, as I confronted the vain symmetries of Spanish style, I have suspected that we differ irrevocably from Spain; but those two lines from the *Quixote* have sufficed to convince me of my error; they are like the calm and secret symbol of our affinity. One night of Argentine literature is enough to confirm this: that desperate night when a rural police sergeant, shouting that he would not condone the crime of killing a brave man, began to fight on the side of the deserter Martín Fierro against his own men.

For the European the world is a cosmos where each person corresponds intimately to the function he performs; for the Argentine it is a chaos. The European and the North American believe that a book which has been awarded any sort of prize must be good; the Argentine acknowledges the possibility that it may not be bad, in spite of the prize. In general, the Argentine is a skeptic. He may not know about the fable that says humanity always includes thirty-six just men—the Lamed Vovniks—who do not know each other but who secretly sustain the universe; if he hears that fable, he will not be surprised that those worthies are obscure and anonymous. His popular hero is the man who fights the multitude alone, either in action (Fierro, Moreira, Hormiga Negra), or in the mind or the past (Segundo Sombra). Other literatures do not record anything quite like that. For example, consider the case of two great European writers, Kipling and Franz Kafka. At first glance the two have nothing in common, but the principal theme of one is the vindication of order—of one order (the highway in *Kim,* the bridge in *The Bridge Builders,* the Roman wall in *Puck of Pook's Hill*); the principal theme of the other is the insupportable and tragic solitude of the person who lacks a place, even a most humble one, in the order of the universe.

Perhaps someone will say that the qualities I have mentioned are merely negative or anarchical ones, and will add that they are not capable of political application. I venture to suggest that the opposite is true. The most urgent problem of our time (already proclaimed with prophetical clarity by the almost forgotten Spencer) is the gradual interference of the state in the acts of the individual; in the struggle against this evil—called Communism and Fascism—Argentine individualism, which has perhaps been useless or even harmful up to now, would find justification and positive value.

Without hope and with nostalgia, I think of the abstract possibility of a political party that has some affinity with the Argentine character; a party that would promise us, say, a rigorous minimum of government.

Nationalism seeks to charm us, but the vision it presents is that of an infinitely importunate state; if that Utopia were established on earth, it would have the providential virtue of making everyone desire, and finally achieve, its antithesis.

With some obvious exceptions (Montaigne, Saint-Simon, Bloy), we can safely affirm that France tends to produce its literature in conformity with the history of that literature. If we compare manuals of French literature (Lanson's, for example, or Thibaudet's) with their English equivalents (Saintsbury's or Sampson's), we discover, not without surprise, that the latter consist of conceivable human beings, and the former, of schools, manifestoes, generations, avant-gardes, rear-guards, lefts and rights, cenacles, and allusions to the tortuous fate of Captain Dreyfus. The strangest part is that reality corresponds to those frantic abstractions: before writing a line, the Frenchman wants to understand, define, classify himself. The Englishman writes in good faith, the Frenchman in favor of *a,* against *b,* conforming to *c,* toward *d* . . . He wonders (let us say): What kind of sonnet would be composed by a young atheist, of a Catholic background, born and bred in Nivernais but of Bretagnais stock, and affiliated with the Communist Party since 1944? Or, more technical: How should one apply the vocabulary and methods of Zola's Rougon-Macquart to the elaboration of an epic poem on the fishermen of Morbihan, adding Fénelon's fervor to Rabelais's garrulous profusion and, of course, without ignoring a psychoanalytical interpretation of the figure of Merlin? This system of premeditation, the mark of French literature, fills its pages with compositions of classical rigor but also with fortunate, or unfortunate, extravagances. In fact, when a Frenchman of letters professes a doctrine, he applies it always to the bitter end, with a kind of ferocious integrity. Racine and Mallarmé are the same writer (I hope this metaphor is acceptable), executing with the same decorum two dissimilar tasks. . . . To mock excessive forethought is not difficult; it is important to remember, however, that it has produced French literature, perhaps the first in the world.

Of all the obligations that an author can impose upon himself, the most common and doubtlessly most harmful is that of being modern. *Il faut être absolument moderne,* Rimbaud decided, a temporal limitation corresponding to the triviality of the nationalist who brags of being hermetically Danish or inextricably Argentine. Schopenhauer *(Welt als Wille und Vorstellung,* II, 15) concludes that the greatest imperfection of the human intellect is its successive, linear character, its tie to the present; to venerate that imperfection is an unfortunate whim. Guillaume Apollinaire embraced, justified, and preached it to his contemporaries. What is more, he devoted himself to that imperfection. He did so— remember the poem *"La jolie roussé"*—with an admirable and clear conscience of the sad dangers of his adventure.

Those dangers were real; today, like yesterday, the general value of Apollinaire's work is more documentary than esthetic. We visit it to recover the flavor of the "modern" poetry of the first decades of our century. Not a single verse allows us to forget the date on which it was written, an error not incurred, for example, in the contemporary works of Valéry, Rilke, Yeats, Joyce. . . . (Perhaps, for the future, the only achievement of "modern" literature will be the unfathomable *Ulysses* which in some way justifies, includes, and goes beyond the other texts).

To place Apollinaire's name next to Rilke's might seem anachronistic, so close is the latter to us, so distant (already) is the former. However, *Das Buch der Bilder,* which includes the inexhaustible *"Herbsttag,"* is from 1902, *Calligrammes,* from 1918. Apollinaire, adorning his compositions with trolleys, airplanes, and other vehicles, did not identify with his times, which are our times.

For the writers of 1918, the war was what Tiberius Claudius Nero was for his professors of rhetoric: "mud kneaded with blood." They all perceived it thus, Unruh as well as Barbusse, Wilfred Owen as well as Sassoon, the solitary Klemm as well as the frequented Remarque. (Paradoxically, one of the first poets to emphasize the monotony, tedium, desperation, and physical humiliations of contemporary war was Rudyard Kipling, in his *Barrack-Room Ballads* of 1903.) For Artillery Lieutenant Guillaume Apollinaire, war was, above all, a beautiful spectacle. His poems, and his letters, express this. Guillermo de Torre, the most devoted and lucid of his critics, observes: "In the long nights of the trenches, the soldier-poet could contemplate the sky starred with mortar, and imagine new constellations." Thus Apollinaire fancied himself attending a dazzling spectacle in *La nuit d'avril 1915:*

> *Le ciel est étoilé par les obus des Boches*
> *La forêt merveilleuse où je vis donne un bal . . .*

A letter dated July 2 confirms this image: "War is decidedly a beautiful thing and, despite all the risks I run, the exhaustion, the total lack of water, of everything, I am not unhappy to be here. . . . The place is very desolate, neither water, nor trees, nor villages are here, only the super-metallic, arch-thundering war."

The meaning of a sentence, like that of an isolated word, depends on the context which, sometimes, can be the entire life of its author. Thus the phrase "war is a beautiful thing" allows for many interpretations. Uttered by a South American dictator, it could express his hope of throwing incendiary bombs on the capital of a neighboring country. Coming from a journalist, it could signify his firm intention of adulating the dictator in order to obtain a good position in his administration. A sedentary man of letters could be suggesting his nostalgia for a life of adventure. For Guillaume Apollinaire, on the battlefields of France, it signifies, I believe, a frame of mind which ignores horror effortlessly, an acceptance of destiny, a kind of fundamental innocence. The same could be said for that Norwegian who conquered six feet of English earth or, what is more, nicknamed the battle *Viking Feast;* the same goes for the immortal and unknown author of the *Chanson de Roland,* singing to the brilliance of a sword:

> *E Durandal, cum ies clere et blanche.*
> *Cuntre soleil si reluis et reflambes.*

Apollinaire's verse, *"La forêt merveilleuse où je vis donne un bal,"* is not a rigorous description of the artillery duels of 1915, but it is an accurate portrait of Apollinaire. Although he lived his days among the *baladins* of Cubism and Futurism, he was not a modern man. He was somewhat simpler and happier,

more ancient, and stronger. He was so unmodern that modernity seemed picturesque, and perhaps even moving, to him. He was the "winged and sacred thing"
of Platonic dialogue, he was a man of elemental and, therefore, eternal feelings;
he was, when the fundaments of the earth and sky vacillated, the poet of ancient
courage and honor. *"La chanson du mal-aimé," "Désir," "Merveille de la guerre,"*
"Tristesse d'une étoile," "La jolie roussé" are the pages which move us like the
nearness of the sea; they are the poet's testimonial.

THE FIRST WELLS   [JLB 56]

Harris relates that when Oscar Wilde was asked about Wells, he called him "a
scientific Jules Verne." That was in 1899; it appears that Wilde thought less of
defining Wells, or of annihilating him, than of changing the subject. Now the
names H. G. Wells and Jules Verne have come to be incompatible. We all feel
that this is true, but still it may be well to examine the intricate reasons on which
our feeling is based.

The most obvious reason is a technical one. Before Wells resigned himself
to the role of a sociological spectator, he was an admirable storyteller, an heir to
the concise style of Swift and Edgar Allan Poe; Verne was a pleasant and industrious journeyman. Verne wrote for adolescents; Wells, for all ages. There is another
difference, which Wells himself once indicated: Verne's stories deal with probable
things (a submarine, a ship larger than those existing in 1872, the discovery of the
South Pole, the talking picture, the crossing of Africa in a balloon, the craters
of an extinguished volcano that lead to the center of the earth); the short stories
Wells wrote concern mere possibilities, if not impossible things (an invisible man,
a flower that devours a man, a crystal egg that reflects the events on Mars, a man
who returns from the future with a flower of the future, a man who returns from
the other life with his heart on the right side, because he has been completely
inverted, as in a mirror). I have read that Verne, scandalized by the license
permitted by *The First Men in the Moon,* exclaimed indignantly, *"Il invente!"*

The reasons I have given seem valid enough, but they do not explain why
Wells is infinitely superior to the author of *Hector Servadac,* and also to Rosney,
Lytton, Robert Paltock, Cyrano, or any other precursor of his methods.[1] Even
his best plots do not adequately solve the problem. In long books the plot can
be only a pretext, or a point of departure. It is important for the composition of
the work, but not for the reader's enjoyment of it. That is true of all genres; the
best detective stories are not those with the best plots. (If plots were everything,
the *Quixote* would not exist and Shaw would be inferior to O'Neill.) In my
opinion, the excellence of Wells's first novels—*The Island of Dr. Moreau,* for
example, or *The Invisible Man*—has a deeper origin. Not only do they tell an

---

[1]In *The Outline of History* (1931) Wells praises the work of two other precursors: Francis
Bacon and Lucian of Samosata.

ingenious story; but they tell a story symbolic of processes that are somehow inherent in all human destinies. The harassed invisible man who has to sleep as though his eyes were wide open because his eyelids do not exclude light is our solitude and our terror; the conventicle of seated monsters who mouth a servile creed in their night is the Vatican and is Lhasa. Work that endures is always capable of an infinite and plastic ambiguity; it is all things for all men, like the Apostle; it is a mirror that reflects the reader's own traits and it is also a map of the world. And it must be ambiguous in an evanescent and modest way, almost in spite of the author; he must appear to be ignorant of all symbolism. Wells displayed that lucid innocence in his first fantastic exercises, which are to me the most admirable part of his admirable work.

Those who say that art should not propagate doctrines usually refer to doctrines that are opposed to their own. Naturally this is not my own case; I gratefully profess almost all the doctrines of Wells, but I deplore his inserting them into his narratives. An heir of the British nominalists, Wells condemns our custom of speaking of the "tenacity of England" or the "intrigues of Prussia." The arguments against that harmful mythology seem to be irreproachable, but not the fact of interpolating them into the story of Mr. Parham's dream. As long as an author merely relates events or traces the slight deviations of a conscience, we can suppose him to be omniscient, we can confuse him with the universe or with God; but when he descends to the level of pure reason, we know he is fallible. Reality is inferred from events, not reasonings; we permit God to affirm "I am that I am" (Exodus, 3:14), not to declare and analyze, like Hegel or Anselm, the *argumentum ontologicum.* God must not theologize; the writer must not invalidate with human arguments the momentary faith that art demands of us. There is another consideration: the author who shows aversion to a character seems not to understand him completely, seems to confess that the character is not inevitable for him. We distrust his intelligence, as we would distrust the intelligence of a God who maintained heavens and hells. God, Spinoza has written, does not hate anyone and does not love anyone (*Ethics,* 5, 17).

Like Quevedo, like Voltaire, like Goethe, like some others, Wells is less a man of letters than a literature. He wrote garrulous books in which the gigantic felicity of Charles Dickens somehow reappears; he bestowed sociological parables with a lavish hand; he constructed encyclopedias, enlarged the possibilities of the novel, rewrote the Book of Job—"that great Hebrew imitation of the Platonic dialogue"; for our time, he wrote a very delightful autobiography without pride and without humility; he combated Communism, Nazism, and Christianity; he debated (politely and lethally) with Belloc; he chronicled the past, chronicled the future, recorded real and imaginary lives. Of the vast and diversified library he left us, nothing has pleased me more than his narration of some atrocious miracles: *The Time Machine, The Island of Dr. Moreau, The Plattner Story, The First Men in the Moon.* They are the first books I read; perhaps they will be the last. I think they will be incorporated, like the fables of Theseus or Ahasuerus, into the general memory of the species and even transcend the fame of their creator or the extinction of the language in which they were written.

One day, or one month, or one Platonic year ago (so infestive is oblivion, so insignificant the event to which I will refer) I worked, though unworthily, as a third-class assistant at a municipal library in the southern suburbs. For nine years I went to that library, nine years which in my memory will be one single afternoon, one monstrous afternoon during which I classified an infinite number of books, during which the Reich devoured France, and the Reich did not devour the British Isles; and the Nazis, driven out of Berlin, sought refuge elsewhere. At some point of that unique afternoon, I valiantly signed some democratic statement; one day, or one month, or one Platonic year ago, they summoned me to the municipal police station. Wonder-struck by such a brusque administrative avatar, I went to the Prefectory. There they confided to me that such a metamorphosis was in punishment for having signed certain statements. While I was receiving the news with due interest, I was distracted by a poster that spruced up the solemn office. It was of rectangular shape, rather laconic, of considerable size, and it contained the interesting epigraph "Hurry, Hurry!" I can't remember my interlocutor's face, I can't remember his name, but until the day I die I shall remember that slovenly inscription. I'll have to resign, I repeated as I went down the stairs; but my personal destiny mattered less than that symbolic poster.

I don't know to what extent the event I have invoked is a parable. But I suspect that memory and oblivion are gods who know full well what they are doing. If they have misplaced the rest, and if they retain that absurd legend, some justification must support them. I formulate it thus: dictatorships foster oppression, dictatorships foster servitude, dictatorships foster cruelty; more abominable is the fact that they foster idiocy. Hotel clerks mumbling orders, effigies of caudillos, prearranged "long live's" and "down with's," walls embellished with names, unanimous ceremonies, mere discipline substituting for lucidity. . . . To combat such sad monotonies is among the writer's many duties. Do I have to remind readers of Martín Fierro and Don Segundo [Sombra] that individuality is an old Argentine virtue? I also want to tell them how proud I am of this bounteous evening and of this active friendship.

THE DEAD MAN [JLB 58]

That a man from the outlying slums of a city like Buenos Aires, that a sorry hoodlum with little else to his credit than a passion for recklessness, should find his way into that wild stretch of horse country between Brazil and Uruguay and become the leader of a band of smugglers, seems on the face of it unbelievable. To those who think so, I'd like to give an account of what happened to Benjamin Otálora, of whom perhaps not a single memory lingers in the neighborhood where he grew up, and who died a fitting death, struck down by a bullet, somewhere on the border of Rio Grande do Sul. Of the details of his adventures I know little;

should I ever be given the facts, I shall correct and expand these pages. For the time being, this outline may prove of some use.

Benjamin Otálora, along about 1891, is a strapping young man of nineteen. He has a low forehead, candid blue eyes, and that country-boy appearance that goes with Basque ancestry. A lucky blow with a knife has made clear to him that he is also brave; his opponent's death causes him no concern, nor does his need to flee the country. The political boss of the district gives him a letter of introduction to a certain Azevedo Bandeira, in Uruguay. Otálora books passage; the crossing is stormy and the ship pitches and creaks. The next day, he wanders the length and breadth of Montevideo, with unacknowledged or perhaps unsuspected homesickness. He does not find Azevedo Bandeira. Getting on toward midnight, in a small saloon out on the northern edge of town, he witnesses a brawl between some cattle drovers. A knife flashes. Otálora has no idea who is in the right or wrong, but the sheer taste of danger lures him, just as cards or music lure other men. In the confusion, he blocks a lunging knife thrust that one of the gauchos aims at a man wearing a rough countryman's poncho and, oddly, the dark derby of a townsman. The man turns out to be Azevedo Bandeira. (As soon as he finds this out, Otálora destroys the letter, preferring to be under no one's obligation.) Azevedo Bandeira, though of stocky build, gives the unaccountable impression of being somehow misshapen. In his large face, which seems always to be too close, are the Jew, the Negro, and the Indian; in his bearing, the tiger and the ape. The scar that cuts across his cheek is one ornament more, like his bristling black mustache.

A fantasy or a mistake born of drunkenness, the fight ends as quickly as it broke out. Otálora takes a drink with the drovers and then goes along with them to an all-night party and after that—the sun high in the sky by now—to a rambling house in the Old Town. Inside, on the bare ground of the last patio, the men laid out their sheepskin saddle blankets to sleep. Dimly, Otálora compares this past night with the night before; here he is, on solid ground now, among friends. A pang of remorse for not missing his Buenos Aires nags at him, however. He sleeps until nightfall, when he is wakened by the same gaucho who, blind drunk, had tried to knife Bandeira. (Otálora recalls that the man has shared the high-spirited night with the rest of them, and that Bandeira had seated him at his right hand and forced him to go on drinking.) The man says the boss has sent for him. In a kind of office opening into the entrance passage (Otálora has never before seen an entrance with doors opening into it from the sides), Azevedo Bandeira, in the company of an aloof and showy red-haired woman, is waiting for him. Bandeira praises him up and down, offers him a shot of rum, tells him he has the makings of a man of guts, suggests that he go up north with the others to bring back a large cattle herd. Otálora agrees; toward dawn they are on the road, heading for Tacuarembó.

For Otálora a new kind of life opens up, a life of far-flung sunrises and long days in the saddle, reeking of horses. It is an untried and at times unbearable life, but it's already in his blood, for just as the men of certain countries worship and feel the call of the sea, we Argentines in turn (including the man who weaves these symbols) yearn for the boundless plains that ring under a horse's hooves. Otálora has grown up in a neighborhood of teamsters and liverymen. In under a year, he makes himself into a gaucho. He learns to handle a horse, to round up and slaughter cattle, to throw a rope for holding an animal fast or bolas for bringing it down, to fight off sleep, to weather storms and frosts and sun, to drive a herd with whistles and hoots. Only once during this whole apprenticeship does he set eyes on Azevedo Bandeira, but he has him always in mind because to be one of Bandeira's men is to be looked up to and feared, and because after any feat or hard job the gauchos always say Bandeira does it better. Somebody has it that Bandeira was born on the Brazilian side of the Cuareim, in Rio Grande do Sul; this, which should lower him in Otálora's eyes, somehow—with its suggestion of dense forests and of marshes and of inextricable and almost endless distances—only adds to him. Little by little, Otálora comes to realize that Bandeira's interests are many and that chief among them is smuggling. To be a cattle drover is to be a servant; Otálora decides to work himself up to the level of smuggler. One night, as two of his companions are about to go over the border to bring back a consignment of rum, Otálora picks a fight with one of them, wounds him, and takes his place. He is driven by ambition and also by a dim sense of loyalty. The man (he thinks) will come to find out that I'm worth more than all his Uruguayans put together.

Another year goes by before Otálora sees Montevideo again. They come riding through the outskirts and into the city (which to Otálora now seems enormous); reaching the boss's house, the men prepare to bed down in the last patio. The days pass, and Otálora still has not laid eyes on Bandeira. It is said, in fear, that he is ailing; every afternoon a Negro goes up to Bandeira's room with a kettle and maté. One evening, the job is assigned to Otálora. He feels vaguely humiliated, but at the same time gratified.

The bedroom is bare and dark. There's a balcony that faces the sunset, there's a long table with a shining disarray of riding crops, bullwhips, cartridge belts, firearms, and knives. On the far wall there's a mirror and the glass is faded. Bandeira lies face up, dreaming and muttering in his sleep; the sun's last rays outline his features. The big white bed seems to make him smaller, darker. Otálora notes his graying hair, his exhaustion, his weakness, the deep wrinkles of his years. It angers him being mastered by this old man. He thinks that a single blow would be enough to finish him. At this moment, he glimpses in the mirror that someone has come in. It's the woman with the red hair; she is barefoot and only half-dressed, and looks at him with cold curiosity. Bandeira sits up in bed; while he speaks of business affairs of the past two years and drinks maté after maté his fingers toy with the woman's braided hair. In the end, he gives Otálora permission to leave.

A few days later, they get orders to head north again. There, in a place that might be anywhere on the face of the endless plains, they come to a forlorn ranch. Not a single tree or a brook. The sun's first and last rays beat down on it. There are stone fences for the lean longhorn cattle. This rundown set of buildings is called "The Last Sigh."

Sitting around the fire with the ranch hands, Otálora hears that Bandeira will soon be on his way from Montevideo. He asks what for, and someone explains that there's an outsider turned gaucho among them who's giving too many orders. Otálora takes this as a friendly joke and is flattered that the joke can be made. Later on he finds out that Bandeira has had a falling out with one of the political bosses, who has withdrawn his support. Otálora likes this bit of news.

Crates of rifles arrive; a pitcher and washbasin, both of silver, arrive for the woman's bedroom; intricately figured damask draperies arrive; one morning, from out of the hills, a horseman arrives—a sullen man with a full beard and a poncho. His name is Ulpiano Suárez and he is Azevedo Bandeira's strong-arm man, or bodyguard. He speaks very little and with a thick Brazilian accent. Otálora does not know whether to put down his reserve to unfriendliness, or to contempt, or to mere backwoods manners. He realizes, however, that to carry out the scheme he is hatching he must win the other man's friendship.

Next into Benjamin Otálora's story comes a black-legged bay horse that Azevedo Bandeira brings from the south, which carries a fine saddle worked with silver and a saddle blanket trimmed with a jaguar skin. This spirited horse is a token of Bandeira's authority and for this reason is coveted by the young man, who comes also—with a desire bordering on spite—to hunger for the woman with the shining hair. The woman, the saddle, and the big bay are attributes or trappings of a man he aspires to bring down.

At this point the story takes another turn. Azevedo Bandeira is skilled in the art of slow intimidation, in the diabolical trickery of leading a man on, step by step, shifting from sincerity to mockery. Otálora decides to apply this ambiguous method to the hard task before him. He decides to replace Azevedo Bandeira, but to take his time over it. During days of shared danger, he gains Suárez's friendship. He confides his plan to him; Suárez pledges to help. Then a number of things begin happening of which I know only a few. Otálora disobeys Bandeira's orders; he takes to overlooking them, changing them, defying them. The whole world seems to conspire with him, hastening events. One noontime, somewhere around Tacuarembó, there is an exchange of gunfire with a gang from Brazil; Otálora takes Bandeira's place and shouts out orders to the Uruguayans. A bullet hits him in the shoulder, but that afternoon Otálora rides back to "The Last Sigh" on the boss's horse, and that evening some drops of his blood stain the jaguar skin, and that night he sleeps with the woman with the shining hair. Other accounts change the order of these events, denying they happened all in the same day.

Bandeira, nevertheless, remains nominally the boss. He goes on giving orders which are not carried out. Benjamin Otálora leaves him alone, out of mixed reasons of habit and pity.

The closing scene of the story coincides with the commotion of the closing night of the year 1894. On this night, the men of "The Last Sigh" eat freshly slaughtered meat and fall into quarreling over their liquor; someone picks out on the guitar, over and over again, a *milonga* that gives him a lot of trouble. At the head of the table, Otálora, feeling his drink, piles exultation upon exultation, boast upon boast; this dizzying tower is a symbol of his irresistible destiny. Bandeira, silent amid the shouting, lets the night flow noisily on. When the clock strikes twelve, he gets up like a man just remembering he has something to do. He gets up and softly knocks at the woman's door. She opens at once, as though waiting to be called. She steps out barefoot and half-dressed. In an almost feminine, soft-spoken drawl, Bandeira gives her an order.

"Since you and the Argentine care so much for each other," he says, "you're going to kiss him right now in front of everyone."

He adds an obscene detail. The woman tries to resist, but two men have taken her by the arms and fling her upon Otálora. Brought to tears, she kisses his face and chest. Ulpiano Suárez has his revolver out. Otálora realizes, before dying, that he has been betrayed from the start, that he has been sentenced to death—that love and command and triumph have been accorded him because his companions already thought of him as a dead man, because to Bandeira he already was a dead man.

Suárez, almost in contempt, fires the shot.

ABOUT OSCAR WILDE [JLB 59]

To mention Wilde's name is to mention a dandy who was also a poet; it is to evoke the image of a gentleman dedicated to the paltry aim of startling people by his cravats and his metaphors. It is also to evoke the notion of art as a select or secret game—like the work of Hugh Vereker and Stefan George—and the poet as an industrious *monstrorum artifex* (Pliny, XXVIII, 2). It is to evoke the weary twilight of the nineteenth century and the oppressive pomp one associates with a conservatory or a masquerade ball. None of these evocations is false, but I maintain that they all correspond to partial truths and contradict, or overlook, well-known facts.

For example, consider the notion that Wilde was a kind of Symbolist. A great many facts support it: around 1881 Wilde directed the Aesthetes and ten years later, the Decadents; Rebecca West falsely accuses him (*Henry James,* III) of imposing the stamp of the middle class on the Decadents; the vocabulary of the poem "The Sphinx" is studiously magnificent; Wilde was a friend of Schwob and of Mallarmé. But one important fact refutes this notion: in verse or in prose Wilde's syntax is always very simple. Of the many British writers, none is so accessible to foreigners. Readers who are incapable of deciphering a paragraph by Kipling or a stanza by William Morris begin and end *Lady Windermere's Fan* on the same afternoon. Wilde's metrical system is spontaneous or simulates spontaneity; his work does not include a single experimental verse, like this solid and wise alexandrine by Lionel Johnson: "Alone with Christ, desolate else, left by mankind."

Wilde's technical insignificance can be an argument in favor of his intrinsic greatness. If his work corresponded to the sort of reputation he had, it would consist merely of artifices like *Les palais nomades* or *Los crepúsculos del jardín,* which abound in Wilde—remember Chapter II of *Dorian Gray* or "The Harlot's House" or "Symphony in Yellow"—but his use of adjectives gave him a certain

177

notoriety. Wilde can dispense with those purple patches—a phrase attributed to him by Ricketts and Hesketh Pearson, but which had already appeared elsewhere earlier. The fact that it was attributed to Wilde confirms the custom of linking his name to decorative passages.

Reading and rereading Wilde through the years, I notice something that his panegyrists do not seem to have even suspected: the provable and elementary fact that Wilde is almost always right. *The Soul of Man under Socialism* is not only eloquent; it is just. The miscellaneous notes that he lavished on the *Pall Mall Gazette* and the *Speaker* are filled with perspicuous observations that exceed the optimum possibilities of Leslie Stephen or Saintsbury. Wilde has been accused of practicing a kind of combinatorial art, in the manner of Raymond Lully; that is perhaps true of some of his jokes ("one of those British faces that, once seen, are always forgotten"), but not of the belief that music reveals to us an unknown and perhaps real past (*The Critic as Artist*), or that all men kill the thing they love (*The Ballad of Reading Gaol*), or that to be repentant for an act is to modify the past (*De Profundis*), or that (and this is a belief not unworthy of Léon Bloy or Swedenborg) there is no man who is not, at each moment, what he has been and what he will be (*ibid.*).[1] I do not say this to encourage my readers to venerate Wilde; but rather to indicate a mentality that is quite unlike the one generally attributed to Wilde. If I am not mistaken, he was much more than an Irish Moréas; he was a man of the eighteenth century who sometimes condescended to play the game of symbolism. Like Gibbon, like Johnson, like Voltaire, he was an ingenious man who was also right. He was "remarkable for the rapidity with which he could utter fatal words."[2] He gave the century what the century demanded—*comédies larmoyantes* for the many and verbal arabesques for the few —and he executed those dissimilar things with a kind of negligent glee. His perfection has been a disadvantage; his work is so harmonious that it may seem inevitable and even trite. It is hard for us to imagine the universe without Wilde's epigrams; but that difficulty does not make them less plausible.

An aside: Oscar Wilde's name is linked to the cities of the plain; his fame, to condemnation and jail. Nevertheless (this has been perceived very clearly by Hesketh Pearson), the fundamental spirit of his work is joy. On the other hand, the powerful work of Chesterton, the prototype of physical and moral sanity, is always on the verge of becoming a nightmare. The diabolical and the horrible lie in wait on his pages; the most innocuous subject can assume the forms of terror. Chesterton is a man who wants to regain childhood; Wilde, a man who keeps an invulnerable innocence in spite of the habits of evil and misfortune.

Like Chesterton, like Lang, like Boswell, Wilde is among those fortunate writers who can do without the approval of the critics and even, at times, without the reader's approval, and the pleasure we derive from his company is irresistible and constant.

---

[1] Compare the curious thesis of Leibniz, which seemed so scandalous to Arnauld: "The notion of each individual includes *a priori* all the events that will happen to him." According to this dialectical fatalism, the fact that Alexander the Great would die in Babylon is a quality of that king, like arrogance.

[2] This sentence is by Reyes, who applies it to the Mexican male (*Reloj de sol,* page 158).

In paragraph 6, he had already stated:

> Some truths there are so near and obvious to the mind that a man need only open his eyes to see them. Such I take this important one to be, viz., that all the choir of heaven and furniture of the earth, in a word all those bodies which compose the mighty frame of the world, have not any subsistence without a mind—that their *being* is *to be perceived or known;* that consequently so long as they are not actually perceived by me, or do not exist in my mind or that of any other created spirit, they must either have no existence at all, or else subsist in the mind of some Eternal Spirit—.

That, in the words of its inventor, is the idealist doctrine. Understanding it is easy; the difficult thing is to think within its limits. Schopenhauer himself, when he explains it, commits culpable negligences. In the first lines of the first book of his *Welt als Wille und Vorstellung*—in 1819—he makes the following statement, which entitles him to the imperishable bewilderment of all men: "The world is my representation. The man who confesses this truth is well aware that he does not know a sun or an earth, but only some eyes that see a sun and a hand that feels the contact of an earth." That is to say, for the idealist Schopenhauer man's eyes and hand are less illusory or apparential than the earth and the sun. In 1844 he published a supplementary volume. In the first chapter he rediscovers and exaggerates the old error: he defines the universe as a cerebral phenomenon and distinguishes "the world in the head" from "the world outside of the head." But in 1713 Berkeley had made Philonous say: "The brain therefore you speak of, being a sensible thing, exists only in the mind. Now, I would fain know whether you think it reasonable to suppose, that one idea or thing existing in the mind, occasions all other ideas. And if you think so, pray how do you account for the origin of that primary idea or brain itself?"

The dualism or cerebralism of Schopenhauer can be opposed effectively to the monism of Spiller. The latter (*The Mind of Man,* 1902, Chapter 8) argues that the retina and the cutaneous surface invoked to explain the visual and the tactile are, in turn, two tactile and visual systems; and that the room we see (the "objective") is no larger than the imagined one (the "cerebral") and does not contain it, since they are two independent visual systems. Berkeley (*The Principles of Human Knowledge,* pages 10 and 116) also denied the primary qualities—the solidity and the extension of things—and absolute space.

Berkeley affirmed the continuous existence of objects, since even if some individual did not perceive them, God perceived them. More logically, Hume denied it (*A Treatise of Human Nature,* I, 4, 2). Berkeley affirmed personal identity, because "I myself am not my ideas, but somewhat else, a thinking, active principle" (*Dialogues,* 3). Hume, the skeptic, refuted it and made each man "a bundle or collection of different perceptions, which succeed each other with an inconceivable rapidity" (*A Treatise,* I, 4, 6). They both affirm time: for Berkeley it is "the succession of ideas in my mind, which flows uniformly and is participated by all beings" (*The Principles of Human Knowledge,* 98); for Hume time 'must be composed of indivisible moments" (*A Treatise,* I, 2, 2).

I have amassed some quotations from the apologists of idealism, I have offered their canonical passages, I have been iterative and explicit, I have censured Schopenhauer (not without ingratitude), to help my reader penetrate that unstable mental world. A world of evanescent impressions; a world without matter or spirit, neither objective nor subjective; a world without the ideal architecture of space; a world made of time, of the absolute uniform time of the *Principia;* an indefatigable labyrinth, a chaos, a dream—the almost complete disintegration to which David Hume came.

Once the idealist argument is admitted, I believe that it is possible—perhaps inevitable—to go further. For Hume it is not licit to speak of the shape of the moon or of its color; the shape and the color *are* the moon; nor can one speak of the perceptions of the mind, since the mind is nothing more than a series of perceptions. The Cartesian "I think, therefore I am" is invalidated. To say "I think" is to postulate the ego; it is a *petitio principii.* In the eighteenth century Lichtenberg proposed that instead of "I think," we should say impersonally "it thinks," as we say "it thunders" or "it rains." I repeat: there is not a secret ego behind faces that governs actions and receives impressions; we are only the series of those imaginary actions and those errant impressions. The series? If we deny spirit and matter, which are continuities, and if we deny space also, I do not know what right we have to the continuity that is time.

Imagine any present. On a Mississippi night Huckleberry Finn awakens. The raft, lost in the partial darkness, is floating down the river. Perhaps the weather is cool. Huckleberry Finn recognizes the quiet relentless sound of the water; he opens his eyes lazily. He sees a vague number of stars, he sees an indistinct streak of trees; then he sinks into an immemorial sleep that envelops him like murky water.[1] The metaphysics of idealism declare that it is risky and futile to add a material substance (the object) and a spiritual substance (the subject) to those perceptions. I maintain that it is no less illogical to think that they are terms of a series whose beginning is as inconceivable as its end. To add to the river and the shore perceived by Huck the notion of another substantive river and another shore, to add another perception to that immediate network of perceptions is, for idealism, unjustifiable. For me, it is no less unjustifiable to add chronological precision: the fact, for example, that the event occurred on June 7, 1849, between 4:10 and 4:11 A.M. Or in other words: I deny, with the arguments of idealism, the vast temporal series that idealism admits. Hume has denied the existence of absolute space, in which each thing has its place; I deny the existence of one time, in which all events are linked together. To deny coexistence is no less difficult than to deny succession.

I deny the successive, in a large number of cases; I deny the contemporaneous also, in a large number of cases. The lover who thinks, "While I was so happy, thinking of my loved one's fidelity, she was deceiving me," deceives himself: if each state we live is absolute, that happiness was not contemporaneous with that

---

[1]For the facility of the reader, I have selected an instant between two dreams, a literary instant, not a historical one. If anyone suspects a fallacy, he can insert another example; from his own life, if he wishes.

deceit; the discovery of that deceit is one more state, incapable of modifying the "previous" ones, but not the remembrance of them. The misfortune of today is no more real than past happiness. I shall give a more concrete example. At the beginning of August 1824 Captain Isidoro Suárez, leading a squadron of Peruvian Hussars, achieved the victory of Junín; at the beginning of August 1824 De Quincey published a diatribe against *Wilhelm Meisters Lehrjahre.* Those events were not contemporaneous (they are now), for the two men died, Suárez in the city of Montevideo, De Quincey in Edinburgh, each without knowing of the other. Every instant is autonomous. Neither revenge nor pardon nor prisons nor even oblivion can modify the invulnerable past. No less vain to me are hope and fear, which always relate to future events: that is, to events that will not happen to us, who are the minutiae of the present. I am told that the present, the "specious present" of the psychologists, lasts between several seconds and a tiny fraction of a second; that is how long the history of the universe lasts. Or rather, there is no such history, as there is no life of a man, nor even one of his nights; each moment we live exists, not its imaginary aggregate. The universe, the sum of all the events, is a collection that is no less ideal than that of all the horses Shakespeare dreamed—one, many, none?—between 1592 and 1594. I might add that if time is a mental process, how can it be shared by thousands, or even two different men?

Interrupted and burdened by examples, the argument of the foregoing paragraphs may seem intricate. I shall try a more direct method. Let us consider a life in which repetitions are abundant; mine, for example. I never pass Recoleta cemetery without remembering that my father, my grandparents, and my great-grandparents are buried there, as I shall be; then I remember that I have already remembered that, many times before. I cannot walk down my neighborhood streets in the solitude of night without thinking that night is pleasing to us because, like memory, it erases idle details. I cannot mourn the loss of a love or a friendship without reflecting that one can lose only what one has never really had. Each time I come to a certain place in the South, I think of you, Helen; each time the air brings me a scent of eucalyptus, I think of Adrogué, in my childhood; each time I remember Fragment 91 of Heraclitus: "You will not go down twice to the same river," I admire his dialectic skill, because the facility with which we accept the first meaning ("The river is different") clandestinely imposes the second one ("I am different") and gives us the illusion of having invented it. Each time I hear a Germanophile vituperating Yiddish, I pause and think that Yiddish is, after all, a German dialect, barely maculated by the language of the Holy Spirit. Those tautologies (and others I shall not disclose) are my whole life. Naturally, they are repeated without precision; there are differences of emphasis, temperature, light, general physiological state. But I suspect that the number of circumstantial variations is not infinite: we can postulate, in the mind of an individual (or of two individuals who do not know each other, but on whom the same process is acting), two identical moments. Having postulated that identity, we must ask: Are those identical moments the same? Is *a single repeated term* enough to disrupt and confound the series of time? Are the enthusiasts who devote a lifetime to a line by Shakespeare not literally Shakespeare?

I am still not certain of the ethics of the system I have outlined. I do not know whether it exists. The fifth paragraph of Chapter 4 in the *Sanhedrin* of the Mishnah declares that, for the Justice of God, he who kills a single man destroys the world; if there is no plurality, he who annihilated all men would be no more guilty than the primitive and solitary Cain, which is orthodox, nor more universal in his destruction, which can be magic. I believe that is true. The tumultuous general catastrophes—fires, wars, epidemics—are but a single sorrow, illusorily multiplied in many mirrors. That is Bernard Shaw's judgment when he states (*Guide to Socialism,* 86) that what one person can suffer is the maximum that can be suffered on earth. If one person dies of inanition, he will suffer all the inanition that has been or will be. If 10,000 persons die with him, he will not be 10,000 hungrier nor will he suffer 10,000 longer. There is no point in being overwhelmed by the appalling total of human suffering; such a total does not exist. Neither poverty nor pain is accumulable. Compare also *The Problem of Pain* (VII) by C. S. Lewis.

Lucretius (*De rerum natura,* I, 830) attributes to Anaxagoras the doctrine that gold consists of particles of gold; fire, of sparks; bone, of imperceptible little bones. Josiah Royce, perhaps influenced by St. Augustine, believes that time consists of time and that "Every *now* within which something happens is therefore *also* a succession" (*The World and the Individual,* II, 139). That proposition is compatible with my own.

II

All language is of a successive nature; it is not an effective tool for reasoning the eternal, the intemporal. Those who were displeased with the foregoing argumentation might prefer this piece from 1928, which is part of the story *"Sentirse en muerte,"* mentioned earlier in this article:

And here I should like to record an experience I had several nights ago: too evanescent and ecstatic a trifle to be called an adventure; too unreasonable and sentimental to be a thought. There is a scene and a word: a word I had said before but never lived with complete dedication until that night. I shall relate it now, with the accidents of time and place that brought about its revelation.

I remember it this way. I had spent the afternoon in Barracas, a place I rarely visited, a place whose very distance from the scene of my later wanderings gave an aura of strangeness to that day. As I had nothing to do in the evening and the weather was fair, I went out after dinner to walk and remember. I did not wish to have a set destination. I followed a random course, as much as possible; I accepted, with no conscious prejudice other than avoiding the avenues or wide streets, the most obscure invitations of chance. But a kind of familiar gravitation drew me toward certain sections I shall always remember, for they arouse in me a kind of reverence. I am not speaking of the precise environment of my childhood, my own neighborhood, but of the still mysterious fringe area beyond it, which I have possessed completely in words and but little in reality, an area that is familiar and mythological at the same time. The opposite of the known—its wrong side, so to speak—are those streets to me, almost as completely hidden as the buried foundation of our house or our invisible skeleton.

The walk brought me to a corner. I breathed the night, feeling the peaceful respite from thought. The sight that greeted my eyes, uncomplicated to be sure, seemed simplified by my fatigue. Its very typicality made it unreal. The street was lined with low houses, and, although the first impression was poverty, the second was surely happiness. The street was very poor and very pretty. None of the houses stood out from the rest; the fig tree cast a shadow; the doors—higher than the elongated lines of the walls—seemed to be made of the same infinite substance as the night. The footpath ran along steeply above the street, which was of elemental clay, clay of a still unconquered America. To the rear the alley was already the pampa, descending toward the Maldonado. On the muddy and chaotic ground a rose-colored adobe wall seemed not to harbor moonglow but to shed a light of its own. I suspect that there can be no better way of denoting tenderness than by means of that rose color.

I stood there looking at that simplicity. I thought, no doubt aloud, "This is the same as it was thirty years ago." I guessed at the date: a recent time in other countries, but already remote in this changing part of the world. Perhaps a bird was singing and I felt for him a small, bird-sized affection. What stands out most clearly: in the already vertiginous silence the only noise was the intemporal sound of the crickets. The easy thought, "I am in the 1800s, " ceased to be a few careless words and deepened into reality. I felt dead—that I was an abstract perceiver of the world; I felt an undefined fear imbued with knowledge, the supreme clarity of metaphysics. No, I did not believe I had traveled across the presumptive waters of time; rather I suspected I was the possessor of the reticent or absent meaning of the inconceivable word "eternity" Only later was I able to define that imagining.

And now I shall write it like this: that pure representation of homogeneous facts—clear night, limpid wall, rural scent of honeysuckle, elemental clay—is not merely identical to the scene on that corner so many years ago; it is, without similarities or repetitions, the same. If we can perceive that identity, time is a delusion: the indifference and inseparability of one moment of time's apparent yesterday and another of its apparent today are enough to disintegrate it.

It is evident that the number of these human moments is not infinite. The basic ones are still more impersonal—moments of physical suffering and physical joy, of the approach of sleep, of the hearing of a single piece of music, of much intensity or much dejection. This is the conclusion I derive: life is too poor not to be immortal. But we do not even possess the certainty of our poverty, since time, easily refutable in the area of the senses, is not so easily refutable in the intellectual sphere, from whose essence the concept of succession seems inseparable. So then, let my intimation of an idea remain as an emotional anecdote. The real moment of ecstasy and the possible insinuation of eternity which that night so generously bestowed on me will be crystallized in the avowed irresolution of these pages.

B

Of the many doctrines recorded by the history of philosophy, idealism is perhaps the most ancient and the most widely divulged. The observation is Carlyle's (*Novalis,* 1829). Without any hope of completing the infinite census, I should like to add to the philosophers he mentioned the Platonists, for whom prototypes are the only reality (Norris, Judah Abrabanel, Gemistus, Plotinus); the theologians, for whom everything that is not the divinity is contingent (Malebranche, Johannes Eckhart); the monists, who make of the universe a vain adjective of the Absolute (Bradley, Hegel, Parmenides). Idealism is as old as metaphysical inquietude. Its most clever apologist, George Berkeley, flourished in the eighteenth century. Contrary to Schopenhauer's statement (*Welt als Wille und Vorstellung,* II, I), Berkeley's merit could not have consisted in the intuitive perception of that doctrine, but in the arguments he conceived to reason it. Berkeley utilized those arguments against the notion of matter; Hume applied them to consciousness. My purpose is to apply them to time. But first I shall summarize briefly the various stages of that dialectic.

Berkeley denied matter. That does not mean, it should be understood, that he denied colors, odors, flavors, sounds, and contacts. What he denied was that, outside of those perceptions or components of the external world, there was an invisible, intangible something called matter. He denied that there were pains that no one feels, colors that no one sees, forms that no one touches. He reasoned that to add matter to perceptions is to add to the world an inconceivable superfluous world. He believed in the apparential world fabricated by the senses, but he considered that the material world (Toland's, say) was an illusory duplication. He observed (*The Principles of Human Knowledge,* 3):

> That neither our thoughts, nor passions, nor ideas formed by the imagination, exist without the mind, is what everybody will allow.—And to me it is no less evident that the various *Sensations,* or *ideas imprinted on the sense,* however blended or combined together (that is, whatever *objects* they compose), cannot exist otherwise than in a mind perceiving them— . . . The table I write on I say exists, that is, I see and feel it; and if I were out of my study I should say it existed—meaning thereby that if I was in my study I might perceive it, or that some other spirit actually does perceive it. . . . For as to what is said of the absolute existence of unthinking things without any relation to their being perceived, that is to me perfectly unintelligible. Their *esse* is *percipi,* nor is it possible they should have any existence out of the minds or thinking things which perceive them.

Foreseeing objections, he added in paragraph 23:

> But, say you, surely there is nothing easier than for me to imagine trees, for instance, in a park, or books existing in a closet, and nobody by to perceive them. I answer, you may so, there is no difficulty in it; but what is all this, I beseech you, more than framing in *your* mind certain ideas

which you call books and trees, and at the same time omitting to frame the idea of any one that may perceive them? But do not you yourself perceive or think of them all the while? This therefore is nothing to the purpose; it only shews you have the power of imagining or forming ideas in your mind; but it does not shew that you can conceive it possible the objects of your thought may exist without the mind.

In paragraph 6 he had already stated:

Some truths there are so near and obvious to the mind that a man need only open his eyes to see them. Such I take this important one to be, viz., that all the choir of heaven and furniture of the earth, in a word all those bodies which compose the mighty frame of the world, have not any subsistence without a mind—that their *being* is *to be perceived or known;* that consequently so long as they are not actually perceived by me, or do not exist in my mind or that of any other created spirit, they must either have no existence at all, or else subsist in the mind of some Eternal Spirit—.

(Berkeley's God is a ubiquitous spectator whose purpose is to give coherence to the world.)

The doctrine I have just expounded has been misinterpreted. Herbert Spencer believes he refutes it (*Principles of Psychology,* VIII, 6) by reasoning that if there is nothing but consciousness, then it must be infinite in time and space. It is true that consciousness is infinite in time if we understand that all time is time perceived by someone, and false if we infer that that time must, necessarily, span an infinite number of centuries. That consciousness must be infinite in space is illicit, since Berkeley (*The Principles of Human Knowledge,* 116; *Siris,* 266) repeatedly denied absolute space. Even more indecipherable is the error Schopenhauer makes (*Welt als Wille und Vorstellung,* II, I) when he teaches that for the idealists the world is a cerebral phenomenon. However, Berkeley had written (*Dialogues Between Hylas and Philonous,* II): "The brain . . . being a sensible thing, exists only in the mind. Now, I would fain know whether you think it reasonable to suppose, that one idea or thing existing in the mind, occasions all other ideas. And if you think so, pray how do you account for the origin of that primary idea or brain itself?" The brain, in fact, is no less a part of the external world than the constellation Centaurus.

Berkeley denied that there was an object behind sense impressions. David Hume denied that there was a subject behind the perception of changes. Berkeley denied matter; Hume denied the spirit. Berkeley did not wish us to add the metaphysical notion of matter to the succession of impressions, while Hume did not wish us to add the metaphysical notion of a self to the succession of mental states. This amplification of Berkeley's arguments is so logical that Berkeley had already foreseen it, as Alexander Campbell Fraser points out, and had even tried to confute it by means of the Cartesian *ergo sum.* Hylas, foreshadowing David Hume, had said in the third and last of the *Dialogues:* ". . . in consequence of your own principles, it should follow that you are only a system of floating ideas, without any substance to support them. . . . And as there is no more meaning in spiritual substance than in material substance, the one is to be exploded as well as the other." Hume corroborates this:

> . . . I may venture to affirm of the rest of mankind, that they are nothing but a bundle or collection of different perceptions, which succeed each other with an inconceivable rapidity . . . The mind is a kind of theatre, where several perceptions successively make their appearance; pass, repass, glide away, and mingle in an infinite variety of postures and situations. . . . The comparison of the theatre must not mislead us. They are the successive perceptions only, that constitute the mind; nor have we the most distant notion of the place where these scenes are represented, or of the materials of which it is composed. (*A Treatise of Human Nature*, I, 4, 6)

Having admitted the idealist argument, I believe it is possible—perhaps inevitable—to go further. For Berkeley, time is "the succession of ideas . . . which flows uniformly and is participated by all beings" (*The Principles of Human Knowledge*, 98); for Hume, it is "composed of indivisible moments" (*A Treatise of Human Nature*, I, 2, 2). Nevertheless, having denied matter and spirit, which are continuities, and having denied space also, I do not know with what right we shall retain the continuity that is time. Outside of each perception (actual or conjectural) matter does not exist; outside of each mental state the spirit does not exist; nor will time exist outside of each present instant. Let us select a moment of the greatest simplicity, that of the dream of Chuang Tzu (Herbert Allen Giles, *Chuang Tzu*, 1889). Around 2400 years ago Chuang Tzu dreamed that he was a butterfly and when he awakened he did not know if he was a man who had dreamed he was a butterfly, or a butterfly dreaming it was a man. Let us not consider the awakening; let us consider the moment of the dream; or one of the moments. "I dreamed that I was a butterfly flying through the air and that I knew nothing of Chuang Tzu," says the ancient text. We shall never know if Chuang Tzu saw a garden over which he seemed to be flying, or a moving yellow triangle, which was undoubtedly he himself, but we know that the image was subjective, although it was supplied by the memory. The doctrine of psychophysical parallelism will avow that this image must have been caused by some change in the dreamer's nervous system; according to Berkeley, at that moment neither Chuang Tzu's body nor the black bedroom in which he dreamed existed, except as a perception in the divine mind. Hume simplifies it even more: at that moment Chuang Tzu's spirit did not exist; only the colors of the dream and the certainty of being a butterfly existed. It existed as a momentary term of the "bundle or collection of different perceptions" which was, some four centuries before Christ, the mind of Chuang Tzu; they existed as term n of an infinite temporal series, between $n - 1$ and $n + 1$. There is no other reality for idealism than that of the mental processes; to add to the butterfly that is perceived an objective butterfly seems to be a vain duplication; to add an ego to the processes seems no less excessive. It acknowledges that there was a dreaming, a perceiving, but not a dreamer or even a dream; and that to speak of objects and of subjects is to gravitate toward an impure mythology. Now then, if each psychic state is self-sufficient, if to connect it to a circumstance or to an ego is an illicit and vain addition, what right have we to impose on it, later, a place in time? Chuang Tzu dreamed that he was a butterfly and during that dream he was not Chuang Tzu —he was a butterfly. How, having abolished space and the ego, shall we connect those instants to the instants of awakening and to the feudal age of Chinese history? That does not mean that we shall never know, even approximately, the date of the dream; it means that the chronological determination of an event, of any event on earth, is alien and exterior to the event. In China, Chuang Tzu's dream is proverbial; imagine that one of its almost infinite readers dreams he is a butterfly and then that he is Chuang Tzu. Imagine that, by a not impossible chance, this dream is an exact repetition of the master's dream. Having postulated that identity, we must ask: Those instants that coincide—are they not the same? Is not *one single repeated term* enough to disrupt and confound the history of the world, to tell us that there is no such history?

To deny time is really two denials: the denial of the succession of the terms of a series, the denial of the synchronism of the terms of two series. In fact, if each term is absolute, its relations are reduced to the consciousness that those relations exist. One state precedes another if it is known to be anterior to it; State G is contemporaneous with State H if it is known to be contemporaneous with it. Contrary to Schopenhauer's declaration[2] in his table of fundamental truths (*Welt als Wille und Vorstellung,* II, 4), each fraction of time does not fill all space simultaneously, time is not ubiquitous. (Naturally, at this stage of the argument, space no longer exists.)

Meinong, in his theory of apprehension, admits the apprehension of imaginary objects: the fourth dimension, say, or the sensible statue of Condillac, or the hypothetical animal of Lotze, or the square root of -1. If the reasons I have indicated are valid, then matter, the ego, the external world, universal history, our lives also belong to that nebulous orb.

Furthermore, the phrase *negation of time* is ambiguous. It can mean the eternity of Plato or Boethius and also the dilemmas of Sextus Empiricus. The latter (*Adversus mathematicos,* XI, 197) denies the past, which already was, and the future, which has not yet been, and argues that the present is divisible or indivisible. It is not indivisible, because in that case it would have no beginning that would connect it to the past nor end that would connect it to the future, nor even a middle, because a thing that has no beginning and end cannot have a middle; neither is it divisible, because in that case it would consist of a part that was and of another part that is not. *Ergo,* the present does not exist, and since the past and the future do not exist either, time does not exist. F. H. Bradley rediscovers and improves that perplexity. He observes (*Appearance and Reality,* IV) that if the now is divisible into other nows it is no less complicated than time, and, if it is indivisible, time is a mere relation between intemporal things. As you see, those reasonings deny the parts in order to deny the whole; I reject the whole

---

[2]And previously by Newton, who affirmed: "Each particle of space is eternal, each indivisible moment of duration is everywhere" (*Principia,* III, 42).

to exalt each one of the parts. By the dialectic of Berkeley and Hume I have arrived at Schopenhauer's statement:

> The form of the appearance of the will is only the present, not the past or the future; the latter do not exist except in the concept and by the linking of the consciousness, submitted to the principle of reason. No one has lived in the past, no one will live in the future; the present is the form of all life, it is a possession that no misfortune can take away . . . Time is like an infinitely rotating circle: the descending arc is the past, the ascending one is the future; above, there is an indivisible point that touches the tangent and is the now. Motionless like the tangent, that extensionless point marks the contact of the object, whose form is time, with the subject, which is formless, because it does not belong to the knowable and is a preliminary condition of knowledge. (*Welt als Wille und Vorstellung,* I, 54)

A Buddhist tract from the fifth century, the *Visuddhimagga* (*Way of Purity*), illustrates the same doctrine with the same figure: "Strictly speaking, the life of a being has the duration of an idea. As a carriage wheel touches the ground in only one place when it turns, life lasts as long as a single idea" (Radhakrishnan, *Indian Philosophy,* I, 373). Other Buddhist texts say that the world is annihilated and resurges again 6,500,000,000 times a day and that every man is an illusion, vertiginously made of a series of momentary and lone men. "The man of a past moment," says the *Way of Purity,* "has lived, but he does not live nor will he live; the man of a future moment will live, but he has not lived nor does he live; the man of the present moment lives, but he has not lived nor will he live" (*Indian Philosophy,* I, 407). We can compare this with the words of Plutarch: "The man of yesterday has died in the man of today, the man of today dies in the man of tomorrow" (*De E apud Delphos, 18*).

And yet, and yet—to deny temporal succession, to deny the ego, to deny the astronomical universe, are apparent desperations and secret assuagements. Our destiny (unlike the hell of Swedenborg and the hell of Tibetan mythology) is not horrible because of its unreality; it is horrible because it is irreversible and ironbound. Time is the substance I am made of. Time is a river that carries me away, but I am the river; it is a tiger that mangles me, but I am the tiger; it is a fire that consumes me, but I am the fire. The world, alas, is real; I, alas, am Borges.

NOTE TO THE PROLOGUE

All expositions of Buddhism mention the *Milinda Pañha,* an apologetic work from the second century, which relates a discussion between the King of the Bactrians, Menander, and the monk Nagasena. The latter reasons that as the king's chariot is not the wheels, nor the body, nor the axis, nor the pole, nor the yoke, neither is man matter, form, impressions, ideas, instincts, or consciousness. He is not the combination of those parts nor does he exist apart from them. After a controversy that lasts for many days, Menander (Milinda) is converted to the faith of the Buddha.

The *Milinda Pañha* has been translated into English by Rhys Davids (Oxford, 1890–94).

NOTE ON WALT WHITMAN [JLB 61]

The whole of Whitman's work is deliberate.
—R. L. Stevenson, *Familiar*
Studies of Men and Books (1882)

The practice of literature sometimes fosters the ambition to construct an absolute book, a book of books that includes all the others like a Platonic archetype, an object whose virtue is not lessened by the years. Those who cherished that ambition have chosen lofty subjects: Apollonius of Rhodes, the first ship that braved the dangers of the deep; Lucan, the struggle between Caesar and Pompey, when the eagles waged war against the eagles; Camoëns, the Portuguese armies in the Orient; Donne, the circle of a soul's transmigrations according to Pythagorean dogma; Milton, the most ancient of sins and Paradise; Firdusi, the thrones of the Sassanidae. Góngora, I believe, was the first to say that an important book can exist without an important theme; the vague story told by the *Soledades* is deliberately trite, according to the observation and reproof of Cascales and Gracián (*Cartas filológicas,* VIII; *El Criticón,* II, 4). Trivial themes did not suffice for Mallarmé; he sought negative ones—the absence of a flower or a woman, the whiteness of the piece of paper before the poem. Like Pater, he felt that all the arts gravitate toward music, the art that has form as its substance; his decorous profession of faith, *Tout aboutit à un livre,* seems to summarize the Homeric axiom that the gods fabricate misfortunes so that future generations will have something to sing about (*Odyssey,* VIII). Around 1900 Yeats searched for the absolute in the manipulation of symbols that would awaken the generic memory, or Great Memory, which pulsates beneath individual minds; those symbols could be compared to the later archetypes of Jung. Barbusse, in *L'Enfer,* a book that has been unjustly neglected, avoided (tried to avoid) the limitations of time by means of the poetical account of man's basic acts. In *Finnegans Wake* Joyce tried to achieve the same objective by the simultaneous presentation of the characteristics of different epochs. The deliberate manipulation of anachronisms to produce an appearance of eternity has also been practiced by Pound and T. S. Eliot.

I have recalled some procedures; none is more curious than the one used by Whitman in 1855. Before considering it, I should like to quote some opinions that more or less prefigure what I am going to say. The first is from the English poet Lascelles Abercrombie, who wrote that Whitman extracted from his noble experience the vivid and personal figure who is one of the few great things in modern literature: the figure of himself. The second is from Sir Edmund Gosse, who said there was no real Walt Whitman, but that Whitman was literature in the protoplasmic state: an intellectual organism that was so simple it only reflected those who approached it. The third one is mine; it is found on page 70 of the book *Discusión* (1932):

> Almost everything that has been written about Whitman is falsified by two persistent errors. One is the summary identification of Whitman, the man of letters, with Whitman, the semidivine hero of *Leaves of Grass,* as Don Quixote is the hero of the *Quixote.* The other is the senseless adoption of the style and vocabulary of his poems by those who write about him, that is to say, the adoption of the same surprising phenomenon one wishes to explain.

Imagine that a biography of Ulysses (based on the testimonies of Agamemnon, Laertes, Polyphemus, Calypso, Penelope, Telemachus, the swineherd, Scylla and Charybdis) indicated that he never left Ithaca. Such a book is fortunately hypothetical, but its particular brand of deception would be the same as the deception in all the biographies of Whitman. To progress from the paradisiacal sphere of his verses to the insipid chronicle of his days is a melancholy transition. Paradoxically, that inevitable melancholy is aggravated when the biographer chooses to overlook the fact that there are two Whitmans: the "friendly and eloquent savage" of *Leaves of Grass* and the poor writer who invented him.[1] The latter was never in California or in Platte Canyon; the former improvises an apostrophe in Platte Canyon ("Spirit that Formed this Scene") and was a miner in California ("Starting from Paumanok," 1). In 1859 the latter was in New York; on December 2 of that year the former was present at the execution of the old abolitionist, John Brown, in Virginia ("Year of Meteors"). The latter was born on Long Island; so was the former ("Starting from Paumanok," 1), but he was also born in one of the Southern states ("Longings for Home"). The latter was chaste, reserved, and somewhat taciturn; the former, effusive and orgiastic. It is easy to multiply such contradictions; but it is more important to understand that the mere happy vagabond proposed by the verses of *Leaves of Grass* would have been incapable of writing them.

Byron and Baudelaire dramatized their unhappiness in famous volumes; Whitman, his joy. (Thirty years later, in Sils-Maria, Nietzsche would discover Zarathustra; that pedagogue is happy or, at any rate, he recommends happiness, but his principal defect is that he does not exist.) Other romantic heroes—Vathek is the first of the series, Edmond Teste is not the last—tediously emphasize their differences; Whitman, with impetuous humility, yearns to be like all men. He says that *Leaves of Grass* "is the song of a great collective, popular individual, man or woman" (*Complete Writings,* V, 192). Or in these immortal words ("Song of Myself," 17):

> These are really the thoughts of all men in all ages and lands,
>> they are not original with me,
> If they are not yours as much as mine they are nothing, or next
>> to nothing,

---

[1] Henry Seidel Canby (*Walt Whitman,* 1943) and Mark Van Doren in the Viking Press anthology (1945) recognize that difference very well, but, to my knowledge, they are the only ones who do.

If they are not the riddle and the untying of the riddle they are
   nothing,
If they are not just as close as they are distant they are nothing.

This is the grass that grows wherever the land is and the water is,
This is the common air that bathes the globe.

Pantheism has disseminated a variety of phrases which declare that God is
several contradictory or (even better) miscellaneous things. The prototype of
such phrases is this: "I am the rite, I am the offering, I am the oblation to the
parents, I am the grass, I am the prayer, I am the libation of butter, I am the
fire" (*Bhagavad-Gita,* IX, 16). Earlier, but ambiguous, is Fragment 67 of Heraclitus: "God is day and night, winter and summer, war and peace, satiety and
hunger." Plotinus describes for his pupils an inconceivable sky, in which "everything is everywhere, anything is all things, the sun is all the stars, and each
star is all the stars and the sun" (*Enneads,* V, 8, 4). Attar, a twelfth-century
Persian, sings of the arduous pilgrimage of the birds in search of their king, the
Simurg; many of them perish in the seas, but the survivors discover that they
are the Simurg and that the Simurg is each one of them and all of them. Extension of the principle of identity seems to have infinite rhetorical possibilities.
Emerson, a reader of the Hindus and of Attar, leaves us the poem "Brahma";
perhaps the most memorable of its sixteen verses is this one: "When me they
fly, I am the wings." Similar but more fundamental is *"Ich bin der Eine und bin
Beide,"* by Stefan George (*Der Stern des Bundes*). Walt Whitman renovated
that procedure. He did not use it, as others had, to define the divinity or to play
with the "sympathies and differences" of words; he wanted to identify himself,
in a sort of ferocious tenderness, with all men. He said ("Crossing Brooklyn
Ferry," 6):

[I] Was wayward, vain, greedy, shallow, sly, cowardly, malignant,
The wolf, the snake, the hog, not wanting in me,

And also, ("Song of Myself," 33):

I am the man, I suffer'd, I was there.
The disdain and calmness of martyrs,
The mother of old, condemn'd for a witch, burnt with dry
   wood, her children gazing on,
The hounded slave that flags in the race, leans by the fence,
   blowing, cover'd with sweat,
The twinges that sting like needles his legs and neck, the
   murderous buckshot and the bullets,
All these I feel or am.

Whitman felt and was all of them, but fundamentally he was—not in mere
history, in myth—what these two lines denote ("Song of Myself," 24):

Walt Whitman, a kosmos, of Manhattan the son,
Turbulent, fleshy, sensual, eating, drinking, and breeding,

He was also the one he would be in the future, in our future nostalgia, which is created by these prophecies that announced it ("Full of Life Now"):

> Full of life now, compact, visible,
> I, forty years old the eighty-third year of the States,
> To one a century hence or any number of centuries hence,
> To you yet unborn these, seeking you.
>
> When you read these I that was visible am become invisible,
> Now it is you, compact, visible, realizing my poems,
>   seeking me,
> Fancying how happy you were if I could be with you and
>   become your comrade;
> Be it as if I were with you. (Be not too certain but I am
>   now with you.)

Or ("Songs of Parting," 4, 5):

> Camerado, this is no book,
> Who touches this touches a man,
> (Is it night? are we here together alone?)
>
> I love you, I depart from materials,
> I am as one disembodied, triumphant, dead.[2]

Walt Whitman, the man, was editor of the *Brooklyn Eagle* and read his basic ideas in the pages of Emerson, Hegel, and Volney; Walt Whitman, the poetic personage, evolved his ideas from contact with America through imaginary experiences in the bedrooms of New Orleans and on the battlefields of Georgia. That does not necessarily imply falsity. A false fact may be essentially true. It is said that Henry I of England never smiled after the death of his son; the fact, perhaps false, can be true as a symbol of the king's grief. In 1914 it was reported that the Germans had tortured and mutilated a number of Belgian hostages; the statement may have been false, but it effectively summarized the infinite and confused horrors of the invasion. Even more pardonable is the case of those who attribute a doctrine to vital experiences and not to a certain library or a certain epitome. In 1874 Nietzsche ridiculed the Pythagorean thesis that history repeats itself cyclically (*Vom Nutzen und Nachtheil der Historie,* 2); in 1881 he suddenly conceived that thesis on a path in the woods of Silvaplana (*Ecce homo,* 9). One could descend to the level of a detective and speak of plagiarism; if he were asked about it, Nietzsche would reply that the important consideration is the change an idea

---

[2]The mechanism of these apostrophes is intricate. We are touched by the fact that the poet was moved when he foresaw our emotion. Compare these lines by Flecker, addressed to the poet who will read him a thousand years later:

> O friend unseen, unborn, unknown,
> Student of our sweet English tongue,
> Read out my words at night, alone:
> I was a poet, I was young.

can cause in us, not the mere formulation of it.[3] The abstract proposition of divine unity is one thing; the flash of light that drove some Arab shepherds out of the desert and forced them into a battle that has not ended and which extended from Aquitaine to the Ganges is another. Whitman's plan was to display an ideal democrat, not to devise a theory.

Since Horace predicted his celestial metamorphosis with a Platonic or Pythagorean image, the theme of the poet's immortality has been classic in literature. Those who utilized it did so from motives of vainglory ("Not marble, nor the gilded monuments"), if not from a kind of bribery or even revenge. From his manipulation of the theme, Whitman derives a personal relationship with each future reader. He identifies himself with the reader, and converses with Whitman ("*Salut au Monde!,*" 3):

What do you hear, Walt Whitman?

And it was thus that he became the eternal Whitman, the friend who is an old American poet of the 1800s and also his legend and also each one of us and also happiness. Vast and almost inhuman was the task, but no less important was the victory.

THE HOUSE OF ASTERION [JLB 62]

And the Queen gave birth to a
son, who was called Asterion.
—Apollodorus, *The Library,* III, 1

I know that I am thought of as proud, as a hater of mankind, and perhaps as a madman. Such charges (which in due time I will avenge) are, of course, groundless. It is true that I seldom venture out of my house, but it is equally true that its gates, whose number is infinite, are open night and day to man and beast alike. Let him who wants come in. Here he will find neither womanish luxuries nor the pomp and gallantries of palaces, but rather, peace and solitude. At the same time, he will find a house unlike any other on earth. (Those who claim that in Egypt there is one similar are liars.) Even my detractors are forced to admit that there's not a single stick of furniture in my house. Another spiteful falsehood has it that I, Asterion, am a captive. Must I repeat that this house has no closed door? Need I add that there are no locks and no keys? As a matter of fact, one afternoon I did step out into the street; if I came back before nightfall I did so out of the horror that the faces of the common people stirred in me—colorless, flattened faces like an open palm. The sun had already set, but the helpless wail of a child

---

[3]Reason and conviction differ so much that the gravest objections to any philosophical doctrine usually preexist in the work that declares it. In the *Parmenides* Plato anticipates the argument of the third man which Aristotle will use to oppose him; Berkeley (*Dialogues,* 3) anticipates the refutations of Hume.

and the crude supplications of the mob showed that they knew me. Men uttered prayers, fled, fell before me on their knees. Some clambered up the steps of the Temple of the Axes, others gathered stones. One or two, I believe, sought refuge beneath the waves. Not for nothing was my mother a queen; I cannot mingle with the crowd, even if my modesty were to allow it.

The fact is that there is nobody like me. I take no stock in what one man may convey to other men; like the philosopher, I believe that nothing is conveyed by the art of writing. Petty, bothersome details find no room in my spirit, whose scope tends to the lofty. I have never been able to tell the difference between one letter and another, and a certain generous impatience has not permitted me to learn to read. Now and then I regret this, for the nights and days are very long.

Of course, I have no lack of pastimes. Like a butting ram, I rush down these stone passages until I fall to the ground in a daze. I crouch in the shadow of a wellhead, or in the bend of a corridor, and play at being hunted. There are flat roofs from which I let myself fall and bloody my knees. At any hour, shutting my eyes and breathing heavily, I can play at being asleep. (Sometimes I really sleep, sometimes the color of the sky is changed when I open my eyes.) But of all these games, I like best the one I play with another Asterion. I pretend he comes to visit me and I am showing him the house. Bowing low, I say to him, "Now we are back at the same crossway," or "Now we find our way into a new courtyard," or "I knew you'd like this water trough," or "Now you're about to see a cistern that has filled with sand," or "Now you'll see how the cellar branches right and left." Sometimes I make a mistake and the two of us have a good long laugh.

Not only have I dreamed up these games; I have also pondered the house. Every part of it is to be found many times, and any particular place may be any other. There is no one cistern, courtyard, watering trough, or manger; there are fourteen [infinite] mangers, troughs, courtyards, cisterns. The house is the same size as the world; or rather, it is the world. Nonetheless, by plodding through courtyard after courtyard and along dusty gray stone corridors, I reached the street and saw the Temple of the Axes and the sea. I failed to understand these things until a night vision revealed to me that the seas and temples are also fourteen [infinite] in number. All things are many, are fourteen, but there are two things in the world that seem to be just one—on high, the intricate sun; on earth, Asterion. Maybe I created the stars and the sun and this sprawling house, but I no longer remember.

Every nine years, nine men enter the house so that I may deliver them from all evil. I hear their footsteps or their voices along the stone passages and, full of joy, I rush to find them. The ceremony lasts only minutes. One after the other they go down, and my hands are unsullied. Where they fall they remain; these corpses help me tell one passageway from another. I do not know who these men are, but I know that one of them, at the hour of his death, foretold that on a certain day my redeemer would come. Since then, I have not suffered loneliness, for I know that my redeemer lives and that someday he shall rise out of the dust. If all the sounds of the world reached my ears I would hear his steps. If only he would take me to a house with fewer passages and fewer gates! What will my redeemer be like? I ask myself. Will he be a bull or a man? Can he possibly be a bull with a man's face? Or will he be like me?

The morning sun glinted off the bronze sword. It no longer showed even a trace of blood.

"Would you believe it, Ariadne?" said Theseus. "The Minotaur barely put up a fight."

THE ZAHIR [JLB 63]

In Buenos Aires the Zahir is an ordinary coin worth 20 centavos. The letters N T and the number 2 are scratched as if with a razor blade or penknife; 1929 is the date on the obverse. (In Guzerat, toward the end of the eighteenth century, the Zahir was a tiger; in Java, a blind man from the mosque of Surakarta whom the Faithful pelted with stones; in Persia, an astrolabe which Nadir Shah caused to be sunk to the bottom of the sea; in the Mahdi's prisons, along about 1892, it was a little compass which Rudolf Carl von Slatin touched, tucked into the fold of a turban; in the mosque of Córdoba, according to Zotenberg, it was a vein in the marble of one of the 1200 pillars; in the Tetuán ghetto, it was the bottom of a well.) Today is November 13; the Zahir came into my possession at dawn on June 7. I am no longer the "I" of that episode; but it is still possible for me to remember what happened, perhaps even to tell it. I am still, however incompletely, Borges.

Clementina Villar died on June 6. Around 1930, her pictures were clogging the society magazines: perhaps it was this ubiquity that contributed to the legend that she was extremely pretty, although not every portrait bore out this hypothesis unconditionally. At any rate, Clementina Villar was interested less in beauty than in perfection. The Hebrews and the Chinese codified every conceivable human eventuality; it is written in the Mishnah that a tailor is not to go out into the street carrying a needle once the Sabbath twilight has set in, and we read in the Book of Rites that a guest should assume a grave air when offered the first cup, and a respectfully contented air upon receiving the second. Something of this sort, though in much greater detail, was to be discerned in the uncompromising strictness which Clementina Villar demanded of herself. Like any Confucian adept or Talmudist, she strove for irreproachable correctness in every action; but her zeal was more admirable and more exigent than theirs because the tenets of her creed were not eternal, but submitted to the shifting caprices of Paris or Hollywood. Clementina Villar appeared at the correct places, at the correct hour, with the correct appurtenances and the correct boredom; but the boredom, the appurtenances, the hour, and the places would almost immediately become passé and would provide Clementina Villar with the material for a definition of cheap taste. She was in search of the Absolute, like Flaubert; only hers was an Absolute of a moment's duration. Her life was exemplary, yet she was ravaged unremittingly by an inner despair. She was forever experimenting with new metamorphoses, as though trying to get away from herself; the color of her hair and the shape of her coiffure were celebratedly unstable. She was always changing her smile, her complexion, the slant of her eyes. After thirty-two she was scrupulously slender. . . . The war gave her much to think about: with Paris occupied by the Germans, how could one follow the fashions? A foreigner whom she had always distrusted presumed so far upon her good faith as to sell her a number of cylindrical hats; a year later it was divulged that those absurd creations *had never been worn in Paris at all!* Consequently they were not hats, but arbitrary, unauthorized eccentricities. And troubles never come singly: Dr. Villar had to move to Aráoz Street, and his daughter's portrait was now adorning advertisements for cold cream and automobiles. (The cold cream that she abundantly applied, the automobiles she *no longer* possessed.) She knew that the successful exercise of her art demanded a large fortune, and she preferred retirement from the scene to halfway effects. Moreover, it pained her to have to compete with giddy little nobodies. The gloomy Aráoz apartment was too much to bear: on June 6 Clementina Villar committed the solecism of dying in the very middle of the southern district. Shall I confess that I—moved by that most sincere of Argentinian passions, snobbery—was enamored of her, and that her death moved me to tears? Probably the reader has already suspected as much.

At a wake, the progress of corruption brings it about that the corpse reassumes its earlier faces. At some stage of that confused night of the sixth, Clementina Villar was magically what she had been twenty years before: her features recovered that authority which is conferred by pride, by money, by youth, by the awareness of rounding off a hierarchy, by lack of imagination, by limitations, by stolidity. Somehow, I thought, no version of that face which has disturbed me so will stay in my memory as long as this one; it is right that it should be the last, since it might have been the first. I left her rigid among the flowers, her disdain perfected by death. It must have been about two in the morning when I went away. Outside, the predictable rows of one- and two-story houses had taken on the abstract appearance that is theirs at night, when darkness and silence simplify them. Drunk with an almost impersonal piety, I walked through the streets. At the corner of Chile and Tacuarí I saw an open shop. And in that shop, unhappily for me, three men were playing cards.

In the figure of speech called oxymoron a word is modified by an epithet which seems to contradict it: thus, the Gnostics spoke of dark light, and the alchemists of a black sun. For me it was a kind of oxymoron to go straight from my last visit with Clementina Villar to buy a drink at a bar; I was intrigued by the coarseness of the act, by its ease. (The contrast was heightened by the circumstance that there was a card game in progress.) I asked for a brandy. They gave me the Zahir in my change. I stared at it for a moment and went out into the street, perhaps with the beginnings of a fever. I reflected that every coin in the world is a symbol of those famous coins which glitter in history and fable. I thought of Charon's obol; of the obol for which Belisarius begged; of Judas's thirty coins; of the drachmas of Laïs, the famous courtesan; of the ancient coin which one of the Seven Sleepers proffered; of the shining coins of the wizard in *The 1001 Nights,* that turned out to be bits of paper; of the inexhaustible penny of Isaac Laquedem; of the 60,000 pieces of silver, one for each line of an epic, which Firdusi sent back to a king because they were not of gold; of the doubloon which Ahab nailed to the mast; of Leopold Bloom's irreversible florin; of the louis whose pictured face betrayed the fugitive Louis XVI near Varennes. As if in a dream, the thought that every piece of money entails such illustrious connotations as these, seemed to me of huge, though inexplicable, importance. My speed increased as I passed through the empty squares and along the empty streets. At length, weariness deposited me at a corner. I saw a patient iron grating and, beyond, the black and white flagstones of the Concepción. I had wandered in a circle and was now a block away from the store where they had given me the Zahir.

I turned back. The dark window told me from a distance that the shop was now closed. In Belgrano Street I took a cab. Sleepless, obsessed, almost happy, I reflected that there is nothing less material than money, since any coin whatsoever (let us say a coin worth 20 centavos) is, strictly speaking, a repertory of possible futures. Money is abstract, I repeated; money is the future tense. It can be an evening in the suburbs, or music by Brahms; it can be maps, or chess, or coffee; it can be the words of Epictetus teaching us to despise gold; it is a Proteus more versatile than the one on the isle of Pharos. It is unforeseeable time, Bergsonian time, not the rigid time of Islam or the Porch. The determinists deny that there is such a thing in the world as a single possible act, i.e. an act that could or could not happen; a coin symbolizes man's free will. (I did not suspect that these "thoughts" were an artifice opposed to the Zahir and an initial form of its demoniacal influence.) I fell asleep after much brooding, but I dreamed that I was the coins guarded by a griffon.

The next day I decided that I had been drunk. I also made up my mind to get rid of the coin that had caused me so much worry. I looked at it: there was nothing out of the ordinary about it except for some scratches. The best thing to do would be to bury it in the garden or hide it in some corner of the library, but I wanted to remove myself from its orbit. I preferred to lose it. I did not go to the Pilar that morning, or to the cemetery; I took the underground to Constitución and from Constitución to the corner of San Juan and Boedo. I got off, on an impulse, at Urquiza and walked west and south. With scrupulous lack of plan I rounded a number of corners, and in a street which looked to me like all the others I went into a wretched little tavern, asked for a drink of brandy, and paid for it with the Zahir. I half-closed my eyes behind my dark spectacles, managing not to see the house numbers or the name of the street. That night I took a Veronal tablet and slept peacefully.

Up till the end of June I was busy writing a tale of fantasy. This contained two or three enigmatic circumlocutions, or kennings: for example, instead of *blood* it says *sword-water,* and *gold* is the *serpent's bed;* the story is told in the first person. The narrator is an ascetic who has abjured the society of men and who lives in a kind of wilderness. (The name of this place is Gnitaheidr.) Because of the simplicity and candor of his life there are those who consider him an angel;

but this is a pious exaggeration, for there is no man who is free of sin. As a matter of fact, he has cut his own father's throat, the old man having been a notorious wizard who by magic arts had got possession of a limitless treasure. To guard this treasure from the insane covetousness of human beings is the purpose to which our ascetic has dedicated his life: day and night he keeps watch over the hoard. Soon, perhaps too soon, his vigil will come to an end: the stars have told him that the sword has already been forged which will cut it short forever. (*Gram* is the name of that sword.) In a rhetoric increasingly more complex he contemplates the brilliance and the flexibility of his body: in one paragraph he speaks distractedly of his scales; in another he says that the treasure which he guards is flashing gold and rings of red. In the end we understand that the ascetic is the serpent Fafnir, that the treasure upon which he lies is the treasure of the Nibelungs. The appearance of Sigurd brings the story to an abrupt end.

I have said that the composition of this trifle (into which I inserted, in a pseudo-erudite fashion, a verse or two from the *Fáfnismál*) gave me a chance to forget the coin. There were nights when I felt so sure of being able to forget it that I deliberately recalled it to mind. What is certain is that I overdid these occasions: it was easier to start the thing than to have done with it. It was in vain that I told myself that that abominable nickel disk was no different from others that pass from one hand to another, alike, countless, innocuous. Attracted by this idea, I tried to think of other coins; but I could not. I remember, too, a frustrated experiment I made with Chilean 5- and 10-centavo pieces and a Uruguayan *vintén*. On July 16 I acquired a pound sterling. I did not look at it during the day, but that night (and other nights) I put it under a magnifying glass and studied it by the light of a powerful electric lamp. Afterward I traced it on paper with a pencil. But the brilliance and the dragon and Saint George were of no help to me: I could not manage to change obsessions.

In August I decided to consult a psychiatrist. I did not tell him the whole of my ridiculous story; I said I was bothered by insomnia, that I was being haunted by the image of something or other . . . let us say a poker chip or a coin. A little later, in a bookshop in Sarmiento Street, I dug up a copy of Julius Barlach's *Urkunden zur Geschichte der Zahirsage* (Breslau, 1899).

In this book my disease was clearly revealed. According to the preface, the author proposed "to gather together in one handy octavo volume all the documents having to do with the Zahir superstition, including four papers from the Habicht collection and the original manuscript of the study by Philip Meadows Taylor." Belief in the Zahir is of Islamic origin, and seems to date from the eighteenth century. (Barlach rejects the passages which Zotenberg attributes to Abulfeda.) *Zahir* in Arabic means "notorious," "visible"; in this sense it is one of the ninety-nine names of God, and the people (in Muslim territories) use it to signify "beings or things which possess the terrible property of being unforgettable, and whose image finally drives one mad." The first irrefutable testimony is that of the Persian Lutf Ali Azur. In the precise pages of the biographical encyclopedia entitled *Temple of Fire* this polygraph dervish writes that in a school at Shiraz there was a copper astrolabe "fashioned in such a way that whoever looked once upon it could thereafter think of nothing else; whence the King ordered that it should be sunk in the deepest part of the sea, lest men forget the universe." The study of Philip Meadows Taylor is more detailed (he was in the service of the Nizam of Hyderabad, and wrote the famous novel, *Confessions of a Thug*). In about 1832, in the outskirts of Bhuj, Taylor heard the unusual expression "Verily he has looked on the Tiger" to signify madness or saintliness. He was informed that the reference was to a magic tiger which was the ruin of whoever beheld it, even from far away, since the beholder continued to think about it to the end of his days. Someone said that one of these unfortunates had fled to Mysore, where he had painted the figure of the tiger on the walls of some palace. Years later, Taylor was inspecting the jails of the kingdom; and in the one at Nittur the governor showed him a cell where the floor, the walls, and the ceiling had been covered, in barbaric colors which time was subtilizing before erasing them, by a Muslim fakir's elaboration of a kind of infinite Tiger. This Tiger was composed of many tigers in the most vertiginous fashion: it was traversed by tigers, scored by tigers, and it contained seas and Himalayas and armies which seemed to reveal still other tigers. The painter had died many years ago in this very cell; he had come from Sind, or maybe Guzerat, and his original purpose had been to design a map of the world. Indeed, some traces of this were yet to be discerned in the monstrous image. . . . Taylor told the story to Mohammed Al-Yemeni, of Fort William; Mohammed informed him that there was no created thing in this world which could not take on the properties of *Zaheer*, [1] but that the All-Merciful does not allow two things to be it at the same time, since one alone is able to fascinate multitudes. He said that there is always a Zahir; that in the Age of Innocence it was an idol named Yaúq; and later, a prophet of Jorasán who used to wear a veil embroidered with stones, or a golden mask. [2] He also said that God is inscrutable.

I read Barlach's monograph—read it and reread it. I hardly need describe my feelings. I remember my despair when I realized that nothing could save me; the sheer relief of knowing that I was not to blame for my predicament; the envy I felt for those whose Zahir was not a coin, but a piece of marble, or a tiger. How easy it would be not to think of a tiger! And I also remember the odd anxiety with which I studied this paragraph: "A commentator on the *Gulshan i Raz* says that he who has seen the Zahir will soon see the Rose; and he cites a verse interpolated in the *Asrar Nama* (Book of Things Unknown) of Attar: 'The Zahir is the shadow of the Rose, and the Rending of the Veil.' "

That night at Clementina's house I had been surprised not to see her younger sister, Mrs. Abascal. In October one of her friends told me about it: "Poor Julie! She got awfully *queer*, and they had to shut her up in the Bosch. She's just going to be the *death* of the nurses who have to *spoon*-feed her! Why, she keeps on talking about a *coin*, just like Morena Sackmann's *chauffeur*."

Time, which generally attenuates memories, only aggravates that of the

---

[1] Such is Taylor's spelling of the word.
[2] Barlach observes that Yaúq is mentioned in the Koran (71, 23) and that the Prophet is Al-Mokanna (the Veiled One), and that no one except Taylor's surprising informant has identified them with the Zahir.

Zahir. There was a time when I could visualize the obverse, and then the reverse. Now I see them simultaneously. This is not as though the Zahir were crystal, because it is not a matter of one face being superimposed upon another; rather, it is as though my eyesight were spherical, with the Zahir in the center. Whatever is not the Zahir comes to me fragmentarily, as if from a great distance: the arrogant image of Clementina; physical pain. Tennyson once said that if we could understand a single flower, we should know what we are and what the world is. Perhaps he meant that there is no fact, however insignificant, that does not involve universal history and the infinite concatenation of cause and effect. Perhaps he meant that the visible world is implicit in every phenomenon, just as the will, according to Schopenhauer, is implicit in every subject. The Cabalists pretend that man is a microcosm, a symbolic mirror of the universe; according to Tennyson, everything would be. Everything, even the intolerable Zahir.

Before 1948 Julia's destiny will have caught up with me. They will have to feed me and dress me, I shall not know whether it is afternoon or morning, I shall not know who Borges was. To call this prospect terrible is a fallacy, for none of its circumstances will exist for me. One might as well say that an anesthetized man feels terrible pain when they open his cranium. I shall no longer perceive the universe: I shall perceive the Zahir. According to the teaching of the Idealists, the words "live" and "dream" are rigorously synonymous. From thousands of images I shall pass to one; from a highly complex dream to a dream of utter simplicity. Others will dream that I am mad; I shall dream of the Zahir. When all the men on earth think, day and night, of the Zahir, which will be a dream and which a reality—the earth or the Zahir?

In the empty night hours I can still walk through the streets. Dawn may surprise me on a bench in Garay Park, thinking (trying to think) of the passage in the *Asrar Nama* where it says that the Zahir is the shadow of the Rose and the Rending of the Veil. I associate that saying with this bit of information: in order to lose themselves in God, the Sufis recite their own names, or the ninety-nine divine names, until they become meaningless. I long to travel that path. Perhaps I shall conclude by wearing away the Zahir simply through thinking of it again and again. Perhaps behind the coin I shall find God.

A CELEBRATION OF THE MONSTER [JLB 64]

Here begins your sorrow.
—Hilario Ascasubi, *The Blood Bath*

I'm telling you, Nelly, it was a regular civic demonstration. Me with my flat feet trouble and with my breath that gets blocked in my short little neck and with my hippo tummy, I had a real opponent in fatigue, specially when you think that the night before I thought I'd hit the sack early, I mean, who wants to look like a jerk on your day off with a big show coming up, you know? This here was my plan: show up in person at the committee at eight-thirty, at nine hit the sack like a sponge, and with the Colt under my pillow, take off on the Big Sleep of the Century, and be up and at 'em with the first cock-a-doodle-doo, when the guys in the truck would come pick me up. But tell me something, don't you think luck is like the lottery, and that somebody else is always winning? On the little plank bridge there that leads to the sidewalk I almost took a swimming lesson in the water flooding there 'cause of the surprise of running into my buddy Milk Tooth, one of those guys you meet once in a while. Soon as I saw his expense-account face, I knew he was going to the committee too, and just in the way of getting a view of the latest developments, we got to talkin' about the distribution of heaters for the great parade and about a Jew, who, no questions asked, would take 'em for scrap iron over in Berazategui. While we got on line we struggled to tell each other in Pig Latin how once we got hold of the firearms we'd get 'em over to Berazategui, even if we had to carry each other piggyback, and there, after we pumped a little pasta into the guts, paid for with the weapon money, we'd buy —to the surprise of the ticket seller guy—two tickets back to Tolosa! But we might as well have been talkin' French, 'cause Milk Tooth didn't catch any of it, me neither, and the fellows on line lent their services as interpreters, they almost busted my eardrums, and they passed us the ballpoint to jot down the Jew's address. A lucky thing Mr. Marforio, who's skinnier than the slot you put the nickel in, is one of them old-timers that while you think he's just a pile of dandruff, he's really in touch with the inside feelings of the masses themselves, so you shouldn't be surprised that he stopped the whole shebang there, putting off the handouts till the big day, with the excuse that there was a delay in the Police Department about giving out the guns. We'd been standing on that there line for an hour and a half, something I wouldn't even do for cooking gas, when from Mr. Pizzurno's very mouth we heard the order to get out of there on the double, which we did cheerin', so full of spirit that even the cripple who works as doorman for the committee couldn't break it up with his raving brooms.

At a safe distance the gang got together again. Loiácomo started talkin', man, worse than the radio of the lady down the hall. The thing about these fatheads with the big mouths is that they get you going and then the guy they get going—the undersigned, follow?—don't know what's hit him, and they got you playing blackjack in Bernardez's store, and maybe you figured I was having a good time but the sad truth is that they skinned me out of my last token, without even saying thanks for the memories.

(Take it easy, Nelly, now that the switchman's finished eatin' you up with his peepers and he's takin' off on the dray like a big jerk, let your little ol' Donald Duck give you another pinch on the cheek.)

When I finally crawled into the sack, my feets were giving off such tired signals that I knew right away that restful sleep was mine for the taking. What I didn't figure on was that member of the opposing team, healthy patriotism. All I could think of was the Monster and that the next day I would see him smilin' and talkin' like the great Argentine worker he is. I swear I got so worked up that I threw off the covers so I could breathe, just like a baby whale. Just about the time the dogcatcher comes around I got to sleep, what turned out to be as exhausting as not sleeping, 'cause I dreamt first about an afternoon when I was a kid, when my dear departed mother took me to a farm. Believe me, Nelly, I hadn't never thought about that afternoon, but in the dream I realized it was the happiest in my life, and all I really remember is some water with leaves shining in it and a very white and very gentle dog who I patted on the back; luckily I got out of that kid stuff and dreamt about more modern things, stuff on the big agenda: the Monster made me his mascot and, later, his Great High Priest Dog. I woke up and it'd taken five minutes to dream all that crazy stuff. I decided to turn over a new leaf: I gave myself a rubdown with the kitchen rag, I stuck my corns into my Buster Browns. I got all tangled like a squid in the sleeves and legs of my suit—my trusty overalls—I put on the wool tie with the cartoon characters you gave me the day of the other demonstration, and I went out sweatin' grease 'cause some big cat came down the street and I thought it was the truck. With every false alarm what could of been a truck or not I popped out like a cork, trottin' like in gym class, covering the sixty yards from the third courtyard to the street entrance. With youthful enthusiasm I sang the march song which is our flag, but at ten of twelve I lost my voice and the millionaires from the first courtyard stopped throwing everything they had at me. At one-twenty the truck came, early, and when the comrades of the crusade were happy to see me, and I didn't even eat the bread the clean-up lady leaves for the parrot, they all voted to leave me, with the excuse that they were riding on a meat truck and not on a crane. I played along and hung on and they told me if I promised not to have a baby before we got to Ezpeleta they would carry me like a sack, but finally they gave in and sorta helped me up. The truck of the country's youth took off like a mad swallow and before it went half a block it stopped in front of the committee. A gray-haired Indian came out, and it was a pleasure how he bossed us around, and before they could give us the complaints book, we was already sweatin' in the clink, like we had necks like grated cheese. A heater per head in alphabetical order was the way it was; meditate on that, Nelly; for every revolver there was one of us. Without even a time limit enough for us to line up outside the *Gentlemen,* or even to try to sell off a pistol in good shape, the Indian put us back into the truck which we couldn't escape without a letter of recommendation for the truck-driver.

Just sittin' there waitin' for the command, "Forward, march!" They had us standin' in the sun for an hour and a half, in plain sight of our beloved Tolosa, and as soon as the police went after them, the kids had us in slingshot range, as if what they appreciated most in us wasn't our selfless patriotism but our bein' blackbirds for the pie. When half of the first hour passed there prevailed in the truck that tension on which all social gatherings is based, but later the gang put me in a good mood when they asked me if I had signed up for the Queen Victoria Prize, for the first man to give birth, you know, an indirect way of referring to this bass drum here in front, you know, they always say it ought to be made out of glass so that I could see, even if it was only the toes, of my size fourteens. I was so hoarse that it looked like I had a muzzle on, but in an hour or so I got back my silver tongue[1] a little, and shoulder to shoulder with the comrades in the

---

[1]While we was recuperating our energies with the help of some buns, Nelly told me[2] the poor sap stuck out the aforementioned tongue. (Note supplied by Young Rabasco.)

breech, I didn't want to hold back my participation in a stereophonic singin' of the Monster's march, and I tried till I sorta croaked, somethin', honest, like a hiccup, that if I didn't open the umbrella I left home I'd have been like in a canoe with all the spit flying around, you'd have took me for Vito Dumas, the Solitary Sailor. Finally we got goin' and then the air started to flow, it was like takin' a bath in a soup pot, and there was a guy eatin' a sausage sandwich, there was somebody else with a salami, another guy with a loaf of bread, another guy with a half a bottle of chocolate milk, and a guy in back with an eggplant parmigian', but maybe I'm thinkin' of another time when we went out to the Ensenada, but since I didn't go I'm better off not talkin'. I couldn't stop thinkin' about the fact that all those modern healthy boys thought everything just like me, 'cause even the laziest has to hear the official radio announcements 'cause that's all you can hear even if you don't want to. We were all Argentines, all young, all from the Southside, and we were all rushin' to meet our twin brothers, who, in the same kind of trucks, was comin' from Fiorito and Villa Dominico, from Ciudadela, from Villa Luro, from La Paternal, but over in Villa Crespo there's too many Jews and I say it would be better for us to say we live in North Tolosa.

What team spirit you missed, Nelly! In every rundown neighborhood a real avalanche, excited with the purest idealism, wanted to come along, but the *capo* of our truckload, Garfunkel, knew how to get rid of the miserable bunch of bastards, specially when you think that in all those bums there could hide a fifth column just like that, guys who could convince you before you go around the world in eighty days that you're a certified jerk and that the Monster is a tool of the telephone company. I wouldn't tell you too much about more than one chicken who tried to take advantage of those purges to slip away in the confusionism and get home just like that; but admit it, some guys got it, some guys don't, 'cause when I've tried to slip out of the truck it was a kick from Mister Garfunkel that restored me to the bosom of those valiant heroes. At the beginning we was received with an enthusiasm that was frankly contagious, but Mister Garfunkel, who don't use his head just to hold up his hat, forbid the driver to slow down so that no wise guy would try to bug out. Another end of the stick was handed to us in Quilmes, where the jerks got permission to flatten out their calluses, but at that distance from home, who was goin' to leave the group? Till that very second, as Zoppi or his mother is my witness, everything went like a charm, but nervousness spread over the gang when the boss, Garfunkel to you, set us to shaking like jelly when he ordered us to write the Monster's name on all the walls and to jump back on the truck as fast as a dose of castor oil before somebody took a swing at us. When the moment of truth arrived, I grabbed my heater and got out, ready for anything, Nelly, even for sellin' it for three bucks. But not even one customer stuck his nose out so I had some fun scribblin' some letters on a wall, and if I'd have spent another minute there, the truck would have gone around a corner and the horizon would have swallowed it up on the way to civic pride, togetherness, brotherhood, the Monsterfest. The truck was set for togetherness when I got back sweatin' like a pig with my tongue hanging out. They had on the brakes and the truck looked like the picture of a truck. Thank God that

[2]She told me first. (Supplemental note by Nano Buttafuoco, Sanitation Dept.)

guy Tabacman, the guy who talks through his nose, the guy they call the Endless Screw, was with us, 'cause he's an ace with engines and after a half-hour looking into the engine and drinkin' all the soda in my camel stomach, that's the nickname I gave to my canteen, he stood up and said, "Beats me," 'cause Ford turned out to be a mystery name for him.

I think I read on a wall somewhere that we should always look for the silver lining, 'cause just then Our Father presented us with a bike left in a vegetable garden, and it looked to me like the owner was gone for a new tire 'cause he didn't show his nostrils when Garfunkel himself hit the seat with his rear end. Then he took off like he smelled a whole block of sausages, like as if Zoppi or his mother shoved a firecracker up his ass. Not a few guys had to loosen their belts from laughin' so hard seeing the guy pedal like that, but after keepin' up with him for four blocks they lost sight of him, 'cause your pedestrian even if he's got Keds on his hands can't keep the victor's laurel when he's up against Mr. Bicycle. The enthusiasm of conscience on the march, in less time than it takes you, pudgy, to gobble up everythin' in front of you, made that guy disappear into the horizon, home to Tolosa, to hit the sack, the way it looked to me.

Now your little Porky's goin' to get confidential, Nelly: he was goin' like mad, runnin' from the Great God Fear, but like I always say whenever a fighter looks like he's sinkin' and the bleakest predictions pile up, suddenly the center forward kicks a good one and makes a goal: that's the way the Monster does it for the Fatherland; and for our bunch that was scatterin' around, the truck-driver. That patriot, I take my hat off to him, took off like a shot and stopped the one who got farthest, right in his tracks. He slipped him a message so that the next day, 'cause of the bruises, everybody took me for the bread man's pinto horse. From down on the ground I gave such loud cheers that the locals had to stick their fingers in their ears. Meantime the truck-driver put us patriots in Indian file and if anybody tried to get away the guy behind had carte blanche to ascribe him a kick in the backside so that it still hurts me to sit down. Figure it out, Nelly, what luck the last guy had, with nobody takin' shots at his rear guard! It was—you guessed it—the truck-driver who drove us like a bunch of flatfooted recruits to a place that I wouldn't hesitate to characterize as the vicinity of Don Bosco, I mean, the Wilde. There, chance put into our hands a bus headin' for Black Lady's Rest, as if made to order. The truck-driver, who had the bus driver's number—they both, in the heroic days of the Villa Dominico People's Zoo, worked as halfs of the same camel—asked that Catalonian guy to take us down. Before you could say go! to Gofreddo, we was already added to the passenger list, laughin' till we showed our tonsils at the impotent jerks waitin' on line that didn't get into the vehicle, bein' left you might say, with a clear pat to go back, with no ill-feelin', to Tolosa. I exaggerate, Nelly, that we was like in a bus, why we was sweatin' like a can of sardines, that if you took a good look, the *Ladies* over in Berazategui would've looked small. What stories of mediocre interest ran around! And I don't have to say nothin' about the beauty broadcast by Potasman the wop, right by Sarandi, and right now I'd applaud the Endless Screw with my four hands 'cause he was right in there winnin' his metal for bein' a comedian by makin' me, after threatening me with a shot in the nuts, open my mouth and close my eyes: a joke where he took advantage by immediately stuffing my mouth with dust balls and other stuff from the seats. But even suckers get tired and when we didn't know what to do anymore, a guy slipped me his penknife and we all used it to make the seat covers look like strainers. To throw suspicion off us, we all laughed at me; and later, sure enough, there was one of those wise guys who jumps like a flea and ends up stuck in the asphalt, tryin' to get out of the bus before the driver spots the damage. The first to hit the ground was Simon Tabacman, who landed right on his ass; right after, Noodles Zoppi or his mother; finally, even if you split open in anger, Rabasco; then Spatola; *doppo,* Speciale the Basque. Meantime, Morpurgo got down and got papers and paper bags together, obsessed with the idea of startin' a true-blue bonfire that would burn up the Brockway bus with the intention of drawin' attention away from the marks left by the penknife. Pirosanto, that nasal, motherless punk who has more matches than dirt in his pockets, took off on the first turn so he wouldn't have to loan me a Lucky, almost tippin' a hand, but at the same time with a Kool he grabbed out of my mouth. Me, without tryin' to show off, but tryin' to show a little style, was just about pullin' my mouth into shape for the first drag when Pirosanto, with a grab, kidnapped the cigarette and Morpurgo, as if he was sweetening the medicine, grabbed the match that was toasting my warts and set fire to the papers. Without even taking off his skimmer, lid, or hat, Morpurgo hit the street, but me, pot and all, beat him out and jumped first, so I was set up as a mattress for him, so I broke his fall and he almost broke the bottom out of my gut with his two hundred pounds. Jeez, when I pulled Manolo M. Morpurgo's boots, which was up to his knees, out of my mouth, the bus was burnin' in the distance, like Rome itself, and the guard-ticket-taker-owner was cryin' like mad about his investment turnin' to black smoke before his very eyes. The guys, tougher than him, was laughin', but we was still ready, I swear by the Monster, to run if the guy got really mad. Screw, the economy-sized joker, thought up a joke that while you're listening there with your mouth open you'll turn to jelly from laughin'. Listen, Nelly. Clean out your ears 'cause here it comes. You said—but don't get distracted by that asshole over there you're makin' eyes at—that the bus was burnin' like Rome. Ha ha ha.

I was as cool as a cucumber, but turnin' yellow inside. You, who should be engraving every word that drops from between my teeth in your brain, maybe you remember the truck-driver who was half a camel with the bus guy. If you get me, we figured that he would get together with that crybaby and punish us for our bad conduct. But don't worry about your little bunny; the truck-driver took it all calmly and figured out that the other guy, without his bus, wasn't no oligarch you had to worry about no more. He smiled like the good-hearted slob he is; just to maintain discipline he nudged a couple of guys in a friendly way (here's the tooth he knocked out that I bought off him later for a souvenir) and then: Close ranks! Double time, march!

What a thing togetherness is! The proud column was advancin' through the backed-up sewers or the piles of garbage that mark the entrance to the capital, with no defections except maybe a third of us guys that started out from Tolosa.

At least one incorrigible dared, with the approval of the truck-driver, to start to light up a Kent. What a picture to color in: Spatola carried the colors, wearin' his T-shirt over his wool clothes, to make himself into a *descamisado*. Screw and the rest followed him in ranks of four.

It was probably around seven when we finally got to Mitre. Morpurgo laughed like hell to think that we was already at Avellaneda. The playboys laughed too, almost fallin' off the balconies, out of cars and open buses, they all laughed to see us on foot with no cars. Luckily, Babuglia thinks of everything, and on the other side of the Riachuelo some trucks was rustin' away, Canadian trucks that the institute, always on the alert, got as puzzles from the demolition section of the American Army. Like monkeys we scrambled up into the khaki-colored one, and harmonizing, "Farewell, for I depart weeping," we waited till a loon from the Autonomous Unit, supervised by Endless Screw, got goin' on installin' the engine. Lucky that Rabasco, despite the backside face he got, made a deal with a guard from the Monopoly, and after payin' for the tickets we filled up a trolley that made more noise than a bagpipe. The trolley headed bangity-bang downtown; it went along proud as a young mother that under the eyes of Granpa carries in her tummy the modern generations that tomorrow will claim their place in the snack bars of life. . . . In its bosom, with one ankle in a stirrup and the other with no legal residence, went your dear clown, me. An innocent bystander would've said that the trolley was singin'; it cut through the air, pushed on by song; we were the singers. Just before Belgrano Street the speed stopped dead after twenty-four minutes: I sweated to understand and also because of the crowd, like ants of more and more cars, that didn't let our means of locomotion take a single step.

    The truck-driver shrieked out the word, "Out, you bums!" and then we got out at the intersection of Tacuarí and Belgrano. After two or three blocks on foot, a question came out in the open: our throats was dry and demanded liquids. The Puga and Gallach Emporium and Dispensary of Beverages presented a means to resolve the problem. But now tell me, bright boy: How was we goin' to pay? At that junction the truck-driver came up with a plan. With the sense and patience of a bulldog, which ended up seein' things the other way, he tripped me up in front of the amused gang, then he stuck a screen over my head like a hat down to my nose, and out of my vest spilled the dough I had, so I wouldn't look so bad when the hot-dog stand came around. The purse went into the common fund and the truck-driver, havin' taken care of me, switched to Souza, who's the right-hand man of Gouvea, from Caravel Caramels—you know, the guys that set themselves up as the Technical Tapioca Corporation. Souza, who lives for Caramels, is paymaster over there, and it's for sure that he's put into circulation so many bills—of up to 50 cents—that not even Crazy Calcamonia had seen so many, and he'd been pulled in for doctorin' up the first bank note he'd ever seen. Souza's, natch, weren't fakes, and they paid in cold cash for our consumption of Virginia Dare, and we went out like you do when the jug's dry. Bo, when he's got the guitar, thinks he's Gardel.[3] He even thinks he's Gotuso.[3] He even thinks he's Garofalo.[3] He even thinks he's Giganti-Tomassoni.[3] There was no guitar in the joint, but Bo gave out with "Farewell, My Beloved Pampa," and we all sang the chorus and the juvenile column was like a single shout. Each guy, in spite of his youth, sang what his body told him to, till we was distracted by a kike that came by lookin' so respectable with his beard. We let that one off with his life, but a smaller one, easier to handle, more practical, handier, didn't get off so easy. He was a miserable four-eyes, without the muscles of an athlete. He had red hair, books under his arms, the studious type. He barely noticed, he was so distracted that he almost knocked over our color guard, Spatola. Bonfirraro, who's a bug for details, said he wasn't goin' to let go unpunished such irreverence for the banner and the picture of the Monster. Right then and there he signaled to Ten-Ton Baby, whose name is Cagnazzo, to go ahead. Ten-Ton, always the same kidder, let go of my ears, which he'd rolled up like peanut shells and, just to be nice to Bonfirraro, told the Jew to show a little more respect for the picture of the Monster. The guy answered with some nonsense about havin' his own ideas. Baby, who gets bored with explanations, shoved him with a hand that if the butcher sees it, the shortage of steak is over. He pushed him into a vacant lot, the kind that one of these days'll get turned into a parking lot, and backs the guy up against a nine-story wall without windows. Meantime, the guys in the back was pushin' us out of curiosity to see, and the guys in the front ended up like a salami sandwich, between the nuts who wanted a panoramic view and the jerks who was surrounded, who, God knows why, was gettin' mad. Ten-Ton, aware of the danger, backpedaled, and we opened up like a fan making a semicircle, but with no exit, 'cause we was all along the wall. We was yellin' like the bears' cage and our teeth was chattering, but the truck-driver, who never missed a single hair in his soup, figured that more or less than one of us had in mind a plan for escape. Everybody was whistlin', then he set us up on a pile of rubble, which was there for anyone to see. You remember that that afternoon the thermometer hit soup temperature, and you're not goin' to argue that a percentage of us took off our coats. We made the Saulino kid our coat guard, so he couldn't take part in the stonin'. The first shot got him right in the head—Tabacman—and it split his gums, and the blood was a black stream. I got hot 'cause of the blood and I hit him with a chunk that smashed his ear and then I lost count of the hits, 'cause the bombardment was massive. It was a riot; the Jew went down on his knees and looked at the sky and prayed in his broken speech like he wasn't there. When the bells of Montserrat rang, he fell down, 'cause he was dead. We kept it up a little more with shots that didn't hurt him anymore. I swear, Nelly, we left the body in a hell of a mess. Then Morpurgo, to make the guys laugh, made me stick the penknife in what used to be his face.

After exercisin', what gets you warmed up, I put on my jacket again, a move to keep me from catchin' cold, that could cost you a fortune in aspirins. Then I tied the scarf that you embroidered with your fairy fingers around my neck and accommodated my ears under my homburg, but the great surprise of the day came from Pirosanto, with the idea of settin' fire to our bleedin' rock pile, after

---

[3]The most popular singers of that season.

auctioning off his eyeglasses and clothes. The auction wasn't a success. The glasses was covered with the slime from the eyes and the suit was sticky with blood. The books too was a bust, saturated as they was with organic remains. Luck had it that the truck-driver (who turned out to be Graffiacane) managed to salvage a seventeen-jewel Bulova, and Bonfirraro snagged a Fabricant watch that had up to three bucks in it and a snapshot of a lady piano teacher, and that sap Rabasco had to be satisfied with the Bausch glass case and a Plumex fountain pen, not to mention the ring from Poplavsky's old shop.

Pretty soon, pudgy, that street episode was relegated to oblivion. Banners fluttering, trumpet blasts excitin', the masses all around, great-arino. In the Plaza de Mayo, the great electric shock that signs his name Dr. Marcelo N. Frogman harangued us. He put us in shape for what came after: the words of the Monster. These very ears heard him, pudgy, just like the rest of the country, 'cause the speech was on national broadcast.

THE MEETING IN A DREAM [JLB 65]

After conquering the circles of Hell and the arduous borders of Purgatory, Dante sees Beatrice at last in the Earthly Paradise. Ozanam conjectures that this scene (certainly one of the most astonishing in all literature) is the primitive nucleus of the *Comedy*. My purpose is to relate it, to repeat what the scholiasts say, and to present an observation, perhaps new, of a psychological nature.

On the morning of April 13, 1300, the day before the last day of his journey, Dante, his tasks accomplished, enters the Earthly Paradise, which flourishes on the summit of Purgatory. He has seen the temporal fire and the eternal one, he has passed through a wall of fire, his will is free and upright. Virgil has crowned and mitered him lord of himself *(per ch'io te sovra te corono e mitrio)*. He follows the paths of the ancient garden to a river that transcends all other waters in purity, although neither the sun nor the moon penetrates the trees to illuminate it. Music floats on the air, and a mysterious procession advances on the opposite bank. Twenty-four elders in white robes and four animals, each with six wings adorned with open eyes, precede a triumphal chariot drawn by a griffon. At the right wheel three women are dancing; one is so ruddy that we would scarcely be able to see her in a fire. Beside the left wheel there are four women in purple raiment, one of whom has three eyes. The chariot stops and a veiled woman appears; her costume is the color of a living flame. Not by sight but by the stupor of his spirit and the fear in his blood, Dante knows that it is Beatrice. On the threshold of glory he feels the love that had transfixed him so many times in Florence. Like a frightened child he looks for Virgil's protection, but Virgil is no longer beside him.

I have mislaid the letter, but a couple of years or so ago Gannon wrote me from his ranch up in Gualeguaychú saying he would send me a translation, perhaps the very first into Spanish, of Ralph Waldo Emerson's poem "The Past," and adding in a P.S. that Don Pedro Damián, whom I might recall, had died of a lung ailment a few nights earlier. The man (Gannon went on), wasted by fever, had in his delirium relived the long ordeal of the battle of Masoller. It seemed to me there was nothing unreasonable or out of the ordinary about this news since Don Pedro, when he was nineteen or twenty, had been a follower of the banners of Aparicio Saravia. Pedro Damián had been working as a hand up north on a ranch in Rio Negro or Paysandú when the 1904 revolution broke out. Although he was from Gualeguaychú, in the province of Entre Ríos, he went along with his friends and, being as cocky and ignorant as they were, joined the rebel army. He fought in one or two skirmishes and in the final battle. Returned home in 1905, Damián, with a kind of humble stubbornness, once more took up his work as a cowhand. For all I know, he never left his native province again. He spent his last thirty years living in a small lonely cabin eight or ten miles from Ñancay. It was in that out-of-the-way place that I spoke with him one evening (that I tried to speak with him one evening) back around 1942; he was a man of few words, and not very bright. Masoller, it turned out, was the whole of his personal history. And so I was not surprised to find out that he had lived the sound and fury of that battle over again at the hour of his death. When I knew I would never see Damián another time, I wanted to remember him, but so poor is my memory for faces that all I could recall was the snapshot Gannon had taken of him. There is nothing unusual in this fact, considering that I saw the man only once at the beginning of 1942, but had looked at his picture many times. Gannon sent me the photograph and it, too, has been misplaced. I think now that if I were to come across it, I would feel afraid.

The second episode took place in Montevideo, months later. Don Pedro's fever and his agony gave me the idea for a tale of fantasy based on the defeat at Masoller; Emir Rodríguez Monegal, to whom I had told the plot, wrote me an introduction to Colonel Dionisio Tabares, who had fought in that campaign. The colonel received me one evening after dinner. From a rocking chair out in the side yard, he recalled the old days with great feeling but at the same time with a faulty sense of chronology. He spoke of ammunition that never reached him and of reserves of horses that arrived worn out, of sleepy dust-covered men weaving labyrinths of marches, of Saravia, who might have ridden into Montevideo but who passed it by "because the gaucho has a fear of towns," of throats hacked from ear to ear, of a civil war that seemed to me less a military operation than the dream of a cattle thief or an outlaw. Names of battles kept coming up: Illescas, Tupambaé, Masoller. The colonel's pauses were so effective and his manner so vivid that I realized he had told and retold these same things many times before, and I feared that behind his words almost no true memories remained. When he stopped for a breath, I managed to get in Damián's name.

"Damián? Pedro Damián?" said the colonel. "He served with me. A little half-breed. I remember the boys used to call him Daymán—after the river." The colonel let out a burst of loud laughter, then cut it off all at once. I could not tell whether his discomfort was real or put on.

In another voice, he stated that war, like women, served as a test of men, and that nobody knew who he really was until he had been under fire. A man might think himself a coward and actually be brave. And the other way around, too, as had happened to that poor Damián, who bragged his way in and out of saloons with his white ribbon marking him as a Blanco, and later on lost his nerve at Masoller. In one exchange of gunfire with the regulars, he handled himself like a man, but then it was something else again when the two armies met face to face and the artillery began pounding away and every man felt as though there were 5000 other men out there grouping to kill him. That poor kid. He'd spent his life on a farm dipping sheep, and then all of a sudden he gets himself dragged along and mixed up in the grim reality of war. . . .

For some absurd reason Tabares's version of the story made me uncomfortable. I would have preferred things to have happened differently. Without being aware of it, I had made a kind of idol out of old Damián—a man I had seen only once on a single evening many years earlier. Tabares's story destroyed everything. Suddenly the reasons for Damián's aloofness and his stubborn insistence on keeping to himself were clear to me. They had not sprung from modesty but from shame. In vain, I told myself that a man pursued by an act of cowardice is more complex and more interesting than one who is merely courageous. The gaucho Martín Fierro, I thought, is less memorable than Lord Jim or Razumov. Yes, but Damián, as a gaucho, should have been Martín Fierro—especially in the presence of Uruguayan gauchos. In what Tabares left unsaid, I felt his assumption (perhaps undeniable) that Uruguay is more primitive than Argentina and therefore physically braver. I remember we said goodbye to each other that night with a marked cordiality.

During the winter, the need of one or two details for my story (which somehow was slow in taking shape) sent me back to Colonel Tabares again. I found him with another man of his own age, a Dr. Juan Francisco Amaro from Paysandú, who had also fought in Saravia's revolution. They spoke, naturally, of Masoller.

Amaro told a few anecdotes, then slowly added, in the manner of someone who is thinking aloud, "We camped for the night at Santa Irene, I recall, and some of the men from around there joined us. Among them a French veterinarian, who died the night before the battle, and a boy, a sheep shearer from Entre Ríos. Pedro Damián was his name."

I cut him off sharply. "Yes, I know," I said. "The Argentine who couldn't face the bullets."

I stopped. The two of them were looking at me, puzzled.

"You are mistaken, sir," Amaro said after a while. "Pedro Damián died as any man might wish to die. It was about four o'clock in the afternoon. The regular troops had dug themselves in on the top of a hill and our men charged them with lances. Damián rode at the head, shouting, and a bullet struck him square in the chest. He stood up in his stirrups, finished his shout, and then rolled to the ground, where he lay under the horses' hooves. He was dead, and the whole last charge of Masoller trampled over him. So fearless, and barely twenty."

He was speaking, doubtless, of another Damián, but something made me ask what it was the boy had shouted.

"Filth," said the colonel. "That's what men shout in action."

"Maybe," said Amaro, "but he also cried out, 'Long live Urquiza!' "

We were silent. Finally the colonel murmured, "Not as if we were fighting at Masoller, but at Cagancha or India Muerta a hundred years ago." He added, genuinely bewildered, "I commanded those troops, and I could swear it's the first time I've ever heard of this Damián."

We had no luck in getting the colonel to remember him.

Back in Buenos Aires, the amazement that his forgetfulness produced in me repeated itself. Browsing through the eleven pleasurable volumes of Emerson's works in the basement of Mitchell's, the English bookstore, I met Patricio Gannon one afternoon. I asked him for his translation of "The Past." He told me that he had no translation of it in mind, and that, besides, Spanish literature was so boring it made Emerson quite superfluous. I reminded him that he had promised me the translation in the same letter in which he wrote me of Damián's death. He asked me who Damián was. I told him in vain. With rising terror, I noticed that he was listening to me very strangely, and I took refuge in a literary discussion on the detractors of Emerson, a poet far more complex, far more skilled, and truly more extraordinary than the unfortunate Poe.

I must put down some additional facts. In April, I had a letter from Colonel Dionisio Tabares; his mind was no longer vague and now he remembered quite well the boy from Entre Ríos who spearheaded the charge at Masoller and whom his men buried that night in a grave at the foot of the hill. In July, I passed through Gualeguaychú; I did not come across Damián's cabin, and nobody there seemed to remember him now. I wanted to question the foreman Diego Abaroa, who saw Damián die, but Abaroa had passed away himself at the beginning of the winter. I tried to call to mind Damián's features; months later, leafing through some old albums, I found that the dark face I had attempted to evoke really belonged to the famous tenor Tamberlik, playing the role of Othello.

Now I move on to conjectures. The easiest, but at the same time the least satisfactory, assumes two Damiáns: the coward who died in Entre Ríos around 1946, and the man of courage who died at Masoller in 1904. But this falls apart in its inability to explain what are really the puzzles: the strange fluctuations of Colonel Tabares's memory, for one, and the general forgetfulness, which in so short a time could blot out the image and even the name of the man who came back. (I cannot accept, I do not want to accept, a simpler possibility—that of my having dreamed the first man.) Stranger still is the supernatural conjecture thought up by Ulrike von Kühlmann. Pedro Damián, said Ulrike, was killed in the battle and at the hour of his death asked God to carry him back to Entre Ríos. God hesitated a moment before granting the request, but by then the man was already dead and had been seen by others to have fallen. God, who cannot unmake the past but can affect its images, altered the image of Damián's violent death into one of falling into a faint. And so it was the boy's ghost that came back to his native province. Came back, but we must not forget that it did so as a ghost. It lived in isolation without a woman and without friends; it loved and possessed everything, but from a distance, as from the other side of a mirror; ultimately it "died" and its frail image just disappeared, like water in water. This conjecture is faulty, but it may have been responsible for pointing out to me the true one (the one I now believe to be true), which is at the same time simpler and more unprecedented. In a mysterious way I discovered it in the treatise *De Omnipotentia* by Pier Damiani, after having been referred to him by two lines in Canto XXI of the *Paradiso,* in which the problem of Damiani's identity is brought up. In the fifth chapter of that treatise, Pier Damiani asserts—against Aristotle and against Fredegarius de Tours—that it is within God's power to make what once was into something that has never been. Reading those old theological discussions, I began to understand Don Pedro Damián's tragic story.

This is my solution. Damián handled himself like a coward on the battlefield at Masoller and spent the rest of his life setting right that shameful weakness. He returned to Entre Ríos; he never lifted a hand against another man, he never cut anyone up, he never sought fame as a man of courage. Instead, living out there in the hill country of Ñancay and struggling with the backwoods and with wild cattle, he made himself tough, hard. Probably without realizing it, he was preparing the way for the miracle. He thought from his innermost self, *If destiny brings me another battle, I'll be ready for it.* For forty years he waited and waited, with an inarticulate hope, and then, in the end, at the hour of his death, fate brought him his battle. It came in the form of delirium, for, as the Greeks knew, we are all shadows of a dream. In his final agony he lived his battle over again, conducted himself as a man, and in heading the last charge he was struck by a bullet in the middle of the chest. And so, in 1946, through the working out of a long, slow-burning passion, Pedro Damián died in the defeat at Masoller, which took place between winter and spring in 1904.

In the *Summa theologica,* it is denied that God can unmake the past, but nothing is said of the complicated concatenation of causes and effects which is so vast and so intimate that perhaps it might prove impossible to annul a *single* remote fact, insignificant as it may seem, without invalidating the present. To modify the past is not to modify a single fact; it is to annul the consequences of that fact, which tend to be infinite. In other words, it involves the creation of two universal histories. In the first, let us say, Pedro Damián died in Entre Ríos in 1946; in the second, at Masoller in 1904. It is this second history that we are living now, but the suppression of the first was not immediate and produced the odd contradictions that I have related. It was in Colonel Dionisio Tabares that the different stages took place. At first, he remembered that Damián acted as a coward; next, he forgot him entirely; then he remembered Damián's fearless death. No less illuminating is the case of the foreman Abaroa; he had to die, as I understand it, because he held too many memories of Don Pedro Damián.

As for myself, I do not think I am running a similar risk. I have guessed at and set down a process beyond man's understanding, a kind of exposure of reason;

but there are certain circumstances that lessen the dangers of this privilege of mine. For the present, I am not sure of having always written the truth. I suspect that in my story there are a few false memories. It is my suspicion that Pedro Damián (if he ever existed) was not called Pedro Damián and that I remember him by that name so as to believe someday that the whole story was suggested to me by Pier Damiani's thesis. Something similar happened with the poem I mentioned in the first paragraph, which centers on the irrevocability of the past. A few years from now, I shall believe I made up a fantastic tale, and I will actually have recorded an event that was real, just as some 2000 years ago in all innocence Virgil believed he was setting down the birth of a man and foretold the birth of Christ.

Poor Damián! Death carried him off at the age of twenty in a local battle of a sad and little-known war, but in the end he got what he longed for in his heart, and he was a long time getting it, and perhaps there is no greater happiness.

NATHANIEL HAWTHORNE[1] [JLB 67]

I shall begin the history of American literature with the history of a metaphor; or rather, with some examples of that metaphor. I don't know who invented it; perhaps it is a mistake to suppose that metaphors can be invented. The real ones, those that formulate intimate connections between one image and another, have always existed; those we can still invent are the false ones, which are not worth inventing. The metaphor I am speaking of is the one that compares dreams to a theatrical performance. Quevedo used it in the seventeenth century at the beginning of the *Sueño de la muerte;* Luis de Góngora made it a part of the sonnet *"Varia imaginación,"* where we read:

> A dream is a playwright
> Clothed in beautiful shadows
> In a theater fashioned on the wind.

In the eighteenth century Addison will say it more precisely. When the soul dreams (he writes) it is the theater, the actors, and the audience. Long before, the Persian Omar Khayyam had written that the history of the world is a play that God—the multiform God of the pantheists—contrives, enacts, and beholds to entertain his eternity; long afterward, Jung the Swiss, in charming and doubtless accurate volumes, compares literary inventions to oneiric inventions, literature to dreams.

If literature is a dream (a controlled and deliberate dream, but fundamentally a dream) then Góngora's verses would be an appropriate epigraph to this story about American literature, and a look at Hawthorne, the dreamer, would be a

---

[1]This is the text of a lecture given at the Colegio Libre de Estudios Superiores in March 1949.

good beginning. There are other American writers before him—Fenimore Cooper, a sort of Eduardo Gutiérrez infinitely inferior to Eduardo Gutiérrez; Washington Irving, a contriver of pleasant Spanish fantasies—but we can skip over them without any consequence.

Hawthorne was born in 1804 in the port of Salem, which suffered, even then, from two traits that were anomalous in America: it was a very old, but poor, city; it was a city in decadence. Hawthorne lived in that old and decaying city with the honest biblical name until 1836; he loved it with the sad love inspired by persons who do not love us, or by failures, illness, and manias; essentially it is not untrue to say that he never left his birthplace. Fifty years later, in London or Rome, he continued to live in his Puritan town of Salem; for example, when he denounced sculptors (remember that this was in the nineteenth century) for making nude statues.

His father, Captain Nathaniel Hawthorne, died in Surinam in 1808 of yellow fever; one of his ancestors, John Hawthorne, had been a judge in the witchcraft trials of 1692, in which nineteen women, among them the slave girl Tituba, were condemned to be executed by hanging. In those curious trials (fanaticism has assumed other forms in our time) Justice Hawthorne acted with severity and probably with sincerity. Nathaniel, our Nathaniel, wrote that his ancestor made himself so conspicuous in the martyrdom of the witches that possibly the blood of those unfortunate women had left a stain on him, a stain so deep as to be present still on his old bones in the Charter Street Cemetery if they had not yet turned to dust. After that picturesque note Hawthorne added that, not knowing whether his elders had repented and begged for divine mercy, he wished to do so in their name, begging that any curse that had fallen on their descendants would be pardoned from that day forward.

When Captain Hawthorne died, his widow, Nathaniel's mother, became a recluse in her bedroom on the second floor. The rooms of his sisters, Louise and Elizabeth, were on the same floor; Nathaniel's was on the top floor. The family did not eat together and they scarcely spoke to one another; their meals were left on trays in the hall. Nathaniel spent his days writing fantastic stories; at dusk he would go out for a walk. His furtive way of life lasted for twelve years. In 1837 he wrote to Longfellow: ". . . I have secluded myself from society; and yet I never meant any such thing, nor dreamed what sort of life I was going to lead. I have made a captive of myself, and put me into a dungeon, and now I cannot find the key to let myself out."

Hawthorne was tall, handsome, lean, dark. He walked with the rocking gait of a seaman. At that time children's literature did not exist (fortunately for boys and girls!). Hawthorne had read *Pilgrim's Progress* at the age of six; the first book he bought with his own money was *The Faërie Queene;* two allegories. Also, although his biographers may not say so, he read the Bible; perhaps the same Bible that the first Hawthorne, William Hathorne, brought from England with a sword in 1630. I have used the word "allegories"; the word is important, perhaps imprudent or indiscreet, to use when speaking of the work of Hawthorne. It is common knowledge that Edgar Allan Poe accused Hawthorne of allegorizing and that Poe deemed both the activity and the genre indefensible. Two tasks confront us: first, to ascertain whether the allegorical genre is, in fact, illicit; second, to ascertain whether Nathaniel Hawthorne's works belong to that category.

The best refutation of allegories I know is Croce's; the best vindication, Chesterton's. Croce says that the allegory is a tiresome pleonasm, a collection of useless repetitions which shows us (for example) Dante led by Virgil and Beatrice and then explains to us, or gives us to understand, that Dante is the soul, Virgil is philosophy or reason or natural intelligence, and Beatrice is theology or grace. According to Croce's argument (the example is not his), Dante's first step was to think: "Reason and faith bring about the salvation of souls" or "Philosophy and theology lead us to heaven" and then, for *reason* or *philosophy* he substituted *Virgil* and for *faith* or *theology* he put *Beatrice,* all of which became a kind of masquerade. By that derogatory definition an allegory would be a puzzle, more extensive, boring, and unpleasant than other puzzles. It would be a barbaric or puerile genre, an esthetic sport. Croce wrote that refutation in 1907; Chesterton had already refuted him in 1904 without Croce's knowing it. How vast and uncommunicative is the world of literature!

The page from Chesterton to which I refer is part of a monograph on the artist Watts, who was famous in England at the end of the nineteenth century and was accused, like Hawthorne, of allegorism. Chesterton admits that Watts has produced allegories, but he denies that the genre is censurable. He reasons that reality is interminably rich and that the language of men does not exhaust that vertiginous treasure. He writes:

> Man knows that there are in the soul tints more bewildering, more num-
> berless, and more nameless than the colours of an autumn forest; . . . Yet
> he seriously believes that these things can every one of them, in all their
> tones and semi-tones, in all their blends and unions, be accurately repre-
> sented by an arbitrary system of grunts and squeals. He believes that an
> ordinary civilized stockbroker can really produce out of his own inside
> noises which denote all the mysteries of memory and all the agonies of
> desire.

Later Chesterton implies that various languages can somehow correspond to the ungraspable reality, and among them are allegories and fables.

In other words, Beatrice is not an emblem of faith, a belabored and arbitrary synonym of the word "faith." The truth is that something—a peculiar sentiment, an intimate process, a series of analogous states—exists in the world that can be indicated by two symbols: one, quite insignificant, the sound of the word "faith"; the other, Beatrice, the glorious Beatrice who descended from Heaven and left her footprints in Hell to save Dante. I don't know whether Chesterton's thesis is valid; I do know that the less an allegory can be reduced to a plan, to a cold set of abstractions, the better it is. One writer thinks in images (Shakespeare or Donne or Victor Hugo, say), and another writer thinks in abstractions (Benda or Bertrand Russell); a priori, the former are just as estimable as the latter. However, when an abstract man, a reasoner, also wants to be imaginative, or to pass as such, then the allegory denounced by Croce occurs. We observe that a logical process has been embellished and disguised by the author to dishonor the reader's understanding, as Wordsworth said. A famous example of that ailment is the case of José Ortega y Gasset, whose good thought is obstructed by difficult and adventitious metaphors; many times this is true of Hawthorne. Outside of that, the two writers are antagonistic. Ortega can reason, well or badly, but he cannot imagine; Hawthorne was a man of continual and curious imagination; but he was refractory, so to speak, to reason. I am not saying he was stupid; I say that he thought in images, in intuitions, as women usually think, not with a dialectical mechanism.

One esthetic error debased him: the Puritan desire to make a fable out of each imagining induced him to add morals and sometimes to falsify and to deform them. The notebooks in which he jotted down ideas for plots have been preserved; in one of them, dated 1836, he wrote: "A snake taken into a man's stomach and nourished there from fifteen years to thirty-five, tormenting him most horribly." That is enough, but Hawthorne considers himself obliged to add: "A type of envy or some other evil passion." Another example, this time from 1838: "A series of strange, mysterious, dreadful events to occur, wholly destructive of a person's happiness. He to impute them to various persons and causes, but ultimately finds that he is himself the sole agent. Moral, that our welfare depends on ourselves." Another, from the same year: "A person, while awake and in the business of life, to think highly of another, and place perfect confidence in him, but to be troubled with dreams in which this seeming friend appears to act the part of a most deadly enemy. Finally it is discovered that the dream-character is the true one. The explanation would be—the soul's instinctive perception." Better are those pure fantasies that do not look for a justification or moral and that seem to have no other substance than an obscure terror. Again, from 1838: "The situation of a man in the midst of a crowd, yet as completely in the power of another, life and all, as if they two were in the deepest solitude." The following, which Hawthorne noted five years later, is a variation of the above: "Some man of powerful character to command a person, morally subjected to him, to perform some act. The commanding person to suddenly die; and, for all the rest of his life, the subjected one continues to perform that act." (I don't know how Hawthorne would have written that story. I don't know if he would have decided that the act performed should be trivial or slightly horrible or fantastic or perhaps humiliating.) This one also has slavery—subjection to another—as its theme: "A rich man left by will his mansion and estate to a poor couple. They remove into it, and find there a darksome servant, whom they are forbidden by will to turn away. He becomes a torment to them; and, in the finale, he turns out to be the former master of the estate." I shall mention two more sketches, rather curious ones; their theme, not unknown to Pirandello or André Gide, is the coincidence or the confusion of the esthetic plane and the common plane, of art and reality. The first one: "Two persons to be expecting some occurrence, and watching for the two principal actors in it, and to find that the occurrence is even then passing, and that they themselves are the two actors." The other is more complex: "A person to be writing a tale, and to find that it shapes itself against his intentions; that the characters act otherwise than he thought; that unforeseen events occur; and a catastrophe comes which he strives in vain to avert. It might shadow forth his own fate—he having made himself one of the personages." These games, these momentary confluences of the imaginative world and the real world—the world we pretend is real when we read—are, or seem to us, modern. Their origin, their ancient origin, is perhaps to be found in that part of the *Iliad* in which Helen of Troy weaves into her tapestry the battles and the disasters of the Trojan War even then in progress. Virgil must have been impressed by that passage, for the *Aeneid* relates that Aeneas, hero of the Trojan War, arrived at the port of Carthage and saw scenes from the war sculpted on the marble of a temple and, among the many images of warriors, he saw his own likeness. Hawthorne liked those contacts of the imaginary and the real, those reflections and duplications of art; and in the sketches I have mentioned we observe that he leaned toward the pantheistic notion that one man is the others, that one man is all men.

Something more serious than duplications and pantheism is seen in the sketches, something more serious for a man who aspires to be a novelist, I mean. It is that, in general, situations were Hawthorne's stimulus, Hawthorne's point of departure—situations, not characters. Hawthorne first imagined, perhaps unwittingly, a situation and then sought the characters to embody it. I am not a novelist, but I suspect that few novelists have proceeded in that fashion. "I believe that Schomberg is real," wrote Joseph Conrad about one of the most memorable characters in his novel *Victory*, and almost any novelist could honestly say that about any of his characters. The adventures of the *Quixote* are not so well planned, the slow and antithetical dialogues—reasonings, I believe the author calls them—offend us by their improbability, but there is no doubt that Cervantes knew Don Quixote well and could believe in him. Our belief in the novelist's belief makes up for any negligence or defect in the work. What does it matter if the episodes are unbelievable or awkward when we realize that the author planned them, not to challenge our credibility, but to define his characters? What do we care about the puerile scandals and the confused crimes of the hypothetical court of Denmark if we believe in Prince Hamlet? But Hawthorne first conceived a situation, or a series of situations, and then elaborated the people his plan required. That method can produce, or tolerate, admirable stories because their brevity makes the plot more visible than the actors, but not admirable novels, where the general form (if there is one) is visible only at the end and a single badly invented character can contaminate the others with unreality. From the foregoing statement it will be inferred that Hawthorne's stories are better than Hawthorne's novels. I believe that is true. The twenty-four chapters of *The Scarlet Letter* abound in memorable passages, written in good and sensitive prose, but none of them has moved me like the singular story of "Wakefield" in the *Twice-Told Tales.*

Hawthorne had read in a newspaper, or pretended for literary reasons that he had read in a newspaper, the case of an Englishman who left his wife without cause, took lodgings in the next street, and there, without anyone's suspecting it, remained hidden for twenty years. During that long period he spent all his days across from his house or watched it from the corner, and many times he caught a glimpse of his wife. When they had given him up for dead, when his wife had been resigned to widowhood for a long time, the man opened the door of his house one day and walked in—simply, as if he had been away only a few hours. (To the day of his death he was an exemplary husband.) Hawthorne read about the curious case uneasily and tried to understand it, to imagine it. He pondered on the subject; "Wakefield" is the conjectural story of that exile. The interpretations of the riddle can be infinite; let us look at Hawthorne's.

He imagines Wakefield to be a calm man, timidly vain, selfish, given to childish mysteries and the keeping of insignificant secrets; a dispassionate man of great imaginative and mental poverty, but capable of long, leisurely, inconclusive, and vague meditations; a constant husband, by virtue of his laziness. One October evening Wakefield bids farewell to his wife. He tells her—we must not forget we are at the beginning of the nineteenth century—that he is going to take the stagecoach and will return, at the latest, within a few days. His wife, who knows he is addicted to inoffensive mysteries, does not ask the reason for the trip. Wakefield is wearing boots, a rain hat, and an overcoat; he carries an umbrella and a valise. Wakefield, and this surprises me, does not yet know what will happen. He goes out, more or less firm in his decision to disturb or to surprise his wife by being away from home for a whole week. He goes out, closes the front door, then half opens it, and, for a moment, smiles. Years later his wife will remember that last smile. She will imagine him in a coffin with the smile frozen on his face, or in paradise, in glory, smiling with cunning and tranquillity. Everyone will believe he has died but she will remember that smile and think that perhaps she is not a widow.

Going by a roundabout way, Wakefield reaches the lodging place where he has made arrangements to stay. He makes himself comfortable by the fireplace and smiles; he is one street away from his house and has arrived at the end of his journey. He doubts; he congratulates himself; he finds it incredible to be there already; he fears that he may have been observed and that someone may inform on him. Almost repentant, he goes to bed, stretches out his arms in the vast emptiness, and says aloud: "I will not sleep alone another night." The next morning he awakens earlier than usual and asks himself, in amazement, what he is going to do. He knows that he has some purpose, but he has difficulty defining it. Finally he realizes that his purpose is to discover the effect that one week of widowhood will have on the virtuous Mrs. Wakefield. His curiosity forces him into the street. He murmurs, "I shall spy on my home from a distance." He walks, unaware of his direction; suddenly he realizes that force of habit has brought him, like a traitor, to his own door and that he is about to enter it. Terrified, he turns away. Have they seen him? Will they pursue him? At the corner he turns back and looks at his house; it seems different to him now, because he is already another man—a single night has caused a transformation in him, although he does not know it. The moral change that will condemn him to twenty years of exile has occurred in his soul. Here, then, is the beginning of the long adventure. Wakefield acquires a reddish wig. He changes his habits; soon he has established a new routine. He is troubled by the suspicion that his absence has not disturbed Mrs. Wakefield enough. He decides he will not return until he has given her a good scare. One day the druggist enters the house, another day the doctor. Wakefield is sad, but he fears that his sudden reappearance may aggravate the illness. Obsessed, he lets time pass; before he had thought, "I shall return in a few days," but now he thinks, "in a few weeks." And so ten years pass. For a long time he has not known that his conduct is strange. With all the lukewarm affection of which his heart is capable, Wakefield continues to love his wife, while she is forgetting him. One Sunday morning the two meet in the street amid the crowds of London. Wakefield has become thin; he walks obliquely, as though hiding or escaping; his low forehead is deeply wrinkled; his face, which was common before, is extraordinary, because of his extraordinary conduct. His small eyes wander or look inward. His wife has grown stout; she is carrying a prayer book and her whole person seems to symbolize a placid and resigned widowhood. She is accustomed to sadness and would not exchange it, perhaps, for joy. Face to face, the two look into each other's eyes. The crowd separates them, and soon they are lost within it. Wakefield hurries to his lodgings, bolts the door, and throws himself on the bed where he is seized by a fit of sobbing. For an instant he sees the miserable oddity of his life. "Wakefield, Wakefield! You are mad!" he says to himself.

Perhaps he is. In the center of London he has severed his ties with the world. Without having died, he has renounced his place and his privileges among living men. Mentally he continues to live with his wife in his home. He does not know, or almost never knows, that he is a different person. He keeps saying, "I shall soon go back," and he does not realize that he has been repeating these words for twenty years. In his memory the twenty years of solitude seem to be an interlude, a mere parenthesis. One afternoon, an afternoon like other afternoons, like the thousands of previous afternoons, Wakefield looks at his house. He sees that they have lighted the fire in the second-floor bedroom; grotesquely, the flames project Mrs. Wakefield's shadow on the ceiling. Rain begins to fall, and Wakefield feels a gust of cold air. Why should he get wet when his house, his home, is there. He walks heavily up the steps and opens the door. The crafty smile we already know is hovering, ghostlike, on his face. At last Wakefield has returned. Hawthorne does not tell us of his subsequent fate, but lets us guess that he was already dead, in a sense. I quote the final words: "Amid the seeming confusion of our mysterious world, individuals are so nicely adjusted to a system, and systems to one another, and to a whole, that by stepping aside for a moment a man exposes himself to a fearful risk of losing his place for ever. Like Wakefield, he may become, as it were, the Outcast of the Universe."

In that brief and ominous parable, which dates from 1835, we have already entered the world of Herman Melville, of Kafka—a world of enigmatic punishments and indecipherable sins. You may say that there is nothing strange about that, since Kafka's world is Judaism, and Hawthorne's, the wrath and punishments of the Old Testament. That is a just observation, but it applies only to ethics, and the horrible story of Wakefield and many stories by Kafka are united not only by a common ethic but also by a common rhetoric. For example, the protagonist's profound *triviality,* which contrasts with the magnitude of his perdition and delivers him, even more helpless, to the Furies. There is the murky background against which the nightmare is etched. Hawthorne invokes a romantic past in other stories, but the scene of this tale is middle-class London, whose crowds serve, moreover, to conceal the hero.

Here, without any discredit to Hawthorne, I should like to insert an observation. The circumstance, the strange circumstance, of perceiving in a story written by Hawthorne at the beginning of the nineteenth century the same quality that distinguishes the stories Kafka wrote at the beginning of the twentieth must not cause us to forget that Hawthorne's particular quality has been created, or determined, by Kafka. "Wakefield" prefigures Franz Kafka, but Kafka modifies and refines the reading of "Wakefield." The debt is mutual; a great writer creates his precursors. He creates and somehow justifies them. What, for example, would Marlowe be without Shakespeare?

The translator and critic Malcolm Cowley sees in "Wakefield" an allegory of Nathaniel Hawthorne's curious life of reclusion. Schopenhauer has written the famous words to the effect that no act, no thought, no illness is involuntary; if there is any truth in that opinion, it would be valid to conjecture that Nathaniel Hawthorne left the society of other human beings for many years so that the singular story of Wakefield would exist in the universe, whose purpose may be variety. If Kafka had written that story, Wakefield would never have returned to his home; Hawthorne lets him return, but his return is no less lamentable or less atrocious than is his long absence.

One of Hawthorne's parables which was almost masterly, but not quite, because a preoccupation with ethics mars it, is "Earth's Holocaust." In that allegorical story Hawthorne foresees a moment when men, satiated by useless accumulations, resolve to destroy the past. They congregate at evening on one of the vast western plains of America to accomplish the feat. Men come from all over the world. They make a gigantic bonfire kindled with all the genealogies, all the diplomas, all the medals, all the orders, all the judgments, all the coats of arms, all the crowns, all the scepters, all the tiaras, all the purple robes of royalty, all the canopies, all the thrones, all the spirituous liquors, all the bags of coffee, all the boxes of tea, all the cigars, all the love letters, all the artillery, all the swords, all the flags, all the martial drums, all the instruments of torture, all the guillotines, all the gallows trees, all the precious metals, all the money, all the titles of property, all the constitutions and codes of law, all the books, all the miters, all the vestments, all the sacred writings that populate and fatigue the earth. Hawthorne views the conflagration with astonishment and even shock. A man of serious mien tells him that he should be neither glad nor sad, because the vast pyramid of fire has consumed only what was consumable. Another spectator —the Devil—observes that the organizers of the holocaust have forgotten to throw away the essential element—the human heart—where the root of all sin resides, and that they have destroyed only a few forms. Hawthorne concludes as follows:

> The heart, the heart—there was the little yet boundless sphere wherein existed the original wrong of which the crime and misery of this outward world were merely types. Purify that inward sphere, and the many shapes of evil that haunt the outward, and which now seem almost our only

realities, will turn to shadowy phantoms and vanish of their own accord; but if we go no deeper than the intellect, and strive, with merely that feeble instrument, to discern and rectify what is wrong, our whole accomplishment will be a dream, so unsubstantial that it matters little whether the bonfire, which I have so faithfully described, were what we choose to call a real event and a flame that would scorch the finger, or only a phosphoric radiance and a parable of my own brain.

Here Hawthorne has allowed himself to be influenced by the Christian, and specifically the Calvinist, doctrine of the inborn depravation of mankind and does not appear to have noticed that his parable of an illusory destruction of all things can have a philosophical as well as a moral interpretation. For if the world is the dream of Someone, if there is Someone who is dreaming us now and who dreams the history of the universe (that is the doctrine of the idealists), then the annihilation of religions and the arts, the general burning of libraries, does not matter much more than does the destruction of the trappings of a dream. The Mind that dreamed them once will dream them again; as long as the Mind continues to dream, nothing will be lost. The belief in this truth, which seems fantastic, caused Schopenhauer, in his book *Parerga und Paralipomena,* to compare history to a kaleidoscope, in which the figures, not the pieces of glass, change; and to an eternal and confused tragicomedy in which the roles and masks, but not the actors, change. The presentiment that the universe is a projection of our soul and that universal history lies within each man induced Emerson to write the poem entitled "History."

As for the fantasy of abolishing the past, perhaps it is worth remembering that this was attempted in China, with adverse fortune, three centuries before Christ. Herbert Allen Giles wrote that the prime minister Li Su proposed that history should begin with the new monarch, who took the title of First Emperor. To sever the vain pretensions of antiquity, all books (except those that taught agriculture, medicine, or astrology) were decreed confiscated and burned. Persons who concealed their books were branded with a hot iron and forced to work on the construction of the Great Wall. Many valuable works were destroyed; posterity owes the preservation of the Confucian canon to the abnegation and valor of obscure and unknown men of letters. It is said that so many intellectuals were executed for defying the imperial edict that melons grew in winter on the burial ground.

Around the middle of the seventeenth century that same plan appeared in England, this time among the Puritans, Hawthorne's ancestors. Samuel Johnson relates that in one of the popular parliaments convoked by Cromwell it was seriously proposed that the archives of the Tower of London be burned, that every memory of the past be erased, and that a whole new way of life should be started. In other words, the plan to abolish the past had already occurred to men and—paradoxically—is therefore one of the proofs that the past cannot be abolished. The past is indestructible; sooner or later all things will return, including the plan to abolish the past.

Like Stevenson, also the son of Puritans, Hawthorne never ceased to feel that the task of the writer was frivolous or, what is worse, even sinful. In the preface to *The Scarlet Letter* he imagines that the shadows of his forefathers are watching him write his novel. It is a curious passage. "What is he?" says one ancient shadow to the other. "A writer of story-books! What kind of a business in life— what mode of glorifying God, or being serviceable to mankind in his day and generation—may that be? Why, the degenerate fellow might as well have been a fiddler!" The passage is curious, because it is in the nature of a confidence and reveals intimate scruples. It harks back to the ancient dispute between ethics and esthetics or, if you prefer, theology and esthetics. One early example of this dispute was in the Holy Scriptures and forbade men to adore idols. Another example, by Plato, was in the *Republic,* Book X: "God creates the Archetype (the original idea) of the table; the carpenter makes an imitation of the Archetype; the painter, an imitation of the imitation." Another is by Mohammed, who declared that every representation of a living thing will appear before the Lord on the day of the Last Judgment. The angels will order the artisan to animate what he has made; he will fail to do so and they will cast him into Hell for a certain length of time. Some Muslim teachers maintain that only images that can project a shadow (sculpted images) are forbidden. Plotinus was said to be ashamed to dwell in a body, and he did not permit sculptors to perpetuate his features. Once, when a friend urged him to have his portrait painted, he replied, "It is enough to be obliged to drag around this image in which nature has imprisoned me. But why shall I consent to the perpetuation of the image of this image?"

Nathaniel Hawthorne solved that difficulty (which is not a mere illusion). His solution was to compose moralities and fables; he made or tried to make art a function of the conscience. So, to use only one example, the novel *The House of the Seven Gables* attempts to show that the evil committed by one generation endures and persists in its descendants, like a sort of inherited punishment. Andrew Lang has compared it to Émile Zola's novels, or to Émile Zola's theory of novels; to me the only advantage to be gained by the juxtaposition of those heterogeneous names is the momentary surprise it causes us to experience. The fact that Hawthorne pursued, or tolerated, a moral purpose does not invalidate, cannot invalidate his work. In the course of a lifetime dedicated less to living than to reading, I have been able to verify repeatedly that aims and literary theories are nothing but stimuli; the finished work frequently ignores and even contradicts them. If the writer has something of value within him, no aim, however trite or erroneous it may be, will succeed in affecting his work irreparably. An author may suffer from absurd prejudices, but it will be impossible for his work to be absurd if it is genuine, if it responds to a genuine vision. Around 1916 the novelists of England and France believed (or thought they believed) that all Germans were devils; but they presented them as human beings in their novels. In Hawthorne the germinal vision was always true; what is false, what is ultimately false, are the moralities he added in the last paragraph or the characters he conceived, or assembled, in order to represent that vision. The characters in *The Scarlet Letter* —especially Hester Prynne, the heroine—are more independent, more autonomous, than those in his other stories; they are more like the inhabitants of most novels and not mere projections of Hawthorne, thinly disguised. This objectivity, this relative and partial objectivity, is perhaps the reason why two such acute (and dissimilar) writers as Henry James and Ludwig Lewisohn called *The Scarlet Letter* Hawthorne's masterpiece, his definitive testimony. But I would venture to differ with those two authorities. If a person longs for objectivity, if he hungers and thirsts for objectivity, let him look for it in Joseph Conrad or Tolstoy; if a person looks for the peculiar flavor of Nathaniel Hawthorne, he will be less apt to find it in the laborious novels than on some random page or in the trifling and pathetic stories. I don't know exactly how to justify my difference of opinion; in the three American novels and *The Marble Faun* I see only a series of situations, planned with professional skill to affect the reader, not a spontaneous and lively activity of the imagination. The imagination (I repeat) has planned the general plot and the digressions, not the weaving together of the episodes and the psychology—we have to call it by some name—of the actors.

Johnson observes that no writer likes to owe something to his contemporaries; Hawthorne was as unaware of them as possible. Perhaps he did the right thing; perhaps our contemporaries—always—seem too much like us, and if we are looking for new things we shall find them more easily in the ancients. According to his biographers, Hawthorne did not read De Quincey, did not read Keats, did not read Victor Hugo—who did not read each other, either. Groussac would not admit that an American could be original; he denounced "the notable influence of Hoffmann" on Hawthorne, an opinion that appears to be based on an impartial ignorance of both writers. Hawthorne's imagination is romantic; in spite of certain excesses, his style belongs to the eighteenth century, to the feeble end of the admirable eighteenth century.

I have quoted several fragments from the journal Hawthorne kept to entertain his long hours of solitude; I have given brief resumés of two stories; now I shall quote a page from *The Marble Faun* so that you may read Hawthorne's own words. The subject is that abyss or well that opened up, according to Latin historians, in the center of the Forum; a Roman, armed and on horseback, threw himself into its blind depths to propitiate the gods. Hawthorne's text reads as follows:

> "Let us settle it," said Kenyon, "that this is precisely the spot where the chasm opened, into which Curtius precipitated his good steed and himself. Imagine the great, dusky gap, impenetrably deep, and with half-shaped monsters and hideous faces looming upward out of it, to the vast affright of the good citizens who peeped over the brim! Within it, beyond a question, there were prophetic visions,—intimations of all the future calamities of Rome,—shades of Goths, and Gauls, and even of the French soldiers of today. It was a pity to close it up so soon! I would give much for a peep into such a chasm."
>
> "I fancy," remarked Miriam, "that every person takes a peep into it in moments of gloom and despondency; that is to say, in his moments of deepest insight.
>
> "The chasm was merely one of the orifices of that pit of blackness that lies beneath us, everywhere. The firmest substance of human happi-

ness is but a thin crust spread over it, with just reality enough to bear up the illusive stage-scenery amid which we tread. It needs no earthquake to open the chasm. A footstep, a little heavier than ordinary, will serve; and we must step very daintily, not to break through the crust at any moment. By and by, we inevitably sink! It was a foolish piece of heroism in Curtius to precipitate himself there, in advance; for all Rome, you see, has been swallowed up in that gulf, in spite of him. The Palace of the Caesars has gone down thither, with a hollow, rumbling sound of its fragments! All the temples have tumbled into it; and thousands of statues have been thrown after! All the armies and the triumphs have marched into the great chasm, with their martial music playing, as they stepped over the brink . . ."

From the standpoint of reason, of mere reason—which should not interfere with art—the fervent passage I have quoted is indefensible. The fissure that opened in the middle of the Forum is too many things. In the course of a single paragraph it is the crevice mentioned by Latin historians and it is also the mouth of Hell "with half-shaped monsters and hideous faces"; it is the essential horror of human life; it is time, which devours statues and armies, and eternity, which embraces all time. It is a multiple symbol, a symbol that is capable of many, perhaps incompatible, values. Such values can be offensive to reason, to logical understanding, but not to dreams, which have their singular and secret algebra, and in whose ambiguous realm one thing may be many. Hawthorne's world is the world of dreams. Once he planned to write a dream, "which shall resemble the real course of a dream, with all its inconsistency, its eccentricities and aimlessness," and he was amazed that no one had ever done such a thing before. The same journal in which he wrote about that strange plan—which our "modern" literature tries vainly to achieve and which, perhaps, has only been achieved by Lewis Carroll—contains his notes on thousands of trivial impressions, small concrete details (the movement of a hen, the shadow of a branch on the wall); they fill six volumes and their inexplicable abundance is the consternation of all his biographers. "They read like a series of very pleasant, though rather dullish and decidedly formal, letters, addressed to himself by a man who, having suspicions that they might be opened in the post, should have determined to insert nothing compromising." Henry James wrote that, with obvious perplexity. I believe that Nathaniel Hawthorne recorded those trivialities over the years to show himself that he was real, to free himself, somehow, from the impression of unreality, of ghostliness, that usually visited him.

One day in 1840 he wrote:

Here I sit in my old accustomed chamber, where I used to sit in days gone by . . . Here I have written many tales—many that have been burned to ashes, many that have doubtless deserved the same fate. This claims to be called a haunted chamber, for thousands upon thousands of visions have appeared to me in it; and some few of them have become visible to the world . . . And sometimes it seems to me as if I were already in the grave, with only life enough to be chilled and benumbed. But oftener I was happy

> . . . And now I begin to understand why I was imprisoned so many years in this lonely chamber, and why I could never break through the viewless bolts and bars; for if I had sooner made my escape into the world, I should have grown hard and rough, and been covered with earthly dust, and my heart might have become callous . . . Indeed, we are but shadows . . .

In the lines I have just quoted, Hawthorne mentions "thousands upon thousands of visions." Perhaps this is not an exaggeration; the twelve volumes of Hawthorne's complete works include more than a hundred stories, and those are only a few of the very many he outlined in his journal. (Among the stories he finished, one—"Mr. Higginbotham's Catastrophe"—prefigures the detective story that Poe was to invent.) Miss Margaret Fuller, who knew him in the utopian community of Brook Farm, wrote later, "Of that ocean we have had only a few drops," and Emerson, who was also a friend of his, thought Hawthorne had never given his full measure. Hawthorne married in 1842, when he was thirty-eight; until that time his life had been almost purely imaginative, mental. He worked in the Boston customhouse; he served as United States consul at Liverpool; he lived in Florence, Rome, and London. But his reality was always the filmy twilight, or lunar world, of the fantastic imagination.

At the beginning of this essay I mentioned the doctrine of the psychologist Jung, who compared literary inventions to oneiric inventions, or literature to dreams. That doctrine does not seem to be applicable to the literatures written in the Spanish language, which deal in dictionaries and rhetoric, not fantasy. On the other hand, it does pertain to the literature of North America, which (like the literatures of England or Germany) tends more toward invention than transcription, more toward creation than observation. Perhaps that is the reason for the curious veneration North Americans render to realistic works, which induces them to postulate, for example, that Maupassant is more important than Hugo. It is within the power of a North American writer to be Hugo, but not, without violence, Maupassant. In comparison with the literature of the United States, which has produced several men of genius and has had its influence felt in England and France, our Argentine literature may possibly seem somewhat provincial. Nevertheless, in the nineteenth century we produced some admirable works of realism—by Echeverría, Ascasubi, Hernández, and the forgotten Eduardo Gutiérrez—the North Americans have not surpassed (perhaps have not equaled) them to this day. Someone will object that Faulkner is no less brutal than our gaucho writers. True, but his brutality is of the hallucinatory sort—the infernal, not the terrestrial sort of brutality. It is the kind that issues from dreams, the kind inaugurated by Hawthorne.

Hawthorne died on May 18, 1864, in the mountains of New Hampshire. His death was tranquil and it was mysterious, because it occurred in his sleep. Nothing keeps us from imagining that he died while dreaming and we can even invent the story that he dreamed—the last of an infinite series—and the manner in which death completed or erased it. Perhaps I shall write it someday; I shall try to redeem this deficient and too digressive essay with an acceptable story.

Van Wyck Brooks in *The Flowering of New England,* D. H. Lawrence in

Studies in Classic American Literature, and Ludwig Lewisohn in *Story of American Literature* analyze and evaluate the work of Hawthorne. There are many biographies. I have used the one Henry James wrote in 1879 for the English Men of Letters Series.

When Hawthorne died, the other writers inherited his task of dreaming. At some future time we shall study, if your indulgence permits, the glory and the torment of Poe, in whom the dream was exalted to a nightmare.

FROM ALLEGORIES TO NOVELS   [JLB 68]

For all of us, the allegory is an esthetic error. (My first impulse was to write "the allegory is nothing more than an error of esthetics," but then I noticed that an allegory had crept into my sentence.) To the best of my knowledge, the allegorical genre has been analyzed by Schopenhauer (*Welt als Wille und Vorstellung,* I, 50), by De Quincey (*Writings,* XI, 198), by Francesco De Sanctis (*Storia della letteratura italiana,* VII), by Croce (*Estetica,* 39), and by Chesterton (*G. F. Watts,* 83). In this essay I shall consider only the last two. Croce denies the allegorical art; Chesterton vindicates it. I agree with the former, but I should like to know how a form we consider unjustifiable could have enjoyed so much favor.

Croce's words are crystalline; let me repeat them now:

> If the symbol is conceived as inseparable from the artistic intuition, it is a synonym of the intuition itself, which always has an ideal character. If the symbol is conceived as separable, if the symbol can be expressed on the one hand and the thing symbolized can be expressed on the other, one falls back into the intellectualist error. The supposed symbol is the exposition of an abstract concept; it is an allegory; it is science, or art that copies science. But in fairness we must point out that in some cases the allegory is innocuous. A moral of sorts can be educed from the *Jerusalén libertada;* and from the *Adone* by Marino, the poet of lust, the reflection that unbridled pleasure will end in pain. The sculptor can place a card on a statue saying that it is Clemency or Kindness. Allegories of this sort added to a finished work have no adverse effect on it. They are expressions added extrinsically to other expressions. A page in prose that relates another thought of the poet is added to the *Jerusalén;* a verse or stanza that tells what the poet wishes to convey is added to the *Adone.* The word "clemency" or the word "kindness" is added to the statue.

On page 222 of the book *La poesia* (Bari, 1946) the tone is more hostile: "The allegory is not a direct mode of spiritual manifestation, but rather a kind of writing or cryptography."

Croce does not admit any difference between the content and the form. The latter is the former and the former is the latter. The allegory seems monstrous to him because it aspires to encipher two contents in one form: the immediate or literal one (Dante, guided by Virgil, comes to Beatrice) and the figurative one (man finally comes to faith, guided by reason). He believes that this way of writing fosters tedious enigmas.

To vindicate the allegory, Chesterton begins by denying that language is the only way to express reality.

> Man knows that there are in the soul tints more bewildering, more num-
> berless, and more nameless than the colours of an autumn forest; . . . Yet
> he seriously believes that these things can every one of them, in all their
> tones and semi-tones, in all their blends and unions, be accurately repre-
> sented by an arbitrary system of grunts and squeals. He believes that an
> ordinary civilized stockbroker can really produce out of his own inside
> noises which denote all the mysteries of memory and all the agonies of
> desire.

With one form of communication declared to be insufficient, there is room for others; allegory may be one of them, like architecture or music. It is made up of words, but it is not a language of language, a sign of other signs. For example, Beatrice is not a sign of the word "faith"; she is a sign of active virtue and the secret illuminations that this word indicates—a more precise sign, a richer and happier sign than the monosyllable "faith."

I am not certain which of the eminent contradictors is right. I know that at one time the allegorical art was considered quite charming (the labyrinthine *Roman de la Rose,* which survives in 200 manuscripts, consists of 24,000 verses) and is now intolerable. We feel that, besides being intolerable, it is stupid and frivolous. Neither Dante, who told the story of his passion in the *Vita nuova;* nor the Roman Boethius, writing his *De consolatione* in the tower of Pavia, in the shadow of his executioner's sword, would have understood our feeling. How can I explain that difference in outlook without simply appealing to the principle of changing tastes?

Coleridge observes that all men are born Aristotelian or Platonist. The latter know by intuition that ideas are realities; the former, that they are generalizations; for the latter, language is nothing but a system of arbitrary symbols; for the former, it is the map of the universe. The Platonist knows that the universe is somehow a cosmos, an order, which, for the Aristotelian, may be an error or a figment of our partial knowledge. Across the latitudes and the ages, the two immortal antagonists change their name and language: one is Parmenides, Plato, Spinoza, Kant, Francis Bradley; the other is Heraclitus, Aristotle, Locke, Hume, William James. In the arduous schools of the Middle Ages they all invoke Aristotle, the master of human reason (*Convivio,* IV, 2), but the nominalists are Aristotle; the realists, Plato. George Henry Lewes has observed that the only medieval debate of any philosophical value is the debate between nominalism and realism. This opinion is rather temerarious, but it emphasizes the importance of the persistent controversy provoked at the beginning of the ninth century by a sentence from Porphyry, which Boethius translated and annotated; a controversy that Anselm and Roscellinus continued at the end of the eleventh century and that William of Occam reanimated in the fourteenth.

As might be supposed, the passage of so many years multiplied the intermediate positions and the distinctions to the point of infinity. Nevertheless, for realism the universals (Plato would say the ideas, forms; we call them abstract concepts) were fundamental; and for nominalism, the individuals. The history of philosophy is not a vain museum of distractions and verbal games; the two theses probably correspond to two manners of intuitively perceiving reality. Maurice de Wulf writes: "Ultrarealism gained the first adherents. The chronicler Heriman (eleventh century) speaks of those who teach dialectic *in re* as *'antiqui doctores';* Abelard calls dialectic an 'ancient doctrine,' and the name of *'moderni'* is applied to its adversaries until the end of the twelfth century." A thesis that is inconceivable now seemed obvious in the ninth century, and it somehow endured until the fourteenth century. Nominalism, which was formerly the novelty of a few, encompasses everyone today; its victory is so vast and fundamental that its name is unnecessary. No one says that he is a nominalist, because nobody is anything else. But we must try to understand that for the people of the Middle Ages reality was not men but humanity, not the individuals but mankind, not the species but the genus, not the genera but God. I believe that allegorical literature has developed from such concepts (of which the clearest manifestation is perhaps the quadruple system of Erigena). The allegory is a fable of abstractions, as the novel is a fable of individuals. The abstractions are personified; therefore, in every allegory there is something of the novel. The individuals proposed by novelists aspire to be generic (Dupin is Reason, Don Segundo Sombra is the Gaucho); an allegorical element inheres in novels.

The passage from the allegory to the novel, from the species to the individual, from realism to nominalism, required several centuries, but I shall attempt to suggest an ideal date when it occurred. That day in 1382 when Geoffrey Chaucer, who perhaps did not believe he was a nominalist, wished to translate a line from Boccaccio into English, *"E con gli occulti ferri i Tradimenti"* ("And Treachery with hidden weapons"), and he said it like this: "The smyler with the knyf under the cloke." The original is in the seventh book of the *Teseide;* the English version, in "The Knightes Tale."

PARTIAL ENCHANTMENTS OF THE QUIXOTE [JLB 69]

It is probable that these observations have been made before at least once and, perhaps, many times; the novelty of them interests me less than their possible truth.

In comparison with other classics (the *Iliad,* the *Aeneid,* the *Pharsalia,* the Dantesque *Comedy,* the tragedies and comedies of Shakespeare), the *Quixote* is realistic; but this realism differs essentially from the nineteenth-century variety.

Joseph Conrad was able to write that he excluded the supernatural from his works, because to include it would seem to be a denial that the quotidian was marvelous. I do not know whether Miguel de Cervantes shared that idea, but I do know that the form of the *Quixote* caused him to counterpose a real, prosaic world with an imaginary, poetic one. Conrad and Henry James incorporated reality into their novels because they deemed it poetic; to Cervantes the real and the poetic are antonyms. To the vast and vague geography of the Amadís, he opposes the dusty roads and sordid inns of Castile; it is as if a novelist of our day were to sketch a satirical caricature of, say, service stations, treating them in a ludicrous way. Cervantes has created for us the poetry of seventeenth-century Spain, but neither that century nor that Spain were poetic for him; men like Unamuno or Azorín or Antonio Machado, whose emotions were stirred by the evocation of La Mancha, he would have found incomprehensible. The plan of his work precluded the marvelous, but still the marvelous had to be there, if only indirectly, as crime and mystery are present in a parody of the detective story. Cervantes could not have had recourse to amulets or sorcery, but he insinuated the supernatural in a subtle and therefore more effective way. In his heart of hearts, Cervantes loved the supernatural. In 1924 Paul Groussac observed: "With his cursory smattering of Latin and Italian, Cervantes derived his literary production primarily from pastoral novels and novels of chivalry, fables that had given solace to him in his captivity." The *Quixote* is less an antidote for those tales than a secret nostalgic farewell.

Every novel is an ideal depiction of reality. Cervantes delights in fusing the objective and the subjective, the world of the reader and the world of the book. In the chapters that consider whether the barber's basin is a helmet and the packsaddle a harness, the problem is treated explicitly; other parts, as I mentioned before, merely hint at it. In the sixth chapter of Part One the priest and the barber inspect Don Quixote's library; astonishingly enough, one of the books they examine is the *Galatea* by Cervantes. It develops that the barber is a friend of his who does not admire him very much, and says that Cervantes is more versed in misfortunes than in verses. He adds that the book has a rather well-constructed plot; it proposes something and concludes nothing. The barber, a dream of Cervantes or a form of one of Cervantes's dreams, passes judgment on Cervantes. It is also surprising to learn, at the beginning of Chapter 9, that the whole novel has been translated from the Arabic and that Cervantes acquired the manuscript in the marketplace of Toledo. It was translated by a Morisco, who lived in Cervantes's house for more than a month and a half while he completed the task. We are reminded of Carlyle, who feigned that the *Sartor Resartus* was a partial version of a work published in Germany by Dr. Diogenes Teufelsdröckh; we are reminded of the Spanish Rabbi Moisés de León, who wrote the *Zohar* or *Book of the Splendor* and divulged it as the work of a Palestinian rabbi of the third century.

The set of strange ambiguities culminates in Part Two. The protagonists of the *Quixote* who are, also, readers of the *Quixote,* have read Part One. Here we inevitably remember the case of Shakespeare, who includes on the stage of *Hamlet* another stage, where a tragedy almost like that of *Hamlet* is being presented. The imperfect correspondence of the principal work and the secondary one lessens the effectiveness of that inclusion. A device analogous to Cervantes's, and even more startling, appears in the *Ramayana,* epic poem by Valmiki, which relates the deeds of Rama and his war with the evil spirits. In the last book, Rama's children, not knowing who their father is, seek refuge in a forest, where a hermit teaches them to read. That teacher, strangely enough, is Valmiki; the book they study is the *Ramayana.* Rama orders a sacrifice of horses; Valmiki comes to the ceremony with his pupils. They sing the *Ramayana* to the accompaniment of the lute. Rama hears his own story, recognizes his children, and then rewards the poet.

Chance has caused something similar to occur in *1001 Nights.* That compilation of fantastic stories duplicates and reduplicates to the point of vertigo the ramification of a central tale into subordinate ones, without attempting to evaluate their realities; the effect (which should have been profound) is superficial, like that of a Persian rug. The first story is well known: the desolate oath of the Sultan, who marries a maiden each night and then orders her to be beheaded at dawn, and the courage of Scheherazad, who delights him with fables until The 1001 Nights have gyrated about them and she shows him their son. The need to complete The 1001 Nights obliged the copyists of the work to make all sorts of interpolations. None is so disturbing as that of Night 602, magic among the nights. That is when the Sultan hears his own story from the Sultana's mouth. He hears the beginning of the story, which embraces all the other stories as well as—monstrously—itself. Does the reader perceive the unlimited possibilities of that interpolation, the curious danger—that the Sultana may persist and the Sultan, transfixed, will hear forever the truncated story of *The 1001 Nights,* now infinite and circular?

The inventions of philosophy are no less fantastic than those of art. In the first volume of *The World and the Individual* (1899) Josiah Royce has formulated the following one:

> . . . let us suppose, if you please, that a portion of the surface of England is very perfectly levelled and smoothed, and is then devoted to the production of our precise map of England. . . . But now suppose that this our resemblance is to be made absolutely exact, in the sense previously defined. A map of England, contained within England, is to represent, down to the minutest detail, every contour and marking, natural or artificial, that occurs upon the surface of England . . . For the map, in order to be complete, according to the rule given, will have to contain, as a part of itself, a representation of its own contour and contents. In order that this representation should be constructed, the representation itself will have to contain once more, as a part of itself, a representation of its own contour and contents; and this representation, in order to be exact, will have once more to contain an image of itself; and so on without limit.

Why does it make us uneasy to know that the map is within the map and the thousand and one nights are within *The 1001 Nights?* Why does it disquiet us to know that Don Quixote is a reader of the *Quixote,* and Hamlet is a spectator of *Hamlet?* I believe I have found the answer: those inversions suggest that if the characters in a story can be readers or spectators, then we, their readers or spectators, can be fictitious. In 1833 Carlyle observed that universal history is an infinite sacred book that all men write and read and try to understand, and in which they too are written.

THE HANDWRITING OF GOD [JLB 70]

The prison is deep and of stone; its form, that of a nearly perfect hemisphere, though the floor (also of stone) is somewhat less than a great circle, a fact that in some way aggravates the feelings of oppression and of vastness. A dividing wall cuts it at the center; this wall, although very high, does not reach the upper part of the vault; in one cell am I, Tzinacán, magician of the pyramid of Qaholom, which Pedro de Alvarado devastated by fire; in the other there is a jaguar measuring with secret and even paces the time and space of captivity. A long window with bars, flush with the floor, cuts the central wall. At the shadowless hour [midday], a trap in the high ceiling opens and a jailer whom the years have gradually been effacing maneuvers an iron sheave and lowers for us, at the end of a rope, jugs of water and chunks of flesh. The light breaks into the vault; at that instant I can see the jaguar.

I have lost count of the years I have lain in the darkness; I, who was young once and could move about this prison, am incapable of more than awaiting, in the posture of my death, the end destined to me by the gods. With the deep obsidian knife I have cut open the breasts of victims and now I could not, without magic, lift myself from the dust.

On the eve of the burning of the pyramid, the men who got down from the towering horses tortured me with fiery metals to force me to reveal the location of a hidden treasure. They struck down the idol of the god before my very eyes, but he did not abandon me and I endured the torments in silence. They scourged me, they broke and deformed me, and then I awoke in this prison from which I shall not emerge in mortal life.

Impelled by the fatality of having something to do, of populating time in some way, I tried, in my darkness, to recall all I knew. Endless nights I devoted to recalling the order and the number of stone-carved serpents or the precise form of a medicinal tree. Gradually, in this way, I subdued the passing years; gradually, in this way, I came into possession of that which was already mine. One night I felt I was approaching the threshold of an intimate recollection; before he sights the sea, the traveler feels a quickening in the blood. Hours later I began to perceive the outline of the recollection. It was a tradition of the god. The god, foreseeing that at the end of time there would be devastation and ruin, wrote on the first day of creation a magical sentence with the power to ward off those evils. He wrote it in such a way that it would reach the most distant generations and not be subject to chance. No one knows where it was written nor with what characters, but it is certain that it exists, secretly, and that a chosen one shall read it. I considered that we were now, as always, at the end of time and that my destiny as the last priest of the god would give me access to the privilege of intuiting the script. The fact that a prison confined me did not forbid my hope; perhaps I had seen the script of Qaholom a thousand times and needed only to fathom it.

This reflection encouraged me, and then instilled in me a kind of vertigo. Throughout the earth there are ancient forms, forms incorruptible and eternal; any one of them could be the symbol I sought. A mountain could be the speech of the god, or a river or the empire or the configuration of the stars. But in the process of the centuries the mountain is leveled and the river will change its course, empires experience mutation and havoc and the configuration of the stars varies. There is change in the firmament. The mountain and the star are individuals and individuals perish. I sought something more tenacious, more invulnerable. I thought of the generations of cereals, of grasses, of birds, of men. Perhaps the magic would be written on my face, perhaps I myself was the end of my search. That anxiety was consuming me when I remembered the jaguar was one of the attributes of the god.

Then my soul filled with pity. I imagined the first morning of time; I imagined my god confiding his message to the living skin of the jaguars, who would love and reproduce without end, in caverns, in cane fields, on islands, in order that the last men might receive it. I imagined that net of tigers, that teeming labyrinth of tigers, inflicting horror upon pastures and flocks in order to perpetuate a design. In the next cell there was a jaguar; in his vicinity I perceived a confirmation of my conjecture and a secret favor.

I devoted long years to learning the order and the configuration of the spots. Each period of darkness conceded an instant of light, and I was able thus to fix in my mind the black forms running through the yellow fur. Some of them included points, others formed cross lines on the inner side of the legs; others, ring-shaped, were repeated. Perhaps they were a single sound or a single word. Many of them had red edges.

I shall not recite the hardships of my toil. More than once I cried out to the vault that it was impossible to decipher that text. Gradually, the concrete enigma I labored at disturbed me less than the generic enigma of a sentence written by a god. What type of sentence (I asked myself) will an absolute mind construct? I considered that even in the human languages there is no proposition that does not imply the entire universe; to say *the tiger* is to say the tigers that begot it, the deer and turtles devoured by it, the grass on which the deer fed, the earth that was mother to the grass, the heaven that gave birth to the earth. I considered that in the language of a god every word would enunciate that infinite concatenation of facts, and not in an implicit but in an explicit manner, and not progressively but instantaneously. In time, the notion of a divine sentence seemed puerile or blasphemous. A god, I reflected, ought to utter only a single word and in that word absolute fullness. No word uttered by him can be inferior to the universe or less than the sum total of time. Shadows or simulacra of that single word

236

equivalent to a language and to all a language can embrace are the poor and ambitious human words, "all," "world," "universe."

One day or one night—what difference between my days and nights can there be?—I dreamed there was a grain of sand on the floor of the prison. Indifferent, I slept again; I dreamed I awoke and that on the floor there were two grains of sand. I slept again; I dreamed that the grains of sand were three. They went on multiplying in this way until they filled the prison and I lay dying beneath that hemisphere of sand. I realized that I was dreaming; with a vast effort I roused myself and awoke. It was useless to awake; the innumerable sand was suffocating me. Someone said to me: *You have not awakened to wakefulness, but to a previous dream. This dream is enclosed within another, and so on to infinity, which is the number of grains of sand. The path you must retrace is interminable and you will die before you ever really awake.*

I felt lost. The sand burst my mouth, but I shouted: *A sand of dreams cannot kill me nor are there dreams within dreams.* A blaze of light awoke me. In the darkness above there grew a circle of light. I saw the face and hands of the jailer, the sheave, the rope, the flesh, and the water jugs.

A man becomes confused, gradually, with the form of his destiny; a man is, by and large, his circumstances. More than a decipherer or an avenger, more than a priest of the god, I was one imprisoned. From the tireless labyrinth of dreams I returned as if to my home to the harsh prison. I blessed its dampness, I blessed its tiger, I blessed the crevice of light, I blessed my old, suffering body, I blessed the darkness and the stone.

Then there occurred what I cannot forget nor communicate. There occurred the union with the divinity, with the universe (I do not know whether these words differ in meaning). Ecstasy does not repeat its symbols; God has been seen in a blazing light, in a sword, or in the circles of a rose. I saw an exceedingly high Wheel, which was not before my eyes, nor behind me, nor to the sides, but every place at one time. That Wheel was made of water, but also of fire, and it was (although the edge could be seen) infinite. Interlinked, all things that are, were, and shall be formed it, and I was one of the fibers of that total fabric and Pedro de Alvarado who tortured me was another. There lay revealed the causes and the effects and it sufficed me to see that Wheel in order to understand it all, without end. O bliss of understanding, greater than the bliss of imagining or feeling. I saw the universe and I saw the intimate designs of the universe. I saw the origins narrated in the Book of the Common. I saw the mountains that rose out of the water, I saw the first men of wood, the cisterns that turned against the men, the dogs that ravaged their faces. I saw the faceless god concealed behind the other gods. I saw infinite processes that formed one single felicity and, understanding all, I was able also to understand the script of the tiger.

It is a formula of fourteen random words (they appear random) and to utter it in a loud voice would suffice to make me all powerful. To say it would suffice to abolish this stone prison, to have daylight break into my night, to be young, to be immortal, to have the tiger's jaws crush Alvarado, to sink the sacred knife into the breasts of Spaniards, to reconstruct the pyramid, to reconstruct the empire. Forty syllables, fourteen words, and I, Tzinacán, would rule the lands

Moctezuma ruled. But I know I shall never say those words, because I no longer remember Tzinacán.

May the mystery lettered on the tigers die with me. Whoever has seen the universe, whoever has beheld the fiery designs of the universe, cannot think in terms of one man, of that man's trivial fortunes or misfortunes, though he be that very man. That man *has been he* and now matters no more to him. What is the life of that other to him, the nation of that other to him, if he, now, is no one. This is why I do not pronounce the formula, why, lying here in the darkness, I let the days obliterate me.

FROM SOMEONE TO NO ONE   [JLB 71]

In the beginning, God is the Gods (Elohim), a plural that some say denotes majesty and others say denotes plenitude and in which some have thought they observed an echo of earlier polytheisms or a prefiguring of the doctrine, declared in Nicaea, that God is One and is Three. Elohim is used with a singular verb; the first verse of the Law says literally: "In the beginning the Gods created the heaven and the earth"—the verb *created* is in the singular. Despite the vagueness suggested by the plural, Elohim is concrete; God is called Jehovah and we read that He walked in the garden in the air of the day, or, as the English versions say, "in the cool of the day." Human qualities define Him; in one part of the Scripture we read: "And it repented Jehovah that He had made man on the earth, and it grieved Him at His heart"; and in another, "For I the Lord thy God am a jealous God"; and in another, "In the fire of My wrath have I spoken." The subject of those locutions is indisputably Someone, a corporeal Someone Whom the centuries will continue to depict and magnify. His titles vary: The Mighty One of Jacob, the Holy One of Israel, I Am That I Am, God of the Armies, King of Kings. The last, which was no doubt the inspiration (by opposition) of the Servant of the Servants of God of Gregory the Great, is a superlative of king in the original text: as Fray Luis de León writes, "It is a property of the Hebrew language to use the same word twice for the sake of emphasis, either favorable or unfavorable. And so, to say 'Song of Songs' is the same as saying 'Song among Songs,' 'he is a man among men,' that is, famous and eminent among all men and more excellent than many others." In the first centuries of our era theologians supply the prefix *omni*, which was previously reserved for adjectives describing nature or Jupiter. They coin words like "omnipotent," "omnipresent," "omniscient," which make of God a respectful chaos of unimaginable superlatives. That nomenclature, like the others, seems to limit the divinity: at the end of the fifth century the obscure author of the *Corpus Dionysiacum* declares that no affirmative predicate is fitting for God. Nothing should be affirmed of Him, everything can be denied. Schopenhauer notes dryly: "That theology is the only true one, but it has no content." Written in Greek, the tracts and letters of the *Corpus Dionysiacum* encounter a reader in the ninth century who puts them into Latin: Johannes Erigena or Scotus, or rather John the Irishman, whose name in history is Scotus Erigena or Irish Irish. He formulates a doctrine of a pantheistic nature: particular things are theophanies (revelations or appearances of the divine) and behind them is God, the only reality, "who does not know what He is, because He is not a what, and is incomprehensible to Himself and to all intelligence." He is not sapient, He is more than sapient; He is not good, He is more than good; inscrutably He exceeds and rejects all attributes. John the Irishman, to define Him, utilized the word *"nihilum,"* which is nothingness; God is the primordial nothingness of the *creatio ex nihilo,* the abyss where first the archetypes and then concrete beings were engendered. He is Nothing and Nobody; those who imagined Him thus did so in the belief that it was more than being a Who, more than being a What. Analogously, Shankara teaches that men in a deep sleep are the universe, are God.

The process I have just illustrated is not, certainly, aleatory. Magnification to nothingness occurs or tends to occur in all cults; unequivocally we observe it in the case of Shakespeare. His contemporary, Ben Jonson, loves him without reaching the point of idolatry, "on this side Idolatry"; Dryden declares that he is the Homer of the dramatic poets of England, but admits that he is often insipid and pompous; the discursive eighteenth century seeks to appraise his virtues and to rebuke his faults; in 1774, Maurice Morgan states that King Lear and Falstaff are nothing but modifications of the mind of their inventor; at the beginning of the nineteenth century that opinion is re-created by Coleridge, for whom Shakespeare is no longer a man but a literary variation of the infinite God of Spinoza. Coleridge wrote that Shakespeare was a *natura naturata,* an effect, but that the universal, potentially present in the particular, was revealed to him—not as abstracted from the observation of a plurality of cases but rather as the substance capable of infinite modifications, of which his personal existence was only one. Hazlitt corroborated or confirmed that, and said that Shakespeare was like other men in every way except in being like other men; and that intimately he was nothing, but he was everything that others were, or could be. Later Hugo compared him to the ocean, the possible forms of which were infinite.[1]

To be one thing is inexorably not to be all the other things. The confused intuition of that truth has induced men to imagine that not being is more than being something and that, somehow, not to be is to be everything. That fallacy is inherent in the words of the legendary king of Hindustan who renounces power and goes out to beg in the streets: "From this day forward I have no realm or my realm is limitless, from this day forward my body does not belong to me or all the earth belongs to me." Schopenhauer has written that history is an intermi-

---

[1]The image is repeated in Buddhism. The first texts relate that the Buddha, under the fig tree, perceives by intuition the infinite concatenation of all the causes and effects of the universe, the past and future incarnations of each being. The last texts, written centuries later, reason that nothing is real and that all knowledge is fictitious and that if there were as many Ganges Rivers as there are grains of sand in the Ganges and again as many Ganges Rivers as grains of sand in those new Ganges Rivers, the number of grains of sand would be smaller than the number of things *not known* by the Buddha.

nable and perplexing dream of human generations; in the dream there are recurring forms, perhaps nothing but forms; one of them is the process described in this essay.

PASCAL'S SPHERE   [JLB 72]

Perhaps universal history is the history of a few metaphors. I should like to sketch one chapter of that history.

Six centuries before the Christian era Xenophanes of Colophon, the rhapsodist, weary of the Homeric verses he recited from city to city, attacked the poets who attributed anthropomorphic traits to the gods; the substitute he proposed to the Greeks was a single God: an eternal sphere. In Plato's *Timaeus* we read that the sphere is the most perfect and most uniform shape, because all points on its surface are equidistant from the center. Olof Gigon (*Ursprung der griechischen Philosophie,* 183) says that Xenophanes shared that belief; the God was spheroid, because that form was the best, or the least bad, to serve as a representation of the divinity. Forty years later, Parmenides of Elea repeated the image ("Being is like the mass of a well-rounded sphere, whose force is constant from the center in any direction"). Calogero and Mondolfo believe that he envisioned an infinite, or infinitely growing sphere, and that those words have a dynamic meaning (Albertelli, *Gli Eleati,* 148). Parmenides taught in Italy; a few years after he died, the Sicilian Empedocles of Agrigentum plotted a laborious cosmogony, in one section of which the particles of earth, air, fire, and water compose an endless sphere, "the round *Sphairos,* which rejoices in its circular solitude."

Universal history followed its course. The too-human gods attacked by Xenophanes were reduced to poetic fictions or to demons, but it was said that one god, Hermes Trismegistus, had dictated a variously estimated number of books (42, according to Clement of Alexandria; 20,000, according to Iamblichus; 36,-525, according to the priests of Thoth, who is also Hermes), on whose pages all things were written. Fragments of that illusory library, compiled or forged since the third century, form the so-called *Hermetica.* In one part of the *Asclepius,* which was also attributed to Trismegistus, the twelfth-century French theologian, Alain de Lille (Alanus de Insulis), discovered this formula, which future generations would not forget: "God is an intelligible sphere, whose center is everywhere and whose circumference is nowhere." The Pre-Socratics spoke of an endless sphere; Albertelli (like Aristotle before him) thinks that such a statement is a *contradictio in adjecto,* because the subject and predicate negate each other. Possibly so, but the formula of the Hermetic books almost enables us to envisage that sphere. In the thirteenth century the image reappeared in the symbolic *Roman de la Rose,* which attributed it to Plato, and in the *Speculum Triplex* encyclopedia. In the sixteenth century the last chapter of the last book of *Pantagruel* referred to "that intellectual sphere, whose center is everywhere and whose circumference nowhere, which we call God." For the medieval mind, the meaning was clear: God is in each one of his creatures, but is not limited by any one of them. "Behold, the heaven and heaven of heavens cannot contain thee," said Solomon (I Kings, 8:27). The geometrical metaphor of the sphere must have seemed like a gloss of those words.

Dante's poem has preserved Ptolemaic astronomy, which ruled men's imaginations for 1400 years. The earth is the center of the universe. It is an immovable sphere, around which nine concentric spheres revolve. The first seven are the planetary heavens (the heavens of the Moon, Mercury, Venus, the Sun, Mars, Jupiter, and Saturn); the eighth, the Heaven of Fixed Stars; the ninth, the Crystalline Heaven (called the *Primum mobile*), surrounded by the Empyrean, which is made of light. That whole laborious array of hollow, transparent, and revolving spheres (one system required fifty-five) had come to be a mental necessity. *De hypothesibus motuum coelestium commentariolus* was the timid title that Copernicus, the disputer of Aristotle, gave to the manuscript that transformed our vision of the cosmos. For one man, Giordano Bruno, the breaking of the sidereal vaults was a liberation. In *La cena de le ceneri* he proclaimed that the world was the infinite effect of an infinite cause and that the divinity was near, "because it is in us even more than we ourselves are in us." He searched for the words that would explain Copernican space to mankind, and on one famous page he wrote: "We can state with certainty that the universe is all center, or that the center of the universe is everywhere and the circumference nowhere" (*De la causa, principio de uno,* V).

That was written exultantly in 1584, still in the light of the Renaissance; seventy years later not one spark of that fervor remained and men felt lost in time and space. In time, because if the future and the past are infinite, there will not really be a when; in space, because if every being is equidistant from the infinite and the infinitesimal, there will not be a where. No one exists on a certain day, in a certain place; no one knows the size of his face. In the Renaissance humanity thought it had reached adulthood, and it said as much through the mouths of Bruno, Campanella, and Bacon. In the seventeenth century humanity was intimidated by a feeling of old age; to vindicate itself it exhumed the belief of a slow and fatal degeneration of all creatures because of Adam's sin. (In Genesis, 5:27, we read that "all the days of Methuselah were nine hundred sixty and nine years"; in 6:4, that "There were giants in the earth in those days.") The elegy *Anatomy of the World,* by John Donne, deplored the very brief lives and the slight stature of contemporary men, who could be likened to fairies and dwarfs. According to Johnson's biography, Milton feared that an epic genre had become impossible on earth. Glanvill thought that Adam, God's medal, enjoyed a telescopic and microscopic vision. Robert South wrote, in famous words, that an Aristotle was merely the wreckage of Adam, and Athens, the rudiments of Paradise. In that jaded century the absolute space that inspired the hexameters of Lucretius, the absolute space that had been a liberation for Bruno, was a labyrinth and an abyss for Pascal. He hated the universe, and yearned to adore God. But God was less real to him than the hated universe. He was sorry that the firmament could not speak; he compared our lives to those of shipwrecked men on a desert island. He felt the incessant weight of the physical world; he felt confused, afraid, and alone; and he expressed his feelings like this: "It [nature] is an infinite sphere, the center of which is everywhere, the circumference nowhere." That is the text of the Brunsch-vicg edition, but the critical edition of Tourneur (Paris, 1941), which reproduces the cancellations and the hesitations of the manuscript, reveals that Pascal started to write *effroyable:* "A frightful sphere, the center of which is everywhere, and the circumference nowhere."

Perhaps universal history is the history of the diverse intonation of a few metaphors.

KAFKA AND HIS PRECURSORS

Once I planned to make a survey of Kafka's precursors. At first I thought he was as singular as the fabulous phoenix; when I knew him better I thought I recognized his voice, or his habits, in the texts of various literatures and various ages. I shall record a few of them here, in chronological order.

The first is Zeno's paradox against movement. A moving body at A (declares Aristotle) will not be able to reach point B, because before it does, it must cover half of the distance between the two, and before that, half of the half, and before that, half of the half of the half, and so on to infinity; the formula of this famous problem is, exactly, that of *The Castle;* and the moving body and the arrow and Achilles are the first Kafkian characters in literature.

In the second text that happened to come to my attention, the affinity is not of form but rather of tone. It is an apologue by Han Yu, a prose writer of the ninth century, and it is included in the admirable *Anthologie raisonnée de la littérature chinoise* by Margouliès (1948). This is the paragraph I marked, a mysterious and tranquil one:

> It is universally admitted that the unicorn is a supernatural being and one of good omen; this is declared in the odes, in the annals, in the biographies of illustrious men, and in other texts of unquestioned authority. Even the women and children of the populace know that the unicorn constitutes a favorable presage. But this animal is not one of the domestic animals, it is not always easy to find, it does not lend itself to classification. It is not like the horse or the bull, the wolf or the deer. And therefore we could be in the presence of the unicorn and we would not know for certain that it was one. We know that a certain animal with a mane is a horse, and that one with horns is a bull. We do not know what the unicorn is like.[1]

The third text proceeds from a more foreseeable source: the writings of Kierkegaard. The mental affinity of both writers is known to almost everyone; what has not yet been brought out, as far as I know, is that Kierkegaard, like

---

[1]The failure to recognize the sacred animal and its opprobrious or casual death at the hands of the populace are traditional themes in Chinese literature. See the last chapter of Jung's *Psychologie und Alchemie* (Zurich, 1944), which includes two curious illustrations.

bear testimony to that brotherhood, according to Lessing. "Monkey of death" (*Affe des Todes*) said Wilhelm Klemm, who likewise wrote: "Death is the first restful night." Previously, Heine had written: "Death is the refreshing night; life the stormy day. . . ." Vigny called death "dream of the earth"; in the language of jazz, "ol' rocking chair" refers to death: it becomes the black man's final rest, his last siesta. Schopenhauer, in his work, repeats the death-sleep equation; enough for me to copy these lines: "What sleep is for the individual, death is for the species" (*Welt als Wille und Vorstellung*, II, 41). The reader will surely recall the words of Hamlet: "To die, to sleep. To sleep: perchance to dream," and his fear that the dreams of death's sleep would be atrocious.

Comparing women to flowers is another eternal or trivial metaphor. Here are a few examples. "I am the rose of Sharon and the lily of the valleys," says the virgin in the Song of Solomon. In the story of Math, which is the fourth "branch" of the Welsh *Mabinogion*, a prince requires a woman that is not of this world, and a magician "through conjurations and illusion makes her out of oak blossoms and furze blossoms and ulmaria flowers." In the fifth "adventure" of *Nibelungenlied*, Siegfried sees Kriemhild for the first time, and the first thing we are told is that her face was shining with the color of roses. Ariosto, inspired by Catullus, compares the maiden to a secret flower (*Orlando*, I, 42); in the garden of Armida, a bird with a purple beak exhorts the lovers never to let that flower wither (*Gerusalemme*, XVI, 13–15). Toward the end of the sixteenth century, Malherbe tries to console a friend over the death of his daughter and in his consolation are found these famous words: "And, a rose, she hath lived that which roses live." Shakespeare, in a garden, admires the deep vermilion of the roses and the whiteness of the lilies, yet their finery, to him, is nothing more than the shadow of his absent love (*Sonnets*, 98). "God, making roses, made my face," says the queen of Samothrace in one of Swinburne's works. This census could go on forever;[3] it suffices to recall the scene from *Weir of Hermiston*, Stevenson's last book, in which the hero wants to know if Christina has a soul "or if she is nothing more than a flower-colored animal."

I have produced ten examples from the first group and nine from the second; sometimes their essential unity is less apparent than their distinguishing characteristics. Who would have previously suspected that "ol' rocking chair" and "David slept with his fathers" came from the same source?

The first monument of Western literature, the *Iliad*, was composed about 3000 years ago; it is possible to conjecture that during this enormous time-span every intimate, necessary analogy (wakefulness-life, sleep-death, rivers and lives that rush by, etc.) was at some time or another noticed and written down. This does not mean, naturally, that the number of metaphors has been exhausted—

---

[3]One also finds this subtle image in the famous verses of Milton (*Paradise Lost*, IV, 268–271) about the abduction of Proserpine, and there are these lines by Dario:

> But in spite of stubborn time,
> My thirst for love persists;
> I approach the garden's roses,
> My hair a greying mist.

the ways of indicating or insinuating these secret similarities among concepts turn out, in fact, to be endless.

Their virtues or weaknesses lie in their words; the curious line in which Dante (*Purgatory,* I, 13), in order to define the eastern sky, invokes an Oriental stone in whose name the Orient, by strange coincidence, is found: "Sweet color of the Oriental sapphire" is, without a shadow of a doubt, remarkable; not so Góngora's line (*Solitude,* I, 6): "In fields of sapphire lie stars," which is, unless I am mistaken, a mere vulgarity, a mere emphasis.[4]

Someday the history of the metaphor will be written and we will know the truth and error contained in these conjectures.

THE MODESTY OF HISTORY [JLB 75]

On September 20, 1792, Johann Wolfgang von Goethe (who had accompanied the Duke of Weimar on a military expedition to Paris) saw the finest army of Europe inexplicably repulsed at Valmy by some French militiamen, and said to his disconcerted friends, "In this place and on this day, a new epoch in the history of the world is beginning, and we shall be able to say that we have been present at its origin." Since that time historic days have been numerous, and one of the tasks of governments (especially in Italy, Germany, and Russia) has been to fabricate them or to simulate them with an abundance of preconditioning propaganda followed by relentless publicity. Such days, which reveal the influence of Cecil B. de Mille, are related less to history than to journalism. I have suspected that history, real history, is more modest and that its essential dates may be, for a long time, secret. A Chinese prose writer has observed that the unicorn, because of its own anomaly, will pass unnoticed. Our eyes see what they are accustomed to seeing. Tacitus did not perceive the crucifixion, although his book recorded it.

Those thoughts came to me after a phrase happened to catch my eye as I leafed through a history of Greek literature. The phrase aroused my interest because of its enigmatic quality: "He brought in a second actor." I stopped; I found that the subject of that mysterious action was Aeschylus and that, as we read in the fourth chapter of Aristotle's *Poetics,* he "raised the number of actors from one to two." It is well known that the drama was an offshoot of the religion of Dionysus. Originally, a single actor, the *hypokritēs,* elevated by the cothurnus, dressed in black or purple and with his face enlarged by a mask, shared the scene with the twelve individuals of the chorus. The drama was one of the ceremonies of the worship and, like all ritual, was in danger of remaining invariable. Aeschylus's innovation could have occurred on but one day, 500 years before the Christian era; the Athenians saw with amazement and perhaps with shock (Victor

---

[4]Both lines are derived from the Scripture: "And they saw the God of Israel; and there was under his feet as it were a paved work of a sapphire stone, as it were the body of heaven in his clearness" (Exodus, 24:10).

Hugo thought the latter) the unannounced appearance of a second actor. On that remote spring day, in that honey-colored theater, what did they think, what did they feel exactly? Perhaps neither amazement nor shock; perhaps only a beginning of surprise. In the *Tusculanae* it is stated that Aeschylus joined the Pythagorean order, but we shall never know if he had a prefiguring, even an imperfect one, of the importance of that passage from one to two, from unity to plurality, and thus to infinity. With the second actor came the dialogue and the indefinite possibilities of the reaction of some characters on others. A prophetic spectator would have seen that multitudes of future appearances accompanied him: Hamlet and Faust and Sigismundo and Macbeth and Peer Gynt and others our eyes cannot yet discern.

I found another historic day in the course of my reading. It occurred in Iceland in the thirteenth century; let us say in 1225. For the instruction of future generations, the historian and polygrapher Snorri Sturlason, at his estate in Borgarfjord, wrote about the last exploit of the famous King Harald Sigurdsson, also called the Implacable (Hardrada), who fought in Byzantium, Italy, and Africa. Tostig, the brother of the Saxon king of England, Harold Godwinson, coveted the power and had obtained the help of Harald Sigurdsson. With an army of Norsemen, they landed on the eastern shore and subdued the castle of Jorvik (York). South of Jorvik they were confronted by the Saxon army. Snorri's text continues:

> Twenty horsemen joined the ranks of the invader; the men and also the horses were covered with mail. One of the horsemen shouted, "Is Earl Tostig here?"
>
> "I do not deny that I am here," said the Earl.
>
> "If you are really Tostig," said the horseman, "I come to tell you that your brother offers you his pardon and a third part of the kingdom."
>
> "If I accept," said Tostig, "what will the King give to Harald Sigurdsson?"
>
> "He has not forgotten him," replied the horseman. "He will give him six feet of English sod and since he is so tall, one more."
>
> "Then," said Tostig, "tell your king we shall fight to the death."
>
> The horsemen galloped away. Harald Sigurdsson asked pensively, "Who was that man who spoke so well?"
>
> "Harold Godwinson."

Other chapters tell that before the sun set that day the Norse army was defeated. Harald Sigurdsson died in the battle and so did the Earl (*Heimskringla*, X, 92).

There is a flavor that our time (perhaps surfeited by the clumsy imitations of professional patriots) does not usually perceive without some suspicion: the fundamental flavor of the heroic. People assure me that the *Poema del Cid* has that flavor; I have found it, unmistakably, in verses of the *Aeneid* ("My son, from me learn valor and true constancy; from others, success"), in the Anglo-Saxon ballad of Maldon ("My people will pay the tribute with lances and with old swords"), in the *Chanson de Roland,* in Victor Hugo, in Whitman, and in

Faulkner ("the single sprig of it [verbena] . . . filling the room, the dusk, the evening with that odor which she said you could smell alone above the smell of horses"), in Housman's "Epitaph on an Army of Mercenaries," and in the "six feet of English sod" of the *Heimskringla.* Behind the apparent simplicity of the historian there is a delicate psychological game. Harold pretends not to recognize his brother, so that the latter, in turn, will perceive that he must not recognize him either; Tostig does not betray him, nor will he betray his ally; Harold, willing to pardon his brother but not to tolerate the meddling of the Norse king, proceeds in a very comprehensible manner. I shall say nothing of the verbal skill of his reply: to give a third of the kingdom, to give six feet of sod.[1]

Only one thing is more admirable than the admirable reply of the Saxon king: that an Icelander, a man of the lineage of the vanquished, has perpetuated the reply. It is as if a Carthaginian had bequeathed to us the memory of the exploit of Regulus. Saxo Grammaticus wrote with justification in his *Gesta Danorum:* "The men of Thule [Iceland] are very fond of learning and of recording the history of all peoples and they are equally pleased to reveal the excellences of others or of themselves."

Not the day when the Saxon said the words, but the day when an enemy perpetuated them, was the historic date. A date that is a prophecy of something still in the future: the day when races and nations will be cast into oblivion, and the solidarity of all mankind will be established. The offer owes its virtue to the concept of a fatherland. By relating it, Snorri surmounts and transcends that concept.

I recall another tribute to an enemy in one of the last chapters of Lawrence's *Seven Pillars of Wisdom.* The author praises the valor of a German detachment and writes that for the first time in the campaign he was proud of the men who had killed his brothers. And he adds: "They were glorious."

THE ENIGMA OF EDWARD FITZGERALD [JLB 76]

A man named Omar ben Ibrāhīm is born in Persia in the eleventh century of the Christian era (for him, that century was the fifth of the Hegira); he learns the Koran and its traditions with Hassan ben Sabbah, the future founder of the sect of the Hashishin or Assassins, and with Nizam-al-Mulk, who will be the vizier of Alp Arslan, conqueror of the Caucasus. The three friends, half in jest, swear that if fortune happens to favor one of them someday, the lucky one will not forget the others. After several years Nizam attains the dignity of a vizier; Omar asks only for a corner in the shadow of his friend's good fortune so that he may pray for his prosperity and meditate on mathematics. (Hassan requests and receives a high position and, in the end, has the vizier stabbed to death.) Omar receives

---

[1]Carlyle (*Early Kings of Norway,* XI) spoils this economy with an unfortunate addition. To the "six feet of English sod" he adds "for a grave."

an annual pension of 10,000 dinars from the treasury of Nishapur, and is able to devote his life to study. He does not believe in judicial astrology, but he cultivates astronomy, collaborates on the reform of the calendar promoted by the Sultan, and writes a famous treatise on algebra, which gives numerical solutions for first- and second-degree equations, and geometric solutions—by the intersection of conics—for third-degree equations. The arcana of numbers and stars do not exhaust his attention; in the solitude of his library he reads the texts of Plotinus, who in the vocabulary of Islam is the Egyptian Plato or the Greek Master, and the fifty-odd epistles of the heretical and mystical encyclopedia of the Brethren of Purity, where it is written that the universe is an emanation of the Unity, and will return to the Unity. They call him a proselyte of Alfarabi, who believed that universal forms did not exist outside of things, and of Avicenna, who taught that the world was eternal. A certain chronicle tells us that he believes, or professes to believe, in transmigrations of the soul, from human to bestial body, and that once he spoke with a donkey as Pythagoras spoke with a dog. He is an atheist, but he knows the orthodox interpretation of the Koran's most difficult passages, because every cultivated man is a theologian, and faith is not a requisite. In the intervals between astronomy, algebra, and apologetics, Omar ben Ibrāhīm al-Khayyāmī writes compositions of four lines whose first, second, and last lines rhyme; he has been credited with 500 of these quatrains—an exiguous number which will be unfavorable for his reputation, because in Persia (as in the Spain of Lope and Calderón) the poet must be prolific. In the year 517 of the Hegira, Omar is reading a tract entitled *The One and the Many;* he is interrupted by an indisposition or a premonition. He gets up, marks the page that his eyes will not see again, and reconciles himself with God—the God Who perhaps exists and Whose favor he has implored on the difficult pages of his algebra. He dies that same day, at the hour of sunset. Around that same time, on a northwesterly island which is unknown to the cartographers of Islam, a Saxon king who defeated a king of Norway is himself defeated by a Norman duke.

Seven centuries pass with their lights and agonies and mutations, and in England a man, FitzGerald, is born; he is less intellectual than Omar, but perhaps more sensitive and more sad. FitzGerald knows that his true destiny is literature, and he practices it with indolence and tenacity. He reads and rereads the *Quixote,* which seems to him almost the best of all books (but he does not wish to be unjust with Shakespeare and with "dear old Virgil"), and his love extends to the dictionary in which he seeks the words. He knows that every man who has any music in his soul can write verses ten or twelve times in the natural course of his life, if the stars are propitious, but he does not propose to abuse that modest privilege. He is a friend of famous persons (Tennyson, Carlyle, Dickens, Thackeray), to whom he does not feel inferior in spite of the fact that he is both modest and courteous. He has published a properly written dialogue, *Euphranor,* and mediocre versions of Calderón and the great Greek tragedians. From the study of Spanish he has progressed to the study of Persian; he has begun a translation of the *Mantiq al-Tayr,* that mystical epic about the birds who are looking for their king, the Simurg. They finally reach his palace, situated in back of seven seas, only to discover that they are the Simurg and the Simurg is all of them and each one of them. Around 1854 he borrows a manuscript collection of Omar's compositions. FitzGerald translates some into Latin and then has a prefiguring of a continuous and organic book made of the verses, with the images of the morning, the rose, and the nightingale at the beginning, and those of the night and the tomb at the end. FitzGerald dedicates his life of an indolent, mad, and solitary man to this improbable and even unbelievable purpose. In 1859 he publishes a first version of the *Rubáiyát,* which is followed by others, rich in variations and scruples. A miracle happens: from the fortuitous conjunction of a Persian astronomer who condescends to write poetry, and an eccentric Englishman who peruses Oriental and Hispanic books, perhaps without completely understanding them, emerges an extraordinary poet who does not resemble either of them. Swinburne writes that FitzGerald has given Omar Khayyam a perpetual place among the greatest poets of England, and Chesterton, sensitive to the romantic and classic aspects of this peerless book, observes that it has both an elusive melody and an enduring inscription. Some critics believe that FitzGerald's *Omar* is, actually, an English poem with Persian allusions; FitzGerald interpolated, refined, and invented, but his *Rubáiyát* seems to demand that we read them as Persian and ancient.

The case invites conjectures of a metaphysical nature. Omar professed (we know) the Platonic and Pythagorean doctrine of the soul's passage through many bodies; centuries later his soul may have been reincarnated in England to fulfill the literary destiny repressed by mathematics in Nishapur, in a distant Germanic language variegated with Latin. Isaac Luria the Lion taught that the soul of a dead man can enter an unhappy soul to sustain or instruct it; perhaps the soul of Omar lodged in FitzGerald's around 1857. In the *Rubáiyát* we read that universal history is a spectacle that God conceives, represents, and contemplates; that speculation (its technical name is pantheism) would permit us to think that the Englishman could have re-created the Persian, because both were, essentially, God—or momentary faces of God. The supposition of a beneficent chance is more credible and no less marvelous than those conjectures of a supernatural sort. Sometimes clouds form the shapes of mountains or lions; Edward FitzGerald's unhappiness and a manuscript of yellow paper with purple letters, forgotten on a shelf of the Bodleian at Oxford, formed the poem for our benefit.

All collaboration is mysterious. That by the Englishman and the Persian was more mysterious than any because the two were very different and perhaps in life they would not have become friends; death and vicissitudes and time caused one to know of the other and made them into a single poet.

A PAGE TO COMMEMORATE COLONEL SUÁREZ, VICTOR AT JUNÍN

What do they matter now, the deprivations,
the alienation, the frustrations of growing old,
the dictator's shadow spreading across the land, the house
in the Barrio del Alto, which his brothers sold while he fought,
the useless days
(those one hopes to forget, those one knows are forgettable),
when he had, at least, his burning hour, on horseback
on the clear plains of Junín, a setting for the future?

What matters the flow of time, if he knew
that fullness, that ecstasy, that afternoon?

He served three years in the American Wars; and then
luck took him to Uruguay, to the banks of the Rio Negro.
In the dying afternoons, he would think
that somehow, for him, a rose had burst into flower,
taken flesh in the battle of Junín, the ever-extending moment
when the lances clashed, the order which shaped the battle,
the initial defeat, and in the uproar
(no less harsh for him than for the army),
his voice crying out at the attacking Peruvians,
the light, the force, the fatefulness of the charge,
the teeming labyrinths of foot soldiers,
the crossing of lances, when no shot resounded,
the Spaniard fighting with a reckless sword,
the victory, the luck, the exhaustion, a dream beginning,
and the men dying among the swamps,
and Bolívar uttering words which were marked for history,
and the sun, in the west by now, and, anew, the taste
of wine and water,
and death, that death without a face,
for the battle had trampled over it, effaced it . . .

His great-grandson is writing these lines,
and a silent voice comes to him out of the past,
out of the blood:

"What does my battle at Junín matter if it is only
a glorious memory, or a date learned by rote
for an examination, or a place in the atlas?
The battle is everlasting, and can do without
the pomp of the obvious armies with their trumpets;
Junín is two civilians cursing a tyrant
on a street corner,
or an unknown man somewhere, dying in prison."

MATTHEW, 25:30

And cast ye the unprofitable servant into outer darkness:
there shall be weeping and gnashing of teeth.

The first bridge on Constitution. At my feet
the shunting trains trace iron labyrinths.
Steam hisses up and up into the night
which becomes, at a stroke, the Night of the Last Judgment.

From the unseen horizon,
and from the very center of my being,
an infinite voice pronounced these things—
things, not words. This is my feeble translation,
time-bound, of what was a single limitless Word:

"Stars, bread, libraries of East and West,
playing cards, chessboards, galleries, skylights, cellars,
a human body to walk with on the earth,
fingernails, growing at nighttime and in death,
shadows for forgetting, mirrors which endlessly multiply,
falls in music, gentlest of all time's shapes,
borders of Brazil, Uruguay, horses and mornings,
a bronze weight, a copy of Grettir Saga,
algebra and fire, the charge at Junín in your blood,
days more crowded than Balzac, scent of the honeysuckle,
love, and the imminence of love, and intolerable remembering,
dreams like buried treasure, generous luck,
and memory itself, where a glance can make men dizzy—

all this was given to you and, with it,
the ancient nourishment of heroes—
treachery, defeat, humiliation.
In vain have oceans been squandered on you, in vain
the sun, wonderfully seen through Whitman's eyes.
You have used up the years and they have used up you,
and still, and still, you have not written the poem."

THE SOUTH   [JLB 79]

The man who landed in Buenos Aires in 1871 bore the name of Johannes Dahlmann and he was a minister in the Evangelical Church. In 1939, one of his
grandchildren, Juan Dahlmann, was secretary of a municipal library on Córdoba
Street, and he considered himself profoundly Argentinian. His maternal grandfa-

ther had been that Francisco Flores, of the Second Line Infantry Division, who had died on the frontier of Buenos Aires, run through with a lance by Indians from Catriel; in the discord inherent between his two lines of descent, Juan Dahlmann (perhaps driven to it by his Germanic blood) chose the line represented by his romantic ancestor, his ancestor of the romantic death. An old sword, a leather frame containing the daguerreotype of a blank-faced man with a beard, the dash and grace of certain music, the familiar strophes of *Martín Fierro,* the passing years, boredom, solitude, all went to foster this voluntary, but never ostentatious nationalism. At the cost of numerous small privations, Dahlmann had managed to save the empty shell of a ranch in the South which had belonged to the Flores family; he continually recalled the image of the balsamic eucalyptus trees and the great rose-colored house which had once been crimson. His duties, perhaps even indolence, kept him in the city. Summer after summer he contented himself with the abstract idea of possession and with the certitude that his ranch was waiting for him on a precise site in the middle of the plain. Late in February 1939 something happened to him.

Blind to all fault, destiny can be ruthless at one's slightest distraction. Dahlmann had succeeded in acquiring, on that very afternoon, an imperfect copy of Weil's edition of *The 1001 Nights.* Avid to examine this find, he did not wait for the elevator but hurried up the stairs. In the obscurity, something brushed by his forehead: a bat, a bird? On the face of the woman who opened the door to him he saw horror engraved, and the hand he wiped across his face came away red with blood. The edge of a recently painted door which someone had forgotten to close had caused this wound. Dahlmann was able to fall asleep, but from the moment he awoke at dawn the savor of all things was atrociously poignant. Fever wasted him and the pictures in *The 1001 Nights* served to illustrate nightmares. Friends and relatives paid him visits and, with exaggerated smiles, assured him that they thought he looked fine. Dahlmann listened to them with a kind of feeble stupor and he marveled at their not knowing that he was in Hell. A week, eight days passed, and they were like eight centuries. One afternoon, the usual doctor appeared, accompanied by a new doctor, and they carried him off to a sanitarium on Ecuador Street, for it was necessary to X-ray him. Dahlmann, in the hackney coach which bore them away, thought that he would, at last, be able to sleep in a room different from his own. He felt happy and communicative. When he arrived at his destination, they undressed him, shaved his head, bound him with metal fastenings to a stretcher; they shone bright lights on him until he was blind and dizzy, auscultated him, and a masked man stuck a needle into his arm. He awoke with a feeling of nausea, covered with a bandage, in a cell with something of a well about it; in the days and nights which followed the operation he came to realize that he had merely been, up until then, in a suburb of Hell. Ice in his mouth did not leave the least trace of freshness. During these days Dahlmann hated himself in minute detail: he hated his identity, his bodily necessities, his humiliation, the beard which bristled upon his face. He stoically endured the curative measures, which were painful, but when the surgeon told him he had been on the point of death from septicemia, Dahlmann dissolved in tears of self-pity for his fate. Physical wretchedness and the incessant anticipation of horrible nights had not allowed him time to think of anything so abstract as death. On another day, the surgeon told him he was healing and that, very soon, he would be able to go to his ranch for convalescence. Incredibly enough, the promised day arrived.

Reality favors symmetries and slight anachronisms: Dahlmann had arrived at the sanitarium in a hackney coach and now a hackney coach was to take him to Constitution Station. The first fresh tang of autumn, after the summer's oppressiveness, seemed like a symbol in nature of his rescue and release from fever and death. The city, at seven in the morning, had not lost that air of an old house lent it by the night; the streets seemed like long vestibules, the plazas were like patios. Dahlmann recognized the city with joy on the edge of vertigo: a second before his eyes registered the phenomena themselves, he recalled the corners, the billboards, the modest variety of Buenos Aires. In the yellow light of the new day, all things returned to him.

Every Argentine knows that the South begins at the other side of Rivadavia. Dahlmann was in the habit of saying that this was no mere convention, that whoever crosses this street enters a more ancient and sterner world. From inside the carriage he sought out, among the new buildings, the iron grille window, the brass knocker, the arched door, the entranceway, the intimate patio.

At the railroad station he noted that he still had thirty minutes. He quickly recalled that in a café on Brazil Street (a few dozen feet from Yrigoyen's house) there was an enormous cat which allowed itself to be caressed as if it were a disdainful divinity. He entered the café. There was the cat, asleep. He ordered a cup of coffee, slowly stirred the sugar, sipped it (this pleasure had been denied him in the clinic), and thought, as he smoothed the cat's black coat, that this contact was an illusion and that the two beings, man and cat, were as good as separated by a glass, for man lives in time, in succession, while the magical animal lives in the present, in the eternity of the instant.

Along the next to the last platform the train lay waiting. Dahlmann walked through the coaches until he found one almost empty. He arranged his baggage in the network rack. When the train started off, he took down his valise and extracted, after some hesitation, the first volume of *The 1001 Nights*. To travel with this book, which was so much a part of the history of his ill fortune, was a kind of affirmation that his ill fortune had been annulled; it was a joyous and secret defiance of the frustrated forces of evil.

Along both sides of the train the city dissipated into suburbs; this sight, and then a view of the gardens and villas, delayed the beginning of his reading. The truth was that Dahlmann read very little. The magnetized mountain and the genie who swore to kill his benefactor are—who would deny it?—marvelous, but not so much more than the morning itself and the mere fact of being. The joy of life distracted him from paying attention to Scheherazad and her superfluous miracles. Dahlmann closed his book and allowed himself to live.

Lunch—the bouillon served in shining metal bowls, as in the remote summers of childhood—was one more peaceful and rewarding delight.

Tomorrow I'll wake up at the ranch, he thought, and it was as if he were two men at a time: the man who traveled through the autumn day and across his native geography, and the other one, locked up in a sanitarium and subject to methodical servitude. He saw unplastered brick houses, long and angled, timelessly watching the trains go by; he saw horsemen along the dirt roads; he saw gullies and lagoons and ranches; he saw great luminous clouds that resembled marble; and all these things were accidental, casual, like dreams of the plain. He also thought he recognized trees and crop fields; but he would not have been able to name them, for his actual knowledge of the countryside was quite inferior to his nostalgic and literary knowledge.

From time to time he slept, and his dreams were animated by the impetus of the train. The intolerable white sun of high noon had already become the yellow sun which precedes nightfall, and it would not be long before it would turn red. The railroad car was now also different; it was not the same as the one which had quit the station siding at Constitution; the plain and the hours had transfigured it. Outside, the moving shadow of the railroad car stretched toward the horizon. The elemental earth was not perturbed either by settlements or other signs of humanity. The country was vast but at the same time intimate and, in some measure, secret. The limitless country sometimes contained only a solitary bull. The solitude was perfect, perhaps hostile, and it might have occurred to Dahlmann that he was traveling into the past and not merely south. He was distracted from these considerations by the railroad inspector who, on reading his ticket, advised him that the train would not let him off at the regular station but at another: an earlier stop, one scarcely known to Dahlmann. (The man added an explanation which Dahlmann did not attempt to understand, and which he hardly heard, for the mechanism of events did not concern him.)

The train laboriously ground to a halt, practically in the middle of the plain. The station lay on the other side of the tracks; it was not much more than a siding and a shed. There was no means of conveyance to be seen, but the station chief supposed that the traveler might secure a vehicle from a general store and inn to be found some ten or twelve blocks away.

Dahlmann accepted the walk as a small adventure. The sun had already disappeared from view, but a final splendor exalted the vivid and silent plain, before the night erased its color. Less to avoid fatigue than to draw out his enjoyment of these sights, Dahlmann walked slowly, breathing in the odor of clover with sumptuous joy.

The general store at one time had been painted a deep scarlet, but the years had tempered this violent color for its own good. Something in its poor architecture recalled a steel engraving, perhaps one from an old edition of *Paul et Virginie*. A number of horses were hitched up to the paling. Once inside, Dahlmann thought he recognized the shopkeeper. Then he realized that he had been deceived by the man's resemblance to one of the male nurses in the sanitarium. When the shopkeeper heard Dahlmann's request, he said he would have the shay made up. In order to add one more event to that day and to kill time, Dahlmann decided to eat at the general store.

Some country louts, to whom Dahlmann did not at first pay any attention, were eating and drinking at one of the tables. On the floor, and hanging on to the bar, squatted an old man, immobile as an object. His years had reduced and polished him as water does a stone or the generations of men do a sentence. He was dark, dried up, diminutive, and seemed outside time, situated in eternity. Dahlmann noted with satisfaction the kerchief, the thick poncho, the long *chiripá,* and the colt boots, and told himself, as he recalled futile discussions with people from the northern counties or from the province of Entre Ríos, that gauchos like this no longer existed outside the South.

Dahlmann sat down next to the window. The darkness began overcoming the plain, but the odor and sound of the earth penetrated the iron bars of the window. The shop owner brought him sardines, followed by some roast meat. Dahlmann washed the meal down with several glasses of red wine. Idling, he relished the tart savor of the wine, and let his gaze, now grown somewhat drowsy, wander over the shop. A kerosene lamp hung from a beam. There were three customers at the other table: two of them appeared to be farmworkers; the third man, whose features hinted at Chinese blood, was drinking with his hat on. Of a sudden, Dahlmann felt something brush lightly against his face. Next to the heavy glass of turbid wine, upon one of the stripes in the tablecloth, lay a spit ball of bread crumb. That was all: but someone had thrown it there.

The men at the other table seemed totally cut off from him. Perplexed, Dahlmann decided that nothing had happened, and he opened the volume of *1001 Nights,* by way of suppressing reality. After a few moments another little ball landed on his table, and now the *peones* laughed outright. Dahlmann said to himself that he was not frightened, but he reasoned that it would be a major blunder if he, a convalescent, were to allow himself to be dragged by strangers into some chaotic quarrel. He determined to leave, and had already gotten to his feet when the owner came up and exhorted him in an alarmed voice:

"Señor Dahlmann, don't pay any attention to those lads; they're half high."

Dahlmann was not surprised to learn that the other man, now, knew his name. But he felt that these conciliatory words served only to aggravate the situation. Previous to this moment, the *peones'* provocation was directed against an unknown face, against no one in particular, almost against no one at all. Now it was an attack against him, against his name, and his neighbors knew it. Dahlmann pushed the owner aside, confronted the *peones,* and demanded to know what they wanted of him.

The tough with a Chinese look staggered heavily to his feet. Almost in Juan Dahlmann's face he shouted insults, as if he had been a long way off. His game was to exaggerate his drunkenness, and this extravagance constituted a ferocious mockery. Between curses and obscenities, he threw a long knife into the air, followed it with his eyes, caught and juggled it, and challenged Dahlmann to a knife fight. The owner objected in a tremulous voice, pointing out that Dahlmann was unarmed. At this point, something unforeseeable occurred.

From a corner of the room, the old ecstatic gaucho—in whom Dahlmann saw a summary and cipher of the South (his South)—threw him a naked dagger, which landed at his feet. It was as if the South had resolved that Dahlmann should accept the duel. Dahlmann bent over to pick up the dagger, and felt two things. The first, that this almost instinctive act bound him to fight. The second, that the weapon, in his torpid hand, was no defense at all, but would merely serve to justify his murder. He had once played with a poniard, like all men, but his idea of fencing and knife play did not go further than the notion that all strokes should be directed upward, with the cutting edge held inward. *They would not have allowed such things to happen to me in the sanitarium,* he thought.

"Let's get on our way," said the other man.

They went out and if Dahlmann was without hope, he was also without fear. As he crossed the threshold, he felt that to die in a knife fight, under the open sky, and going forward to the attack, would have been a liberation, a joy, and a festive occasion, on the first night in the sanitarium, when they stuck him with the needle. He felt that if he had been able to choose, then, or to dream his death, this would have been the death he would have chosen or dreamed.

Firmly clutching his knife, which he perhaps would not know how to wield, Dahlmann went out into the plain.

THE DAGGER [JLB 80]

A dagger lies in a drawer.

It was forged in Toledo toward the end of last century.
Luis Melián Lafinur gave it to my father, who brought it
from Uruguay. Evaristo Carriego once handled it.

People who catch sight of it cannot resist playing with it,
almost as if they had been looking for it for some time.
The hand eagerly grasps the expectant hilt. The powerful,
passive blade slides neatly into the sheath.

The dagger itself is after something else.

It is more than a thing of metal. Men dreamed it up and fashioned it for
a very precise purpose. In some eternal way, it is the
same dagger that last night killed a man in Tacuarembó,
the same daggers that did Caesar to death. Its will is to
kill, to spill sudden blood.

In a desk drawer, among rough drafts and letters, the dagger
endlessly dreams its simple tiger's dream, and, grasping it,
the hand comes alive because the metal comes alive, sensing
in every touch the killer for whom it was wrought.

Sometimes it moves me to pity. Such force, such purpose,
so impassive, so innocently proud, and the years go past,
uselessly.

257

Forty playing cards would displace life. The deck in the fingers crackles with newness or is sticky from use. The pasteboard hodgepodges animate themselves: an ace of swords that becomes as omnipotent as Don Juan Manuel, big-bellied little horses from which Velázquez copied his. The dealer shuffles these little paintings. The thing is easy to tell about, and even to do, but what is magical and outrageous about the game, the act of playing, is revealed in the action. Forty is the number of playing cards, and 1 by 2 by 3 by 4 . . . by 40, the ways in which they can come out. It is a figure pointedly delicate in its enormity, with immediate predecessor and sole successor, but not written out ever. It is a remote dizzying figure which seems to dissolve those who shuffle the cards into its muchness. Thus, from the beginning, the central mystery of the game is seen to be adorned with another mystery—that of there being numbers.

On the table, the cloth removed so that the cards will slide, wait the garbanzos, used as counters, in their pile, they too arithmetized. The game is on —suddenly, the players disburden themselves of their habitual I's, become indigenous. A different I, an I virtually ancestral, vernacular, entwines the designs of the game. Language is other, suddenly. Tyrannical prohibitions, cunning possibilities, and impossibilities hover over every act of speech. To mention the word "flower," without holding three cards of a suit, is a criminal act, punishable; but if one has already said, "I open," then it doesn't matter. To mention one of the holdings of the game is to be bound to it—a bond that goes on unfolding in euphemisms at each turn. "I'll beat you" might stand for "I'll see you," "I hope" for "I open," "perfume" or "flower bed" for "flower." One often hears, booming in the mouths of the losers, this pronouncement of the courtyard party boss: "By the law of the game, everything has been spoken; I'll see you open and now we'll play out our tricks, and if you're holding a flower, then it's mine against yours for the pot!" More than once, dialogue is excited to verse. *Truco* has verbal formulas for endurance for the losers, verses for exultation for the winners. *Truco* is as memorable as a red-letter day. Crooning *milongas* of the kitchen and the café, bluesy songs of the wake, bragging political songs of the Roquists or the Tejedorists, raucous songs from the houses on Junín and its godmother-street Temple, are its human commerce. *Truco* is a great singer, most of all when winning or bluffing a win—it sings out at dusk from the lighted cafés on the street corners.

The great habit of *truco* is lying. The manner of its deception is not poker's —mere deanimation, the stiffness not to quiver, and hazarding a stack of chips every few hands. Rather it is the action of a lying voice, of a face that puts on and keeps up an expression of *seeming,* of a deceptive and reckless chatter. There is an exponentiation of deceit that occurs in *truco*—that grumbling player who has thrown his cards down on the table might be concealing a good hand (elementary cunning) or, perhaps, is lying to us with the truth, so that we believe it (cunning squared). Relaxed and talkative, this native player, but his calm is that of native cunning, a superposition of masks, and his spirit is that of the two peddlers Mosche and Daniel who greeted each other in the middle of the Russian steppes.

"Where are you going, Daniel?" said one.

"To Sebastopol," said the other.

At that, Mosche looked hard at him and uttered his judgment:

"You're lying, Daniel. You answer me that you're going to Sebastopol so I'll think you're going to Nizhni-Novgorod, but the truth is that you really *are* going to Sebastopol. You lie, Daniel!"

I regard the players of *truco*. They are as though hidden in the noisy lingo of the dialogue—they want to shock life with shouts. Forty playing cards (amulets of painted pasteboard, cheap mythology, exorcisms) suffice them to ward off common life. They play with their backs to the trafficking hours of the world. The urgent public reality in which we all live edges on their gathering but does not cross; the precinct of their table is another country. "I open" and "I'll see you" people it, the perfumed crusade, the unhoped-for gift of it, the sharp melodrama of each deal, the seven of coins tinkling hope, the other impassioned bagatelles of the repertory. The tricksters live out this hallucinated little world. They foster it with desultory native bombast, they tend it like a fire. It is a narrow world, I know, a phantom of ward politics and rogueries, a world invented finally by the do-nothings of the stockyards and the con men of the barrio, but, for all that, still replacing this real world, and no less inventive and diabolical in its ambitions.

To think up a local argument like this one about *truco*—and not to abandon it or go deeper into it—the two tropes might here mean the same thing, such is their precision—seems to me very serious trifling. I would not omit here a thought about the poverty of *truco*. The diverse stages of its polemics, the flights and falls, the heartiness, the cabalism, cannot come back, they must experientially be repeated. What is *truco* for one drilled in it but a custom? Look, too, at the memoriousness of the game, at its devotion to traditional formulas. Every player, in truth, does no more than revert into remote plays. His game is a repetition of past games, which is to say past times of living. Generations of player natives now invisible are as it were buried alive in it; they *are* it, we might affirm without metaphor. It may be inferred, from that thought, that time is a fiction. Thus from the painted pasteboard labyrinths of *truco*, we have approached metaphysics: sole justification and end of all subjects.

Vicente Rossi, Carlos Vega, and Carlos Muzzi Saénz Peña, all accurate researchers, have chronicled in their different ways the origin of the tango. I can easily declare that I subscribe to all their conclusions, and even to some others. There is a history of the course of the tango's life, periodically put forward by the filmmaker; the tango, according to that sentimental version, would have been born in the suburbs, in the tenements (at the mouth of the Riachuelo, generally, for the photographic virtues of that area); the patrician caste would have rejected it at the beginning; around 1910, taught by the good example of Paris, they would at last have thrown open their doors to that *orillero,* the interesting young native of the riverbank settlements. That *Bildungsroman,* that "novel of the young man of poverty," is now a sort of incontestable truth or axiom; my memories (and I have seen fifty birthdays) and the researches of an oral nature that I have undertaken assuredly do not support it.

I have spoken about that account with José Saborido, author of *Felicia* and *The Well-Preserved Lady,* with Ernesto Poncio, author of *Don Juan,* with the brothers of Vicente Greco, author of *The Wood-Chip* and *The Boards,* with Nicolás Paredes, party chief who came from Palermo, and with an itinerant singer. I let them talk; I carefully avoided formulating questions which might suggest determined answers. About the derivations of the tango, the topography and even geography of their communications were singularly diverse: Saborido (who was from the east) preferred a Montevidean cradle; Poncio (who was from Retiro) opted for Buenos Aires and for his own neighborhood; those from the south of the port area invoked Chile Street, those from the north, raucous Temple Street or Junín Street.

In spite of the divergences that I have enumerated and that would be easy to add to by asking people from Rio Plata or from around Rosario, my advisers concur in one essential fact—that the tango was born in brothels. (So, too, with the date of that origin, which no one felt was very much before 1880 or after 1890.) The primitive instrumentation of the orchestras—piano, flute, violin, later concertina—confirms, with its extravagance, that testimony; proof of the hypothesis that the tango did not arise in the riverbank communities is that, as no one denies, they always contented themselves with the six strings of the guitar. There is no lack of other confirmation—the lasciviousness of the steps, the evident suggestiveness of certain titles (the Corn-Cob, the Big Iron), the circumstance that I observed, as a boy in Palermo and years later in La Chacarita and Boedo, that in corners pairs of men would dance, since the women of the town would not want to take part in a dance that so much suggested lasciviousness. Evaristo Carriego got it in his *Heresy Masses:*

> In the street, the gentlefolk turn up their noses
> and let fall all their withering remarks.
> To the beat of a tango, something like *Red Roses,*
> two men are dancing close, and striking sparks.

On another page, Carriego shows, with a wealth of affecting detail, a poor wedding reception; the groom's brother is in jail; there are two rowdy boys that the tough guy has to quiet down with threats; there is suspicion, anger, and ribaldry, but

> The bride's uncle thinks it is his duty
> to see the dancing is controlled, though festive.
> There'll be no slithering tangos here, he says,
> even in fun, nothing the least suggestive.

> They won't forget their modesty, the dancers,
> and glue themselves together, like bottle and stopper.
> This house may be poor, I grant it you, he answers,
> whatever you like, but one thing—at least it's proper!

The momentary glimpse of the severe man that the two stanzas permanently fix for us symbolizes very well the first reaction of the town to the tango, *that reptile of the brothel,* as Lugones was to define it with laconic contempt (*The Itinerant Singer,* page 117). It took many years for the Barrio Norte to impose the tango, by then somewhat civilized by Paris, it is true, on the tenements, and I do not know if all in all it has entirely succeeded. Before it was an orgiastic deviltry; today it is a way of walking.

THE FIGHTING TANGO

The sexual character of the tango was noted by many; not so its aggressiveness. It is true that both are modes or manifestations of one impulse, and thus the word "man," in all the languages I know, connotes both sexual and fighting ability, and the word *"virtus,"* which in Latin means courage, comes from *vir,* which means male. Similarly, on one of the pages of *Kim,* an Afghan declares, "When I was fifteen, I had shot my man and begot my man," as if the two acts were, essentially, one.

To speak of the tango as aggressive is not enough; I would say that the tango and the other Argentine dance, the *milonga,* express something directly that poets have often tried to say with words—their sense that fighting can be a celebration. In the famous *History of the Goths* that Jordanes composed in the sixth century, we read that Attila, before the rout of Châlons, harangued his armies and told them that fortune had reserved for them the joys of this battle *(certamines huius gaudia).* The *Iliad* speaks of Achaeans for whom war was sweeter than returning in hollowed ships to their beloved native land, and it is said that Paris, son of Priam, ran with rapid feet into battle, like a horse with stirring mane in search of mares. In the old Saxon epic which begins Germanic literature, *Beowulf,* the rhapsody calls battle *sweorda gelac* (game of swords). It was called "vikings-feast" by Scandinavian poets in the eleventh century. At the beginning of the seventeenth century, Quevedo, in one of his romances, called a duel a sword dance *(danza de espadas),* which is almost the "sword game" of the anonymous Anglo-Saxon. The splendid Hugo, in his evocation of the Battle of Waterloo, said that the soldiers, understanding that they were going to die in that festivity *(comprenant qu'ils allaient mourir dans cette fête),* saluted their god as they stood in the storm.

These examples, which I have been noting down at random from my readings, could without great diligence be multiplied, and perhaps in the *Chanson de Roland* or in the vast poem of Ariosto there are like instances. Any one of those listed here—Quevedo's or the one about Attila, let us say—has an unimpeachable strength; all, however, are afflicted with the original sin of the literary thing: they are structures of words, forms made of symbols. Sword dance, for example, invites us to join two disparate representations—that of dance and that of combat, so that the first saturates the second with joy, but does not speak directly to our blood, does not re-create in us that joy. Schopenhauer (*Welt als Wille und Vorstellung,* I, 52) has written that music is no less immediate than the world itself is; without the world, without the common stock of memories that language evokes, there would be, certainly, no literature, but music is detached from the world; there could be music and not world. Music is will, passion—the old tango, as music, is wont to transmit directly that bellicose joy which, in remote ages, Greek and German rhapsodies tried to put into words. Certain composers of today seek that valiant tone and concoct, sometimes felicitously, *milongas* of the lower Battery or of the Barrio Alto, but their works, music and lyrics studiously antiquated, are exercises in nostalgia for what was, laments for what is lost, essentially sad though happy in tone. They are to the rough and innocent *milongas* that Rossi's book contains what *Don Segundo Sombra* is to *Martín Fierro* or to *Paulino Lucero.*

In a dialogue by Oscar Wilde we read that music reveals to us a personal past that until that moment we were unaware of and that moves us to lament mischances that never occurred to us and wrongs we did not commit; for myself, I will confess that I can never hear The Marne or Don Juan without remembering in detail an apocryphal past, at once stoic and orgiastic, in which I have been defiant and have fought and fallen at last, silent, in an obscure knife fight. Perhaps the mission of the tango is just that: to give Argentines the assurance of having been brave, of having met the demands of valor and honor.

A PARTIAL MYSTERY

Having conceded one compensatory function to the tango, there remains a slight mystery to solve. The independence of South America was, in great part, an Argentine enterprise; Argentine men fought in distant battles on the continent, at Maipú, at Ayacucho, at Junín. Later there were the civil wars, the war in Brazil, the campaigns against Rosas and Urquizas, the war in Paraguay, the frontier war with the Indians. . . . Our military past is copious, but it is indisputable that the Argentine, when he wants to think himself brave, does not identify himself with that past (in spite of the preference that in school is given to the study of history), but rather with the vast generic figures of the gaucho and the more-than-friend, the *compadre.* If I do not deceive myself, this instinctive and paradoxical trait has its explanation. The Argentine tends to find his symbol in the gaucho and not the military man because the bravery figured in the former by oral tradition is not at the service of a cause, and is pure. The gaucho and the *compadre* are seen as rebels; the Argentine, unlike North Americans and almost

262

all Europeans, does not identify himself with the state. That may be attributed to the general fact that the state is an inconceivable abstraction;[1] it is certain that the Argentine is an individual, not a citizen. Aphorisms such as Hegel's "The State is the reality of the moral idea" seem to him sinister jests. Films made in Hollywood repetitively propose for our admiration the case of a man (generally, a journalist) who befriends a criminal so as later to turn him in to the police. The Argentine, for whom friendship is a passion and the police a mafia, feels that that "hero" is an incomprehensible swine. He feels with Don Quixote that *"up there, each man will have to answer for his own sins"* and that *"it is not right for honorable men to be the hangmen of others, with whom they have nothing to do"* (*Quixote,* I, 22). More than once, faced with the empty symmetries of the Spanish style, I have suspected that we differ irredeemably from Spain; those two lines from *Quixote* have sufficed to convince me of my error. They are as it were the secret quiet symbol of an affinity. One night from Argentine literature confirms that affinity—that desperate night in which a sergeant of the rural police cried that he was not going to commit the crime of killing a brave man and began to fight, together with the deserter Martín Fierro, against his own soldiers.

THE LYRICS

Of unequal value, since, notoriously, they proceed from hundreds, thousands of heterogeneous pens, the tango lyrics which inspiration or industry has turned out come together to form, right at midcentury, an almost inextricable *corpus poeticum* that historians of Argentine literature will read or, in any case, will vindicate. That which is popular, even though people no longer understand it, even though the years have made it antiquated, gains the nostalgic veneration of the erudite and permits polemics and glossaries. It is likely that around 1990 the suspicion or certitude will arise that the true poetry of our time is not in *La Urna* by Banchs or *Luz de Provincia* by Mastronardi, but rather in the imperfect and human pieces that are treasured up in *The Soul that Sings.* A culpable negligence has deprived me of the acquisition and study of this chaotic repertory, but I am not unacquainted with its variety and the growing compass of its themes. At the beginning the tango had no lyrics, or else had obscene and casual ones. Some had rustic ones ("I am the girlfriend, ever true/ Of the noble gaucho Argentino") because composers were looking for the popular, and low life and the outlying districts were not then poetic material. Others, like the related *milongas,*[2] were happy, showy, bragging-songs ("In the tango I'm so tough/ That when I do my

---

[1]The state is impersonal; the Argentine conceives only a personal relationship. Therefore, for him, stealing public monies is not a crime. I state the fact, I do not justify or excuse it.

[2]I'm from the Barrio Alto,
from the Retiro, me.
I choose never to see
the man I'm fighting with,
the girl I'm dancing with.
Nobody fools with me.

sensuous dips/ My voice carries to the North/ When in the South I move my hips"). Later the genre chronicled, like certain French naturalist novels or certain Hogarth engravings, the local vicissitudes of the "harlot's progress" ("Later you were the 'little friend'/ Of an aging pharmacist/ And the son of the commissioner/ Knocked out of you all your wind"); later, the deplored turnover of violent slum districts to decency ("Alsina Bridge—/ Where is that scoundrel?" or "Where are those men and China girls/ Red scarves and slouch hats that Requeña knew?/ Where's the Villa Crespo I knew before?/ There came the Jews, the Triumvirate flew"). From very early on, the anxieties of clandestine or sentimental love had burdened the pens ("Don't you remember that you wore/ The hat with me, and more,/ That leather belt around your waist/ I'd made you at the other mining place?"). Tangos of guilt, tangos of hate, tangos of mockery and anger were written, difficult to transcribe and to remember; some, too, perhaps a little more tolerable, in which vengeance takes the form of pardon, and delights in acts of magnanimity ("Come in, come in, now you've come back./ Don't be afraid of my foolish slaps"). Every aspect of the city began entering into the tango; low life and the suburbs were not the only subjects and I remember pieces called (this is around nineteen-twenty-something) The Rose Garden and My Nights in Colón. In the prologue to his *Satires,* Juvenal wrote memorably that everything that moves man—desire, fear, anger, carnal pleasure, intrigues, happiness— would be matter for his book; with pardonable exaggeration we might apply his famous *quidquid agunt homines* to the sum total of tango lyrics. We might also say that these lyrics form an unconnected, vast *comédie humaine* of the life of Buenos Aires. One knows that Wolf, at the end of the eighteenth century, wrote that the *Iliad* was a series of songs and rhapsodies before it was an epic; that allows, perhaps, the prophecy that tango lyrics will in time form a long civil poem, or will suggest to some ambitious person the writing of that poem.

Andrew Fletcher's similar statement is well known: "If they let me write all a nation's ballads, I don't care who writes the laws"; the dictum suggests that common or traditional poetry can influence feelings and dictate conduct. Were the conjecture applied to the Argentine tango, we might see that it is a mirror of our realities and at the same time a mentor or model, with, certainly, maleficent power. The first *milongas* and tangos could be stupid or, at least, reckless, but they were brave and happy; the later tango is a resentful thing that deplores miseries close by with sentimental excess and celebrates distant ones with diabolic impudence.

I remember that around 1926 I would persist in blaming the Italians (and more concretely the Genovese of the Barrio de la Boca) for the degeneration of the tango. In that myth, or fantasy, of a "native" tango corrupted by the "gringos," I see a clear symptom, now, of certain nationalistic heresies which have devastated the world since then—coming from the gringos, naturally. It is not the concertina, which I once ridiculed as contemptible, nor the hardworking composers that have made the tango what it is, but the republic as a whole. Moreover, the old "natives" who engendered the tango were named Bevilacqua, Greco, de Bassi. . . .

To my denigration of the tango in the state that it is in today, someone will wish to object that the passage from valor or braggadocio to sadness is not necessarily a bad thing and might be an indication of maturity. My imaginary contender might well add that the innocent and valiant Ascasubi is to the complaining Hernández what the first tango is to the last and that no one—save, perhaps, Jorge Luis Borges—has exercised himself to infer from that diminution of happiness that *Martín Fierro* is inferior to *Paulino Lucero*. The answer is easy: the difference is not only in hedonistic tone, it is in moral tone. In the usual Buenos Aires tango, in the tango of family wakes and decent confectioners' shops, there is a trivial coarseness, a savor of infamy that the tangos of the knife and the brothel never even suspected.

Musically, the tango should not be important; its only importance is that which we give it. The reflection is just, but perhaps is applicable to everything —to our personal death, for example, or to the woman who scorns us. . . . The tango may be discussed, and we discuss it, but it still guards, as does all the really real, a secret. Musical dictionaries register their brief, sufficient definition, approved by everyone; that definition is elementary, and promises no difficulties, but the French or Spanish composer who, having trusted in it, correctly works out a "tango" discovers, not without a kind of shock, that he has put together something which our ears don't recognize, which our memory offers no lodging to, and which our body rejects. That is to say that without the evenings and nights of Buenos Aires, a tango cannot be made, and that in heaven there waits for us Argentines the Platonic idea of the tango, its universal form (that form which the Boards or the Corn-Cob barely spell out), and that that valiant species has its place, albeit humble, in the universe.

THE CHALLENGE

There is an account—legendary or historical, or made of history and legend both (which, perhaps, is another way of saying legendary)—which supports the idea of the cult of courage. The best of written versions may be pursued in the novels of Eduardo Gutiérrez, *The Black Ant* or *Juan Moreira,* unjustly forgotten now; the first oral version I heard came out of a ward called Tierra del Fuego that was demarcated by a jail, a river, and a cemetery. The protagonist of that version was Juan Muraña, carter and knife fighter, in whom converge all the stories of courage that circulate through the riverbanks of the North. A man of Los Corrales or Las Barracas, knowing the fame of Juan Muraña, whom he has never seen, comes from his suburb in the South to fight him; he provokes him in a little store, the two come out into the street to fight; they wound each other; Muraña, finally, *marks* him and tells him, "I leave you with your life so you can come looking for me again."

The disinterestedness of that duel engraved it in my memory; my conversations (as my friends, thoroughly tired of it, knew) would not let it alone; about 1927, I wrote it and with emphatic brevity titled it *Men Fought;* years later the anecdote helped me imagine a lucky, since not good, story, *Man from the Slums;* in 1950, Adolfo Bioy Casares and I took it up again to work out the script of a film the studios emphatically rejected and which was to have been called *The Men from Along the River.* I thought, at the end of such extended labors, that I had said goodbye to the story of the generous duel; this year, in Chivilcoy, I picked up a version superior enough that it may well be the true one, though both could very well be, since destiny likes to repeat forms and what happened once happens often. Two mediocre stories and a film that I think was very good came out of the deficient version; nothing can come out of the other, which is perfect and complete. As I was told it I shall tell it, without addition of metaphor or landscape. The story, so they told me, occurred in Chivilcoy in the 1870s. Wenceslao Suárez was the name of the hero, who works as a rope maker and lives on a little ranch. He is forty or fifty years old; he has a reputation for bravery and it would surely be unlikely (given the facts of the story I narrate) that he could not claim one or two killings, but, committed in honor, they do not bother his conscience or sully his fame. One afternoon, in the placid life of the man, an unusual event occurs; in the general store, they inform him that a letter has come for him. Don Wenceslao does not know how to read; the ceremonious missive, which likewise seems not to be in the handwriting of the man who sent it, is slowly deciphered by the proprietor. As though they were friends who know how to value agility with the knife and true serenity, a stranger salutes Don Wenceslao, rumors of whose fame have crossed the Arroyo del Medio, and offers him the hospitality of his humble house, in a little town in the province of Santa Fe. Wenceslao Suárez dictates an answer to the proprietor; he thanks the stranger for his expressions of friendship, explains that he cannot think of leaving his mother alone, much along in years as she is now, and invites the other man to Chivilcoy, to his ranch, where there will be no lack of beef to roast and glasses of wine. Months pass and a man on a farm horse of a breed somewhat different from those of the region asks in the general store for directions to Suárez's house. Suárez, who has come to buy meat, overhears the question and tells him who he is; the stranger recalls to him the letters they wrote each other a while ago. Suárez is delighted that the other man has decided to come; later the two of them go to a little camp and Suárez prepares some roast meat. They eat and drink and talk. About what? I suspect about themes of blood, rude themes, but with civility and politeness.

They have eaten lunch and the heavy warmth of siesta time hangs over the land when the stranger suggests to Don Wenceslao that they trade a few little parries. To refuse would be dishonorable. The two men get ready and play at fighting at first, but Wenceslao before long feels that the stranger intends to kill him. He understands at last the meaning of the ceremonious letter and is sorry that he has eaten and drunk so much. He knows that he will tire before the other, who is still a young man. With feigned lethargy or courtesy, the stranger proposes that they rest. Don Wenceslao accepts, and, when they rejoin the duel, he permits the other to wound him in the left hand, which has the poncho rolled about it.[3] The knife enters his wrist, his hand hangs there deadened. Suárez, with a great

[3]Montaigne in his *Essays* (I, 49) speaks of that old manner of combat with cape and sword, and cites a passage from Caesar: *Sinistras sagis involvunt, gladiosque distringunt.* Lugones, on page 54 of *The Itinerant Singer,* has an analogous citation from the romance of Bernardo del Carpio:

Wrapping the mantle round his arm
He would go to draw his sword.

leap, falls back, lays his bloodied hand on the ground, steps on it with his boot, tears it off, fakes a blow to the stranger's chest, and with one thrust opens his belly. Thus ends the story, save that in one version, the man from Santa Fe stays there in the field and in another (which begrudges him the dignity of dying) he returns to his province. In this last version, Suárez gives him first aid with the sugarcane left from lunch. . . .

In the gesture of Wenceslao the One-Handed—for such is the epithet connected with Suárez now—the modesty or courtesy of certain traits (the work of a rope maker, the scruples over leaving his mother alone, the two florid letters, the conversation, the dinner) soften or happily accentuate the tremendous fable; such traits give it an epic or even chivalric character that we will not find, for example, unless we are bent on finding it, in the drunken fights of *Martín Fierro* or in the similar and poorer version of Juan Muraña and the man from the South. One trait common to both is, perhaps, significant. In both, the one who provokes the fight is destroyed. That may be due to the simple, miserable necessity that the local champion triumph, but also, and thus we would prefer it, to a tacit condemnation of provocation in these heroic fictions, or, and this would be best of all, to the dark and tragic conviction that man is always the artificer of his own doom, like the Ulysses of Canto XXVI of the *Inferno*. Emerson, who extolled in Plutarch's biographies "a stoicism that comes not from schools, but from the blood," would not have disdained this story.

We would have, then, the poorest level of life, gauchos and men from the regions of the banks of the Rio Plata and Paraná, creating, all unknowingly, a religion, with its mythology and its martyrs—the hard, blind religion of courage, of being ready to kill and to die. That religion is as old as the world, but it would have been discovered, and have been lived, by shepherds, slaughterers, soldiers, profligates, and ruffians in these republics. Its music would be in the styles of the *milongas* and the first tangos. I have written that it is an old religion; in a saga of the twelfth century one may read:

> "Tell me what is thy faith?" said the count.
> "I believe in my strength," said Sigmund.

Wenceslao Suárez and his anonymous opponent, and others whom the mythology has forgotten or has incorporated into those two, undoubtedly professed that virile faith, which well may be not a vanity but rather the consciousness that, in any man whatever, is God.

PART TWO
THE DICTATOR

THE DICTATOR

In spite of several operations, Borges gradually lost the use of his right eye, with the vision in the left severely impaired. His ophthalmologist ordered him to stop reading and writing. The world became increasingly gray; colors disappeared, with the exception of persistent yellow. For a man who was used to writing in a minute hand, there was no hope. He had to learn a new craft, that of dictation. The writer became a dictator.

He learned to rehearse each line in his mind. When the whole text was memorized, he would dictate it to Mother and then would have it read and reread until he was satisfied. Soon, friends and relatives began to help Mother in her exacting task. Borges trained them to read in at least one of the languages he knew. Little by little, a sort of school of readers, translators, and secretaries began to gather around him. To thank them for the gift of their time, he sometimes included their names as coauthors of his work.

One of these collaborators stands apart: Adolfo Bioy Casares, a novelist who was fifteen years younger than Borges. They had met in the early 1930s when Borges was already one of the leading Argentine writers and Bioy a mere beginner. Soon, however, the latter was to develop into an original and subtle writer. Their collaboration created many pseudonymous books and, especially, a deadly satire of Perón's regime, "A Celebration of the Monster" (JLB 64).

With the help of his collaborators, Borges eventually learned to compose and dictate not only poems but even fiction and essays.

THE OLD POET'S VOICE

Blindness privileged poetry. Now, it was easier for Borges to compose a poem in his head than a story or an essay. The predictable rhythms and even the rhymes, the musical structure of verse, favored the memorizing and rewriting of it. Because he was virtually blind, Borges could go on endlessly composing his poems. But the man who returned to poetry in his mid-fifties was a completely different craftsman. His young ambition of being able to write *the* poem had been forgotten. Now he favored a more conventional, almost classical diction. In returning to the old craft, he wrote about some of the subjects he had already explored in fiction and essays, but the tone was more relaxed or casual, the revelations more explicit. Tension had almost disappeared, self-irony had been toned down. Little by little, out of the ruins of the writer, the old bard emerged. His likes and dislikes, his foibles and manias, were all still there, but the mood was softer. The older Borges assumed the mask of the blind poet.

THE GOLEM (I)   [JLB 83]

In a book inspired by infinite wisdom, nothing can be left to chance, not even the number of words it contains or the order of the letters; this is what the Cabalists thought, and they devoted themselves to the task of counting, combining, and permutating the letters of the Scriptures, fired by a desire to penetrate the secrets of God. Dante stated that every passage of the Bible has a fourfold meaning— the literal, the allegorical, the moral, and the spiritual. Johannes Scotus Erigena, closer to the concept of divinity, had already said that the meanings of the Scriptures are infinite, like the hues in a peacock's tail. The Cabalists would have approved this view; one of the secrets they sought in the Bible was how to create living beings. It was said of demons that they could make large and bulky creatures like the camel but were incapable of creating anything delicate or frail, and Rabbi Eliezer denied them the ability to produce anything smaller than a barley grain. Golem was the name given to the man created by combinations of letters; the word means, literally, a shapeless or lifeless clod.

In the Talmud (*Sanhedrin,* 65b) we read:

> If the righteous wished to create a world, they could do so. By trying different combinations of the letters of the ineffable names of God, Raba succeeded in creating a man, whom he sent to Rabbi Zera. Rabbi Zera spoke to him, but as he got no answer, he said: "You are a creature of magic; go back to your dust."
>
> Rabbi Hanina and Rabbi Oshaia, two scholars, spent every Sabbath eve studying the Book of Creation, by means of which they brought into being a three-year-old calf that they then used for the purposes of supper.

Schopenhauer, in his book *Will in Nature,* writes (Chapter 7): "On page 325 of the first volume of his *Zauberbibliothek* [Magic Library], Horst summarizes the teachings of the English mystic Jane Lead in this way: Whoever possesses magical powers can, at will, master and change the mineral, vegetable, and animal kingdoms; consequently, a few magicians, working in agreement, could make this world of ours return to the state of Paradise."

The Golem's fame in the West is owed to the work of the Austrian writer Gustav Meyrink, who in the fifth chapter of his dream novel *Der Golem* (1915) writes:

> It is said that the origin of the story goes back to the seventeenth century. According to lost formulas of the Kabbalah, a rabbi [Judah Loew ben Bezabel] made an artificial man—the aforesaid Golem—so that he would ring the bells and take over all the menial tasks of the synagogue.
>
> He was not a man exactly, and had only a sort of dim, half-conscious, vegetative existence. By the power of a magic tablet which was placed under his tongue and which attracted the free sidereal energies of the universe, this existence lasted during the daylight hours.
>
> One night before evening prayer, the rabbi forgot to take the tablet out of the Golem's mouth, and the creature fell into a frenzy, running out into the dark alleys of the ghetto and knocking down those who got in his way, until the rabbi caught up with him and removed the tablet.
>
> At once the creature fell lifeless. All that was left of him is the dwarfish clay figure that may be seen today in the New Synagogue.

Eleazar of Worms has preserved the secret formula for making a Golem. The procedures involved cover some twenty-three folio columns and require knowledge of the "alphabets of the 221 gates," which must be recited over each of the Golem's organs. The word *emet,* which means "truth," should be marked on its forehead; to destroy the creature, the first letter must be obliterated, forming the word *met,* whose meaning is "death."

THE GOLEM (II)

If (as the Greek asserts in the *Cratylus*)
the name is archetype to the thing,
the rose is in the letters of "rose"
and the length of the Nile in "Nile."

Thus, compounded of consonants and vowels,
there must be a terrible Name, which essence
ciphers as God and Omnipotence
preserves in consummate letters and syllables.

Adam, and the stars, knew it
in the Garden. The iron rust of sin
(say the Cabalists) has effaced it
and the generations have lost the word.

The artifices and candor of man
are endless. We know that there came a day
on which the People of God sought the Name
in the vigils of the ghetto:

The memory is still green and vivid—
not in the manner of other memories like
vague shadows insinuated in a vague history—
of Judah Lion, rabbi of Prague.

Burning to know what God knew,
Judah Lion gave himself up to permutations
of letters and complex variations:
and at length pronounced the Name which is the Key,

the Portal, the Echo, the Host, the Palace,
over a doll which, with torpid hands,
He wrought to teach the arcana
of Letters, Time, and Space.

The simulacrum raised its heavy
lids and saw forms and colors
it did not understand, lost in a din,
and attempted fearsome movements.

Gradually it saw itself (even as we)
imprisoned in that sonorous net
of Before, After, Yesterday, While, Now,
Left, Right, I, Thou, Those, Others.

(The Cabalist who officiated as divinity
called his farfetched creature "Golem":

A POET OF THE THIRTEENTH CENTURY

Think of him laboring in the Tuscan halls
on the first sonnet (that word still unsaid),
the undistinguished pages, filled with sad
triplets and quatrains, without heads or tails.

Slowly he shapes it; yet the impulse fails.
He stops, perhaps at a strange slight music shed
from time coming and its holy dread,
a murmuring of far-off nightingales.

Did he sense that others were to follow,
that the arcane, incredible Apollo
had revealed an archetypal thing,

a whirlpool mirror that would draw and hold
all that night could hide or day unfold:
Daedalus, labyrinth, riddle, Oedipus King?

MIRRORS

I have been horrified before all mirrors,
not just before the impenetrable glass,
the end and the beginning of that space,
inhabited by nothing but reflections,

but faced with specular water, mirroring
the other blue within its bottomless sky,
incised at times by the illusory flight
of inverted birds, or troubled by a ripple,

or face to face with the unspeaking surface
of ghostly ebony whose very hardness
reflects, as if within a dream, the whiteness
of spectral marble or a spectral rose.

Now, after so many troubling years
of wandering underneath the wavering moon,
I ask myself what accident of fortune
handed to me this terror of all mirrors—

mirrors of metal and the shrouded mirror
of sheer mahogany which in the twilight
of its uncertain red softens the face
that watches and in turn is watched by it.

I look on them as infinite, elemental
fulfillers of a very ancient pact
to multiply the world, as in the act
of generation, sleepless and dangerous.

They extenuate this vain and dubious world
within the web of their own vertigo.
Sometimes at evening they are clouded over
by someone's breath, someone who is not dead.

The glass is watching us. And if a mirror
hangs somewhere on the four walls of my room,
I am not alone. There's an other, a reflection
which in the dawn enacts its own dumb show.

Everything happens, nothing is remembered
in those dimensioned cabinets of glass
in which, like rabbis in fantastic stories,
we read the lines of text from right to left.

Claudius, king for an evening, king in a dream,
did not know he was a dream until that day
on which an actor mimed his felony
with silent artifice, in a tableau.

Strange, that there are dreams, that there are mirrors.
Strange that the ordinary, worn-out ways
of every day encompass the imagined
and endless universe woven by reflections.

God (I've begun to think) implants a promise
in all that insubstantial architecture
that makes light out of the impervious surface
of glass, and makes the shadow out of dreams.

God has created nights well-populated
with dreams, crowded with mirror-images,
so that man may feel that he is nothing more
than vain reflection. That's what frightens us.

BORGES AND I   [JLB 88]

It's to the other man, to Borges, that things happen. I walk along the streets of
Buenos Aires, stopping now and then—perhaps out of habit—to look at the arch
of an old entranceway or a grillwork gate; of Borges I get news through the mail
and glimpse his name among a committee of professors or in a dictionary of

biography. I have a taste for hourglasses, maps, eighteenth-century typography, the roots of words, the smell of coffee, and Stevenson's prose; the other man shares these likes, but in a showy way that turns them into stagy mannerisms. It would be an exaggeration to say that we are on bad terms; I live, I let myself live, so that Borges can weave his tales and poems, and those tales and poems are my justification. It is not hard for me to admit that he has managed to write a few worthwhile pages, but these pages cannot save me, perhaps because what is good no longer belongs to anyone—not even the other man—but rather to speech or tradition. In any case, I am fated to become lost once and for all, and only some moment of myself will survive in the other man. Little by little, I have been surrendering everything to him, even though I have evidence of his stubborn habit of falsification and exaggerating. Spinoza held that all things try to keep on being themselves; a stone wants to be a stone and the tiger, a tiger. I shall remain in Borges, not in myself (if it is so that I am someone), but I recognize myself less in his books than in those of others or than in the laborious tuning of a guitar. Years ago, I tried ridding myself of him and I went from myths of the outlying slums of the city to games with time and infinity, but those games are now part of Borges and I will have to turn to other things. And so, my life is a running away, and I lose everything and everything is left to oblivion or to the other man.

Which of us is writing this page I don't know.

POEM OF THE GIFTS   [JLB 89]

No one should read self-pity or reproach
into this statement of the majesty
of God; who with such splendid irony
granted me books and blindness at one touch.

Care of this city of books he handed over
to sightless eyes, which now can do no more
than read in libraries of dream the poor
and senseless paragraphs that dawns deliver

to wishful scrutiny. In vain the day
squanders on these same eyes its infinite tomes,
as distant as the inaccessible volumes
which perished once in Alexandria.

From hunger and from thirst (in the Greek story),
a king lies dying among gardens and fountains.
Aimlessly, endlessly, I trace the confines,
high and profound, of this blind library.

Cultures of East and West, the entire atlas,
encyclopedias, centuries, dynasties,

279

symbols, the cosmos, and cosmogonies
are offered from the walls, all to no purpose.

In shadow, with a tentative stick, I try
the hollow twilight, slow and imprecise—
I, who had always thought of Paradise
in form and image as a library.

Something, which certainly is not defined
by the word *fate,* arranges all these things;
another man was given, on other evenings
now gone, these many books. He too was blind.

Wandering through the gradual galleries,
I often feel with vague and holy dread
I am that other dead one, who attempted
the same uncertain steps on similar days.

Which of the two is setting down this poem—
a single sightless self, a plural I?
What can it matter, then, the name that names me,
given our curse is common and the same?

Groussac or Borges, now I look upon
this dear world losing shape, fading away
into a pale uncertain ashy-gray
that feels like sleep, or else oblivion.

CHESS   [JLB 90]

I

In their serious corner, the players
move the gradual pieces. The board
detains them until dawn in its hard
compass: the hatred of two colors.

In the game, the forms give off a severe
magic: Homeric castle, gay
knight, warlike queen, king solitary,
oblique bishop, and pawns at war.

Finally, when the players have gone in,
and when time has eventually consumed them,
surely the rites then will not be done.

In the east, this war has taken fire.
Today, the whole earth is its provenance.
Like that other, this game is forever.

II

Tenuous king, slant bishop, bitter queen,
straightforward castle and the crafty pawn—
over the checkered black and white terrain
they seek out and enjoin their armed campaign.

They do not realize the dominant
hand of the player rules their destiny.
They do not know an adamantine fate
governs their choices and controls their journey.

The player, too, is captive of caprice
(the sentence is Omar's) on another ground
crisscrossed with black nights and white days.

God moves the player, he, in turn, the piece.
But what god beyond God begins the round
of dust and time and dream and agonies?

THE OTHER TIGER   [JLB 91]

And the craft createth a semblance.
—Morris, *Sigurd the Volsung* (1876)

I think of a tiger. The half-light enhances
the vast and painstaking library
and seems to set the bookshelves at a distance;
strong, innocent, bloodstained, and new-made,
it will move through its jungle and its morning,
and leave its track across the muddy
edge of a river, unknown, nameless
(in its world, there are no names, nor past, nor future—
only the sureness of the passing moment)
and it will cross the wilderness of distance
and sniff out in the woven labyrinth
of smells the smell peculiar to morning
and the scent of deer, delectable.
Among the slivers of bamboo, I notice
its stripes, and I have an inkling of the skeleton
under the magnificence of the skin, which quivers.
In vain, the convex oceans and the deserts
spread themselves across the earth between us;
from this one house in a remote lost seaport
in South America, I dream you, follow you,
oh tiger on the fringes of the Ganges.

281

Afternoon creeps in my spirit and I keep thinking
that the tiger I am conjuring in my poem
is a tiger made of symbols and of shadows,
a sequence of prosodic measures,
scraps remembered from encyclopedias,
and not the deadly tiger, the luckless jewel
which in the sun or the deceptive moonlight
follows its paths, in Bengal or Sumatra,
of love, of indolence, of dying.
Against the symbolic tiger, I have put
the real one, whose blood runs hot,
and today, 1959, the third of August,
a slow shadow spreads across the prairie,
but still, the act of naming it, of guessing
what is its nature and its circumstances
creates a fiction, not a living creature,
not one of those who wander on the earth.

Let us look for a third tiger. This one
will be a form in my dream like all the others,
a system and arrangement of human language,
and not the flesh-and-bone tiger
which, out of reach of all mythology,
paces the earth. I know all this, but something
drives me to this ancient and vague adventure,
unreasonable, and still I keep on looking
throughout the afternoon for the other tiger,
the other tiger which is not in this poem.

THE BORGES   [JLB 92]

I know little or nothing of the Borges,
my Portuguese forebears. They were a ghostly race,
who still ply in my body their mysterious
disciplines, habits, and anxieties.
Shadowy, as if they had never been,
and strangers to the processes of art,
indecipherably they form a part
of time, of earth, and of oblivion.
Better so. When everything is said,
they are Portugal, they are that famous people
who forced the Great Wall of the East, and fell
to the sea, and to that other sea of sand.

They are that king lost on the mystic strand
and those at home who swear he is not dead.

ADROGUÉ   [JLB 93]

Let no one fear in the bewildering night
that I will lose my way among the borders
of dusky flowers that weave a cloth of symbols
appropriate to old nostalgic loves

or the sloth of afternoons—the hidden bird
forever whittling the same thin song,
the circular fountain and the summerhouse,
the indistinct statue and the hazy ruin.

Hollow in the hollow shade, the coach house
marks (I know well) the insubstantial edges
of this particular world of dust and jasmine
so dear to Julio Herrera and Verlaine.

The shade is thick with the medicinal smell
of the eucalyptus trees, that ancient balm
which, beyond time and ambiguities
of language, brings back vanished country houses.

My step feels out and finds the anticipated
threshold. Its darkened limit is defined
by the roof, and in the chessboard patio
the water tap drips intermittently.

On the far side of the doorways they are sleeping,
those who through the medium of dreams
watch over in the visionary shadows
all that vast yesterday and all dead things.

Each object in this venerable building
I know by heart—the flaking layers of mica
on that gray stone, reflected endlessly
in the recesses of a faded mirror,

and the lion head which holds an iron ring
in its mouth, and the multicolored window glass,
revealing to a child the early vision
of one world colored red, another green.

Far beyond accident and death itself
they endure, each one with its particular story,

283

but all this happens in the strangeness of
that fourth dimension which is memory.

In it and it alone do they exist,
the gardens and the patios. The past
retains them in that circular preserve
which at one time embraces dawn and dusk.

How could I have forgotten that precise
order of things both humble and beloved,
today as inaccessible as the roses
revealed to the first Adam in Paradise?

The ancient aura of an elegy
still haunts me when I think about that house—
I do not understand how time can pass,
I, who am time and blood and agony.

EMERSON   [JLB 94]

Closing the heavy volume of Montaigne,
the tall New Englander goes out
into an evening which exalts the fields.
It is a pleasure worth no less than reading.
He walks toward the final sloping of the sun,
toward the landscape's gilded edge;
he moves through darkening fields as he moves now
through the memory of the one who writes this down.
He thinks: I have read the essential books
and written others which oblivion
will not efface. I have been allowed
that which is given mortal man to know.
The whole continent knows my name.
I have not lived. I want to be someone else.

CAMDEN, 1892   [JLB 95]

The fragrance of coffee and newspapers.
Sunday and its tedium. This morning,
on the uninvestigated page, that vain

column of allegorical verses
by a happy colleague. The old man lies
prostrate, pale, even white in his decent
room, the room of a poor man. Needlessly
he glances at his face in the exhausted
mirror. He thinks, without surprise now,
That face is me. One fumbling hand touches
the tangled beard, the devastated mouth.
The end is not far off. His voice declares:
I am almost gone. But my verses scan
life and its splendor. I was Walt Whitman.

SPINOZA   [JLB 96]

The Jew's hands, translucent in the dusk,
polish the lenses time and again.
The dying afternoon is fear, is
cold, and all afternoons are the same.
The hands and the hyacinth-blue air
that whitens at the Ghetto edges
do not quite exist for this silent
man who conjures up a clear labyrinth—
undisturbed by fame, that reflection
of dreams in the dream of another
mirror, nor by maidens' timid love.
Free of metaphor and myth, he grinds
a stubborn crystal: the infinite
map of the One who is all His stars.

POEM WRITTEN IN A COPY OF BEOWULF   [JLB 97]

At various times, I have asked myself what reasons
moved me to study, while my night came down,
without particular hope of satisfaction,
the language of the blunt-tongued Anglo-Saxons.

Used up by the years, my memory
loses its grip on words that I have vainly

285

repeated and repeated. My life in the same way
weaves and unweaves its weary history.

Then I tell myself: it must be that the soul
has some secret, sufficient way of knowing
that it is immortal, that its vast, encompassing
circle can take in all, can accomplish all.

Beyond my anxiety, beyond this writing,
the universe waits, inexhaustible, inviting.

PART THREE
A BRIEF RETURN
TO REALISM

A BRIEF RETURN TO REALISM

In spite of his theorizing about fantastic literature and his love for Kafka (JLB 73) and Wells (JLB 52, JLB 56), Borges had always had a nostalgia for old-fashioned realistic literature. In younger days, he attempted a few stories ("Emma Zunz" is perhaps the best) in which a sort of naturalism prevails. But only in his old age, when theories and inventions mattered less to him, did he feel free to try his hand at realism. "The Intruder" (1966) was his first attempt (JLB 98). Four years later he published a book of stories, *Doctor Brodie's Report,* whose prologue contains a manifesto in favor of realism (JLB 102). Borges's concept of it is very idiosyncratic, to say the least. Some of the stories in the book are fantastic, and even those which have nothing unreal in them have characters whose attitudes are very peculiar. Once, in discussing Melville (JLB 47), Borges pointed out that he had been able to create characters, such as Bartleby, whose behavior was fantastic. The same could be said about many of Kafka's and Borges's characters. What was really important in his attempt to turn to realism was the fact that he went back to writing stories. With the coaxing and the help of his American translator, Norman Thomas di Giovanni, Borges produced *Doctor Brodie's Report.* After parting company with Di Giovanni in 1972, he published in 1975 another collection of stories, *The Book of Sand,* in which he returned to the fantastic. But he did not stop writing poems and essays.

In his eighties, frail and resilient, Borges continues to add small volumes to his works. A writer who had once seemed destined to produce only short pieces and slim, beautiful fragments is now immortalized in the two large volumes of his incomplete *Complete Works* in Spanish. A third volume, equally robust, could be made out of the earlier books of essays he has eliminated from the canon, plus the many articles, reviews, poems, and occasional pieces he wrote while he was an eager, irreverent, younger writer.

THE INTRUDER

2 Samuel 1:26

They claim (improbably) that the story was told by Eduardo, the younger of the Nilsen brothers, at the wake for Cristian, the elder, who died of natural causes at some point in the 1890s, in the district of Morón. Someone must certainly have heard it from someone else, in the course of that long, idle night, between servings of maté, and passed it on to Santiago Dabove, from whom I learned it. Years later, they told it to me again in Turdera, where it had all happened. The second version, considerably more detailed, substantiated Santiago's, with the usual small variations and departures. I write it down now because, if I am not wrong, it reflects briefly and tragically the whole temper of life in those days along the banks of the River Plate. I shall put it down scrupulously; but already I see myself yielding to the writer's temptation to heighten or amplify some detail or other.

In Turdera, they were referred to as the Nilsens. The parish priest told me that his predecessor remembered with some astonishment seeing in that house a worn Bible, bound in black, with Gothic characters; in the end pages, he glimpsed handwritten names and dates. It was the only book in the house. The recorded misfortunes of the Nilsens, lost as all will be lost. The old house, now no longer in existence, was built of unstuccoed brick; beyond the hallway, one could make out a patio of colored tile, and another with an earth floor. In any case, very few ever went there; the Nilsens were jealous of their privacy. In the dilapidated rooms, they slept on camp beds; their indulgences were horses, riding gear, short-bladed daggers, a substantial fling on Saturdays, and belligerent drinking. I know that they were tall, with red hair which they wore long. Denmark, Ireland, places they would never hear tell of, stirred in the blood of those two *criollos*. The neighborhood feared them, as they did all red-haired people; nor is it impossible that they might have been responsible for someone's death. Once, shoulder to shoulder, they tangled with the police. The younger one was said to have had an altercation with Juan Iberra in which he did not come off worst; which, according to what we hear, is indeed something. They were cowboys, team drivers, rustlers, and, at times, cheats. They had a reputation for meanness, except when drinking and gambling made them expansive. Of their ancestry or where they came from, nothing was known. They owned a wagon and a yoke of oxen.

Physically, they were quite distinct from the roughneck crowd of settlers who lent the Costa Brava their own bad name. This, and other things we do not know, helps to explain how close they were; to cross one of them meant having two enemies.

The Nilsens were roisterers, but their amorous escapades had until then been confined to hallways and houses of ill fame. Hence, there was no lack of local comment when Cristian brought Juliana Burgos to live with him. True enough, in that way he got himself a servant; but it is also true that he showered her with gaudy trinkets, and showed her off at fiestas—the poor tenement fiestas, where the more intimate figures of the tango were forbidden and where the dancers still kept a respectable space between them. Juliana was dark-complexioned, with large wide eyes; one had only to look at her to make her smile. In a poor neighborhood, where work and neglect wear out the women, she was not at all bad looking.

At first, Eduardo went about with them. Later, he took a journey to Arrecifes on some business or other; he brought back home with him a girl he had picked up along the way. After a few days, he threw her out. He grew more sullen; he would get drunk alone at the local bar, and would have nothing to do with anyone. He was in love with Cristian's woman. The neighborhood, aware of it possibly before he was, looked forward with malicious glee to the subterranean rivalry between the brothers.

One night, when he came back late from the bar at the corner, Eduardo saw Cristian's black horse tethered to the fence. In the patio, the elder brother was waiting for him, all dressed up. The woman came and went, carrying maté. Cristian said to Eduardo:

"I'm off to a brawl at the Farías'. There's Juliana for you. If you want her, make use of her."

His tone was half-commanding, half-cordial. Eduardo kept still, gazing at him; he did not know what to do. Cristian rose, said goodbye to Eduardo but not to Juliana, who was an object to him, mounted, and trotted off, casually.

From that night on, they shared her. No one knew the details of that sordid conjunction, which outraged the proprieties of the poor locality. The arrangement worked well for some weeks, but it could not last. Between them, the brothers never uttered the name of Juliana, not even to summon her, but they sought out and found reasons for disagreeing. They argued over the sale of some skins, but they were really arguing about something else. Cristian would habitually raise his voice, while Eduardo kept quiet. Without realizing it, they were growing jealous. In that rough settlement, no man ever let on to others, or to himself, that a woman would matter, except as something desired or possessed, but the two of them were in love. For them, that in its way was a humiliation.

One afternoon, in the Plaza de Lomos, Eduardo ran into Juan Iberra, who congratulated him on the beautiful "dish" he had fixed up for himself. It was then,

I think, that Eduardo roughed him up. No one, in his presence, was going to make fun of Cristian.

The woman waited on the two of them with animal submissiveness; but she could not conceal her preference, unquestionably for the younger one, who, although he had not rejected the arrangement, had not sought it out.

One day, they told Juliana to get two chairs from the first patio, and to keep out of the way, for they had to talk. Expecting a long discussion, she lay down for her siesta, but soon they summoned her. They had her pack a bag with all she possessed, not forgetting the glass rosary and the little crucifix her mother had left her. Without any explanation, they put her on the wagon, and set out on a wordless and wearisome journey. It had rained; the roads were heavy going and it was eleven in the evening when they arrived at Morón. There they passed her over to the *patrona* of the house of prostitution. The deal had already been made; Cristian picked up the money, and later on he divided it with Eduardo.

In Turdera, the Nilsens, floundering in the meshes of that outrageous love (which was also something of a routine), sought to recover their old ways, of men among men. They went back to their poker games, to fighting, to occasional binges. At times, perhaps, they felt themselves liberated, but one or other of them would quite often be away, perhaps genuinely, perhaps not. A little before the end of the year, the younger one announced that he had business in Buenos Aires. Cristian went to Morón; in the yard of the house we already know, he recognized Eduardo's piebald. He entered; the other was inside, waiting his turn. It seems that Cristian said to him, "If we go on like this, we'll wear out the horses. It's better that we do something about her."

He spoke with the *patrona,* took some coins from his money belt, and they went off with her. Juliana went with Cristian; Eduardo spurred his horse so as not to see them.

They returned to what has already been told. The cruel solution had failed; both had given in to the temptation to dissimulate. Cain's mark was there, but the bond between the Nilsens was strong—who knows what trials and dangers they had shared—and they preferred to vent their furies on others. On a stranger, on the dogs, on Juliana, who had brought discord into their lives.

March was almost over and the heat did not break. One Sunday (on Sundays it is the custom to retire early), Eduardo, coming back from the corner bar, saw Cristian yoking up the oxen. Cristian said to him, "Come on. We have to leave some hides off at the Pardos'. I've already loaded them. Let us take advantage of the cool."

The Pardo place lay, I think, to the south of them; they took the Camino de las Tropas, and then a detour. The landscape was spreading out slowly under the night.

They skirted a clump of dry reeds. Cristian threw away the cigarette he had lit and said casually, "Now, brother, to work. Later on, the buzzards will give us a hand. Today I killed her. Let her stay here with all her finery, and not do us any more harm."

They embraced, almost in tears. Now they shared an extra bond; the woman sorrowfully sacrificed and the obligation to forget her.

292

Old age (this is the name that others give it)
may prove a time of happiness.
The animal is dead or nearly dead;
man and soul go on.
I live among vague whitish shapes
that are not darkness yet.
Buenos Aires,
which once broke up in a tatter of slums and open lots
out toward the endless plain,
is now again the graveyard of the Recoleta, the Retiro square,
the shabby streets of the old Westside,
and the few vanishing decrepit houses
that we still call the South.
All through my life things were too many.
To think, Democritus tore out his eyes;
time has been my Democritus.
This growing dark is slow and brings no pain;
it flows along an easy slope
and is akin to eternity.
My friends are faceless,
women are as they were years back,
one street corner is taken for another,
on the pages of books there are no letters.
All this should make me uneasy,
but there's a restfulness about it, a going back.
Of the many generations of books on earth
I have read only a few,
the few that in my mind I go on reading still—
reading and changing.
From south and east and west and north,
roads coming together have led me
to my secret center.

These roads were footsteps and echoes,
women, men, agonies, rebirths,
days and nights,
falling asleep and dreams,
each single moment of my yesterdays
and of the world's yesterdays,
the firm sword of the Dane and the moon of the Persians,
the deeds of the dead,
shared love, words,
Emerson, and snow, and so many things.
Now I can forget them. I reach my center,

293

my algebra and my key,
my mirror.
Soon I shall know who I am.

MILONGA OF MANUEL FLORES [JLB 100]

Manuel Flores is doomed to die.
That's as sure as your money.
Dying is a custom
well known to many.

But even so, it pains me
to say goodbye to living,
that state so well known now,
so sweet, so solid-seeming.

I look at my hand in the dawning.
I look at the veins contained there.
I look at them in amazement
as I would look at a stranger.

Tomorrow comes the bullet,
oblivion descending.
Merlin the magus said it:
being born has an ending.

So much these eyes have seen,
such things, such places!
Who knows what they will see
when I've been judged by Jesus.

Manuel Flores is doomed to die.
That's as sure as your money.
Dying is a custom
well known to many.

INVOCATION TO JOYCE [JLB 101]

Scattered over scattered cities,
alone and many
we played at being that Adam
who gave names to all living things.

Down the long slopes of night
that border on the dawn,
we sought (I still remember) words
for the moon, for death, for the morning,
and for man's other habits.
We were imagism, cubism,
the conventicles and sects
respected now by credulous universities.
We invented the omission of punctuation
and capital letters,
stanzas in the shape of a dove
from the librarians of Alexandria.
Ashes, the labor of our hands,
and a burning fire our faith.
You, all the while,
in cities of exile,
in that exile that was
your detested and chosen instrument,
the weapon of your craft,
erected your pathless labyrinths,
infinitesimal and infinite,
wondrously paltry,
more populous than history.
We shall die without sighting
the twofold beast or the rose
that are the center of your maze,
but memory holds its talismans,
its echoes of Virgil,
and so in the streets of night
your splendid hells survive,
so many of your cadences and metaphors,
the treasures of your darkness.
What does our cowardice matter if on this earth
there is one brave man,
what does sadness matter if in time past
somebody thought himself happy,
what does my lost generation matter,
that dim mirror,
if your books justify us?
I am the others. I am all those
who have been rescued by your pains and care.
I am those unknown to you and saved by you.

Kipling's last stories were no less tormented and mazelike than the stories of Kafka or Henry James, which they doubtless surpass; but in 1885, in Lahore, the young Kipling began a series of brief tales, written in a straightforward manner, that he was to collect in 1890. Several of them—"In the House of Suddhoo," "Beyond the Pale," "The Gate of the Hundred Sorrows"—are laconic masterpieces. It occurred to me that what was conceived and carried out by a young man of genius might modestly be attempted by a man on the borders of old age who knows his craft. Out of that idea came the present volume, which I leave to the reader to judge.

I have done my best—I don't know with what success—to write straightforward stories. I do not dare state that they are simple; there isn't anywhere on earth a single page or single word that is, since each thing implies the universe, whose most obvious trait is complexity. I want to make it quite clear that I am not, nor have I ever been, what used to be called a preacher of parables or a fabulist and is now known as a committed writer. I do not aspire to be Aesop. My stories, like those of *The 1001 Nights,* try to be entertaining or moving but not persuasive. Such an intention does not mean that I have shut myself up, according to Solomon's image, in an ivory tower. My political convictions are quite well known; I am a member of the Conservative Party—this in itself is a form of skepticism—and no one has ever branded me a Communist, a nationalist, an anti-Semite, a follower of Billy the Kid or of the dictator Rosas. I believe that someday we will deserve not to have governments. I have never kept my opinions hidden, not even in trying times, but neither have I ever allowed them to find their way into my literary work, except once when I was buoyed up in exultation over the Six-Day War. The art of writing is mysterious; the opinions we hold are ephemeral, and I prefer the Platonic idea of the Muse to that of Poe, who reasoned, or feigned to reason, that the writing of a poem is an act of the intelligence. It never fails to amaze me that the classics advance a romantic theory of poetry, and romantic poets a classical theory.

Apart from the text that gives this book its title and that obviously derives from Lemuel Gulliver's last voyage, my stories are—to use the term in vogue today—realistic. They follow, I believe, all the conventions of that school, which is as conventional as any other and of which we shall soon grow tired if we have not already done so. They are rich in the required invention of circumstances. Splendid examples of this device are to be found in the tenth-century Old English ballad of Maldon and in the later Icelandic sagas. Two stories—I will not give their names—hold the same fantastic key. The curious reader will notice certain close affinities between them. The same few plots, I am sorry to say, have pursued me down through the years; I am decidedly monotonous.

I owe to a dream of Hugo Rodríguez Moroni the general outline of the story —perhaps the best of this collection—called "The Gospel According to Mark." I fear having spoiled it with the changes that my fancy or my reason judged fitting. But after all, writing is nothing more than a guided dream.

I have given up the surprises inherent in a Baroque style as well as the surprises that lead to an unforeseen ending. I have, in short, preferred to satisfy an expectation rather than to provide a startling shock. For many years, I thought it might be given me to achieve a good page by means of variations and novelties; now, having passed seventy, I believe I have found my own voice. Slight rewording neither spoils nor improves what I dictate, except in cases of lightening a clumsy sentence or toning down an exaggeration. Each language is a tradition, each word a shared symbol, and what an innovator can change amounts to a trifle; we need only remember the splendid but often unreadable work of a Mallarmé or a Joyce. It is likely that this all-too-reasonable reasoning is only the fruit of weariness. My now advanced age has taught me to resign myself to being Borges.

I am impartially indifferent to both the dictionary of the Spanish Royal Academy—*dont chaque édition fait regretter la précédente,* according to the sad observation of Paul Groussac— and those weighty Argentine dictionaries of local usage. All, I find—those of this and those of the other side of the ocean—have a tendency to emphasize differences and to fragment the Spanish language. In connection with this, I recall that when it was held against the novelist Roberto Arlt that he had no knowledge of Buenos Aires slang, he replied, "I grew up in Villa Luro, among poor people and hoodlums, and I really had no time to learn that sort of thing." Our local slang, in fact, is a literary joke concocted by writers of popular plays and tango lyrics, and the people who are supposed to use it hardly know what it means, except when they have been indoctrinated by phonograph records.

I have set my stories some distance off in time and in space. The imagination, in this way, can operate with greater freedom. Who, in 1970, is able to remember with accuracy what at the end of the last century the outskirts of Buenos Aires around Palermo and Lomas were like? Unbelievable as it may seem, there are those who go to the length of playing policeman and looking for a writer's petty slips. They remark, for example, that Martín Fierro would have spoken of a "bag" and not a "sack" of bones, and they find fault, perhaps unjustly, with the roan piebald coat of a certain horse famous in our literature.

God spare thee, reader, long prologues. The words are Quevedo's, who, careful not to fall into an anachronism which in the long run would have been detected, never read those of Bernard Shaw.

DOCTOR BRODIE'S REPORT   [JLB 103]

Among the pages of one of the volumes of Lane's *Arabian Nights' Entertainments* (London, 1839), a set of which my dear friend Paul Keins turned up for me, we made the discovery of the manuscript I am about to transcribe below. The neat handwriting—an art that typewriters are now helping us to forget—suggests that it was composed some time around that same date. Lane's work, as is well known, is lavish with extensive explanatory notes; in the margins of my copy there are a number of annotations, interrogation marks, and now and then emendations written in the same hand as the manuscript. We may surmise that the wondrous tales of Scheherazad interested the annotator less than the customs of the Mohammedans Of David Brodie, D.D., whose signature adorns the bottom of the last page with a fine flourish, I have been unable to uncover any information except that he was a Scottish missionary, born in Aberdeen, who preached the Christian faith first in the heart of Africa and later on in certain backlying regions of Brazil, a land he was probably led to by his knowledge of Portuguese. I am unaware of the place and date of his death. The manuscript, as far as I know, was never given to the press.

What follows is a faithful transcription of his report, composed in a rather colorless English, with no other omissions than two or three Bible verses jotted in the margins and a curious passage concerning the sexual practices of the Yahoos, which our good Presbyterian discreetly committed to Latin. The first page is missing.

. . . of the region infested by Ape-men dwell the "Mlch,"[1] whom I shall call Yahoos so that my readers will be reminded of their bestial nature and also because, given the total absence of vowels in their harsh language, an exact transliteration is virtually impossible. Including the "Nr," who dwell farther to the south in the thorn-bush, the numbers of the tribe do not, I believe, exceed 700. The cipher which I propose is a mere conjecture, since, save for the king and queen and the witch doctors, the Yahoos sleep in no fixed abode but wherever night overtakes them. Swamp fever and the continual incursions of the Ape-men diminish their number. Only a very few individuals have names. In order to address one another, it is their custom to fling a small handful of mud. I have also noticed Yahoos who, to attract a friend's attention, throw themselves on the ground and wallow in the dust. Save for their lower foreheads and for having a peculiar copperish hue that reduces their blackness, in other physical respects they do not noticeably differ from the "Kroo." They take their nourishment from fruits, root-stalks, and the smaller reptiles; they imbibe the milk of cats and of chiropterans; and they fish with their hands. While eating, they normally conceal themselves or else close their eyes. All other physical habits they perform in open view, much the same as the Cynics of old. . . . So as to partake of their wisdom, they devour the raw corpses of their witch doctors and of the royal family. When I admonished them for this evil custom they touched their lips and their bellies, perhaps to indicate that the dead are also edible, or—but this explanation may be farfetched—in order that I might come to understand that everything we eat becomes, in the long run, human flesh. In their warfare they employ stones, which they gather for that purpose, and magical spells and incantations. They go about quite naked, the arts of clothing and tattooing being altogether unknown to them.

It is worthy of note that, though they have at hand a wide, grassy plateau on which there are springs of clear water and shade-dispensing trees, they prefer

---

[1] I give the "ch" the value it has in the word "loch." [Author's note.]

to swarm in the marshlands which surround this eminence, as if delighting in the rigors of the hot climate and the general unwholesomeness. The slopes of the plateau are steep and could easily be utilized as a natural bulwark against the onslaughts of the Ape-men. The clans of Scotland, in similar circumstances, erected their castles on the summits of hills; I advised the witch doctors to adopt this simple defensive measure, but my words were of no avail. They allowed me, however, to build a hut for myself on higher ground, where the night air is cooler.

The tribe is ruled over by a king, whose power is absolute, but it is my suspicion that the true rulers are the witch doctors, who administer to him and who have chosen him. Every male born into the tribe is subjected to a painstaking examination; if he exhibits certain stigmata, the nature of which were not revealed to me, he is elevated to the rank of king of the Yahoos. So that the physical world may not lead him from the paths of wisdom, he is gelded on the spot, his eyes are burned, and his hands and feet are amputated. Thereafter, he lives confined in a cavern called the castle ("Qzr"), into which only the four witch doctors and the two slave women who attend him and anoint him with dung are permitted entrance. Should war arise, the witch doctors remove him from his cavern, display him to the tribe to excite their courage, and bear him, lifted onto their shoulders after the manner of a flag or a talisman, to the thick of the fight. In such cases, he dies almost immediately under the hail of stones flung at him by the Ape-men.

In another castle lives the queen, who is not permitted to see her king. During my sojourn, this lady was kind enough to receive me; she was smiling, young, and, insofar as her race allowed, graceful. Bracelets of metalwork and of ivory and necklaces of teeth adorned her nakedness. She inspected me, sniffed me, and, after touching me with a finger, ended by offering herself to me in the presence of all her retinue. My cloth and my ethics, however, forbade me that honor, which commonly she grants only to the witch doctors and to the slave hunters, for the most part Muslims, whose caravans journey across the kingdom. Twice or thrice she sank a gold pin into my flesh; such prickings being tokens of royal favor, the number of Yahoos are more than a few who stick themselves with pins to encourage the belief that the queen herself pricked them. The ornaments she wore, and which I have described, come from other regions. Since they lack the capacity to fashion the simplest object, the Yahoos regard such ornaments as natural. To the tribe my hut was a tree, despite the fact that many of them saw me construct it and even lent me their aid. Among a number of other items, I had in my possession a watch, a cork helmet, a mariner's compass, and a Bible. The Yahoos stared at them, weighed them in their hands, and wanted to know where I had found them. They customarily reached for my cutlass not by the hilt but by the blade, seeing it, undoubtedly, in their own way, which causes me to wonder to what degree they would be able to perceive a chair. A house of several rooms would strike them as a maze, though perhaps they might find their way inside it in the manner of the cat, though the cat does not imagine the house. My beard, which then was red, was a source of wonderment to them all, and it was with obvious fondness that they stroked it.

The Yahoos are insensitive to pain and pleasure, save for the relishment they get from raw and rancid meat and evil-smelling things. An utter lack of imagination moves them to cruelty.

I have spoken of the queen and the king; I shall speak now of the witch doctors. I have already recorded that they are four, this number being the largest that their arithmetic spans. On their fingers they count thus: one, two, three, four, *many.* Infinity begins at the thumb. The same, I am informed, occurs among the Indian tribes who roam in the vicinity of Buenos-Ayres on the South American continent. In spite of the fact that four is the highest number at their disposal, the Arabs who trade with them do not swindle them, because in the bartering everything is divided into lots—which each of the traders piles by his side—of one, two, three, and four. Such transactions are cumbersome, but they do not admit of error or fraudulence. Of the entire nation of the Yahoos, the witch doctors are the only persons who have aroused my interest. The tribesmen attribute to them the power of transforming into ants or into turtles anyone who so desires; one individual, who detected my disbelief, pointed out an anthill to me, as though that constituted a proof.

Memory is greatly defective among the Yahoos, or perhaps is altogether nonexistent. They speak of the havoc wrought by an invasion of leopards, but do not know who witnessed the event, they or their fathers, nor do they know whether they are recounting a dream. The witch doctors show some signs of memory, albeit to a reduced degree; they are able to recollect in the evening things which took place that morning or the preceding evening. They are also endowed with the faculty of foresight, and can state with quiet confidence what will happen ten or fifteen minutes hence. They convey, for example, that "A fly will graze the nape of my neck" or "In a moment we shall hear the song of a bird." Hundreds of times I have borne witness to this curious gift, and I have also reflected upon it at length. Knowing that past, present, and future already exist, detail upon detail, in God's prophetic memory, in His eternity, what baffles me is that men, while they can look indefinitely backward, are not allowed to look one whit forward. If I am able to remember in all vividness that towering four-master from Norway which I saw when I was scarcely four, why am I taken aback by the fact that man may be capable of foreseeing what is about to happen? To the philosophical mind, memory is as much a wonder as divination; tomorrow morning is closer to us than the crossing of the Red Sea by the Hebrews, which, nevertheless, we remember.

The tribesmen are proscribed from lifting their gaze to the stars, a privilege accorded only to the witch doctors. Each witch doctor has a disciple, whom he instructs from childhood in secret lore and who succeeds him upon his death. In this wise they are always four, a number of magical properties, since it is the highest to which the Yahoo mind attains. They profess, in their own fashion, the doctrines of heaven and hell. Both places are subterranean. Hell, which is dry and filled with light, harbors the sick, the aged, the ill-treated, the Ape-men, the Arabs, and the leopards; heaven, which is depicted as marshy and beclouded, is the dwelling-place of the king and queen, the witch doctors, and those who have been happy, merciless, and bloodthirsty on earth. They worship as well a god whose name is Dung, and whom possibly they have conceived in the image and semblance of the king; he is a blind, mutilated, stunted being, and enjoys limitless powers. Dung is wont to take the form of an ant or a serpent.

After the foregoing remarks, it should cause no one to wonder that during my long stay among them I did not contrive to convert a single Yahoo. The words "Our Father," owing to the fact that they have no notion of fatherhood, left them puzzled. They cannot, it seems, accept a cause so remote and so unlikely, and are therefore uncomprehending that an act carried out several months before may bear relation to the birth of a child. Moreover, all the women engage in carnal commerce, and not all are mothers.

The Yahoo language is complex, having affinities with no others of which I have any knowledge. We cannot speak even of parts of speech, for there are no parts. Each monosyllabic word corresponds to a general idea whose specific meaning depends on the context or upon accompanying grimaces. The word "nrz," for example, suggests dispersion or spots, and may stand for the starry sky, a leopard, a flock of birds, smallpox, something bespattered, the act of scattering, or the flight that follows defeat in warfare. "Hrl," on the other hand, means something compact or dense. It may stand for the tribe, a tree trunk, a stone, a heap of stones, the act of heaping stones, the gathering of the four witch doctors, carnal conjunction, or a forest. Pronounced in another manner or accompanied by other grimaces, each word may hold an opposite meaning. Let us not be unduly amazed; in our own tongue, the verb "to cleave" means both to divide asunder and to adhere. Of course, among the Yahoos, there are no sentences, nor even short phrases.

The intellectual power to draw abstractions which such a language assumes has led me to believe that the Yahoos, for all their backwardness, are not a primitive but a degenerate nation. This conjecture is borne out by the inscriptions I discovered on the heights of the plateau and whose characters, which are not unlike the runes carved by our forefathers, are no longer within the tribe's capacity to decipher. It is as though the tribe had forgotten written language and found itself reduced now only to the spoken word.

The diversions of these people are the fights which they stage between trained cats, and capital executions. Someone is accused of an attempt against the queen's chastity, or of having eaten in the sight of another; without either the testimony of witnesses or a confession, the king finds a verdict of guilty. The condemned man suffers tortures that I shall do my best to forget, and then is stoned to death. The queen is privileged to cast the first stone and, what is usually superfluous, the last. The throng applauds her skill and the beauty of her parts, and, all in a frenzy, acclaims her, pelting her with roses and fetid things. The queen, without uttering a sound, smiles.

Another of the tribe's customs is the discovery of poets. Six or seven words, generally enigmatic, may come to a man's mind. He cannot contain himself and shouts them out, standing in the center of a circle formed by the witch doctors and the common people, who are stretched out on the ground. If the poem does not stir them, nothing comes to pass, but if the poet's words strike them they all draw away from him, without a sound, under the command of a holy dread. Feeling then that the spirit has touched him, nobody, not even his own mother, will either speak to him or cast a glance at him. Now he is a man no longer but a god, and anyone has license to kill him. The poet, if he has his wits about him, seeks refuge in the sand dunes of the North.

I have already described how I came to the land of the Yahoos. It will be recalled that they encircled me, that I discharged my firearm into the air, and that they took the discharge for a kind of magical thunderclap. In order to foster that error, I strove thereafter to go about without my weapon. One spring morning, at the break of day, we were suddenly overrun by the Ape-men; I started down from the highlands, gun in hand, and killed two of these animals. The rest fled in amazement. Shot, it is known, is invisible. For the first time in my life I heard myself cheered. It was then, I believe, that the queen received me. The memory of the Yahoos, as I have mentioned, being undependable, that very afternoon I made good an escape. My subsequent adventures in the jungle are of little account. In due course, I came upon a village of black men who knew how to plow, to sow, and to pray, and with whom I made myself understood in Portuguese. A Romish missionary, Father Fernandes, offered me the hospitality of his hut, and cared for me until I was able to continue on my hard journey. At first I found it revolting to see him open his mouth without the slightest dissimulation and put into it pieces of food. I still covered my mouth with my hand, or averted my eyes; a few days later, however, I had readjusted myself. I recall with distinct pleasure our debates in topics theological, but I had no success in turning him to the true faith of Jesus.

I set down this account now in Glasgow. I have told of my visit among the Yahoos, but have not dwelt upon the essential horror of the experience, which never ceases entirely to be with me, and which visits me yet in dreams. In the street, upon occasion, I feel that they still surround me. Only too well do I know the Yahoos to be a barbarous nation, perhaps the most barbarous to be found upon the face of the earth, but it would be unjust to overlook certain traits which redeem them. They have institutions of their own; they enjoy a king; they employ a language based upon abstract concepts; they believe, like the Hebrews and the Greeks, in the divine nature of poetry; and they surmise that the soul survives the death of the body. They also uphold the truth of punishments and rewards. After their fashion, they stand for civilization much as we ourselves do, in spite of our many transgressions. I do not repent having fought in their ranks against the Ape-men. Not only is it our duty to save their souls, but it is my fervent prayer that the government of Her Majesty will not ignore what this report makes bold to suggest.

POEM OF QUANTITY   [JLB 104]

I think of the stark and puritanical sky
with its remote and solitary stars

which Emerson so many nights would look at
from the snow-bound severity of Concord.
Here, the night sky overflows with stars.
Man is too numerous. Endless generations
of birds and insects, multiplying themselves,
of serpents and the spotted jaguar,
of growing branches, weaving, interweaving,
of grains of sand, of coffee and of leaves
descend on every day and re-create
their minuscule and useless labyrinth.
It may be every ant we trample on
is single before God, Who counts on it
for the unfolding of the measured laws
which regulate His curious universe.
The entire system, if it was not so,
would be an error and a weighty chaos.
Mirrors of water, mirrors of ebony,
the all-inventive mirror of our dreams,
lichens, fishes, and the riddled coral,
the clawmarks left by tortoises in time,
the fireflies of a single afternoon,
the dynasties of the Auraucarians,
the delicate shapes of letters in a volume
which night does not blot out, unquestionably
are no less personal and enigmatic
than I, who mix them up. I would not venture
to judge the lepers or Caligula.

PEDRO SALVADORES [JLB 105]

I want to leave a written record (perhaps the first to be attempted) of one of the strangest and grimmest happenings in Argentine history. To meddle as little as possible in the telling, to abstain from picturesque details or personal conjectures is, it seems to me, the only way to do this.

A man, a woman, and the overpowering shadow of a dictator are the three characters. The man's name was Pedro Salvadores; my grandfather Acevedo saw him days or weeks after the dictator's downfall in the battle of Caseros. Pedro Salvadores may have been no different from anyone else, but the years and his fate set him apart. He was a gentleman like many other gentlemen of his day. He owned (let us suppose) a ranch in the country and, opposed to the tyranny, was on the Unitarian side. His wife's family name was Planes; they lived together on Suipacha Street near the corner of Temple in what is now the heart of Buenos

Aires. The house in which the event took place was much like any other, with its street door, long arched entranceway, inner grillwork gate, its rooms, its row of two or three patios. The dictator, of course, was Rosas.

One night, around 1842, Salvadores and his wife heard the growing, muffled sound of horses' hooves out on the unpaved street and the riders shouting their drunken *vivas* and their threats. This time Rosas's henchmen did not ride on. After the shouts came repeated knocks at the door; while the men began forcing it, Salvadores was able to pull the dining-room table aside, lift the rug, and hide himself down in the cellar. His wife dragged the table back in place. The *mazorca* broke into the house; they had come to take Salvadores. The woman said her husband had run away to Montevideo. The men did not believe her; they flogged her, they smashed all the blue chinaware (blue was the Unitarian color), they searched the whole house, but they never thought of lifting the rug. At midnight they rode away, swearing that they would soon be back.

Here is the true beginning of Pedro Salvadores's story. He lived nine years in the cellar. For all we may tell ourselves that years are made of days and days of hours and that nine years is an abstract term and an impossible sum, the story is nonetheless gruesome. I suppose that in the darkness, which his eyes somehow learned to decipher, he had no particular thoughts, not even of his hatred or his danger. He was simply there—in the cellar—with echoes of the world he was cut off from sometimes reaching him from overhead: his wife's footsteps, the bucket clanging against the lip of the well, a heavy rainfall in the patio. Every day of his imprisonment, for all he knew, could have been the last.

His wife let go all the servants, who could possibly have informed against them, and told her family that Salvadores was in Uruguay. Meanwhile, she earned a living for them both sewing uniforms for the army. In the course of time, she gave birth to two children; her family turned from her, thinking she had a lover. After the tyrant's fall, they got down on their knees and begged to be forgiven.

What was Pedro Salvadores? Who was he? Was it his fear, his love, the unseen presence of Buenos Aires, or—in the long run—habit that held him prisoner? In order to keep him with her, his wife would make up news to tell him about whispered plots and rumored victories. Maybe he was a coward and she loyally hid it from him that she knew. I picture him in his cellar perhaps without a candle, without a book. Darkness probably sank him into sleep. His dreams, at the outset, were probably of that sudden night when the blade sought his throat, of the streets he knew so well, of the open plains. As the years went on, he would have been unable to escape even in his sleep; whatever he dreamed would have taken place in the cellar. At first, he may have been a man hunted down, a man in danger of his life; later (we will never know for certain), an animal at peace in its burrow or a sort of dim god.

All this went on until that summer day of 1852 when Rosas fled the country. It was only then that the secret man came out into the light of day; my grandfather spoke with him. Flabby, overweight, Salvadores was the color of wax and could not speak above a low voice. He never got back his confiscated lands; I think he died in poverty.

As with so many things, the fate of Pedro Salvadores strikes us as a symbol of something we are about to understand, but never quite do.

For years now, I have been telling people I grew up in that part of Buenos Aires known as Palermo. This, I've come to realize, is mere literary bravado; the truth is that I really grew up on the inside of a long iron picket fence in a house with a garden and with my father's and his father's library. The Palermo of knife fights and of guitar playing lurked (so they say) on street corners and down back alleys. In 1930, I wrote a study of Evaristo Carriego, a neighbor of ours, a poet and glorifier of the city's outlying slums. A little after that, chance brought me face to face with Emilio Trápani. I was on the train to Morón. Trápani, who was sitting next to the window, called me by name. For some time I could not place him, so many years had passed since we'd been classmates in a school on Thames Street. Roberto Godel, another classmate, may remember him.

Trápani and I never had any great liking for each other. Time had set us apart, and also our mutual indifference. He had taught me, I now recall, all the basic slang words of the day. Riding along, we struck up one of those trivial conversations that force you to unearth pointless facts and that lead up to the discovery of the death of a fellow-schoolmate who is no longer anything more than a name. Then, abruptly, Trápani said to me, "Someone lent me your Carriego book, where you're talking about hoodlums all the time. Tell me, Borges, what in the world can you know about hoodlums?" He stared at me with a kind of wonder.

"I've done research," I answered.

Not letting me go on, he said, "Research is the word, all right. Personally, I have no use for research—I know these people inside out." After a moment's silence, he added, as though he were letting me in on a secret, "I'm Juan Muraña's nephew."

Of all the men around Palermo famous for handling a knife way back in the 1890s one with the widest reputation was Muraña. Trápani went on: "Florentina —my aunt—was his wife. Maybe you'll be interested in this story."

Certain devices of a literary nature and one or two longish sentences led me to suspect that this was not the first time he had told the story.

My mother [Trápani said] could never quite stomach the fact that her sister had linked herself up with a man like Muraña, who to her was just a big brute, while to Aunt Florentina he was a man of action. A lot of stories circulated about my uncle's end. Some say that one night when he was dead drunk he tumbled from the seat of his wagon, making the turn around the corner of Coronel, and cracked his skull on the cobblestones. It's also said that the law was on his heels and he ran away to Uruguay. My mother, who couldn't stand her brother-in-law, never explained to me what actually happened. I was just a small boy then and have no memories of him.

Along about the time of the Centennial, we were living in a long, narrow house on Russell Alley. The back door, which was always kept locked, opened on the other side of the block, on San Salvador Street. My aunt, who was well along in years and a bit queer, had a room with us up in our attic. Big-boned but

305

thin as a stick, she was—or seemed to me—very tall. She also wasted few words. Living in fear of fresh air, she never went out; nor did she like our going into her room. More than once, I caught her stealing and hiding food. The talk around the neighborhood was that Muraña's death, or disappearance, had affected her mind. I remember her always in black. She had also fallen into the habit of talking to herself.

Our house belonged to a certain Mr. Luchessi, the owner of a barbershop on the Southside, in Barracas. My mother, who did piecework at home as a seamstress, was in financial straits. Without being able to understand them, I heard whispered terms like "court order" and "eviction notice." My mother was really at her wit's end, and my aunt kept saying stubbornly that Juan was not going to stand by and let the gringo, that wop, throw us out. She recalled the incident—which all of us knew by heart—of a bigmouthed tough from the Southside who had dared doubt her husband's courage. Muraña, the moment he found out, took all the trouble to go clear across the town, ferret the man out, put him straight with a blow of his knife, and dump his body into the Riachuelo. I don't know if the story's true; what matters is that it was told and that it became accepted.

I saw myself sleeping in empty lots on Serrano Street or begging handouts or going around with a basket of peaches. Selling on the streets tempted me, because it would free me from school. I don't know how long our troubles lasted. Your late father once told us that you can't measure time by days, the way you measure money by dollars and cents, because dollars are all the same while every day is different and maybe every hour as well. I didn't quite understand what he meant, but the words stuck in my mind.

One night, I had a dream that ended in a nightmare. I dreamed of my Uncle Juan. I had never got to know him, but I thought of him as a burly man with a touch of the Indian about him, a sparse mustache and his hair long. He and I were heading south, cutting through huge stone quarries and scrub, but these quarries and thickets were also Thames Street. In the dream, the sun was high overhead. Uncle Juan was dressed in a black suit. He stopped beside a sort of scaffolding in a narrow mountain pass. He held his hand under his jacket, around the level of his heart—not like a person who's about to pull a knife but as though he were keeping the hand hidden. In a very sad voice, he told me, "I've changed a lot." He withdrew the hand, and what I saw was the claw of a vulture. I woke up screaming in the dark.

The next day, my mother made me go with her to Luchessi's. I know she was going to ask him for extra time; she probably took me along so that our landlord would see her helplessness. She didn't mention a word of this to her sister, who would never have let her lower herself in such a way. I hadn't ever set foot in Barracas before; it seemed to me there were a lot more people around than I imagined there'd be, and a lot more traffic and fewer vacant lots. From the corner, we saw several policemen and a flock of people in front of the house we were looking for. A neighbor went from group to group telling everyone that around three o'clock that morning he had been awakened by someone thumping on a door. He heard the door open and someone go in. Nobody shut the door, and as soon as it

side, the wind was rocking the Australian pines. Listening to the first heavy drops of rain, Espinosa thanked God. All at once, cold air rolled in. That afternoon, the Salado overflowed its banks.

The next day, looking out over the flooded fields from the gallery of the main house, Baltasar Espinosa thought that the stock metaphor comparing the pampa to the sea was not altogether false—at least, not that morning—though W. H. Hudson had remarked that the sea seems wider because we view it from a ship's deck and not from a horse or from eye level.

The rain did not let up. The Gutres, helped or hindered by Espinosa, the town dweller, rescued a good part of the livestock, but many animals were drowned. There were four roads leading to La Colorada; all of them were under water. On the third day, when a leak threatened the foreman's house, Espinosa gave the Gutres a room near the toolshed, at the back of the main house. This drew them all closer; they ate together in the big dining room. Conversation turned out to be difficult. The Gutres, who knew so much about country things, were hard put to it to explain them. One night, Espinosa asked them if people still remembered the Indian raids from back when the frontier command was located there in Junín. They told him yes, but they would have given the same answer to a question about the beheading of Charles I. Espinosa recalled his father's saying that almost every case of longevity that was cited in the country was really a case of bad memory or of a dim notion of dates. Gauchos are apt to be ignorant of the year of their birth or of the name of the man who begot them.

In the whole house, there was apparently no other reading matter than a set of the *Farm Journal,* a handbook of veterinary medicine, a deluxe edition of the Uruguayan epic *Tabaré,* a history of shorthorn cattle in Argentina, a number of erotic or detective stories, and a recent novel called *Don Segundo Sombra.* Espinosa, trying in some way to bridge the inevitable after-dinner gap, read a couple of chapters of this novel to the Gutres, none of whom could read or write. Unfortunately, the foreman had been a cattle drover, and the doings of the hero, another cattle drover, failed to whet his interest. He said that the work was light, that drovers always traveled with a packhorse that carried everything they needed, and that, had he not been a drover, he would never have seen such far-flung places as the Laguna de Gómez, the town of Bragado, and the spread of the Núñez family in Chacabuco. There was a guitar in the kitchen; the ranch hands, before the time of the events I am describing, used to sit around in a circle. Someone would tune the instrument without ever getting around to playing it. This was known as a guitarfest.

Espinosa, who had grown a beard, began dallying in front of the mirror to study his new face, and he smiled to think how, back in Buenos Aires, he would bore his friends by telling them the story of the Salado flood. Strangely enough, he missed places he never frequented and never would: a corner of Cabrera Street on which there was a mailbox; one of the cement lions of a gateway on Jujuy Street, a few blocks from the Plaza del Once; an old barroom with a tiled floor, whose exact whereabouts he was unsure of. As for his brothers and his father, they would already have learned from Daniel that he was isolated—etymologically, the word was perfect—by the floodwaters.

Exploring the house, still hemmed in by the watery waste, Espinosa came across an English Bible. Among the blank pages at the end, the Guthries—such was their original name—had left a handwritten record of their lineage. They were natives of Inverness; had reached the New World, no doubt as common laborers, in the early part of the nineteenth century; and had intermarried with Indians. The chronicle broke off sometime during the 1870s, when they no longer knew how to write. After a few generations, they had forgotten English; their Spanish, at the time Espinosa knew them, gave them trouble. They lacked any religious faith, but there survived in their blood, like faint tracks, the rigid fanaticism of the Calvinist and the superstitions of the pampa Indian. Espinosa later told them of his find, but they barely took notice.

Leafing through the volume, his fingers opened it at the beginning of the Gospel according to Saint Mark. As an exercise in translation, and maybe to find out whether the Gutres understood any of it, Espinosa decided to begin reading them that text after their evening meal. It surprised him that they listened attentively, absorbed. Maybe the gold letters on the cover lent the book authority. It's still there in their blood, Espinosa thought. It also occurred to him that the generations of men, throughout recorded time, have always told and retold two stories—that of a lost ship which searches the Mediterranean seas for a dearly loved island, and that of a god who is crucified on Golgotha. Remembering his lessons in elocution from his schooldays in Ramos Mejía, Espinosa got to his feet when he came to the parables.

The Gutres took to bolting their barbecued meat and their sardines so as not to delay the Gospel. A pet lamb that the girl adorned with a small blue ribbon had injured itself on a strand of barbed wire. To stop the bleeding, the three had wanted to apply a cobweb to the wound, but Espinosa treated the animal with some pills. The gratitude that this treatment awakened in them took him aback. (Not trusting the Gutres at first, he'd hidden away in one of his books the 240 pesos he had brought with him.) Now, the owner of the place away, Espinosa took over and gave timid orders, which were immediately obeyed. The Gutres, as if lost without him, liked following him from room to room and along the gallery that ran around the house. While he read to them, he noticed that they were secretly stealing the crumbs he had dropped on the table. One evening, he caught them unawares, talking about him respectfully, in very few words.

Having finished the Gospel according to Saint Mark, he wanted to read another of the three Gospels that remained, but the father asked him to repeat the one he had just read, so that they could understand it better. Espinosa felt that they were like children, to whom repetition is more pleasing than variations or novelty. That night—this is not to be wondered at—he dreamed of the Flood; the hammer blows of the building of the Ark woke him up, and he thought that perhaps they were thunder. In fact, the rain, which had let up, started again. The cold was bitter. The Gutres had told him that the storm had damaged the roof of the toolshed, and that they would show it to him when the beams were fixed. No longer a stranger now, he was treated by them with special attention, almost to the point of spoiling him. None of them liked coffee, but for him there was always a small cup into which they heaped sugar.

The new storm had broken out on a Tuesday. Thursday night, Espinosa was awakened by a soft knock at his door, which, just in case, he always kept locked. He got out of bed and opened it; there was the girl. In the dark he could hardly make her out, but by her footsteps he could tell she was barefoot, and moments later, in bed, that she must have come all the way from the other end of the house naked. She did not embrace him or speak a single word; she lay beside him, trembling. It was the first time she had known a man. When she left, she did not kiss him; Espinosa realized that he didn't even know her name. For some reason that he did not want to pry into, he made up his mind that upon returning to Buenos Aires he would tell no one about what had taken place.

The next day began like the previous ones, except that the father spoke to Espinosa and asked him if Christ had let Himself be killed so as to save all other men on earth. Espinosa, who was a freethinker but who felt committed to what he had read to the Gutres, answered, "Yes, to save everyone from Hell."

Gutre then asked, "What's Hell?"

"A place under the ground where souls burn and burn."

"And the Roman soldiers who hammered in the nails—were they saved, too?"

"Yes," said Espinosa, whose theology was rather dim.

All along, he was afraid that the foreman might ask him about what had gone on the night before with his daughter. After lunch, they asked him to read the last chapters over again.

Espinosa slept a long nap that afternoon. It was a light sleep, disturbed by persistent hammering and by vague premonitions. Toward evening, he got up and went out onto the gallery. He said, as if thinking aloud, "The waters have dropped. It won't be long now."

"It won't be long now," Gutre repeated, like an echo.

The three had been following him. Bowing their knees to the stone pavement, they asked his blessing. Then they mocked at him, spat on him, and shoved him toward the back part of the house. The girl wept. Espinosa understood what awaited him on the other side of the door. When they opened it, he saw a patch of sky. A bird sang out. A goldfinch, he thought. The shed was without a roof; they had pulled down the beams to make the cross.

GUAYAQUIL   [JLB 108]

Now I shall not journey to the Estado Occidental; now I shall not set eyes on snow-capped Higuerota mirrored in the waters of the Golfo Plácido; now I shall not decipher Bolívar's manuscripts in that library, which doubtless has its own shape and its own lengthening shadows but which from here in Buenos Aires I picture in so many different ways.

Rereading the above paragraph preparatory to writing the next, its at once melancholy and pompous tone troubles me. Perhaps one cannot speak of that

Caribbean republic without, even from afar, echoing the monumental style of its most famous historian, Captain Joseph Korzeniowski—but in my case there is another reason. My opening paragraph, I suspect, was prompted by the unconscious need to infuse a note of pathos into a slightly painful and rather trivial episode. I shall with all probity recount what happened, and this may enable me to understand it. Furthermore, to confess to a thing is to leave off being an actor in it and to become an onlooker—to become somebody who has seen it and tells it and is no longer the doer.

The actual event took place last Friday, in this same room in which I am writing, at this same—though now slightly cooler—evening hour. Aware of our tendency to forget unpleasant things, I want to set down a written record of my conversation with Dr. Edward Zimmerman, of the University of Córdoba, before oblivion blurs the details. The memory I retain of that meeting is still quite vivid.

For the better understanding of my story, I shall have to set forth briefly the curious facts surrounding certain letters of General Bolívar found among the papers of Dr. José Avellanos, whose *History of Fifty Years of Misrule*—thought to be lost under circumstances that are only too well known—was ultimately unearthed and published by his grandson, Dr. Ricardo Avellanos. To judge from references I have collected from various sources, these letters are of no particular interest, except for one dated from Cartagena on August 13, 1822, in which the Liberator places upon record details of his celebrated meeting with the Argentine national hero General San Martín. It is needless to underscore the value of this document; in it, Bolívar reveals—if only in part—exactly what had taken place during the two generals' interview the month before at Guayaquil. Dr. Ricardo Avellanos, embattled opponent of the government, refused to turn the correspondence over to his own country's Academy of History, and, instead, offered it for initial publication to a number of Latin American republics. Thanks to the praiseworthy zeal of our ambassador, Dr. Melaza-Mouton, the Argentine government was the first to accept Dr. Avellanos' disinterested offer. It was agreed that a delegate should be sent to Sulaco, the capital of the Estado Occidental, to transcribe the letters so as to see them into print upon return here. The rector of our university, in which I hold the chair of Latin American History, most generously recommended to the Minister of Education that I be appointed to carry out this mission. I also obtained the more or less unanimous vote of the National Academy of History, of which I am a member. The date of my audience with the minister had already been fixed when it was learned that the University of Córdoba—which, I would rather suppose, knew nothing about these decisions —had proposed the name of Dr. Zimmerman.

Reference here, as the reader may be well aware, is to a foreign-born historian expelled from his country by the Third Reich and now an Argentine citizen. Of the noteworthy body of his work, I have glanced only at a vindication of the Semitic republic of Carthage—which posterity judges through the eyes of Roman historians, its enemies—and a sort of polemical essay which holds that government should be neither visible nor emotional. This proposal drew the unanswerable refutation of Martin Heidegger, who, using newspaper headlines, proved that the modern chief of state, far from being anonymous, is rather the protagonist, the choragus, the dancing David, who acts out the drama of his people with all the pomp of stagecraft, and resorts unhesitatingly to the overstatement inherent in the art of oration. He also proved that Zimmerman came of Hebrew, not to say Jewish, stock. Publication of this essay by the venerated existentialist was the immediate cause of the banishment and nomadic activities of our guest.

Needless to say, Zimmerman had come to Buenos Aires to speak to the minister, who personally suggested to me, through one of his secretaries, that I see Zimmerman and, so as to avoid the unpleasant spectacle of two universities in disagreement, inform him of exactly how things stood. I of course agreed. Upon return home, I was told that Dr. Zimmerman had telephoned to announce his visit for six o'clock that same afternoon. I live, as everyone knows, on Chile Street. It was the dot of six when the bell rang.

With republican simplicity, I myself opened the door and led him to my private study. He paused along the way to look at the patio; the black and white tiles, the two magnolias, and the wellhead stirred him to eloquence. He was, I believe, somewhat ill at ease. There was nothing out of the ordinary about him. He must have been forty or so, and seemed to have a biggish head. His eyes were hidden by dark glasses, which he once or twice left on the table, then snatched up again. When we first shook hands, I remarked to myself with a certain satisfaction that I was the taller, and at once I was ashamed of myself, for this was not a matter of a physical or even a moral duel but was simply to be an explanation of where things stood. I am not very observant—if I am observant at all—but he brought to mind what a certain poet has called, with an ugliness that matches what it defines, an "immoderate sartorial inelegance." I can still see garments of electric blue, with too many buttons and pockets. Zimmerman's tie, I noticed, was one of those conjurer's knots held in place by two plastic clips. He carried a leather portfolio, which I presumed was full of documents. He wore a short military mustache, and when in the course of our talk he lit a cigar I felt that there were too many things on that face. *Trop meublé,* I said to myself.

The successiveness of language—since every word occupies a place on the page and a moment in the reader's mind—tends to exaggerate what we are saying; beyond the visual trivia that I have listed, the man gave the impression of having experienced an arduous life.

On display in my study are an oval portrait of my great-grandfather, who fought in the wars of Independence, and some cabinets containing swords, medals, and flags. I showed Zimmerman those old glorious things, explaining as I went along; his eyes passed over them quickly, like one who is carrying out a duty, and, not without a hint of impoliteness that I believe was involuntary and mechanical, he interrupted and finished my sentences for me. He said, for example:

"Correct. Battle of Junín. August 6, 1824. Cavalry charge under Juárez."

"Under Suárez," I corrected.

I suspect his error was deliberate. He spread his arms in an Oriental gesture and exclaimed, "My first mistake, and certainly not my last! I feed on texts and slip up on facts—in you the interesting past lives." He pronounced his *v*'s like *f*'s.

Such flatteries displeased me. He was far more interested in my books, and let his eyes wander almost lovingly over the titles. I recall his saying, "Ah, Schopenhauer, who always disbelieved in history. This same set, edited by Grisebach, was the one I had in Prague. I thought I'd grow old in the friendship of those portable volumes, but it was history itself, in the flesh of a madman, that evicted me from that house and that city. Now here I am, with you, in South America, in this hospitable house of yours."

He spoke inelegantly but fluently, his noticeable German accent going hand in hand with a Spanish lisp. By then we were seated, and I seized upon what he had said in order to take up our subject. "History here in the Argentine is more merciful," I said. "I was born in this house and I expect to die here. Here my great-grandfather lay down his sword, which saw action throughout the continent. Here I have pondered the past and have compiled my books. I can almost say I've never been outside this library, but now I shall go abroad at last and travel to lands I have only traveled in maps." I cut short with a smile my possible rhetorical excess.

"Are you referring to a certain Caribbean republic?" said Zimmerman.

"So I am," I answered. "And it's to this imminent trip that I owe the honor of your visit."

Trinidad served us coffee. I went on slowly and confidently. "You probably know by now that the minister has entrusted me with the mission of transcribing and writing an introduction to the new Bolívar letters, which have accidentally turned up in Dr. Avellanos' files. This mission, by a happy stroke, crowns my lifework—the work that somehow runs in my blood."

It was a relief having said what I had to say. Zimmerman appeared not to have heard me; his averted eyes were fixed not on my face but on the books at my back. He vaguely assented, and then spoke out, saying, "In your blood. You are the true historian. Your people roamed the length and breadth of this continent and fought in the great battles, while in obscurity mine were barely emerging from the ghetto. You, according to your own eloquent words, carry history in your blood; you have only to listen closely to an inner voice. I, on the other hand, must go all the way to Sulaco and struggle through stacks of perhaps apocryphal papers. Believe me, sir, I envy you."

His tone was neither challenging nor mocking; his words were the expression of a will that made of the future something as irrevocable as the past. His arguments hardly mattered. The strength lay in the man himself, not in them. Zimmerman continued, with a schoolteacher's deliberation: "In this matter of Bolívar—I beg your pardon, San Martín—your stand, *cher maître*, is known to all scholars. *Votre siège est fait.* As yet, I have not examined Bolívar's pertinent letter, but it is obvious, or reasonable to guess, that it was written as a piece of self-justification. In any case, this much-touted letter will show us only Bolívar's side of the question, not San Martín's. Once made public, it should be weighed in the balance, studied, passed through the sieve of criticism, and, if need be, refuted. No one is better qualified for that final judgment than you, with your magnifying glass. The scalpel, the lancet—scientific rigor itself demands them! Allow me at the same time to point out that the name of the editor of the letter will remain linked to the letter. Such a link is hardly going to stand you in good stead. The public at large will never bother to look into these subtleties."

I realize now that what we argued after that, in the main, was useless. Maybe I felt it at the time. In order to avoid an outright confrontation I grasped at a detail, and I asked him whether he really thought the letters were fakes.

"That they are in Bolívar's own hand," he said, "does not necessarily mean that the whole truth is to be found in them. For all we know, Bolívar may have tried to deceive the recipient of the letter or, simply, may have deceived himself. You, a historian, a thinker, know far better than I that the mystery lies in ourselves, not in our words."

These pompous generalities irritated me, and I dryly remarked that within the riddle that surrounded us, the meeting at Guayaquil—in which General San Martín renounced mere ambition and left the destiny of South America in the hands of Bolívar—was also a riddle possibly not unworthy of our attention.

"The interpretations are so many," Zimmerman said. "Some historians believe San Martín fell into a trap; others, like Sarmiento, have it that he was a European soldier at loose ends on a continent he never understood; others again —for the most part Argentines—ascribe to him an act of self-denial; still others, weariness. We also hear of the secret order of who knows what Masonic lodge."

I said that, at any rate, it would be interesting to have the exact words spoken between San Martín, the Protector of Peru, and Bolívar, the Liberator. Zimmerman delivered his judgment.

"Perhaps the words they exchanged were irrelevant," he said. "Two men met face to face at Guayaquil; if one of them was master, it was because of his stronger will, not because of the weight of arguments. As you see, I have not forgotten my Schopenhauer." He added, with a smile, "Words, words, words. Shakespeare, insuperable master of words, held them in scorn. In Guayaquil or in Buenos Aires —in Prague, for that matter—words always count less than persons."

At that moment I felt that something was happening between us, or, rather, that something had already happened. In some uncanny way we were already two other people. The dusk entered into the room, and I had not lit the lamps. By chance, I asked, "You are from Prague, Doctor?"

"I *was* from Prague," he answered.

To skirt the real subject, I said, "It must be an unusual city. I've never been there, but the first book I ever read in German was Meyrink's novel *Der Golem.*"

"It's the only book by Gustav Meyrink worth remembering," Zimmerman said. "It's wiser not to attempt the others, compounded as they are of bad writing and worse theosophy. All in all, something of the strangeness of Prague stalks the pages of that book of dreams within dreams. Everything is strange in Prague, or, if you prefer, nothing is strange. Anything may happen there. In London, on certain evenings, I have had the same feeling."

"You have spoken of the will," I said. "In the tales of the *Mabinogion,* two kings play chess on the summit of a hill, while below them their warriors fight. One of the kings wins the game; a rider comes to him with the news that the army of the other side has been beaten. The battle of the men was a mirror of the battle of the chessboard."

"Ah, a feat of magic," said Zimmerman.

"Or the display of a will in two different fields," I said. "Another Celtic legend tells of the duel between two famous bards. One, accompanying himself on the harp, sings from the twilight of morning to the twilight of evening. Then, under the stars or moon, he hands his harp over to his rival. The second bard lays the instrument aside and gets to his feet. The first bard acknowledges defeat."

"What erudition, what power of synthesis!" exclaimed Zimmerman. Then he added, more calmly, "I must confess my ignorance, my lamentable ignorance, of Celtic lore. You, like the day, span East and West, while I am held to my little Carthaginian corner, complemented now with a smattering of Latin American history. I am a mere plodder."

In his voice were both Jewish and German servility, but I felt, insofar as victory was already his, that it cost him very little to flatter me or to admit I was right. He begged me not to trouble myself over the arrangements for his trip. ("Provisions" was the actual word he used.) On the spot, he drew out of his portfolio a letter addressed to the minister. In it, I expounded the motives behind my resignation, and I acknowledged Dr. Zimmerman's indisputable merits. Zimmerman put his own fountain pen in my hand for my signature. When he put the letter away, I could not help catching a glimpse of his passage aboard the next day's Buenos Aires–Sulaco flight.

On his way out he paused again before the volumes of Schopenhauer, saying, "Our master, our common master, denied the existence of involuntary acts. If you stay behind in this house—in this spacious, patrician home—it is because down deep inside you want to remain here. I obey, and I thank you for your will."

Taking this last pittance without a word, I accompanied him to the front door. There, as we said goodbye, he remarked, "The coffee was excellent."

I go over these hasty jottings, which will soon be consigned to the flames. Our meeting had been short. I have the feeling that I shall give up any future writing. *Mon siège est fait.*

THE BLIND MAN   [JLB 109]

I

He is divested of the diverse world,
of faces, which still stay as once they were,
of the adjoining streets, now far away,
and of the concave sky, once infinite.
Of books, he keeps no more than what is left him
by memory, that brother of forgetting,
which keeps the formula but not the feeling
and which reflects no more than tag and name.
Traps lie in wait for me. My every step
might be a fall. I am a prisoner
shuffling through a time which feels like dream,
taking no note of mornings or of sunsets.

It is night. I am alone. In verse like this,
I must create my insipid universe.

II

Since I was born, in 1899,
beside the concave vine and the deep cistern,
frittering time, so brief in memory,
kept taking from me all my eye-shaped world.
Both days and nights would wear away the profiles
of human letters and of well-loved faces.
My wasted eyes would ask their useless questions
of pointless libraries and lecterns.
Blue and vermilion both are now a fog,
both useless sounds. The mirror I look into
is gray. I breathe a rose across the garden,
a wistful rose, my friends, out of the twilight.
Only the shades of yellow stay with me
and I can see only to look on nightmares.

THINGS   [JLB 110]

The fallen volume, hidden by the others
from sight in the recesses of the bookshelves,
and which the days and nights muffle over
with slow and noiseless dust. Also, the anchor
of Sidon, which the seas surrounding England
press down into its blind and soft abyss.
The mirror which shows nobody's reflection
after the house has long been left alone.
Fingernail filings which we leave behind
across the long expanse of time and space.
The indecipherable dust, once Shakespeare.
The changing figurations of a cloud.
The momentary but symmetric rose
which once, by chance, took substance in the shrouded
mirrors of a boy's kaleidoscope.
The oars of *Argus,* the original ship.
The sandy footprints which the fatal wave
as though asleep erases from the beach.
The colors of a Turner when the lights
are turned out in the narrow gallery

317

and not a footstep sounds in the deep night.
The other side of the dreary map of the world.
The tenuous spiderweb in the pyramid.
The sightless stone and the inquiring hand.
The dream I had in the approaching dawn
and later lost in the clearing of the day.
The ending and beginning of the epic
of Finsburh, today a few sparse verses
of iron, unwasted by the centuries.
The mirrored letter on the blotting paper.
The turtle in the bottom of the cistern.
And that which cannot be. The other horn
of the unicorn. The Being, Three in One.
The triangular disk. The imperceptible moment
in which the Eleatic arrow,
motionless in the air, reaches the mark.
The violet pressed between the leaves of Becquer.
The pendulum which time has stayed in place.
The weapon Odin buried in the tree.
The volume with its pages still unslit.
The echo of the hoofbeats at the charge
of Junín, which in some enduring mode
never has ceased, is part of the webbed scheme.
The shadow of Sarmiento on the sidewalks.
The voice heard by the shepherd on the mountain.
The skeleton bleaching white in the desert.
The bullet which shot dead Francisco Borges.
The other side of the tapestry. The things
which no one sees, except for Berkeley's God.

TANKAS

[JLB III]

1
High on the summit,
the garden is all moonlight,
the moon is golden.
More precious is the contact
of your lips in the shadow.

2
The sound of a bird
which the twilight is hiding
has fallen silent.

You wander in your garden.
I know that you miss something.

3
The curious goblet,
the sword which was a sword once
in another grasp,
the street under the moonlight—
tell me, are they not enough?

4
Underneath the moon,
tiger of gold and shadow
looks down at his claws,
unaware that in the dawn
they lacerated a man.

5
Wistful is the rain
falling upon the marble,
sad to become earth,
sad no longer to be part
of man, of dream, of morning.

6
Not to have fallen,
like others of my lineage,
cut down in battle.
To be in the fruitless night
he who counts the syllables.

THE THREATENED ONE [JLB 112]

It is love. I will have to hide or flee.

Its prison walls grow larger, as in a fearful dream. The alluring mask
has changed, but as usual it is the only one. What use now are my talismans,
my touchstones: the practice of literature, vague learning, an apprenticeship
to the language used by the flinty Northland to sing of its seas and its
swords, the serenity of friendship, the galleries of the library, ordinary things,
habits, the young love of my mother, the soldierly shadow cast by my dead
ancestors, the timeless night, the flavor of sleep and dream?

Being with you or without you is how I measure my time.

Now the water jug shatters above the spring, now the man rises to the

sound of birds, now those who look through the windows are
indistinguishable, but the darkness has not brought peace.

It is love, I know it; the anxiety and relief at hearing your voice, the
hope and the memory, the horror at living in succession.

It is love with its own mythology, its minor and pointless magic.

There is a street corner I do not dare to pass.

Now the armies surround me, the rabble.

(This room is unreal. She has not seen it.)

A woman's name has me in thrall.

A woman's being afflicts my whole body.

TO THE GERMAN LANGUAGE

[JLB 113]

My destiny is in the Spanish language,
the bronze words of Francisco de Quevedo,
but in the long, slow progress of the night,
different, more intimate musics move me.
Some have been handed down to me by blood—
voices of Shakespeare, language of the Scriptures—
others by chance, which has been generous;
but you, gentle language of Germany,
I chose you, and I sought you out alone.
By way of grammar books and patient study,
through the thick undergrowth of the declensions,
the dictionary, which never puts its thumb on
the precise nuance, I kept moving closer.
My nights were full of overtones of Virgil,
I once said; but I could as well have named
Hölderlin, Angelus Silesius.
Heine lent me his lofty nightingales;
Goethe, the good fortune of late love,
at the same time both greedy and indulgent;
Keller, the rose which one hand leaves behind
in the closed fist of a dead man who adored it,
who will never know if it is white or red.
German language, you are your masterpiece:
love interwound in all your compound voices
and open vowels, sounds which accommodate
the studious hexameters of Greek
and undercurrents of jungles and of nights.
Once, I had you. Now, at the far extreme
of weary years, I feel you have become
as out of reach as algebra and the moon.

THE WATCHER

The light enters and I remember who I am; he is there.

He begins by telling me his name which (it should now be clear) is mine.

I revert to the servitude which has lasted more than seven times ten years.

He saddles me with his rememberings.

He saddles me with the miseries of every day, the human condition.

I am his old nurse; he requires me to wash his feet.

He spies on me in mirrors, in mahogany, in shop windows.

One or another woman has rejected him, and I must share his anguish.

He dictates to me now this poem, which I do not like.

He insists I apprentice myself tentatively to the stubborn Anglo-Saxon.

He has won me over to the hero worship of dead soldiers, people with whom I could scarcely exchange a single word.

On the last flight of stairs, I feel him at my side.

He is in my footsteps, in my voice.

Down to the last detail, I abhor him.

I am gratified to remark that he can hardly see.

I am in a circular cell and the infinite wall is closing in.

Neither of the two deceives the other, but we both lie.

We know each other too well, inseparable brother.

You drink the water from my cup and you wolf down my bread.

The door to suicide is open, but theologians assert that, in the subsequent shadows of the other kingdom, there will I be, waiting for myself.

THE OTHER

It was in Cambridge, back in February 1969, that the event took place. I made no attempt to record it at the time, because, fearing for my mind, my initial aim was to forget it. Now, some years later, I feel that if I commit it to paper others will read it as a story and, I hope, one day it will become a story for me as well. I know it was horrifying while it lasted—and even more so during the sleepless nights that followed—but this does not mean that an account of it will necessarily move anyone else.

It was about ten o'clock in the morning. I sat on a bench facing the Charles River. Some 500 yards distant, on my right, rose a tall building whose name I never knew. Ice floes were borne along on the gray water. Inevitably, the river made me think about time—Heraclitus' millennial image. I had slept well; my class on the previous afternoon had, I thought, managed to hold the interest of my students. Not a soul was in sight.

All at once, I had the impression (according to psychologists, it corresponds to a state of fatigue) of having lived that moment once before. Someone had sat down at the other end of the bench. I would have preferred to be alone, but not wishing to appear unsociable I avoided getting up abruptly. The other man had begun to whistle. It was then that the first of the many disquieting things of that morning occurred. What he whistled, what he tried to whistle (I have no ear for music), was the tune of "La Tapera," an old *milonga* by Elías Regules. The melody took me back to a certain Buenos Aires patio, which has long since disappeared, and to the memory of my cousin Álvaro Melián Lafinur, who has been dead for so many years. Then came the words. They were those of the opening line. It was not Álvaro's voice but an imitation of it. Recognizing this, I was taken aback.

"Sir," I said, turning to the other man, "are you an Uruguayan or an Argentine?"

"Argentine, but I've lived in Geneva since 1914," he replied.

There was a long silence. "At number seventeen Malagnou—across from the Orthodox church?" I asked.

He answered in the affirmative.

"In that case," I said straight out, "your name is Jorge Luis Borges. I, too, am Jorge Luis Borges. This is 1969 and we're in the city of Cambridge."

"No," he said in a voice that was mine but a bit removed. He paused, then became insistent. "I'm here in Geneva, on a bench, a few steps from the Rhône. The strange thing is that we resemble each other, but you're much older and your hair is gray."

"I can prove I'm not lying," I said. "I'm going to tell you things a stranger couldn't possibly know. At home we have a silver maté cup with a base in the form of entwined serpents. Our great-grandfather brought it from Peru. There's also a silver washbasin that hung from his saddle. In the wardrobe of your room are two rows of books: the three volumes of Lane's *1001 Nights,* with steel engravings and with notes in small type at the end of each chapter; Quicherat's Latin dictionary; Tacitus' *Germania* in Latin and also in Gordon's English translation; a *Don Quixote* published by Garnier; Rivera Indarte's *Tablas de Sangre,* inscribed by the author; Carlyle's *Sartor Resartus;* a biography of Amiel; and, hidden behind the other volumes, a book in paper covers about sexual customs in the Balkans. Nor have I forgotten one evening on a certain second floor of the Place Dubourg."

"Dufour," he corrected.

"Very well—Dufour. Is this enough now?"

"No," he said. "These proofs prove nothing. If I am dreaming you, it's natural that you know what I know. Your catalog, for all its length, is completely worthless."

His objection was to the point. I said, "If this morning and this meeting are dreams, each of us has to believe that he is the dreamer. Perhaps we have stopped dreaming, perhaps not. Our obvious duty, meanwhile, is to accept the dream just as we accept the world and being born and seeing and breathing."

"And if the dream should go on?" he said anxiously.

To calm him and to calm myself, I feigned an air of assurance that I certainly did not feel. "My dream has lasted seventy years now," I said. "After all, there isn't a person alive who, on waking, does not find himself with himself. It's what is happening to us now—except that we are two. Don't you want to know something of my past, which is the future awaiting you?"

He assented without a word. I went on, a bit lost. "Mother is healthy and well in her house on Charcas and Maipú, in Buenos Aires, but Father died some thirty years ago. He died of heart trouble. Hemiplegia finished him; his left hand, placed on his right, was like the hand of a child on a giant's. He died impatient for death but without complaint. Our grandmother had died in the same house. A few days before the end, she called us all together and said, 'I'm an old woman who is dying very, very slowly. Don't anyone become upset about such a common, everyday thing.' Your sister, Norah, married and has two sons. By the way, how is everyone at home?"

"Quite well. Father makes his same antireligious jokes. Last night he said that Jesus was like the gauchos, who don't like to commit themselves, and that's why he preached in parables." He hesitated and then said, "And you?"

"I don't know the number of books you'll write, but I know they'll be too many. You'll write poems that will give you a pleasure that others won't share and stories of a somewhat fantastic nature. Like your father and so many others of our family, you will teach."

It pleased me that he did not ask about the success or failure of his books. I changed my tone and went on. "As for history, there was another war, almost among the same antagonists. France was not long in caving in; England and America fought against a German dictator named Hitler—the cyclical Battle of Waterloo. Around 1946, Buenos Aires gave birth to another Rosas, who bore a fair resemblance to our kinsman. In 1955, the province of Córdoba came to our rescue, as Entre Ríos had in the last century. Now things are going badly. Russia is taking over the world; America, hampered by the superstition of democracy, can't make up its mind to become an empire. With every day that passes, our country becomes more provincial. More provincial and more pretentious—as if its eyes were closed. It wouldn't surprise me if the teaching of Latin in our schools were replaced by that of Guaraní."

I could tell that he was barely paying attention. The elemental fear of what is impossible and yet what is so dismayed him. I, who have never been a father, felt for that poor boy—more intimate to me even than a son of my flesh —a surge of love. Seeing that he clutched a book in his hands, I asked what it was.

"*The Possessed,* or, as I believe, *The Devils,* by Feodor Dostoevsky," he answered, not without vanity.

"It has faded in my memory. What's it like?" As soon as I said this, I felt that the question was a blasphemy.

"The Russian master," he pronounced, "has seen better than anyone else into the labyrinth of the Slavic soul."

This attempt at rhetoric seemed to me proof that he had regained his compo-

323

sure. I asked what other volumes of the master he had read. He mentioned two or three, among them *The Double.* I then asked him if on reading them he could clearly distinguish the characters, as you could in Joseph Conrad, and if he thought of going on in his study of Dostoevsky's work.

"Not really," he said with a certain surprise.

I asked what he was writing and he told me he was putting together a book of poems that would be called *Red Hymns.* He said he had also considered calling it *Red Rhythms.*

"And why not?" I said. "You can cite good antecedents. Rubén Darío's blue verse and Verlaine's gray song."

Ignoring this, he explained that his book would celebrate the brotherhood of man. The poet of our time could not turn his back on his own age, he went on to say. I thought for a while and asked if he truly felt himself a brother to everyone—to all funeral directors, for example, to all postmen, to all deep-sea divers, to all those who lived on the even-numbered side of the street, to all those who were aphonic, and so on. He answered that his book referred to the great mass of the oppressed and alienated.

"Your mass of oppressed and alienated is no more than an abstraction," I said. "Only individuals exist—if it can be said that anyone exists. 'The man of yesterday is not the man of today,' some Greek remarked. We two, seated on this bench in Geneva or Cambridge, are perhaps proof of this."

Except in the strict pages of history, memorable events stand in no need of memorable phrases. At the point of death, a man tries to recall an engraving glimpsed in childhood; about to enter battle, soldiers speak of the mud or of their sergeant. Our situation was unique and, frankly, we were unprepared for it. As fate would have it, we talked about literature; I fear I said no more than the things I usually say to journalists. My alter ego believed in the invention, or discovery, of new metaphors; I, in those metaphors that correspond to intimate and obvious affinities and that our imagination has already accepted. Old age and sunset, dreams and life, the flow of time and water. I put forward this opinion, which years later he would put forward in a book. He barely listened to me. Suddenly, he said, "If you have been me, how do you explain the fact that you have forgotten your meeting with an elderly gentleman who in 1918 told you that he, too, was Borges?"

I had not considered this difficulty. "Maybe the event was so strange I chose to forget it," I answered without much conviction.

Venturing a question, he said shyly, "What's your memory like?"

I realized that to a boy not yet twenty a man of over seventy was almost in the grave. "It often approaches forgetfulness," I said, "but it still finds what it's asked to find. I study Old English, and I am not at the bottom of the class."

Our conversation had already lasted too long to be that of a dream. A sudden idea came to me. "I can prove at once that you are not dreaming me," I said. "Listen carefully to this line, which, as far as I know, you've never read."

Slowly I intoned the famous verse, *"L'hydre-univers tordant son corps écaillé d'astres."* I felt his almost fearful awe. He repeated the line, low-voiced, savoring each resplendent word.

"It's true," he faltered. "I'll never be able to write a line like that."

324

Victor Hugo had brought us together.

Before this, I now recall, he had fervently recited that short piece of Whitman's in which the poet remembers a night shared beside the sea when he was really happy.

"If Whitman celebrated that night," I remarked, "it's because he desired it and it did not happen. The poem gains if we look on it as the expression of a longing, not the account of an actual happening."

He stared at me open-mouthed. "You don't know him!" he exclaimed. "Whitman is incapable of telling a lie."

Half a century does not pass in vain. Beneath our conversation about people and random reading and our different tastes, I realized that we were unable to understand each other. We were too similar and too unalike. We were unable to take each other in, which makes conversation difficult. Each of us was a caricature copy of the other. The situation was too abnormal to last much longer. Either to offer advice or to argue was pointless, since, unavoidably, it was his fate to become the person I am.

All at once, I remembered one of Coleridge's fantasies. Somebody dreams that on a journey through paradise he is given a flower. On awaking, he finds the flower. A similar trick occurred to me. "Listen," I said. "Have you any money?"

"Yes," he replied. "I have about twenty francs. I've invited Simon Jichlinski to dinner at the Crocodile tonight."

"Tell Simon that he will practice medicine in Carouge and that he will do much good. Now, give me one of your coins."

He drew out three large silver pieces and some small change. Without understanding, he offered me a five-franc coin. I handed him one of those not very sensible American bills that, regardless of their value, are all the same size. He examined it avidly.

"It can't be," he said, his voice raised. "It bears the date 1964. All this is a miracle, and the miraculous is terrifying. Witnesses to the resurrection of Lazarus must have been horrified."

We have not changed in the least, I thought to myself. Ever the bookish reference. He tore up the bill and put his coins away. I decided to throw mine into the river. The arc of the big silver disk losing itself in the silver river would have conferred on my story a vivid image, but luck would not have it so. I told him that the supernatural, if it occurs twice, ceases to be terrifying. I suggested that we plan to see each other the next day, on this same bench, which existed in two times and in two places. He agreed at once and, without looking at his watch, said that he was late. Both of us were lying and we each knew it of the other. I told him that someone was coming for me.

"Coming for you?" he said.

"Yes. When you get to my age, you will have lost your eyesight almost completely. You'll still make out the color yellow and lights and shadows. Don't worry. Gradual blindness is not a tragedy. It's like a slow summer dusk."

We said goodbye without having once touched each other. The next day, I did not show up. Neither would he.

I have brooded a great deal over that meeting, which until now I have related to no one. I believe I have discovered the key. The meeting was real, but the other man was dreaming when he conversed with me, and this explains how he was able to forget me; I conversed with him while awake, and the memory of it still disturbs me.

The other man dreamed me, but he did not dream me exactly. He dreamed, I now realize, the date on the dollar bill.

PREFACE TO THE UNENDING ROSE [JLB 116]

The romantic notion of a Muse who inspires poets was advanced by classical writers; the classical idea of the poem as a function of the intelligence was put forward by a romantic, Poe, around 1846. The fact is paradoxical. Apart from isolated cases of oneiric inspiration—the shepherd's dream referred to by Bede, the famous dream of Coleridge—it is obvious that both doctrines are partially true, unless they correspond to distinct stages in the process. (For Muse, we must read what the Hebrews and Milton called Spirit, and what our own woeful mythology refers to as the Subconscious.) In my own case, the process is more or less unvarying. I begin with the glimpse of a form, a kind of remote island, which will eventually be a story or a poem. I see the end and I see the beginning, but not what is in between. That is gradually revealed to me, when the stars or chance are propitious. More than once, I have to retrace my steps by way of the shadows. I try to interfere as little as possible in the evolution of the work. I do not want it to be distorted by my opinions, which are the most trivial things about us. The notion of art as compromise is a simplification, for no one knows entirely what he is doing. A writer can conceive a fable, Kipling acknowledged, without grasping its moral. He must be true to his imagination, and not to the mere ephemeral circumstances of a supposed "reality."

Literature starts out from poetry and can take centuries to arrive at the possibility of prose. After 400 years, the Anglo-Saxons left behind a poetry which was not just occasionally admirable and a prose which was scarcely explicit. The word must have been in the beginning a magic symbol, which the usury of time wore out. The mission of the poet should be to restore to the word, at least in a partial way, its primitive and now secret force. All verse should have two obligations: to communicate a precise instance and to touch us physically, as the presence of the sea does. I have here an example from Virgil:

sunt lacrimae rerum et mentem mortalia tangunt

One from Meredith:

> Not till the fire is dying in the grate
> Look we for any kinship with the stars

Or this alexandrine from Lugones, in which the Spanish is trying to return to the Latin:

El hombre numeroso de penas y de días.

326

Such verses move along their shifting path in the memory.

After so many—too many—years of practicing literature, I do not profess any esthetic. Why add to the natural limits which habit imposes on us those of some theory or other? Theories, like convictions of a political or religious nature, are nothing more than stimuli. They vary for every writer. Whitman was right to do away with rhyme; that negation would have been stupid in Victor Hugo's case.

Going over the proofs of this book, I notice with some distaste that blindness plays a mournful role, which it does not play in my life. Blindness is a confinement, but it is also a liberation, a solitude propitious to invention, a key and an algebra.

THINGS THAT MIGHT HAVE BEEN [JLB 117]

I think of the things that might have been and were not.
The treatise on Saxon mythology that Bede did not write.
The unimaginable work that Dante glimpsed fleetingly
when the last verse of the Comedia was corrected.
History without the afternoon of the Cross and the afternoon of the hemlock.
History without the face of Helen.
Man without the eyes which have shown the moon to us.
In the three labored days of Gettysburg, the victory of the South.
The love we do not share.
The vast empire which the Vikings did not wish to found.
The world without the wheel or without the rose.
The judgment of John Donne on Shakespeare.
The other horn of the unicorn.
The fabled bird of Ireland, in two places at once.
The son I did not have.

A HISTORY OF NIGHT [JLB 118]

Through the course of generations
men brought the night into being.
In the beginning were blindness and dream
and thorns which gash the bare foot
and fear of wolves.
We shall never know who fashioned the word
for the interval of darkness
which divides the two half-lights.

We shall never know in what century it stood
for the starry spaces.
Others began the myth.
They made night mother of the tranquil Fates
who weave all destiny
and sacrificed black sheep to her
and the rooster which announced her end.
The Chaldeans gave her twelve houses;
infinite worlds, the Stoic Portico.
Latin hexameters molded her,
and Pascal's dread.
Luis de León saw in her the homeland
of his shivering soul.
Now we feel her inexhaustible
as an old wine
and no one can think of her without vertigo,
and time has charged her with eternity.

And to think that night would not exist
without those tenuous instruments, the eyes.

PART FOUR

CHRONOLOGY
BORGES IN ENGLISH
NOTES
LIST OF TRANSLATORS

CHRONOLOGY

1899 *August 24.* Born, an eight-month baby, in Buenos Aires at the home of his maternal grandfather, Isidoro Acevedo (JLB 6). His father, Jorge Guillermo Borges, a lawyer and teacher of psychology, was an occasional poet. His mother, Leonor Acevedo Suárez, had close relatives in Uruguay, on the north bank of the River Plate. Both his parents were descended from old Spanish stock and from men who fought bravely in the Wars of Independence and the Civil Wars (JLB 48, JLB 77). From his father's side he had mixed Portuguese (JLB 92) and English blood. (His paternal grandmother, Fanny Haslam, was born in Northumberland.) He learned both Spanish and English at home, and was taught to read first in the latter language. He had a very close relationship with his younger sister Norah, who was born in 1902. The childhood games (in which he always played the part of the Prince protected by her, the Queen Mother) anticipated some of his tales of the hunted and the monstrous. From infancy too dates his fear of mirrors (JLB 87) and carnival masks, and his love of tigers (JLB 91) and fables. A younger brother died in infancy.

1905 He announced to his father his determination to be a writer and was encouraged by him. His first works (at seven) were a summary of Greek mythology, in English, and a short story, "The Fateful Helmet," in Spanish, which he borrowed from *Don Quixote* (JLB 30, JLB 69). At nine he translated Wilde's *The Happy Prince*. His father was a friend of the popular poet Evaristo Carriego (JLB 8), and Georgie loved to stay awake in the evenings to hear him recite his and other Argentine poets' verses.

1914 Because he was losing his sight, Father decided on an early retirement and resolved to spend a few years in Europe with the family. They visited Paris, London, and the north of Italy, before arriving in Geneva, where Georgie and Norah started their formal French studies. The outbreak of World War I made the visit a four-year sojourn. Georgie attended the Lycée Calvin where he was taught French and Latin. On his own, he learned German (JLB 113). In those years, and with the help of Maurice Abramowicz, he read the Symbolists (especially Rimbaud) and even attempted to write some verses in French. He continued his explorations in English literature, adding the works of Chesterton (JLB 23, JLB 26) and Carlyle (JLB 69) to those of Stevenson (JLB 43) and Wells (JLB 52, JLB 56) which had haunted his childhood. In a magazine edited by the German Expressionists, he found some poems by Whitman (JLB 61, JLB 95) and soon was avidly reading the original texts. He also read German philosophy: Schopenhauer (JLB 60), Nietzsche (JLB 22, JLB 33), and Fritz Mauthner (JLB 44); and discovered the legend of the Golem (JLB 83, JLB 84) in a rambling and haunting novel by Gustav Meyrink.

1919 After the war the Borgeses moved to Lugano for one year, and then went to

Barcelona and on to Majorca. Georgie continued to study Latin and prepared two books (one of poems, in the Expressionist vein, and another of essays) which he never published. From Majorca, the family moved first to Seville (where Georgie met some avant-garde poets) and to Madrid. There he discovered Rafael Cansinos Asséns (born 1883), a poet and scholar who became his first master of curious lores and soulful poetry. He also participated in the activities of the Ultraists and struck up a friendship with Guillermo de Torre (born 1900), a promoter of his and other people's avant-garde theories, who married Norah Borges in 1928. Georgie discovered Spanish literature: Quevedo, Gracián, Góngora, Villarroel, Unamuno. To the Ultraist magazines he contributed poems, articles, and translations of the Expressionists.

1921   The Borgeses returned to Buenos Aires for one year. Georgie rediscovered his native city (JLB 4) and took on a new master, the homemade philosopher and wit, Macedonio Fernández (born 1874), an old friend of his father. A group of young Ultraist poets coalesced around Georgie. He launched a little magazine which carried the new poetical gospel: *Prisma* ("Prism"), a posterlike poetry sheet illustrated with Norah's woodcuts.

1922   With Macedonio Fernández and a group of young poets he founded *Proa* ("Prow"), a little magazine.

1923   Second trip to Europe with the family. After visiting London and Paris, they settled in Spain. His first book of poems, *Fervor de Buenos Aires* ("Passion for B.A."), with Norah's woodcuts.

1924   With Ricardo Güiraldes (born 1886) he founded the second *Proa* which anticipated some chapters of *Don Segundo Sombra,* the gauchesque novel Güiraldes was then writing, and which became, on its publication in 1926, a classic of Argentine literature. Borges collaborated actively in *Martín Fierro,* the widely read avant-garde magazine.

1925   His second book of poems, *Luna de enfrente* ("Moon Across the Way"), and his first book of essays, *Inquisiciones* ("Inquisitions"). Borges forbade the reissue of the second. Güiraldes introduced the Borgeses to Victoria Ocampo (born 1893), a patron of the arts and an original essayist in her own right. It was the beginning of a long and fruitful literary association.

1926   His second book of essays, *El tamaño de mi esperanza* ("The Measure of My Hope"). It was never reissued.

1928   His third book of essays, *El idioma de los argentinos* ("The Language of the Argentines"). Only the title essay was reprinted in 1952. He made friends with Alfonso Reyes (born 1889), the Mexican poet and scholar who was then ambassador in Buenos Aires. Borges later admitted that it was Reyes who helped him to leave behind the avant-garde and Baroque excesses of his early prose and learn how to write in a classic style.

1929   His third book of poems, *Cuaderno San Martín* ("San Martín Copybook"). It received the second prize in a municipal literary competition. With the prize money, Borges bought a set of the eleventh edition of the *Encyclopaedia Britannica.*

1930   *Evaristo Carriego,* a literary biography. Victoria Ocampo introduced Adolfo Bioy Casares (born 1914) to him: they became close friends and collaborators (JLB 64).

1931   January: Victoria Ocampo founded *Sur,* which became Argentina's most important literary magazine. Borges remained one of its most frequent contributors.

1932   His fourth book of essays, *Discusión* ("Discussion").

1933   The magazine *Megáfono* ("Megaphone") devoted part of its August issue to a discussion of Borges's work. He was appointed literary editor of the Saturday supplement of *Crítica,* a scandal sheet.

332

1935 His first book of stories, *Historia universal de la infamia* (*A Universal History of Infamy*). It collects many pieces already published in *Crítica* (JLB 17, JLB 18, JLB 19, JLB 20).

1936 His fifth book of essays, *Historia de la eternidad* ("History of Eternity"). He was in charge of the biweekly section, *"Libros y autores extranjeros"* ("Foreign Books and Authors"), in *El Hogar* ("Home"), a position he held until 1939. He translated for *Sur* Virginia Woolf's *A Room of One's Own.*

1937 He edited, with Pedro Henríquez Ureña (born 1884), a didactic *Antología clásica argentina* ("Anthology of Argentine Literature"). According to Borges, Ureña did all the work. He translated for *Sur* Virginia Woolf's *Orlando* (JLB 27). Because his father's health was declining, Borges found a position as a first assistant at the Miguel Cané Municipal Library on the outskirts of Buenos Aires (JLB 29). He was promoted once and remained there until 1946.

1938 He prefaced and edited a collection of Kafka's stories, *La metamorfosis* (*The Metamorphosis*). February: Borges's father died and he became the head of the household. Christmas Eve: An accident he fictionalized in "The South" (JLB 79) almost cost him his life.

1940 Bioy married Silvina Ocampo (born 1906), sister of Victoria and a poet and short-story writer. Borges was best man. The three edited and published an *Antología de la literatura fantástica* ("Anthology of Fantastic Literature"). He wrote a prologue to Bioy's science-fiction novel, *La invención de Morel* (*The Invention of Morel*) (JLB 35), which is a manifesto for fantastic literature.

1941 His second book of stories, *El jardín de senderos que se bifurcan* (*The Garden of Forking Paths*). With Silvina and Bioy, he edited an *Antología de la poesía argentina* ("Anthology of Argentine Poetry"). He translated for *Sur* Henri Michaux's *Un barbare en Asie* ("A Barbarian in Asia"), and for *Sudamericana,* William Faulkner's *The Wild Palms* (JLB 28).

1942 He published with Bioy, under the pseudonym H. Bustos Domecq, a book of detective stories, *Seis problemas para don Isidro Parodi* (*Six Problems for Don Isidro Parodi*), in which they put to parodic use the lessons learned from Poe and Chesterton (JLB 23, JLB 46). July: *Sur* devoted part of the month's issue to a "Reparation for Borges" because the *Garden* did not receive any prize in that year's literary competition. Important writers and critics of the Hispanic world contributed to it.

1943 His first collected poems, *Poemas* (1922–1943), in which he eliminated many of the earlier texts and rewrote others. With Bioy, he edited *Los mejores cuentos policiales* ("The Best Detective Stories").

1944 His third book of stories, *Ficciones.* It included the eight already published in the *Garden,* thus superseding that book.

1945 With Silvina Bullrich Palenque, Borges edited an anthology of prose and verse about Buenos Aires' hoodlums, *El compadrito. Ficciones* was awarded the Grand Prix d'Honneur by the Argentine Society of Writers.

1946 With Bioy, under the pseudonym B. Suárez Lynch, he published a parodic detective novel, *Un modelo para la muerte* ("A Model for Death"); under the pseudonym Bustos Domecq, they published two fantastic short stories: *Dos fantasías memorables* ("Two Memorable Fantasies"). The two books were privately printed in editions limited to 300 copies and were not reissued commercially until 1970. August: He was promoted by the Fascist Perón government to inspector of poultry and rabbits at the municipal market, an indignity to punish him for signing some democratic manifestoes. On his resignation, the Argentine Society of Letters, then presided over by the left-wing intellectual Leonidas Barletta, offered him a reparation banquet at which Borges read a short pointed speech (JLB 57). To survive economically, Borges began a new career as a lecturer and public speaker. A policeman was assigned to attend his lectures and take notes. A newly founded magazine, *Los Anales de Buenos Aires* ("The Annals of B.A."), appointed Borges its editor. He remained in that post until the magazine ended in 1948. Felisberto Hernández (born 1902) and Julio Cortázar (born 1914) were among the new writers he introduced to Argentine readers.

1947 In a privately printed edition, he published a long metaphysical essay, *Nueva refutación del tiempo* ("New Refutation of Time") (JLB 60), which he later collected in *Other Inquisitions.*

1948 September 8: For their participation in a public demonstration against the Perón regime, Borges's mother and sister were imprisoned. For a month, his mother remained under house arrest while Norah spent her time in the prostitutes' section of the local prison. She taught them to draw and to sing old French songs.

1949 His fourth book of stories, *El Aleph* (*The Aleph*). Because of copyright problems, the American translation with the same title did not reproduce all the stories from the original edition and included material from other sources.

1950 He was appointed President of the Argentine Society of Writers, a position he held until 1953. He was appointed Professor of English and American literature at the Argentine Association of English Culture.

1951 He published an anthology of his own fiction under the title *La muerte y la brújula* ("Death and the Compass"). With Delia Ingenieros he published in Mexico *Antiguas literaturas germánicas* ("Ancient German Literatures"), a didactic book he rewrote and published in 1965 with María Esther Vázquez. With Bioy he edited a second anthology of *Los mejores cuentos policiales* ("The Best Detective Stories").

1952 His sixth book of essays, *Otras inquisiciones* (*Other Inquisitions*). "The Language of the Argentines" was reissued in a small volume with José Edmundo Clemente's complementary essay on the language of Buenos Aires.

1953 With Margarita Guerrero he published a didactic study of *El Martín Fierro,* the Argentine gauchesque poet. Edited by Clemente, the first volume of his *Obras completas* ("Complete Works"): *Historia de la eternidad* (1936). Nine more volumes were published separately before the works were collected in one single tome in 1974.

1954 *Poemas 1923–1953* and *Historia universal de la infamia* (1935) were reissued in the *Works.* "Emma Zunz" was made into a movie by Argentine director Leopoldo Torre Nilsson, under the title *Días de odio* ("Days of Wrath").

1955 He was appointed head of the National Library by the military government which took over from Perón (JLB 89). *Evaristo Carriego* (1930) is reissued in the *Works.* With Bioy he published several books: two rejected film scripts, *Los orilleros* ("The Hoodlums") (*see* 1975) and *El paraíso de los creyentes* ("The Believers' Paradise"), in one volume; two anthologies: *Cuentos breves y extraordinarios* ("Short and Extraordinary Tales") and *Poesía gauchesca* ("Gauchesque Poetry"), the latter one published in Mexico. With Luisa Mercedes Levinson (born 1914) he published *La hermana de Eloísa* ("Eloísa's Sister"), a collection of their stories. (Only the one that gave the book its title was written in collaboration.) With Betina Edelberg he published a didactic study of *Leopoldo Lugones,* the famous Argentine poet (1871–1938), whom Borges had hailed as his master.

1956 He was appointed Professor of English Literature at the Faculty of Philosophy and Letters, Buenos Aires. The University of Cuyo (Argentina) awarded him a doctorate *honoris causa,* the first of many to come. He was also awarded the National Prize for literature. Because he was becoming increasingly blind, on medical advice, he had to stop reading and writing. From this date on, Borges's mother became his private secretary. *Ficciones* (1944) is reissued in the *Works*.

1957 With Margarita Guerrero he published in Mexico *Manual de zoología fantástica* ("Manual of Fantastic Zoology"), later to be reissued and enlarged in 1968. *Discusión* (1932) and *El Aleph* (1949) were reissued in the *Works*.

1960 *Otras inquisiciones* (1952) was reissued in the *Works*. For the ninth volume, Borges compiled a new book of prose and verse, *El hacedor* ("The Maker," translated into English as *Dreamtigers*). With Bioy he edited another anthology, *Libro del cielo y del infierno* ("Book of Heaven and Hell"). He edited *Antología personal* (*A Personal Anthology*).

1961 He was awarded, *ex aequo* with Samuel Beckett, the Formentor Prize by a group of avant-garde publishers from Europe and the United States. His international reputation began at this point. The Italian government awarded him the title of Commendatore. He was invited by the University of Texas at Austin to occupy for a year the Tinker chair. He traveled in the United States, lecturing and giving recitals of his poetry. The Argentine movie *Hombre de la esquina rosada* (based on his tale "Man from the Slums" [JLB 17] and directed by René Múgica) was released.

1962 First translations in book form in English: *Labyrinths* (a selection of his prose and verse) and *Ficciones*. Elected member of the Argentine Academy of Letters. Awarded France's Commander of the Order of Arts and Letters.

1963 Third trip to Europe. He lectured in England and Scotland, in France and Spain, and in Switzerland. Awarded the Prize of the National Endowment for the Arts in Argentina.

1964 His fourth book of poems, *El uno, el mismo* ("The One, the Same"), was collected as part of his *Obra poética (1953–1964)* ("Collected Poems"). *L'Herne* published in Paris a large collection of international testimonies and essays on his life and work, the first book of such a scope. The Argentine weekly *Primera Plana* ("First Page") devoted a cover story to him on the occasion of his sixty-fifth birthday. Fourth trip to Europe to visit Spain and the Scandinavian countries, and to participate both in the International Congress of Writers in Berlin and to give the keynote speech at the UNESCO celebration of Shakespeare's fourth centenary.

1965 With the help of María Esther Vázquez, he published a didactic *Introducción a la literatura inglesa* ("Introduction to English Literature") and a second version of his 1951 book, *Literaturas germánicas medievales* ("Medieval German Literatures"). He published a collection of his own lyrics for tangos and *milongas*, *Para las seis cuerdas* ("For the Six Strings") (JLB 100). He visited for the first time other South American countries: Peru, Colombia, Chile. He was awarded the Order of the British Empire.

1966 A new collection of his *Obra poética (1923–1966)* ("Collected Poems"), in a large illustrated volume. He was appointed Professor of English Literature at the Stella Maris Catholic University of La Plata, Argentina. He was awarded the International Prize Madonnina by the Comune of Milano, Italy, and the 1965 Literary Prize by the Ingram Merrill Foundation of New York.

1967 With Bioy he published a collection of parodical essays, *Crónicas de Bustos Domecq* (*Chronicles of Bustos Domecq*). With Esther Zemborain de Torres, he published a didactic *Introducción a la literatura norteamericana* (*An Introduction to American literature*). Second trip to the United States to deliver the Charles Eliot Norton lectures at Harvard University. He traveled in the States, lecturing and giving recitals of his poetry. September 21: He married Elsa Astete Millán, one of his childhood sweethearts whom he met again after the death of her husband.

1968 With Margarita Guerrero he edited *El libro de los seres imaginarios* (*The Book of Imaginary Beings*) and on his own, *Nueva antología personal* ("A New Personal Anthology"). He was awarded the decoration of the Order of Merit by the Italian government.

1969 He published his fifth book of poems, *Elogio de la sombra* (*In Praise of Darkness*). Third trip to the States, invited by the University of Oklahoma to give some lectures and to participate in a symposium on his work. Dutton began the publication of his collected works in English with a new version of *The Book of Imaginary Beings*, edited and translated by Norman Thomas di Giovanni with the author. Two new film versions of his fiction: *Invasión* ("Invasion," Argentina, directed by Hugo Santiago, on an idea by Borges and Bioy) and *Emma Zunz* (France, TV, directed by Alain Magrou, on a story collected in the Spanish *El Aleph*).

1970 His "Autobiographical Essay" was published in the September 19 issue of *The New Yorker*. It was later included in the American edition of *The Aleph* (1970). He traveled to Israel to lecture. He was awarded the Inter-American Prize of Literature ($25,000) given by the government of São Paulo, Brazil. He published his fourth book of pseudorealist stories, *El informe de Brodie* (*Doctor Brodie's Report*) (JLB 103) He divorced Elsa Astete Millán. Bernardo Bertolucci adapted for Italian television "El tema del traidor y del héroe" ("Theme of the Traitor and Hero") (JLB 49): *La strategia de la ragna* (*The Spider's Stratagem*).

1971 Fourth trip to the States. He was awarded a doctorate *honoris causa* by Columbia University, New York, and participated in a scholarly discussion of his work at Yale University. He traveled to Scotland, Iceland (whose literature was the subject of his new research), England (to receive a doctorate *honoris causa* at Oxford), and Israel (to receive the Jerusalem Prize).

1972 He published his sixth book of poems, *El oro de los tigres* (*The Gold of the Tigers*). Fifth trip to the States to receive a doctorate *honoris causa* from the University of Michigan, East Lansing.

1973 Sixth trip to Europe, to lecture in Spain and Italy. Returning to Latin America, he stopped in Mexico City to receive the Alfonso Reyes International Prize. To avoid embarrassment at home, he asked and obtained his retirement from the position of head of the National Library from the new Perón government.

1974 A new movie, based on an original script by Borges and Bioy: *Les autres* (France, directed by Hugo Santiago).

1975 Death of Mother, at ninety-nine. He published his seventh book of poems, *La rosa profunda* (*The Unending Rose*); his fifth book of stories, *El libro de arena* (*The Book of Sand*), and an incomplete collection of his *Prólogos* ("Prologues"). He was appointed editor of a collection of exotica, *La biblioteca di Babele* ("The Library of Babel"), published by Franco Maria Ricci in Torino, Italy. Two of his stories were filmed in Argentina: *Los orilleros* (directed by Ricardo Luna) (*see* 1955) and *El muerto* (directed by Héctor Olivera) (JLB 58).

1976 He published his eighth book of poems, *La moneda de hierro* ("The Iron Coin"); a collection of his and other people's dreams, *Libro de los sueños* ("Book of Dreams"), and a didactic book, *¿Qué es el budismo?* ("What Is Buddhism?"), with Alicia Jurado. Sixth trip to the States to teach at the University of Michigan, East Lansing, and to participate in a symposium on his work at the University of Maine, Orono. He was awarded a doctorate *honoris causa* by the University of Cincinnati. He was the keynote speaker at the First International Shakespeare Congress, at the

336

Folger Library, Washington, D.C. On his way back, he was awarded a doctorate *honoris causa* by the University of Chile and the Order of Bernardo O'Higgins by the government. Seventh trip to Europe to participate in a special program on Spanish television.

1977   His ninth book of poems, *Historia de la noche* ("History of Night"). He collected in a privately printed edition, *Adrogué* (JLB 93), poems and prose dedicated to the town he used to visit with his family during vacations. With Bioy he published, *Nuevos cuentos de Bustos Domecq* ("New Bustos Domecq Stories"). Eighth trip to Europe. He was invited to Italy by his publisher, Franco Maria Ricci, and also visited Paris (where the Sorbonne gave him a doctorate *honoris causa*) and Geneva. On his return to Argentina, he was given another doctorate by the University of Tucumán.

1978   With María Kodama, his secretary for the last few years, he edited a *Breve antología anglosajona* ("Short Anglo-Saxon Anthology") (JLB 97). Invited by Mexican television officials, he visited Mexico for the second time. On his return, he stopped at Bogotá, Colombia, to receive the keys of the city and to be decorated by the government. A second movie version of *Emma Zunz: Splits* (USA, directed by Leonard Katz).

1979   A collection of his most recent lectures, *Borges oral* ("Oral B."). His *Obras Completas en colaboración* ("Complete Works in Collaboration") which only included work done with Bioy, Betina Edelberg, Margarita Guerrero, Alicia Jurado, María Kodama, and María Esther Vázquez. He received a gold medal from the French Academy, the Order of Merit from the German Federal Republic, and the Icelandic Falcon Cross. On his eightieth birthday, he received a national homage at the Cervantes Theater in Buenos Aires. He visited Colombia and Ecuador (to attend a literary congress), and later Japan.

1980   Eighth trip to the States, invited by the P.E.N. Club, New York. The Ministry of Education in Spain awarded him, *ex aequo* with fellow Ultraist Gerardo Diego, the Miguel de Cervantes Prize. Film version of "La intrusa" ("The Intruder") (JLB 98) (Brazil, directed by Carlos Hugo Christensen).

337

BORGES IN ENGLISH

1962 *Ficciones.* Edited and with an introduction by Anthony Kerrigan. New York: Grove Press.

Labyrinths. Selected Stories and Other Writings. Edited by Donald A. Yates and James E. Irby. New York: New Directions.

1964 *Other Inquisitions 1937–1952.* Translated by Ruth L. C. Simms. Austin: University of Texas Press.

Dreamtigers. Translated by Mildred Boyer and Harold Morland. Austin: University of Texas Press.

1967 *A Personal Anthology.* Edited by Anthony Kerrigan. New York: Grove Press.

1969 *The Book of Imaginary Beings.* Revised, enlarged and translated by Norman Thomas di Giovanni, in collaboration with the author. New York: Dutton.

1970 *The Aleph and Other Stories 1933–1969.* Edited and translated by Norman Thomas di Giovanni, in collaboration with the author. New York: Dutton.

1971 *Doctor Brodie's Report.* Translated by Norman Thomas di Giovanni, in collaboration with the author. New York: Dutton.

An Introduction to American Literature. Translated and edited by L. Clark Keating and Robert O. Evans. Lexington: University Press of Kentucky.

1972 *A Universal History of Infamy.* Translated by Norman Thomas di Giovanni. New York: Dutton.

Selected Poems 1923–1967. Edited with an introduction and notes by Norman Thomas di Giovanni. A bilingual edition. Boston: Delacorte Press/A Seymour Lawrence Book.

1973 *Borges on Writing.* Edited by Norman Thomas di Giovanni, Daniel Halpern, and Frank MacShane. New York: Dutton.

1974 *In Praise of Darkness.* Translated by Norman Thomas di Giovanni. A bilingual edition. New York: Dutton.

1976 *Chronicles of Bustos Domecq.* With Adolfo Bioy Casares. Translated by Norman Thomas di Giovanni. New York: Dutton.

1977 *The Book of Sand.* Translated by Norman Thomas di Giovanni. New York: Dutton.

The Gold of the Tigers. Selected Later Poems. Translated by Alastair Reid. (It also includes poems from *The Unending Rose.*) New York: Dutton.

1981 *Six Problems for Don Isidro Parodi.* Translated by Norman Thomas di Giovanni. New York: Dutton.

5. "Horse-Wagon Inscriptions"†
   Sp. title: "Las inscripciones de carros." Pub. *Síntesis,* Dec. 1928, col. *E.C.* (2d ed., 1955).
   The original title, "Séneca en las orillas" ("S. in the Slums"), indicated better B.'s preoccupation with the conceits or happy turns of phrase inscribed on the sides of old horse wagons. A sort of poetics of the folkloric is attempted here. (See also JLB 11, JLB 16.)

6. "Isidoro Acevedo"
   Same Sp. title. Pub. *C.*
   A poem devoted to the memory of his maternal grandfather in whose house B. was born. He had fought in the civil war against Rosas (JLB 2). After the tyrant's defeat in 1852, Acevedo retired to a long secluded life in Buenos Aires. He died in 1905, in his bed and dreaming of heroic actions he had accomplished half a century ago. Forty-four years later, B. wrote a story in which a man dies in bed dreaming that he is dying in the heat of battle (JLB 66).

7. "La Recoleta"
   Same Sp. title. Pub. *C.*
   One of Buenos Aires' older cemeteries, it contains the tomb where B.'s ancestors are buried. One of B.'s favorite spots, he has repeatedly expressed a longing for the day he will rest there. The family piety which impregnates so much of his poetry is the emotion which silently motivates the poem.

REDISCOVERING FICTION

8. "Palermo, Buenos Aires"†
   Same Sp. title. Pub. *E.C.*
   One of the Argentine capital's most popular neighborhoods, it was founded by an Italian from Palermo. It was already in decay at the time the Borgeses lived there (1900–14). But for Georgie, it was the source of a private mythology which included a magic garden and a protective younger sister, Norah. The poet to whom the original book was dedicated was a sentimental lyricist who become popular through songs devoted to poor unmarried working girls and rough predatory males. He came from Father's home town and used to visit the family every Sunday. In writing objectively about Palermo, B. was vicariously revisiting his lost paradise. But the real Palermo had little to do with Georgie. In an earlier poem, there are many allusions to B.'s other, more intimate memories of Palermo (JLB 4), The word *criollo* used by B. in this and other texts does not mean Creole, but is used to identify an Argentine of old Spanish stock. It is also applied generally to gauchos.

9. "A Vindication of the Cabala."†
   Sp. title: "Una Vindicación de la Cábala." Dated 1931 and pub. *D.*
   One of B.'s earliest articles on the subject, it shows his inexhaustible appetite for strange and cryptic lore. As usual, he does not pretend to be a scholar and writes about a formidable subject with the ease and familiarity of a Montaigne. In later texts ("Three Versions of Judas," "The Cult of Books," and JLB 34) he returned to similar topics with the same unscholarly and witty approach. In a famous short story, "Death and the Compass," a parody of the detective story as it was codified by Poe

---

†As noted in the Introduction, p. x, those pieces never before translated into English or published in book form have a dagger next to the title.

and Chesterton (JLB 23, JLB 46), he uses fragments of Hebrew lore to confuse and literally to *amaze* the reader. In a note to that story, he lightly admits that he invented a murderous sect of the Hasidim only to suit the plot. That warning did not prevent solemn Latin American scholars, of Jewish extraction, discussing eloquently and at length, B.'s debt to the Cabala.

10. "A Vindication of Basilides the False"†

Sp. title: "Una vindicación del falso B." Dated 1931 and pub. *D.*

Contemporary with the previous essay, it shows that Gnosticism was one of B.'s most permanent preoccupations. In two stories later included in *F.* ("Three Versions of Judas" and JLB 34), he takes advantage of the Gnostics' view of the world having been created by inferior demons, to build some of his most labyrinthine arguments.

11. "Our Inadequacies"†

Sp. title: "Nuestras imposibilidades." Pub. *Sur,* 1931 and col. *D.*

Written at the time the army had stopped the Argentine democratic process for the first time in this century, this essay represents B. at his most pessimistic. With a Juvenal's eye, he compiles a catalog of native imbecilities and grotesqueries, including the rather brutal and naïve handling of unorthodox sexual mores that slang reveals (JLB 54). When *D.* was reissued (1957), B. eliminated this essay because he was more optimistic about the generals' new role. They were the ones that got rid of Perón, a fact that B. would never forget (JLB 57).

12. "The Postulation of Reality"

Sp. title: "La postulación de la realidad." Pub. *Azul,* June 1931 and col. *D.*

A fascinating and exasperating article, closely connected to JLB 13 but less commented on by B.'s critics, it is devoted primarily to discussing the subject of verisimilitude; that is, the problem of how to present reality in literature and make it believable. B. uses Benedetto Croce's theories about the identification between the esthetic and the expressive to point out the differences between the classicists, who seem to shun expression, and the romantics, who emphasize it. B. empties these categories of any historical sense; they represent for him different ways of handling literature. Cervantes (JLB 30, JLB 69) is presented as a classicist in spite of the fact that he belongs to the Baroque period. From B.'s point of view, it is obvious that the realists are also romantics. According to him, verisimilitude cannot be defined as what conforms to the real, or to what a certain literary epoch or genre claims to be real. It is what gives more feeling or expresses more reality in a certain text. Verisimilitude has less to do with reality than with the conventions of any given culture about how to portray reality.

13. "Narrative Art and Magic"

Sp. title: "El arte narrativo y la magia." Pub. *D.*

This is one of B.'s most important theoretical pieces and decisive to the understanding of his later fiction. In the same way as T. S. Eliot rehearsed in critical essays the views he was later to explore in his poetry, B. advanced in this and other essays what he was to put into practice in his fictional prose. A theory of magical or fantastic literature is sketched out here with some help from texts taken from the most unexpected places: the only novel Poe wrote, a Victorian verse novel, Mallarmé's and Sir James Frazer's views, G. K. Chesterton's detective stories (JLB 23, 26), and even some striking images from Josef von Sternberg's early films. Generally neglected by Latin American scholars until Gerard Genette's brilliant use of it in a 1968 article on verisimilitude, this essay is seen now as a cornerstone of the poetics of narrative. Many of his viewpoints were later developed in the "Prologue" B. wrote to Adolfo Bioy Casares's *The Invention of Morel* (1940, JLB 35).

342

14. "Elements of Rhetoric,"†
    Sp. title: "Elementos de preceptiva." Pub. *Sur,* April 1933; never col. in book form. Already in an earlier piece, "The Literary Fruition" (1927, col. *Id.*), B. had analyzed a famous line without revealing its author and suggesting different and even opposite meanings according to whom it was attributed. At the time, he came to the correct conclusion that the "meaning" of a literary text depends heavily on what we already know about the author and his times, that it depends on its context. The present essay continues and develops this kind of poetics of reading. But the best practical presentation of his views on the matter was reserved for JLB 30.

15. "The Dread Redeemer Lazarus Morell"
    Sp. title: "El espantoso redentor L.M." Pub. *Crítica,* Aug. 12, 1933 and col. *H.I.* One of B.'s earliest and most successful excercises in fiction, it is loosely based on a disreputable historical character. The model for this and similar stories (col. in *H.I.*) was Marcel Schwob's *Imaginary Lives,* as B. later admitted. But he not only distorted facts and invented circumstances beyond anything ever done by Schwob: he produced a Baroque style of storytelling which was heavily indebted to von Sternberg's early gangster films and to some of the most elaborate of Chesterton's stories. Later, he dismissed the book as too badly written to be taken seriously. Latin American critics have taken some time to recognize the unusual merits of this type of story. But some readers—in particular, the Cuban novelist Alejo Carpentier and the Colombian Gabriel García Márquez—were easier to persuade, as can be seen by the tacit tribute to B. in *The Kingdom of This World* and *One Hundred Years of Solitude.*

16. "The Art of Verbal Abuse"†
    Sp. title: "Arte de injuriar." Pub. *Sur,* Sept. 1933 and col. *H.E.*
    One of B.'s most comic articles, it contains a treasury of abusive writing taken from the most unexpected sources. Under its flippancy there is a subtle contribution to B.'s general poetics (JLB 5, JLB 12, JLB 13, JLB 14).

17. "Man from the Slums"
    Sp. title: "Hombre de la esquina rosada." Pub. *Crítica,* Sept. 1933, under the pseudonym "F. Bustos" and with the title, "Hombre de las orillas" ("Man from the Slums"), and col. *H.I.*
    Based on a real anecdote told by one of the protagonists (Nicolás Paredes in real life), it is the third but not the last version of a knife fight of the 1890s. The first, "Police Legend," was published February 26, 1927, in *Martín Fierro;* the second, "Men Fought," was included in a book of essays (*Id.,* 1928). In spite of the popularity of the present version—it was the subject of a 1961 folkloric film version—B. is on record as disliking its excesses both in slang and in local color (JLB 2). It is also one of the few stories of his with an explicitly erotic subject. Years later, B. wrote a much better story about a woman disputed over by two men (JLB 98). Even later, he attempted a fourth version of the first tale, under the title of "Rosendo Juárez's Story" (in *Br.*). In it, as in Ryunosuke Akutagawa's *Rashomon,* the men are really cowards, and it is the woman who kills. The use of a pseudonym in the first publication of "Man from the Slums" helped B. to hide from his parents both the fact that he was indulging in a bit of literary slumming and that he was writing fiction. The paradox is that to mask himself better he used the name of one of Mother's ancestors.

18. "The Mirror of Ink"
    Sp. title: "El espejo de tinta." Pub. *Crítica,* Sept. 30, 1933, and col. *H.I.*
    This text, which was originally attributed to Richard Burton's *The Lake Regions of Central Equatorial Africa* (a book B. admitted to having never read), is really based,

343

according to Di Giovanni, on Edward Lane's *Manners and Customs of the Modern Egyptians.* In thus "mistaking" the correct source, B. changed the adaptation into a different text (JLB 30). By displacement, he gave it a new meaning. Taking into account his well-known childhood obsession with mirrors (JLB 87), the "quotation" becomes an effective disguise to mask the subjectivity of the text. From B.'s point of view, what really mattered was that in this text, the mirror is made of ink, tying together his old fears and the act of writing.

19. "Tom Castro, the Implausible Impostor"
Sp. title: "El impostor inverosímil T.C." Pub. *Crítica,* Sept. 30, 1933, and col. *H.I.*
The source for this story is the *Encyclopaedia Britannica,* as it was acknowledged by B. in the first edition of the book. Unfortunately, from the second (1955) onward, a misprint changed the attribution to Philip Gosse's *The History of Piracy,* a book totally unconnected with Tom Castro, as two different commentators found out after a strenuous scrutiny of that "source." In retelling the story of the Tichborne Claimant (as he is identified in the *Britannica,* 11th ed.), B. altered the role of the manservant Boyle (or Bogle, as he preferred to name him), who became the intellectual impostor, a black Iago to his obese white Othello. One of B.'s wittiest stories, it deserves to be read as a Jamesian exercise on the paradoxes of human behavior (JLB 53).

20. "The Masked Dyer, Hakim of Merv"
Sp. title: "El tintorero enmascarado, H. de M." Pub. *Crítica,* Jan. 20, 1934, and col. *H.I.*
Again, the sources are remote or unreliable. Thomas Moore's romantic poem *Lalla Rookh* is almost unreadable today. B. owes less to it than to the suggestively erotic atmosphere of Richard Burton's *The 1001 Nights,* whose explicitly sexual footnotes he read in Father's copy when the latter was absent. The observation, attributed to Hakim, that mirrors and fatherhood are abominable because they multiply the number of men is nowhere to be found in the sources, but it is used again by B. (in a different context and attributed to another source) in JLB 34. The second text being also imaginary, it is legitimate to suspect that B. is the real author of that memorable statement. Because of his monstrosity, Hakim can be symbolically linked to another of B.'s saddest heroes (JLB 62).

21. "I, a Jew"†
Sp. title: "Yo, judío." Pub. *Megáfono,* April 1934.
To respond to some accusations in a Fascist magazine *Crisol* ("The Crucible") about his supposed Jewish origins, B. wrote this satirical piece. In his list of lost nations he even includes the mythological centaurs. The joke helps to defuse the nastiness of the subject. If to be a Jew means that somewhere in the past a Jewish ancestor looms, then who can be sure, in Spain and Portugal, in Latin America, of not having at least one great-grandparent of that origin? From that point of view, to be a Jew has no meaning. A hidden irony is contained in B.'s mock search for a Jewish ancestor. It was the very Catholic and bigoted maternal branch of his family (the Acevedos) that seemed the most likely carrier of Jewish blood. In later years, B. would devote more time to reading and writing about Jewish culture and literature (JLB 37, JLB 51, JLB 83, JLB 84).

22. "The Doctrine of Cycles"†
Sp. title: "La doctrina de los ciclos." Dated 1934, pub. *Sur,* May 1936, and col. *H.E.*
B.'s reading of Nietzsche and in particular of his theory of the eternal return (in centuries to come we will be reborn and relive the lives we have already lived) is here given an ironic twist. Many things connected B. to N.—the gift of insomnia, a deep

sense of despair, the habit of coining striking images—but while N. was hounded and went beyond the bounds of reason, B. (always in strict control of himself) accepted the world's follies and never relinquished the protective mask of irony. Six years later he returned to a discussion of N. (JLB 33).

23. "Chesterton and the Labyrinths of the Detective Story"†
Sp. title: "Los laberintos policiales y C." Pub. *Sur,* July 1935, never col. in book form. B.'s early interest in the detective story as a literary genre can be traced to this article and many others he wrote for *Sur* and *El Hogar* during the 1930s, but also to his editing in the 1940s and 1950s, with the help of Bioy Casares, collections of detective stories for Emecé. It can also be seen in two of his most popular short stories: "The Garden of Forking Paths" and "Death and the Compass" (both included in *F.*). The present article is the first to comment in detail on C.'s contribution to the genre (JLB 26). (See also JLB 46.)

24. "The Translators of *The 1001 Nights*"†
Sp. title: "Los traductores de las *Mil y una noches.*" Dated 1935 and pub. *H.E.* In discussing some French, English, and German translators of the book, B. not only shows an encyclopedic if faulty scholarship; he also reveals how deeply the boyhood reading of the book had influenced his imagination. It is one of his most important texts on the art of translation, a subject he had already approached in reviewing some of "The Homeric Versions" (also included in *H.E.*) and to which he returned in JLB 76.

25. "Oswald Spengler: A Capsule Biography"†
Sp. title: "Biografías sintéticas: O.S." Pub. *El Hogar,* Dec. 23, 1936, never col. in book form.
One of the many capsule biographies B. produced for the book section he edited in *El Hogar,* it is a good specimen of his capacity to summarize a writer's life and work in a few witty lines. In this case, he succeeds in conveying the sense of adventure and wonder the production of the *Decline of the West* implied. This apocalyptic book influenced not only B. but his entire generation deeply.

26. "Modes of G. K. Chesterton"†
Sp. title: "Modos de G.K.C." Pub. *Sur,* July 1936, never col. in book form.
Written at the time of C.'s death, it is the second article B. devoted to one of his favorite authors (JLB 23). A third, even more all encompassing, was published in *O.I.* But the best homage B. ever paid to C. was in a remark recorded by Richard Burgin in his 1969 book of interviews. When asked about the precision of the visual images in his stories, he acknowledged that they didn't come from reality: they came from C.'s prose.

27. "Virginia Woolf: A Capsule Biography"†
Sp. title: "Biografías sintéticas: V.W." Pub. *El Hogar,* Oct. 30, 1936, never col. in book form.
Using the same format as his capsule biography of Spengler (JLB 25), B. introduces his readers to the work of V.W., a writer he translated twice in 1937: *A Room of One's Own, Orlando.* Commenting on the latter in his *A.E.* B. would maintain that the translation was entirely Mother's work. It is hard to believe that she, on her own, could match the poetic quality of the original. Probably B. was trying in his usual self-deprecatory way to thank his mother for her help with the translation.

28. "William Faulkner: Three Reviews"†
"Tres Reseñas sobre Faulkner." Pub. *El Hogar,* Jan. 22, 1937, Jan. 21, 1938, and May 5, 1939, never col. in book form.
On at least three occasions, B. reviewed books by F. in *El Hogar.* The present text

puts together these reviews with no attempt to edit them. They show not only B.'s high appreciation of F.'s work, but a witty understanding of its uniqueness. The commentary on *The Wild Palms,* one of F.'s neglected masterpieces, has the added value of giving some insight into a book he translated memorably into Spanish in 1941, thus making his intense, Baroque style and views available to younger Latin American writers, such as the Uruguayan Juan Carlos Onetti, the Mexican Juan Rulfo, and the Colombian Gabriel García Márquez.

29. "The Total Library"†

Sp. title: "La biblioteca total." Pub. *Sur,* August 1939, never col. in book form.

Less famous than the story "The Library of Babel" (from *F.*), this essay, which preceded it by a couple of years, provides the philosophical background for it. Here are reviewed the theories about an infinite library which B. found in Leucippus, Lasswitz, and Lewis Carroll, as well as in the classic texts of Aristotle and Cicero; here is the absurd invention of Thomas Henry Huxley, those thousand monkeys typing through eternity. The biographical background to both the story and the essay is the Municipal Library where B. spent "nine years of solid unhappiness," as he put it in *A.E.* Located in a "drab and dreary part" of town, the library provided B. with a meager salary and the ambiguous title of first assistant (above him, he had, in a Kafkaesque progression, not only the director but three officials). In due time, B. would ascend to the dizzy heights of third official. His work was stultifying. To avoid the hostility of his colleagues (more interested in smutty stories, rape, and sports) he had to agree to classify not more than a hundred books per day. (The first day he did without any effort four hundred, and was almost lynched.) The women who worked there were interested in society gossip and B. acquired some status only when they found out he was a friend of Elvira de Alvear, a beautiful and despotic woman he loved hopelessly and who was at the time Buenos Aires' *arbiter elegantiarum.* (In JLB 51, B. used some of Elvira's more telling traits to create the imaginary Beatriz Viterbo.) To underline the menial nature of the job, once in a while the assistants were given two pounds of maté to take home. B. used to cry all the way back to the tramway stop. In spite of this and other miseries, he managed to isolate himself either in the basement or, if weather permitted, on the roof to read and write. From the hell of that library came some of his best stories: "Death and the Compass," and JLB 36, and JLB 39. At the time, he also read Kafka, whose invisible presence can be detected in the fabric of his essay (JLB 73). He also put to good use the long tramway journey by reading, among other works, Dante's *Divine Comedy* (JLB 65) and Ariosto's *Orlando Furioso.* For an account of how his time in hell ended, see JLB 57.

30. "Pierre Menard, Author of the *Quixote*"

Sp. title: "P.M., autor del *Q.*" Pub. *Sur,* May 1939 and col. *F.*

In his *A.E.* B. has described the almost mortal accident he had on Christmas Eve 1938 and which he used as part of one of his stories (JLB 79). While convalescing, he believed his intelligence might have been impaired. To test it, he decided to attempt a genre he had never tried before; the result was "P. M." If B. was wrong in believing this was his first story (see JLB 17), he was right on another count: he had never before attempted to write anything as complex as this text. The conclusion of it—reading is more decisive than writing because it always writes the text anew —was developed by Gerard Genette in 1964 and made into one of the basic tenets of modern criticism. This story is also one of the most effective parodies of literary life ever attempted. Mixing adroitly French and Argentine literary mores, B. produces a caricature of what Mallarmé and Valéry (whose Monsieur Teste is a precursor of P.M.), or Unamuno and Enrique Larreta (both wrote sequels or parallels to the *Q.*), had already attempted. "P.M." had been preceded by a similar hoax: "The Approach to Al'Mutásim" (see Introduction to this book). In 1940, and for the third time, B. would attempt a similar joke. He published as an essay in *Sur* "An Examination of Herbert Quain's Work." It pretended to be an evaluation of a well-known English writer and it began by quoting the *T.L.S.*'s too short obituary. Needless to say, H.Q., like P.M. or Mir Bahadur Ali (the "author" of "Al'Mutásim") existed only in B.'s witty texts. For another view of reading as rewriting, see JLB 73.

31. "Joyce and Neologisms"†
Sp. title: "J. y los neologismos." Pub. *Sur,* Nov. 1939, never col. in book form.
At the time *Finnegans Wake* was published, B. wrote this very short note to elucidate some of its portmanteau words and comment on J.'s linguistic and poetic views. His interest in the Irish storyteller was not new. In his first book of essays, he included a brilliant article on *Ulysses* (see 1925). He returned to the subject in a 1941 article (JLB 40) and in two more recent poems (JLB 101). For B., J. more than Pound or Eliot was the symbol of the Modernists, the one who had explored and discovered new forms for the language.

32. "Avatars of the Tortoise"†
Sp. title: "Avatares de la tortuga." Pub. *Sur,* Dec. 1939, col. *D.,* 1957.
When Georgie was still a boy, Father used to teach him the paradoxes of Zeno, with the aid of a chessboard. From those didactic games, B. moved in his youth and early manhood to philosophical debate on the matter. The present article is the second explicitly dedicated to this subject. An earlier one, "The Perpetual Race Between Achilles and the Tortoise," was included in the first edition of *D.* Another echo of the famous paradoxes can be found in JLB 73.

33. "Some of Nietzsche's Opinions"†
Sp. title: "Algunos pareceres de N." Pub. *La Nación,* Feb. 11, 1940, never col. in book form.
Using the *Notebooks* he had already quoted in JLB 22, B. develops here some views on N.'s thoughts. Years later, influenced by British attacks which presented Nietzsche as a proto-Nazi, B. rejected his philosophy. Today we know that N.'s posthumous works were doctored by his sister Elisabeth, who had married a German nationalist.

34. "Tlön, Uqbar, Orbis Tertius"
Same Sp. title. Pub. *Sur,* May 1940, col. *F.*
The second story written after the 1938 accident (JLB 30), "Tlön" shows B. at his most complex best. A parody of the attempts to reduce the chaos of the universe to a rational explanation (literally based on Berkeley's description of the "real" world), "Tlön" is also a sort of detective story. The searchers are amateur researchers; the adventure is bibliographical; the quest is centered on rare or imaginary books. Strange words are capable of altering reality and of producing uncanny objects called *hrönirs.* The deliberate use of procedures taken from science-fiction stories may be attributed to the fact that the first book B. read after his accident was C. S. Lewis's *Out of the Silent Planet,* a novel in which a Cambridge linguist unwittingly explores Mars. When the story was first published in 1940 it already had a note, dated 1947, which stated that the text was a reproduction of one published in 1940. The reader was then confronted with an uncomfortable simultaneity of two times and two texts which were one yet different. This chronological game played with the reader was another dimension of "Tlön's" magic. In reprinting the story, B. didn't bother to update the futuristic note; after 1947, that magical dimension was lost. The story has another, almost submerged meaning. Written at the time Hitler was destroying

Western Europe with the benevolent complicity of Stalin, it denounced effectively all ideologies which attempt to enslave men under a dogma (JLB 37, JLB 50). At a more autobiographical level, the quotation about mirrors and copulation which serves as a polemical opening ought to be read in connection with a similar unorthodox statement B. had already used in JLB 20.

35. "Prologue to *The Invention of Morel*"
    Sp. title: "Prólogo" a *La invención de Morel.* Pub. in first ed. of that novel (1940), col. in *Pr.*
    This text amounts to a manifesto for a literature of the fantastic and was published the same year the *Antología de la literatura fantástica* B. had compiled with Bioy and Silvina Ocampo was launched. It attacks realism in literature (including the "psychological" novel) and defends the so-called minor narrative genres: the adventure novel, the detective story, and science fiction. The list of the writers he now dislikes or finds merely exasperating includes classics such as Cervantes (to whom he had devoted some praise, JLB 30, JLB 69), Dostoevsky, and Proust. But the main attack is concentrated on the narrative theories of the Spanish philosopher José Ortega y Gasset, whose prose B. viewed as very poor. In praising Bioy Casares's novel, he does not forget to mention some of his sources: James's "The Turn of the Screw," Kafka's *The Trial,* Julien Green's *Le voyageur sur la terre* ("The Earthly Traveler"), and, of course, Wells's *The Island of Dr. Moreau.* They all share with Bioy's fiction the unusual trait of having admirable plots. This article may be read as a development on the narrative theory already advanced in JLB 13 about magic in literature, a theory also advanced in JLB 52 and JLB 69. But it is especially in the fiction B. wrote in the 1930s and 1940s (JLB 20, JLB 30, JLB 34, JLB 36, JLB 39, JLB 49, JLB 51, JLB 66, JLB 70) that his theory is really grounded.

36. "The Circular Ruins"
    Sp. title: "Las ruinas circulares." Pub. *Sur,* Dec. 1940, col. *F.*
    One of B.'s most "narrative" stories and a good example of his fictional prose. The subject, of a man created by another, and the horror of his final discovery that we are all inhabitants of dreams dreamed by somebody else, is connected with B.'s most primeval fears. In a paragraph of an essay on metaphor ("After the Images," col. in *I.*) he had anticipated by some fifteen years the theme of the man who discovers he is only a simulacrum. The epigraph from Carroll's *Through the Looking Glass* connects that paragraph to the story. Many years later, in a poem (JLB 84), B. gave a different twist to the subject. In his personal mythology, the theme of the double —already exhausted by romanticism—was deeply linked to his fears of being but a creature of Father, the quiet and unassuming Jorge Guillermo Borges. The paradox is that now we know him only as Borges's father.

37. "Portrait of the Germanophile"†
    Sp. title: "Definición del germanófilo." Pub. *El Hogar,* Dec. 13, 1940, never col. in book form.
    At the time B. published this essay as an editorial in *El Hogar,* German armies were occupying a large part of Western Europe and seemed invincible. A powerful sector of Argentine society leaned toward Fascism and the Nazis because those were the enemies of England—a country that had refused to hand back to Argentina the Falkland Islands. The present text may have been one of the many that did not endear B. to the future Perón regime. Today it is more important in providing a sort of political background against which to read JLB 34, JLB 39, JLB 64, and "The Library of Babel."

348

38. "The Cyclical Night"

Sp. title: "La noche cíclica." Dated 1940 and col. *P.*

One of B.'s best "metaphysical" poems, it versifies a subject he had already discussed in an article (JLB 22). The poem was dedicated to Silvina Bullrich Palenque, a writer and one of B.'s closest friends at the time. Together, they compiled an anthology in 1945.

39. "The Lottery in Babylon"

Sp. title: "La lotería en Babilonia." Pub. *El jardín de senderos que se bifurcan* (*The Garden of Forking Paths,* 1941), col. *F.*

In a Prologue to the *Garden,* B. stated that this story was not "innocent of symbolism." The game it describes is meant to symbolize destiny, the lottery to which all of us are unwitting subscribers. But it also contains a wealth of hidden allusions and private jokes. The game is modeled on the Argentine lottery. There is a comic reference to a privy called Qaphqa where "malignant or benevolent people deposited accusations" to denounce or praise people. That exotic name, when read aloud, becomes Kafka (JLB 29, JLB 73).

40. "Fragment on Joyce"†

Sp. title: "Fragmento sobre J." Pub. *Sur,* Feb. 1941, never col. in book form.

An unusual obituary, it further develops B.'s evaluation of one of the few Modernists he always admired (JLB 31, JLB 101). The first paragraph anticipates the plot of one of his most famous stories, "Funes the Memorious," published in 1944 in *F.* The trick of talking about a story he will one day write is perfected in JLB 49.

41. "About *The Purple Land*"

Sp. title: "Nota sobre *TPL.*" Pub. *La Nación,* Aug. 3, 1941, col. *O.I.*

William Henry Hudson is the best known English writer in Argentina, whereas he is almost unread in England today. But some of his books (such as the one B. comments on, or *Green Mansions*) were once praised by the likes of Conrad (JLB 3). B.'s admiration for H. can be linked to his lifelong interest in gaucho life, so masterfully described by H. in this and other books (JLB 58).

42. "*Citizen Kane*"†

Sp. title: "El ciudadano." Pub. *Sur,* Aug. 1941, never col. in book form.

B. has always been a film buff. Already in the late 1920s, he was writing about movies. When Victoria Ocampo started *Sur* in 1931, he began contributing film reviews to the periodical, in spite of Victoria's rather reluctant attitude toward the seventh art. Even now, when he can no longer see much on the screen, he goes to the cinema to hear the sound track. The present article is one of his best: laudatory and iconoclastic at the same time, full of tantalizing asides and unexpected references (*The Power and the Glory* is a 1933 Spencer Tracy vehicle which has nothing to do with Graham Greene's novel; in fact, it precedes it by seven years). For another exercise in movie criticism, see JLB 43.

43. "Dr. Jekyll and Edward Hyde, Transformed"†

Sp. title: "El Dr. Jekyll y Edward Hyde, transformados." Pub. *Sur.* Dec. 1941, col. *D.* (2d ed., 1955).

The theme of the double (JLB 36) is here tackled once more with humor. The article shows B.'s familiarity not only with Stevenson's classic but with movies in general (JLB 42). In the last sentence of the present article, B. returns to another of his cherished subjects: that all men are one. Already in a note (attached to "The Approach to Al' Mutásim" in *F.*) he had written about the famous poem by the Persian Attar.

44. "The Analytical Language of John Wilkins"

Sp. title: "El lenguaje analítico de J.W." Pub. *La Nación,* Feb. 8, 1941, col. *O.I.*
B.'s preoccupations with the philosophy of language (evident in JLB 34) are here used
to review the bizarre experiment of the English linguist. From one of B.'s quotations
(that of the highly improbable Chinese encyclopedia), the French philosopher Michael Foucault took a hint, later developed in *Les mots et les choses* (1966).

45. "Almafuerte"†

Sp. title: "Teoría de A." Pub. *La Nación,* Feb. 22, 1942; later included as a prologue
to a selection of A.'s poetry (1962), col. *Pr.*
A popular Argentine poet of the 1890s, A.'s fame never really transcended his
country's boundaries. But for B., he was one of the first poets he thoroughly admired
as a child. In later years he was to deplore his pathetic stance and love of abstractions.
(Even his pseudonym, Strong Soul, is telling.) A less obvious link between the two
is insinuated in the article: like A., B. also was afflicted with the longing to consummate passion and the practical impossibility of doing it. In a poem published in
Dreamtigers and attributed to a certain Gasper Camerarius, B. once said:

> I, who have been so many men, have never been
> The one in whose embrace Matilde Urbach swooned.

46. "On the Origins of the Detective Story"†

Sp. title: "Roger Caillois: *Le roman policier.* " Pub. *Sur,* April 1942, never col. in book
form.
The biographical background of this review is almost as curious as its texts. In 1942,
Caillois was not only a brilliant young French sociologist but the protégé of Victoria
Ocampo. She had invited him on the eve of World War II for an extended visit to
Argentina. When war started, Caillois, very wisely, decided to stay. To contribute
to the cause of Free France, he edited a little magazine, *Lettres françaises,* sponsored
by Victoria. It was as a pamphlet of that magazine that his long essay on the detective
novel was published. Being friends with Victoria did not prevent B. from savaging
C.'s half-baked literary theories. Implacably, he dismissed the notion that the chief
of the French police was the inventor of the detective novel: a literary genre invariably begins with a literary text, B. pointed out, giving to Poe what rightfully belonged
to him (JLB 23). Caillois did not let things stand and challenged B. to a polemic which
had no meaning. Because he was more energetic, or lacked some scruples, he took
advantage of his familiarity with *Sur*'s offices to reply to B. in the same issue. B. never
forgave him. In spite of the fact that C. was responsible for the publication in his
magazine of some of the best French translations of B.'s stories, he cut him in public.
Many years later, C. managed to persuade the international jury of the Formentor
Prize that B. was worthy of sharing the prize with Beckett. Unflinchingly, B. stuck
to his guns.

47. "Melville"

Sp. title: "Prólogo a *Bartleby.* " Pub. as an introduction to B.'s translation of "Bartleby the Scrivener," col. *Pr.*
A capsule biography of M. which also contains an allegorical reading of *Moby-Dick*
and "Bartleby." The latter is very much seen as a precursor of Kafka's stories
(JLB 73). The prologue shows B.'s familiarity with American literature.

48. "Conjectural Poem"

Sp. title: "Poema conjetural." Pub. *La Nación,* July 4, 1943, col. *P.*
Using a device already made famous by Robert Browning's *Dramatis Personae,* B.
re-creates the monologue of one of his ancestors at the moment he is going to be

murdered by gauchos. Connected with the elegiac poetry inspired by family piety (JLB 6), the text once more reduces the life of a man to one single extraordinary event. B.'s nostalgia for a life of action and the ever-present conflict between arms and letters are dramatized here. (JLB 79).

49. "Theme of the Traitor and Hero"
Sp. title: "Tema del traidor y del héroe." Pub. *F.*
A dazzling exercise in narrative, in which B. pretends he is writing a note about a story he will write one day but which he is actually writing. The parodical use of conjecture (JLB 48) helps to lay bare the structure of this and all narratives. It shows how the tale and the telling are produced simultaneously by the author, to be simultaneously decoded by the reader. The story is closely linked to other tales on the theme of the double, a constant topic in B.'s works: "Three Versions of Judas" and "The Shape of the Sword" (both in *F.*), or "The Theologians" (from *A.*). Out of the present story, Bernardo Bertolucci and Eduardo de Gregorio extracted the plot for one of the former's best films: *The Spider's Stratagem* (1970). In changing the action to Fascist Italy, they kept B.'s ironies about historical and metaphysical fallacies intact.

50. " A Comment on August 23, 1944"
Sp. title: "Anotación al 23 de agosto de 1944." Pub. *Sur,* Sept. 1944, col. *O.I.*
The liberation of Paris by Allied troops was celebrated in almost all countries of Latin America as a national feast. For B. it was not only the occasion to comment on his own surprise at being deeply moved by a collective emotion (he who believed in being an individualist to the point of solipsism), but an occasion to recall forcefully the days when Nazism was triumphant in Argentina. An important text for those who pretend to believe B. was always apolitical, or, even worse, that he was always a Fascist.

51. "The Aleph"
Sp. title: "El A." Pub. *Sur,* Sept. 1945, col. *A.*
A satire on Argentine literary mores (JLB 30), it also contains a hidden parody of Dante's *Divine Comedy,* a fact that B. explicitly denied in a commentary to this story included in the American edition (1970). In spite of it, the story is about a man ("Borges") who is hopelessly in love with a woman called Beatriz and who is guided to a vision of the world, contained in a cellar, by a poet called Carlos Argentino Daneri. (*Dan*te's surname was Alighi*eri.*) To compound things even further, Daneri is writing a poem describing the entire world. An article written at the time and published as part of a prologue to an Argentine edition of the *Comedy* (JLB 65) gives a clue to the story. In presenting Dante's love for his Beatrice as hopeless and viewing the actual encounter between the two in Purgatory as a real nightmare, B. gives away the concept behind his story. Being a parody—that is, an inverted and displaced version of the original—his story makes the meeting of the two lovers even more impossible and humiliating. The fragment in which the Aleph is described is one of B.'s most famous prose poems. The story was originally dedicated to Estela Canto, a young writer who was B.'s constant companion at the time, and whose real name seemed to allude to Dante ("I sing to Stella, or to the Star"), as Haroldo de Campos has suggested. But the Beatriz of this story owes more to the style and social standing of another of B.'s close friends, Elvira de Alvear (JLB 29). The references to Hebrew scholarship contained in the title (it is the first letter of the alphabet and also represents man) only add to the complexity of one of B.'s condensed masterpieces.

52. "The Flower of Coleridge"
Sp. title: "La flor de C." Pub. *La Nación,* Sept. 23, 1945, col. *O.I.*

351

Taking a hint from one text found in C.'s *Notebooks,* in which the English poet suggests a disturbing playing with time, B. develops a view of fantastic literature, also illustrated with texts by Henry James (JLB 53) and H. G. Wells (JLB 56). Some of B.'s own stories ("The Secret Miracle," JLB 34, and JLB 66) also play with time. There is another article on C.: a study of *Kubla Khan,* and the mysterious way it was produced, in *O.I.* It confirms B.'s predilection for the work of one of his "precursors."

53. "Henry James"†

Sp. title: "Prólogo a *La humillación de los Northmore.*" Pub. in the Sp. translation of that story (1945), col. *Pr.*

Introducing a minor story by J. ("The Abasement of the N."), B. discusses his entire work, and wittily suggests a paradoxical reading of it. His interest in H. J.'s stories, which he preferred to his more elaborate novels, reflects an interest in the ironical, almost parodical way of composing tales, in particular those about art and artists, poets and poetry (JLB 30, JLB 51). It may also be linked to Father's long and lasting devotion to William James's *Psychology,* a book he used to introduce B. to that branch of knowledge.

54. "Our Poor Individualism"

Sp. title: "Nuestro pobre individualismo." Pub. *Sur,* July 1949, col. *O.I.*

To be read in conjunction with JLB 11 and with some of his most satirical stories (JLB 30, JLB 51) as an example of B.'s social criticism. A writer who had been abusively connected with the Argentine establishment proves once more to be a lucid and witty critic of his native land's saddest mores.

55. "The Paradox of Apollinaire"†

Sp. title: "La paradoja de A." Pub. *Los Anales de Buenos Aires,* Aug. 1946, col. *O.I.*

In writing about one of the founders of French Modernism, B. shows how well and intimately he knew that literature, a fact that will hardly surprise those readers who recall he was educated at a French school in Geneva, but which has been less advertised by himself than his love for Anglo-American letters.

56. "The First Wells"

Sp. title: "El primer W." Pub. *Los Anales de B.A.,* Sept. 1946, col. *O.I.*

Written at the time of Wells's death, B. wisely concentrates the analysis on his early science-fiction novels which counted among the books he read as a child. In *El Hogar* (1936–39) he reviewed with sadness and affection Wells's later work.

57. "Hurry, Hurry!"

Sp. title: "Dele-dele." Pub. *Argentina libre,* Aug. 15, 1946, never col. in book form.

The anecdote behind this text is worth retelling. From 1937 to 1946, B. worked as minor clerk in a municipal library (JLB 29). An allegorical rendering of the horrors he had to endure daily there can be found in "The Library of Babel"; a more factual one in his *A.E.* At the time of Perón's first ascent to power, B. was suddenly promoted to inspector of chickens and rabbits at the municipal market. He declined the honor and was summarily fired. As a form of reparation, the Argentine Society of Letters (at the time presided over by a Communist) organized a dinner at which B. read this text. The paradox is that he was then being hailed as a civic hero by the very people who later rallied around Perón on his return to power in 1973 and denounced B. as a Fascist.

58. "The Dead Man"

Sp. title: "El muerto." Pub. *Sur,* Nov. 1946, col. *A.*

In 1934, B. visited for a few days the north of Uruguay in the company of Enrique Amorim, the Uruguayan novelist. B. already knew the areas around Montevideo and

had no choice. He was invited to teach a course on Anglo-American literature and his first lecture was on Hawthorne. With the help of Mother (who coached him), he learned the present lecture by heart. With practice, he would come to use only some very short and cryptic notes. Later, he grew into a strange, almost hypnotic kind of speaker. His reading of H. is highly personal. In selecting for detailed examination some of his most Kafkaesque stories (such as "Wakefield"), B. creates his own anthology of the master.

68. "From Allegories to Novels"
Sp. title: "De las alegorías a las novelas." Pub. *La Nación,* Aug. 7, 1949, col. *O.I.*
In studying the transition from allegories to novels, B. seems to favor the latter. But, behind his condemnation of allegory, it is possible to detect a fascination with it. B.'s fictional practice at the time seems to correct and even contradict the stand he takes here. There is something of the allegorical process in many of his tales (JLB 34, JLB 36, JLB 51, JLB 66, JLB 79). His concern with Dante may also be taken as a sign of fascination with allegory (JLB 65). Besides, the distance between parody (a genre in which B. excels) and allegory is not great. Both deal with a text which mirrors another; in both, the full understanding of the visible text depends very much on the reader's recognition of the hidden one. In both there is an inversion of values. The main difference (parody generally belongs to the comic mode, allegory to the serious) has been erased many times by the likes of Cervantes or Sterne. B.'s name also may be added to that list. His parodies are deadly serious.

69. "Partial Enchantments of the *Quixote*"
Sp. title: "Magias parciales del *Q.*" Pub. Nov. 6, 1949, col. *O.I.*
In 1939, B. published in *El Hogar* an article, "When Fiction Lives Inside Fiction," which anticipated many of the viewpoints presented here. In ten years, his thoughts on the matter were refined; the practice of storytelling developed his views even further. To the concept of fiction reflecting itself, as if the text were a mirror (a view French criticism would later systematize), B. added his own belief that we are all creatures of fiction, dreamed or magically produced by others (JLB 36). B.'s concern with C.'s masterpiece can be traced back to an early and witty essay on the first paragraph of the *Q.* (collected in *Id.*). In 1947, as a contribution to the celebration of C.'s fourth centenary, he wrote a short evaluation. Several years later, he wrote a few poems underlying some paradoxes in C.'s life and work. But the most famous of all his tributes to the master is, of course, JLB 30. What B. admired most in C. was the freedom with which he played around with narrative conventions and invented new ways of handling a complex story. What he disliked was the devotion paid by the "cervantophiles" to the master's rather casual style, to the moral commonplaces in which he carelessly indulged, to his belief that Christianity was destined to win the battle against the infidels. For B., C.'s best work was above those pieties.

70. "The Handwriting of God"
Sp. title: "La escritura del Dios." Pub. *A.*
Born in a part of South America in which Indian traditions were sparse, educated by Father to love English culture, conversant since adolescence with French, German, and Latin literature, a master of Spanish prose, B. was never a devotee of Indianism, a sentimental branch of pastoral, espoused mainly by foreigners. (Rousseau and Chateaubriand were mainly responsible for its excesses.) B.'s Indians—who fought savagely against the no less savage gauchos, and who were responsible for the death of Colonel Francisco Borges, his paternal grandfather—are never soft or sublime. B. looked at them from the cold distance of a descendant of European settlers. One of the few exceptions to this attitude is the present story, in which

pre-Columbian myths are used to illustrate one of his recurring themes: that there is a secret code, a hidden cipher to the universe, an idea also found in the Cabalists.

71. "From Someone to No One"

Sp. title: "De alguien a nadie." Pub. *Sur,* March 1950, col. *O.I.*

To illustrate the nothingness of individuality (a subject he tackled in his first book of essays, and one which runs through his work), B. traces to ancient cosmologies the notion of a plurality of gods which will later be reduced to one, even later to nobody. Instead of a being there is only a nonbeing (JLB 60).

72. "Pascal's Sphere"

Sp. title: "La esfera de P." Pub. *La Nación,* Jan. 14, 1951, col. *O.I.*

Tracing the origins of one of P.'s most celebrated metaphors—the world as an unending, monstrous sphere—B. travels through time and philosophies. As in some of his most famous stories (JLB 34 and "The Library of Babel") the view of the infinite he presents here is terrifying. (In 1953 Maurice Blanchot pointed out in an article, B.'s infinite is evil.) But in rendering P.'s terrors in a lucid, understated prose, B. seems to exorcise them. As he himself wrote once, echoing Chesterton, "This is the horrid lucidity of insomnia."

73. "Kafka and His Precursors"

Sp. title: "K. y sus precursores." Pub. *La Nación,* Aug. 19, 1951, col. *O.I.*

The first Spanish publication in book form of Kafka's writings (*The Metamorphosis,* 1938) was the work of B. He had already published in *El Hogar* some articles on K., and had translated one of his parables. But his greatest tribute to a writer whose influence on him was decisive is this very short text. Using a well-known 1920 article by T. S. Eliot ("Tradition and the Individual Talent") as one of his sources, B. adds to the diachronic view advanced by the Anglo-American poet a synchronic view produced by the simultaneity of all writers in the actual experience of the reader. Thus, reviewing Zeno's paradoxes *after* reading K., one may recognize a touch of him in the old philosopher. This retroactive view of literature developed in essay form an idea already fictionalized in JLB 30. The present text has become one of the most quoted in contemporary criticism. Both Gerard Genette in 1964 and Harold Bloom in 1970 have extended and enlarged the views it contains.

74. "The Metaphor"

Sp. title: "La metáfora." Pub. *La Nación,* Nov. 9, 1952, col. *O.I.*

Since his young Ultraist poet's days, B. was preoccupied with metaphors. One of his first essays on the subject was published in a Spanish little magazine as early as 1924. In a book published in 1925 there is a second article. In 1932 an article in *Sur* was dedicated to the old Scandinavian poets' ways of handling images. But his best presentation to date is this piece he wrote twenty years later, when he no longer believed in the need for striking or Baroque imagery. The conclusion about the limited number of affinities which one can discover between life's essential things confirms B.'s philosophical intuition that the number of authentic experiences a man may have is small.

75. "The Modesty of History"

Sp. title: "El pudor de la historia." Dated 1952 and col. *O.I.*

In the Middle Ages, it was not only acceptable but also commendable to write a book made only of quotations from other books. Romanticism and its banal insistence on originality forced writers to conceal their models and sources and pretend they were producing truly "original" texts. B. has exploded that notion. In resorting to endless quotation, he has restored to the essay the civilized and ironic structure it had when Montaigne invented, or rather rediscovered, its formal potentialities. The present text is a good example of that long-established but half-forgotten formula.

76. "The Enigma of Edward FitzGerald"
Sp. title: "El engima de E.F." Col. *O.I.*
One of B.'s most cherished notions—one man is all men—here takes the form of a short biographical portrait of a Victorian gentleman whose only claim to fame was the translation of a Persian lyric poet. In demonstrating how F. gave new life to Omar Khayyam, B. stresses the notion Valéry had anticipated—that literature is really impersonal. What he omits to tell here is that another Victorian gentleman, his own father, translated into Spanish F.'s translation, enlarging and complicating the abysmal perspective opened by the first author of the *Rubáiyát.*

77. "A Page to Commemorate Colonel Suárez, Victor at Junín"
Sp. title: "Página para recordar al coronel Suárez, vencedor en J." Pub. *Sur,* Jan-Feb. 1953, col. *O.P.*
Already in his first book, *Fe.,* B. included a poem to celebrate this maternal ancestor. What is new in this poem is the context: it was written at the time Perón's dictatorship was at its worst. Although B. had been spared the worst—the firing from the Municipal Library (JLB 57) and the constant police surveillance of his lectures were enough to humiliate him—his mother and sister were once taken to jail with other ladies from Argentina's best society, for singing the national anthem in downtown Buenos Aires. This 1948 episode stuck in B.'s throat. Thus, while celebrating the centenary of one of Argentina's most famous battles, in which his ancestor leads the decisive cavalry charge, B. swiftly moves the action to the present. Battles can also be fought by civilians who curse a tyrant on a street corner and are ready to die for their convictions. The publication of the poem in *Sur* was an act of open defiance. The real battlefield was then the streets of Buenos Aires.

78. "Matthew, 25:30"
Sp. title: "Mateo, XXV, 30." Dated 1953 and col. *Po.*
Using once more the rhetorical device known as "chaotic enumeration" (JLB 51), B. summarizes his life and comes to the conclusion that he has been a failure, a "worthless servant," in the words of Matthew. For him, as well as for Mallarmé, the world seemed to be destined to lead to *a* book, or *a* poem. Like the French Symbolist poet, he also discovered the impossibility of achieving that sublime goal. His failures and miseries in the art of love are also dutifully registered. (JLB 45, JLB 51). But in thus exposing himself, B. avoids all sentimentality. Confession has never been his forte.

79. "The South"
Sp. title: "El Sur." Pub. *La Nación,* Feb. 8, 1953, col. 2d ed. *F.* (1956).
For many years, B. referred to this story as his best. Based on an accident he had on Christmas Eve 1938 (JLB 30), it handles a topic dear to him: the intellectual's nostalgia for a life of action. Books and knives are here symmetrically opposed, as antagonists in a symbolic drama. Even the old gaucho who plays a decisive role at the end is more allegorical than real: he represents the pampa culture at its purest. (The story can also be seen as a subtle parody of the protagonist of *Don Segundo Sombra,* a novel by Ricardo Güiraldes which Argentinians admire.) In a short statement about this story, B. has indicated that it can be read realistically and also in a different manner, which he did not reveal. The second reading may be fantastic: Juan Dahlmann actually dies in the operating room, dreaming about an impossible return to the South. Thus, the second half of the story uses characters and episodes from the first part in a parodic, nightmarish way. In spite of the simplicity of its writing and the apparent straightforwardness of the plot, it is one of B.'s most complex texts. The actual incident which starts the narrative involved not an imperfect copy of *The 1001 Nights* in a German translation (JLB 24) but a young Chilean

woman B. was going to take to lunch at Mother's house on Christmas Eve. By displacing the focus to a book and by eliminating any reference to Christmas, B. suppressed any suggestion of an erotic or personal involvement, a strategy he has practiced more than once (JLB 51).

80. "The Dagger"

Sp. title: "El puñal." Pub. *Marcha,* Montevideo, June 25, 1954, col. *O.P.*

In the poem to commemorate Isidoro Suárez (JLB 77), B. had already advanced the notion that two civilians who curse a tyrant on a street corner are also participating in a civil war. At the time the present poem was written it was considered too dangerous to be published in Buenos Aires (Perón was then very much in power) and *La Nación* refused to print it. It was published in a Uruguayan weekly whose literary editor I was. The publication did not endear B. to the Argentine ruler (JLB 57).

81. *"Truco"*†

Sp. title: "El truco." Pub. in the 2d ed. *E.C.* (1955).

The title refers to a card game which is unlike those known to English and American cardplayers, though it combines features from rummy, from pinochle, from poker, and from bidding games. Bridge might be thought of as an "exponentiation," though a quieter one, apparently, of *truco. Truco* players do, in actuality, sing elaborate extemporized songs when they win. The Spanish deck, of forty rather than fifty-two cards, with its more realistic and charming pictures and suits, and its obvious affinity with the magical Tarot deck, here furnishes B. with the numerology, the charm and mysteries, the sense of autochthony and deep history, of mingled destiny and magic control, and the sense of the wonderful and frightening "other" world which he uses to produce the effect called "Borgesian." The last sentence might surely be a touchstone for B.'s entire corpus: *truco* is serious trifling indeed. (*Note by Andrew Hurley.*) For B., the *truco* (like chess, JLB 90) is a symbol of the cyclical nature of reality. The number of combinations being limited, any game of *truco* potentially contains all games, and any player all the players. B. included a poem on the same subject in *Fe.*

82. "History of the Tango"†

Sp. title: "Historia del t." Pub. in the 2d ed. *E.C.* (1955).

On his return to Buenos Aires in 1923, B. rediscovered not only his native city (JLB 4) but, especially, the slums where the tango was still king. Soon he learned to reject its sentimentality, which he wrongly attributed to the influence of the Italian lyricists. His view of the tango is highly colored by the stories one of his uncles, Alvaro Melián Lafinur, used to tell him when he was a boy still living in Palermo. The informant was not only wise in tango folklore but especially on its origins in the River Plate brothels he patronized. The tango was then considered so obscene that only men dared to dance it in public. From the protection of his family garden, B. saw male couples perfecting the intricate sexual geometry of its steps.

PART TWO: THE DICTATOR
THE OLD POET'S VOICE

83. *"The Golem* (I)"

Sp. title: "El G.," col. *I.B.*

This text was originally written for an early collection of oddities: the *Manual of Fantastic Zoology* (Mexico, 1957) which B. compiled with Margarita Guerrero's help.

358

It was expanded into *The Book of Imaginary Beings* (1967) and later revised and edited for the American edition (1969). See also JLB 84.

84. "The Golem (II)"

Sp. title: "El G." Dated 1958 and col. *Po.*

Another version of the same legend but this time in verse and in a more personal vein. The main source was Gershom Scholem's 1941 book on *Major Trends in Jewish Mysticism.* (In homage to the author, B. uses his name as the only possible rhyme in Spanish to Golem.) B.'s first encounter with the legend was a chaotic and proliferating novel, *The Golem,* by Gustav Meyrink, which he read in Geneva in 1917. Echoes of the Gothic horror of that book have been carefully erased by B.'s polite diction. The one that remains, and gives a final chill to the poem, is the rabbi's unawareness of being God's Golem, a feeling which was not spared the protagonist of JLB 36.

85. "Limits"

Sp. title: "Límites." Pub. *Po.*

An elegy to the things old age takes from us, this poem shows B. attempting to face blindness and decay. A former, shorter version of the same subject was published in *Dr.,* as the work of an unknown Uruguayan poet, "Julio Platero Haedo," a pseudonym composed of the Christian name of a famous real poet (*Julio* Herrera y Reissig), the second surname of a Uruguayan friend of B. (Emma Risso *Platero*), and a surname (*Haedo*) taken from Mother's side of the family. (A "Francisco Haedo" is mentioned in "Funes the Memorious.")

86. "A Poet of the Thirteenth Century"

Sp. title: "A un poeta del siglo XIII." Col. *Po.*

One of B.'s best erudite poems, written to celebrate the invention of the sonnet form, which is attributed to several Italian poets of that century. B. is less interested in identifying one than in stressing how a new poetic prototype was formed. The ending suggests that this perfect form was needed to imprison adequately other poetic archetypes: the labyrinth, Oedipus, both very close to B.'s imagination (JLB 62).

87. "Mirrors"

Sp. title: "Los espejos." Pub. *La Nación,* Aug. 30, 1959, col. *Dr.*

B.'s obsession with mirrors can be traced back to childhood (JLB 18, JLB 20, JLB 34) but only when he reached sixty did he feel free to handle the subject in this long and self-explanatory poem.

88. "Borges and I"

Sp. title: "B. y yo." Pub. *Dr.*

One of B.'s most quoted texts, it carries the theme of the double to its most literary conclusion. Here the poetic persona has finally obliterated the real individual: B. disappears to let "Borges" be (JLB 36, JLB 43, JLB 66, JLB 79, JLB 84, JLB 114, JLB 115).

89. "Poem of the Gifts"

Sp. title: "Poema de los dones." Pub. *Dr.*

Another reflective view of the ironies of existence. Here B. underlines the paradox that he was appointed head of the National Library in 1955 at the time he was becoming blind. He finds some consolation in the fact that one of his predecessors, Paul Groussac (whose critical strictures he quotes with glee in JLB 16), was also blind. There is a second, less interesting, version in *O.P.*

90. "Chess"

Sp. title: "Ajedrez." Pub. *Dr.*

Father loved chess and, using a chessboard, taught B. the paradoxes of Zeno. A similar conceit to the one presented in JLB 81, is at work here: chess players are really pawns in a symbolic game of fate which mirrors the one played by God.

91. "The Other Tiger"

Sp. title: "El otro tigre." Pub. *Dr.*

B. was always obsessed by tigers. When he was a boy, he loved to be taken to the zoo in Palermo, where he spent hours watching them. Mother recalled that sometimes she had to use force to carry him away. At home, he spent hours drawing them: clumsy distorted specimens with frail legs. No horror came from his pencil. For B., as for Blake, whose "Tiger, Tiger" he loves to quote, tigers represent the pure force of nature, an energy civilized man has entirely lost. A similar feeling was inspired by more elementary men: the gauchos, the Buenos Aires hoodlums, the Vikings. They were as swift and deadly as the tiger in using knives or swords. It is no coincidence that General Juan Facundo Quiroga (JLB 2) was called "The Tiger of the Pampas." Even his educated ancestors, who fought bravely for the independence of his native country, had in them a touch of the tiger (JLB 48). Compared to them —and B. was always making the comparison (JLB 79)—he was only a librarian.

92. "The Borges"

Sp. title: "Los B." Pub. *Dr.*

Borges is a Portuguese surname which (according to B.) means "bourgeois." The first B. came to Latin America at the time of the colonization. In evoking the long line of ancestors, B. now recalls some of their epic moments: Vasco da Gama's exploits in the East (sung by Camoẽs in *The Lusiads*) and the legend of King Sebastian, a Portuguese King Arthur. The poem does not mention another Portuguese branch of the family: the Ramalhos, probably related to the famous "bandeirante" (or flag carrier) who opened for king and country the hinterland of São Paulo, Brazil. He also omits any reference to the possibility he discusses in JLB 21, that these ancestors were of Jewish extraction.

93. "Adrogué"

Same Sp. title. Pub. *Dr.*

Ten or fifteen miles to the south of Buenos Aires there is a small town, Adrogué, where B. used to spend summers as a child when he was not visiting relatives in Uruguay (JLB 58). At the beginning, the family rented a house; later, they stayed at the Delicias (The Pleasures) Hotel, a place celebrated by B. in several stories: "Death and the Compass" climaxes in a villa modeled after the hotel; while staying there, Herbert Ashe quietly waits for a mysterious package with another volume of the encyclopedia of Tlön (JLB 34). His sister Norah has left many imaginative drawings of its elegant, symmetrical balconies and gardens. The hotel was demolished many years ago.

94. "Emerson"

Same Sp. title. Pub. *O.P.*

Although E.'s poetry is out of fashion, B. has remained faithful to it. In JLB 66, he quotes one of his favorite poems, "The Past," to suggest another possible reading of the story. In the present text, E. becomes a mask for B. The poem was written after B.'s first visit to New England in 1962.

95. "Camden, 1892"

Same Sp. title. Pub. *O.P.*

Another old favorite, Whitman, is the subject of this poem. As Emerson in the previous text, W. functions here as a mask for old B. (JLB 61).

96. "Spinoza."

Same Sp. title. Pub. *O.P.*

In this poem, S. is seen as the symbol of the artifex, totally dedicated to the one and only task of perfecting his craft, in his case the definition of the one infinite Being.

97. "Poem Written in a Copy of *Beowulf*"
Sp. title: "Composición escrita en un ejemplar de la gesta de *B.*" Pub. *O.P.*
B.'s interest in primitive poetry had already produced in 1939 "The Kenningars," an elaborate analysis of the system of metaphors used by Scandinavian poets in the Middle Ages (JLB 74). In the 1950s, he became more and more interested in Anglo-Saxon poetry, and even later he turned to the Icelandic sagas. This poem dramatizes his love for these ancient forms and lores. In the 1960s and 1970s, he fulfilled his wish by visiting not only Anglo-Saxon ruins but also Scandinavia and Iceland. In 1978 he edited and translated with María Kodama a short anthology of Anglo-Saxon poetry which includes a fragment of *Beowulf.*

PART THREE: A BRIEF RETURN TO REALISM.

98. "The Intruder"
Sp. title: "La intrusa." Pub. privately, 1966, col. *A.* (1966) and *Br.*
This story marks B.'s return to narrative. The text was dictated to Mother. In spite of the fact that she disliked the plot intensely (it was another variation on the old gaucho conviction that women are worthless), she provided the last line of dialogue. The story was based on a real anecdote. B.'s chief alteration was to make the protagonists brothers instead of close friends, to avoid any homosexual connotations. (Perhaps unwillingly, he added incest.) The epigraph gives only the location of the biblical text about David's love for his brother. The actual quotation is revealing:

> I am distressed for you, my brother Jonathan;
> very pleasant have you been to me;
> your love to me was wonderful,
> passing the love of women.

The story has been turned into a 1980 Brazilian movie; the director, an Argentine, changed the place to Rio Grande do Sul, Brazil's gaucho state. He also made too obvious the brothers' latent homosexuality. What B. had wanted to stress was the fact that in the pampas, a friend is more important than a woman. For a complementary view of gaucho folklore, see JLB 58.

99. "In Praise of Darkness"
Sp. title: "Elogio de la sombra." Pub. *I.P.*
B.'s acceptance of his increasing blindness (JLB 85) implied also an acceptance of the inevitable end. As the Greeks knew, to study philosophy is to learn how to die. In his poetry, B. was already rehearsing that old notion he may have read in Montaigne.

100. "*Milonga* of Manuel Flores"
Sp. title: "M. de M.F." Pub. *I.P.*
Less popular internationally than the tango, the *milonga* was always B.'s favorite. He preferred its quicker, more agile rhythm and its incisive critical lyrics to the tango's more sentimental and morose philosophy (JLB 82). The mythology of courage he had already explored in *E.C.* and in JLB 17 also inspired this poem.

101. "Invocation to Joyce"
Sp. title: "Invocación a J." Pub. *I.P.*
A retrospective view of J. as the central figure of Modernism (JLB 31).

102. "Prologue to *Doctor Brodie's Report*"
Sp. title: "Prólogo" a *El informe de B.* Pub. *Br.*
To mark his return to narrative, B. preceded his new volume of stories with what

amounts to a manifesto in favor of realism and against the kind of fantastic literature he practiced in his best fiction. The paradoxical nature of that manifesto is made obvious in the fact that it introduces a book which contains at least two fantastic stories (that much B. admits) and includes several others dealing with strange if not unbelievable behavior (JLB 107). This prologue also contains some political asides which prove the alacrity with which B. parades his more unpopular opinions.

103. "Doctor Brodie's Report"
Sp. title: "El informe de B." Pub. *Br.*
The connections between this story and the fourth book of *Gulliver's Travels* are obvious and have been acknowledged by B. Although a similar corrosive irony marks both texts, B. is less savage than Dean Swift in fictionalizing his nausea.

104. "Poem of Quantity"
Sp. title: "Poema de la cantidad." Dated 1970 and col. *G.*
Another of B.'s "chaotic enumerations" to celebrate the infinite and absurd complexity of the world (JLB 51, JLB 89, JLB 110).

105. "Pedro Salvadores"
Same Sp. title. Col. *I.P.*
Based on a real anecdote from Rosas's time (JLB 2), it is another exploration of the kind of strange behavior B. has already detected in Melville's "Bartleby" (JLB 47), in Hawthorne's "Wakefield" (JLB 67), and in many Kafka stories (JLB 73). In this retelling, he may have remembered the days when to live in Perón's Buenos Aires was to repeat Pedro Salvadores's humiliating experience (JLB 57).

106. "Juan Muraña"
Same Sp. title. Pub. *La Prensa,* March 29, 1970, col. *Br.*
If, in other stories, B. has accepted the old gaucho view of women as mere objects —an attitude shared by Buenos Aires hoodlums (JLB 17, JLB 98)—in this story, it is the woman who kills. Although B. rewrote the myth, he did it at the expense of creating another: the actual murderer is less the woman than the knife.

107. "The Gospel According to Mark"
Sp. title: "El Evangelio según San Marcos." Pub. *La Nación,* Aug. 2, 1970, col. *Br.*
B.'s agnosticism shows up clearly in this story. Beneath its Gothic surface, it is possible to detect the conviction (also expressed in JLB 103) that all faiths, all beliefs, all cultures are basically the same, and that to crucify a Christian missionary is in fact to reenact an ancient ritual already performed in the historical event the Gospels celebrate. For B., Jesus is really a *pharmakós,* an expiatory victim, like Prometheus or Orpheus (see "Three Versions of Judas" in *F.* for a more complex presentation of the subject).

108. "Guayaquil"
Same Sp. title. Pub. *Periscopio,* Aug. 4, 1970, col. *Br.*
When Bolivar and San Martín met at the equatorial port of Guayaquil in 1822, they divided the still unfinished task of liberating South America from Spain. They behaved very much as the old Roman generals did when carving up the empire. But Latin American historical piety would never accept that reading, and would continue to dispute which of the two heroes was more unselfish. Facing this formidable task, B. takes a different line. Instead of reconstructing the meeting, he transforms it into a clash between two rival historians. By thus changing the scale of the incident, he mocks not only the greediness that pervades scholarship but also the solemn patriotic feelings involved. History has been turned into parody. B. had once attempted a similar operation in a story, "The Theologians," which reconstructs briefly the endless and murderous dispute between two medieval interpreters of the Bible to the chilling conclusion that, in God's eyes, they are the same man.

109. "The Blind Man"
Sp. title: "El ciego." Pub. *La Nación,* June 6, 1971, col. *G.*
Obsessively, B. returns to writing about his blindness, a subject he had explored in JLB 89 and JLB 99.

110. "Things"
Sp. title: "Cosas." Pub. *G.*
Another "chaotic enumeration" (JLB 51, JLB 89, JLB 104, JLB 117). Those now invisible things still populate the gray spaces of B.'s blindness.

111. "Tankas"
Same Sp. title. Pub. *G.*
Based on a five-line Japanese strophe (a first verse of five syllables, a second of seven, a third of five, the last two of seven, as B. explains in a note to this sequence of poems), the subjects he tackles here reveal his basic preoccupations: love, loneliness, alienation, death, resignation to the fate of being a writer. Perhaps his friendship with María Kodama, the young Argentine woman of Japanese origin who has been his secretary for the last few years, determined his interest in tankas. To Ms. Kodama, he dedicated his 1977 *History of Night;* with her, he published in 1978 a short anthology of Anglo-Saxon poetry.

112. "The Threatened One"
Sp. title: "El amenazado." Pub. *G.*
Only in old age has B. dared to describe explicitly the ravages of love. In spite of his reticence, it is well known that he loved and even idolized women (JLB 51, JLB 63). Some of his friends have humorously criticized him for being too prone to falling in love, furiously and forever. "An artichoke heart," was the diagnosis of his friend Silvina Ocampo. In this recent poem, B. proves that it is not fidelity that matters but the fury and possession of love.

113. "To the German Language"
Sp. title: "Al idioma alemán." Pub. *G.*
During the 1930s and 1940s, B. was on record as denouncing one of Germany's most catastrophic inventions: Nazism (JLB 37, JLB 50). But he had also been on record for his admiration for Schopenhauer (JLB 60) and Heine, for Nietzsche (JLB 22, JLB 33) and Mauthner (JLB 44), for Kafka (JLB 73) and Rilke. Of all the languages he studied when he was young—they included English, French, Latin, and Italian—German was the only one he learned by himself. This poem is a long tribute to that language and literature.

114. "The Watcher"
Sp. title: "El centinela." Pub. *G.*
A variation on the theme of the double (JLB 88), this poem adds a strange and pathetic note to it. In growing old, the watcher realizes he is his own slavemaster.

115. "The Other"
Sp. title: "El otro." Pub. *S.*
The second book of stories to be published by B. after the long interval forced by blindness, *S.* contains some curious texts. None is more revealing of B.'s obsession with the theme of the double than this dialogue between his two different selves (JLB 88, JLB 114). Some tantalizing allusions to his discovery of sex in Geneva add to the chilly autobiographical lucidity of the story.

116. "Prologue to *The Unending Rose*"
Sp. title: "Prologo" a *La rosa profunda.* Pub. in the same book.
The book for which B. wrote these pages was the second of his to be baptized originally with an English title. In 1960, B. had thought of calling *El hacedor* (*Dreamtigers*) "The Maker"; but he had to settle for a Sp. translation of that title.

(The joke was that in translating the book, the American publishers did not accept the original title.) This time B. first thought of *The Unending Rose,* and only later found the more banal Sp. title, which literally means "The Deep Rose." The present prologue can be read as a paradoxical *ars poetica* of the old bard: skeptical, ironic, self-critical, repetitive.

117. "Things that Might Have Been"
Original title in English. Pub. *H.N.*
In this erudite and chaotic catalog (JLB 110), two things at least are intimate and disturbing: the love that was never shared, the son that never was. B.'s elegiac tone is at his saddest here.

118. "History of Night"
Sp. title: "Historia de la noche." Pub. *H.N.*
There is a personal paradox behind this poem: B. writes about the darkness of night at the time his blindness has canceled all colors except gray and yellow, thus obliterating for him the possibility of experiencing that total darkness poets call night.

BIBLIOGRAPHY

Here are listed only the articles and books quoted in the Notes. For further information see my *Jorge Luis Borges: A Literary Biography* (New York: Dutton, 1978).
Blanchot 1953 = Maurice Blanchot: *Le livre á venir* (Paris, 1959); *see* "Pascal's Sphere."
Bloom 1970 = Harold Bloom: *Yeats* (New York, 1970); *see* "Kafka and His Precursors."
Burgin 1969 = Richard Burgin: *Conversations with Jorge Luis Borges* (New York, 1969); *see* "Modes of G. K. Chesterton."
De Campos 1978 = Haroldo de Campos, in a conversation with me; *see* "The Aleph."
Foucault 1966 = Michel Foucault: *Les mets et les choses* (Paris, 1966); *see* "The Analytical Language of John Wilkins."
Genette 1964 = Gerard Genette: *Figures I* (Paris, 1966); *see* "Pierre Menard."
Genette 1968 = Gerard Genette: *Figures II* (Paris, 1969); *see* "Narrative Art and Magic."

Emir Rodriguez Monegal

Yale University.

LIST OF TRANSLATORS

1. N. T. di Giovanni
2. Alastair Reid
3. Alastair Reid
4. Alastair Reid
5. Mark Larsen *
6. N. T. di Giovanni
7. Ben Belitt
8. Elizabeth Macklin *
9. Karen Stolley *
10. Andrew Hurley *
11. Suzanne Jill Levine *
12. Karen Stolley *
13. N. T. di Giovanni
14. Alastair Reid *
15. N. T. di Giovanni
16. Suzanne Jill Levine *
17. N. T. di Giovanni
18. N. T. di Giovanni
19. N. T. di Giovanni
20. N. T. di Giovanni
21. Karen Stolley *
22. Karen Stolley *
23. Mark Larsen *
24. Andrew Hurley *
25. Karen Stolley *
26. Mark Larsen *
27. Karen Stolley *
28. Karen Stolley *
    Suzanne Jill Levine *
29. Alfred J. McAdam*
30. Anthony Bonner
31. Mark Larsen *
32. Karen Stolley *
33. Mark Larsen *
34. Alastair Reid
35. Suzanne Jill Levine
36. Anthony Bonner
37. Karen Stolley *
38. Alastair Reid
39. Anthony Kerrigan
40. Mark Larsen *
41. Ruth L. C. Simms
42. Alastair Reid*
43. Karen Stolley *
44. Ruth L. C. Simms
45. Mark Larsen *
    Alastair Reid *
46. Karen Stolley *
47. Suzanne Jill Levine*
48. Anthony Kerrigan
49. Anthony Kerrigan
50. Ruth L. C. Simms
51. N. T. di Giovanni
52. Ruth L. C. Simms
53. Suzanne Jill Levine *
54. Ruth L. C. Simms
55. Suzanne Jill Levine *
56. Ruth L. C. Simms
57. Enrico Mario Santí *
58. N. T. di Giovanni
59. Ruth L. C. Simms
60. Ruth L. C. Simms
61. Ruth L. C. Simms
62. N. T. di Giovanni
63. Dudley Fitts
64. Alfred J. McAdam*
    Suzanne Jill Levine*
    Emir Rodriguez Monegal*

*An asterisk indicates that a new translation was prepared especially for this collection.

365

65. Ruth L. C. Simms
66. N. T. di Giovanni
67. Ruth L. C. Simms
68. Ruth L. C. Simms
69. Ruth L. C. Simms
70. L. A. Murillo
71. Ruth L. C. Simms
72. Ruth L. C. Simms
73. Ruth L. C. Simms
74. Mark Larsen *
75. Ruth L. C. Simms
76. Ruth L. C. Simms
77. Alastair Reid
78. Alastair Reid
79. Anthony Kerrigan
80. Alastair Reid *
81. Andrew Hurley *
82. Andrew Hurley *
83. N. T. di Giovanni
84. John Hollander
85. Alastair Reid
86. William Ferguson
87. Alastair Reid *
88. N. T. di Giovanni
89. Alastair Reid
90. Alastair Reid
91. Alastair Reid
92. Alastair Reid

93. Alastair Reid
94. Mark Strand
95. Richard Howard
    César Rennert
96. Richard Howard
    César Renner'
97. Alastair Reid
98. Alastair Reid
99. N. T. di Giovanni
100. Alastair Reid
101. N. T. di Giovanni
102. N. T. di Giovanni
103. N. T. di Giovanni
104. Alastair Reid
105. N. T. di Giovanni
106. N. T. di Giovanni
107. N. T. di Giovanni
108. N. T. di Giovanni
109. Alastair Reid
110. Alastair Reid
111. Alastair Reid
112. Alastair Reid
113. Alastair Reid
114. Alastair Reid
115. N. T. di Giovanni
116. Alastair Reid
117. Alastair Reid
118. Alastair Reid

Grateful acknowledgment is made to the following for permission to reprint copyrighted material:

DELACORTE PRESS-SEYMOUR LAWRENCE: "Dawn," "General Quiroga Rides to His Death in a Carriage," "Manuscript Found in a Book of Joseph Conrad," "The Mythical Founding of Buenos Aires," "Isidoro Acevedo," "II La Recoleta" ["The Recoleta"], "The Cyclical Night," "Conjectural Poem," "A Page to Commemorate Colonel Suárez, Victor at Junín," "Matthew, 25:30," "The Golem (II)," "Limits," "A Poet of the Thirteenth Century," "Poem of the Gifts," "Chess," "The Other Tiger," "Emerson," "Camden, 1892," "Spinoza," and "Poem Written in a Copy of *Beowulf*," from *Selected Poems 1923–1967* by Jorge Luis Borges, edited with an introduction and notes by Norman Thomas di Giovanni. Copyright © 1968, 1969, 1970, 1971, 1972 by Jorge Luis Borges, Emecé Editores, S.A., and Norman Thomas di Giovanni.

E. P. DUTTON: "Pedro Salvadores," "The Aleph," "Borges and Myself" ["Borges and I"], "The Dead Man," "Streetcorner Man" ["Man from the Slums"], and "The Other Death," from *The Aleph and Other Stories 1933–1969*. English translations copyright © 1968, 1969, 1970 by Emecé Editores, S.A., and Norman Thomas di Giovanni; copyright © 1970 by Jorge Luis Borges, Adolfo Bioy Casares, and Norman Thomas di Giovanni.
    "The Other," from *The Book of Sand*. Copyright © 1971, 1975, 1976, 1977 by Emecé Editores, S.A., and Norman Thomas di Giovanni.
    "The Golem," from *The Book of Imaginary Beings*. Copyright © 1969 by Jorge Luis Borges and Norman Thomas di Giovanni.
    "Guayaquil," "The Gospel According to Mark," "Juan Muraña," "Doctor Brodie's Report," and "Preface" to *Doctor Brodie's Report* ["Prologue to *Doctor Brodie's Report*"], from *Doctor Brodie's Report*. Copyright © 1970, 1971, 1972 by Emecé Editores, S.A., and Norman Thomas di Giovanni.
    "*Milonga* of Manual Flores," "Poem of Quantity," "The Blind Man," "Things," "Tankas," "The Threatened One," "To the German Language," "The Watcher," and "Preface to *The Unending Rose,*" from *The Gold of the Tigers*. English translations copyright © 1976, 1977 by Alastair Reid.
    "Invocation to Joyce" and "In Praise of Darkness," from *In Praise of Darkness*. Copyright © 1969, 1970, 1971, 1972, 1973, 1974 by Emecé Editores, S.A., and Norman Thomas di Giovanni.
    "Tom Castro, the Implausible Impostor," "The Masked Dyer, Hakim of Merv," "The Dread Redeemer Lazarus Morell," and "The Mirror of Ink," from *The Universal*

ABOUT THE EDITORS

EMIR RODRIGUEZ MONEGAL is Chairman of the Latin American Studies Council and Professor of Contemporary Latin American Literature at Yale University. He is the biographer of Jorge Luis Borges and has worked closely with the master for several decades. Professor Monegal is also the editor of the two-volume *Borzoi Anthology of Latin American Literature*.

ALASTAIR REID is a poet, writer, and translator. He has published more than twenty books and has been a staff writer on *The New Yorker* since 1959. His translations of Borges and Neruda are among the finest in English. Born in Scotland, Mr. Reid lived in Europe and Latin America for many years and has worked closely with Jorge Luis Borges and Pablo Neruda and a number of other Latin American writers.

mLib

Jeanne
Titherington

A PLACE
FOR BEN

GREENWILLOW BOOKS

NEW YORK

Colored pencils were used for the full-color art.
The text type is ITC Usherwood.

PSALMS 51:12

Library of Congress Cataloging-in-Publication Data

Titherington, Jeanne.
A place for Ben.
Summary: When his baby brother is moved into
his bedroom, Ben goes elsewhere in search of
a place of his own but finds himself longing
for company of some kind.
[1. Babies—Fiction.   2. Brothers—Fiction]
I. Title.
PZ7.T53P1 1987   [E]   86-7656
ISBN 0-688-06493-0
ISBN 0-688-06494-9 (lib. bdg.)

TO MY BROTHERS

Ezra's crib was moved into Ben's room. Ben didn't feel as if he had a place of his own anymore. Wherever Ben turned, there was Ezra.

Ben decided that he had to find a place where he could be alone. He looked all over the house, in the attic, and in the basement. Finally he found the perfect place— the back corner of the garage, behind his father's car.

Ben got everything he needed—
a stool to sit on, a box of cereal
to eat, and his favorite toys.
Then he made a sign with a
big red X on it. It meant:
PRIVATE!
BEN'S PLACE!

Everything was ready, but still something wasn't right.

Ben tried to coax Mewmew, his cat, to stay with him. But she was happy right where she was.

Ben got his dog, Allie, but Allie was only interested in Ben's box of cereal.

Ben asked his mother to come and visit him, but she was too busy.

He couldn't ask his father
because his father was asleep.

Ben sat down on the front steps. Maybe someone would come by who would want to visit him.

And finally someone did.